Bad Boy

THE LOYAL BOYS BOOK TWO

CHARLI MEADOWS

SYNOPSIS

Linc

This small town is stifling, and my parents are overbearing. They only care about how others perceive us and sustaining the family legacy. I'm drowning from the pressure they've placed on me to be the perfect son, have perfect grades, and wear perfect, preppy clothes. No parties, no friends, no trouble, and certainly no *fun*.

But everything changes when chaos storms into town in the form of Remington Michaels. The mysterious and dangerous new kid everyone is whispering about. They say he killed someone at his old school. That he's a brutal fighter. But I don't believe it. Not with the way he's always there—protecting me, watching me, *touching* me.

I have no idea what's brewing between us, but I'm helpless to stop it when we find ourselves sharing a cabin and becoming friends with benefits all in the first week. You see, he really is a bad boy. But maybe, just maybe, I could be good for him.

Remi

After getting arrested and expelled from my old school in Detroit, Mom had no choice but to move us back to her hometown. Somewhere I've never even been. And we're staying with my eccentric grandpa, whom I've never even met.

This new neighborhood—this new school—isn't what I expected for a place tucked deep in the mountains of North Carolina. The elitism, the bullies, the social structures—I want no part of it. But then I meet the shy, stumbling Lincoln Anderson. He ignites something inside of me, and I'm drawn to him—his goodness, his quiet resolution. I can't leave him alone. Won't leave him alone. Even when an unknown threat from my past endangers everything.

I'm no stranger to putting my fists up, and it doesn't take long to decide that I'll wreck anyone who steps near Linc. The thing is, he doesn't want me to. They say I'm a bad boy, but I think maybe I could be good for him.

Bad Boy is a 96,000-word friends-with-benefits-to-lovers gay romance. It is book two in The Loyal Boys Series, a collection of standalone contemporary M/M romances. You can expect opposites attract, forced proximity, hurt/comfort, and steamy first times. This novel is intended for 18+ readers and contains explicit scenes, violence, language, and bullying from outside sources. See Author's Note for a full list of Content Warnings.

AUTHOR'S NOTE

Let's talk for a second!

First of all, thank you so much for picking up my second book and giving this brand-new story a chance! It really means so much to me, as do these boys!

Bad Boy has similar vibes to *Cali Boy* in that they are seniors attending a private high school—meeting for the first time and hitting it off—struggling with different issues in their lives. More importantly, while our boys are sweet and spicy and loyal, they will also face more physical dangers, especially in the second half, making this book a little darker. I have included a list of content warnings if you want to know what to expect.

I'm so excited to share Remi and Linc's story with you! I hope you enjoy!

Content Warnings: Language, explicit sexual scenes (both MCs are eighteen the entire story), violence, fighting, bullying (outside of the MCs), parental neglect, brief homophobia, brief flashback to physical abuse by a parent (this happens after the first scene break in chapter thirty-two—it is in italics and can be skipped), mentions of a past teenage pregnancy and an unsupportive family (Raina's pregnancy with Remi).

PLAYLIST

Available on Spotify

affection by BETWEEN FRIENDS
Eyes on You by Vwillz
I Like You (A Happier Song) by Post Malone and Doja Cat
Anti-Hero by Taylor Swift
Love Me For Me by MASN
Sleepless by Dutch Melrose
Treacherous Twins by Drake and 21 Savage
love. by Kid Cudi
Bad Habit by Steve Lacy
Not a Home by Pardyalone
Criminals by Xuitcasecity
carpool by Zachary Knowles
Above the Clouds by Luca
Push Up by Ne-Yo feat. Trippie Redd
soda stream sky by Powfu feat. KNOWN
slow down my thoughts by Zachary Knowles
Looking at the Sky With You by Roiael, Monty Datta, and
Skinny Atlas

Live Fast Die Numb by iann dior
cherry wine by Zachary Knowles
snowflake by Powfu feat. Jaden & Sarcastic Sounds
80 Proof by Eric Reprid
Another Love by Tom Odell
where do we go when we fall in love by SVMP, Zabtin, and
Fallen Oceans

DEDICATION

For the bad boys, who are probably just big softies underneath it all.

CHAPTER ONE

REMI

Red and blue flashing lights illuminate the dark alleyway I'm currently sprinting down. Discarded glass bottles and cardboard boxes line the piss-stained concrete, and even in my haste, I wrinkle my nose at the offensive stench. I reach a dead end, throw my hands up, and slam into the chain link fence blocking my way to the other side of the alley and sidewalk beyond.

Shit.

Bouncing on my toes, I glance behind me, ensuring I haven't been found yet. I focus my attention back on the hurdle in front of me. My eyes scan the height, calculating the distance to gauge whether I can make it up and over before the spotlights alert every cop out here to my presence.

Someone snitched tonight, and everyone fled the abandoned automotive warehouse where my boy Hydro was hosting this week's fight night. I had just whooped Derek's ass—laid him flat on the floor, out fucking cold—when the first bullhorn demanded that we exit the premises with our hands up. Yeah fucking right, assholes. This is Detroit; we run. It's not like they can catch fifty kids, anyway. I'll take my chances running the streets over surrendering to these fuckers any day.

I can't change directions now, so I back up several paces and give a running leap at the flimsy metal fence. I land, clinging on like a fucking koala, the chain links rattling loudly as I quickly scale the remaining six feet. I swing my leg over very, *very* carefully; the pointy tops of the fence are *way* too fucking close to my junk right now. I'm still in my tight black jeans, black combat boots, and no shirt—my go-to fight gear. Sweat runs down my face and chest in rivulets, even though it's a cool sixty-five degrees in mid-September.

The police still haven't spotted me, but the flashing lights and wailing sirens give me anxiety, so I frantically descend the other side of the fence to my freedom. I jump down the last couple of feet and land with a splat, right into a dirty puddle on the broken concrete below. I spin on my heel and take off, dodging the overflowing city dumpsters, like this is a fucking obstacle course and not just a normal Friday night for me in the slums of Detroit.

Just as I think I'm home free, I'm completely blindsided and tackled to the ground. My already bruised cheek grinds against the rough cement, and I grit my teeth as my arms are yanked behind me and handcuffed forcefully. My jaw aches with the force of keeping my mouth shut and my protests internalized while I'm roughly manhandled and read my rights simultaneously. Although they completely go in one ear and out the other.

Son of a bitch.

Mom's gonna be so pissed at me.

Again.

My earbuds are in, my eyes are closed, and I'm ignoring any conversation Mom tries to strike up with me. I'm not even upset we're moving to North Carolina—back home was a shithole, and I won't miss anyone except maybe Hydro. And that's mainly because he had the best weed in Michigan.

I'm hoping they grow some good bud here in the mountains, and I'm also hoping this isn't some backward ass town with fuck all to do. Mom didn't tell me much; she's still pretty mad. Okay, scratch that. She's fucking livid.

Getting arrested last month spiraled into a mess of unintended consequences, including getting expelled and Mom losing her job. Franklin Park Public High, the actual shittiest place on earth, kicked me out for supposedly aiding and abetting these fight nights and using school grounds to promote violence and anarchy. A fucking joke if you ask me. I fight. For money. That's it. I'm not the ring-leader of *shit*. But what can I do? One look at my juvie record, and I wouldn't believe me either.

Mom says she spent half her savings on my lawyer, which is why I'm not in jail right now. Also because I was still seventeen when I got arrested last month. I turned eighteen a couple of weeks later. Happy fucking birthday to me. My gift was being on house arrest with a mom who currently hates my guts.

I'm lucky Terry is the best lawyer in Metro Detroit. And I'm lucky Mom had enough in her bank account to pay for him. I owe her five thousand dollars and intend to pay every fucking penny back, even if it takes a few well-planned risks to get there. I'll do it for her. She's had a shitty life, to be honest, and half of it is probably my fault.

Pregnant at sixteen, she was kicked out by her parents

and left town to live with my father, who was two years older than her and had friends with a cheap place to rent all the way up in Detroit.

They took a risk and built the best life they could out there, but the asshole turned into a drunk and left a few months ago—for his twenty-year-old mistress. This is nothing new. He's done this my whole life, and I hate that Mom put up with it for so long.

I have no idea where he is, and I don't give a single fuck, either. I'll beat the shit out of him if I ever see him again, so it's for the best. I don't think I have another "get out of jail free" card.

Mom had to take so much time off from the cafe, dealing with my lawyer and the court, that they let her go. She could have easily found another restaurant or diner to waitress at, and I could have gotten my GED. But I think she's just tired. I don't blame her. I'm tired, too. And I've only been doing this for eighteen years.

The lease on our crappy one-bedroom apartment ended, and apparently, Mom finally made the call she's been avoiding since she left at sixteen. This leads us to where we are now—on the road to her hometown.

Hunter Springs, North Carolina.

I have no fucking clue what to expect. Mom's been pretty tight-lipped about everything, including her relationship with her dad. And I haven't asked about her mother—I know when to shut my mouth. Sometimes.

"Remi, did you hear me?" Mom's annoyed tone pulls me from my thoughts. I open my eyes, focusing back on the green pastures speeding by my passenger window.

Cows. Cows. And more fucking cows.

I tap my earbud, pausing my newest moody mix, and turn to face her. "Sorry, Ma. What?"

"You need to go to the high school first thing tomorrow morning. They'll help you register, and a student guide will show you around." She impatiently drums her short pink nails on the steering wheel, even though we still have a good five hours left on this ten-hour journey. Her shiny dark hair is pulled back into two French braids, making her look even younger than her already youthful thirty-four years. I've had people ask my entire life if she's my big sister or babysitter. It's fucking annoying.

I bite the inside of my cheek to stop the unnecessary comments from bursting out of me. I don't need a fucking *guide*. What is this? The Oregon Trail? I can read a map just fine. "Okay, but I don't need to waste anyone's time showing me around. I can handle a campus map on my own."

"It's part of orientation, Remi. It's not a choice. They assign you a student guide, and that person is also your advisor. You have to keep in mind that you're starting in October, and honey, your old school isn't quite up to par with Blue Ridge Prep."

"It's not up to par with shit," I mutter. The place was a dump, and I worried every day whether the ceiling would cave in on us. Any school would be a. . . transition, to say the least. Plus, I'm not the greatest student.

"Please, Rem. Just go along with it, for me," she pleads.

She's already sacrificed so much for me, lost so much *because* of me. I sigh deeply, "Okay, Mom. Promise I'll go."

"Thanks, baby." She smiles, even though it doesn't quite reach her eyes, and focuses back on the road, turning the volume up and bobbing her head to her favorite rap songs circa 2006. I shake my head at her, a grin tugging at my lips.

My mind is instantly scheming and twisting the angles

to figure out how to get what I want. I'll find this student advisor and make him sign off on whatever the fuck he needs to mark the tour as complete. And if this fucker thinks he's going to advise me on *shit*, he has another thing coming.

I make my own decisions, fuck anyone else.

CHAPTER TWO

REMI

The sun dips low, night on its way, as the last of the day's light shines through the tall pines ahead. The sketchy mountain roads have gotten narrower and windier as we neared our new home in Hunter Springs, North Carolina. I really have no clue what to expect, and I'm starting to feel a little anxious the closer we get. I hope I didn't leave one shithole for another one.

"It's only about two more miles down this road, if I remember correctly," Mom muses.

"Two miles away? From here?" I ask incredulously, making an obnoxious point of craning my neck to peer out every window like I'm searching for something when there's literally *nothing* out there. No buildings, no people, no street lights. I can't even remember the last time I saw a speed limit sign.

"Town is on the other side, Rem. Don't be a smartass. And there's a mall and a movie theater," she says, rolling her eyes like she always does.

Oh, thank fuck.

"We take a left here, and as soon as we crest this ridge, you'll see the estate."

"The estate? What the hell is that?"

Before Mom can answer, we get to the top of the hill, and a sprawling mountain-style Craftsman home comes into view, surrounded by a forest of vibrantly hued trees. Although *home* is an understatement. Mom's right—it *is* an estate. It looks like a fucking ski resort styled as a log cabin. The setting sun reflects off the sea of autumn leaves, gleaming with some of the most beautiful colors I've ever seen in nature, making this whole thing all the more breathtaking. . . and *shocking*.

A giant, circular fountain with a koi fish statue in the center spitting water sits in front of the main house, the driveway wrapping around it in a loop. Solar lanterns line the path to the brick staircase leading up to the ten-foot-tall, imposing front doors—probably solid oak. There are four garage doors and a smaller house off to the side, meaning there's probably a pool back there.

"What the actual *fuck* have you been hiding, Mom?" My wide eyes dart between the unreal sight before me and my *liar* of a mother.

"Just listen to me for a second," Mom pleads as she pulls up right in front of the staircase and puts our beat-up old Honda into park, "before we go in there and you meet my. . . *dad*."

It's like she can barely choke the word out. Fucking hell, can this woman carry a grudge. I understand that she was sixteen, pregnant, and scared and that her mother kicked her out. But I also get the sense that she hasn't been around for a while, and poor old Gramps has still been getting the cold shoulder from Raina Michaels.

"I left because my mother was toxic. She abandoned me

—kicked me out—and I wasn't going to let her control me or my decisions. She gave me some pretty twisted ultimatums, so I decided to leave and be with your father. I never wanted you to be controlled by her the way I was. And yeah, maybe in hindsight, that wasn't the best decision. Maybe I gave you too much freedom, but that's beside the point now. Just know that I only kept this from you to protect you. To keep these hateful people away from you." Her dark brown eyes glisten in the dimming light.

"Did Dad know?" I wonder aloud, referring to the fact that she obviously comes from money. There's no fucking way he knew about this, or he would have figured out a way to siphon money from them like the parasite he is.

"No. He wasn't from my hometown. I've told you that. We met on spring break at the beach, and you know the rest."

"No, Mom. I'm one hundred percent certain I do *not* know the rest. In fact, I am so beyond fucking confused right now, I'm starting to get a headache."

I rub my forehead and bite my tongue to keep from spilling every intrusive thought I wish I could tell her—like how keeping me away from her overbearing, *rich-as-fuck* parents instead kept me with a drunk and abusive dad. But I've never told her that. She doesn't even know the half of it. Well, she obviously knew he was a drunk, but I hid everything else pretty well. She worked all the time and was hardly home. He never put his hands on her, only me. I made sure of it.

It started a couple years ago, shortly after I turned sixteen. Mom always assumed I got into fights running around the city, which in all fairness, was usually true as well. Bruises and butterfly bandages are nothing new to me.

But the worst of what she saw was usually *his* doing. I had to walk on eggshells, never knowing what would set him off. Did I forget to empty the dishwasher? Take out the trash? Even looking at him wrong could earn me a punch to the gut. So I started going out more and staying out later, just to avoid being home. Even if the streets weren't any better.

At seventeen, I started working out regularly and got into the underground fight leagues for extra cash. Dad backed off some; he had no choice when I started fighting back. But it was pretty out of hand for over a year, and Mom has no fucking clue.

"I don't know, Ma. Seems like this would have been a better alternative to the last few years in Detroit." Financially, things were bad. Dad couldn't hold a job down, which gave Mom and me no choice but to pick up the slack. And look where that got us—arrested, expelled, and fired.

"I'm not having this conversation with you right now, Remington. It's been a long ten hours," she sighs wearily, completely defeated. And it fucking has, so I drop it.

"Let's go in, then. I won't deny this place looks pretty fucking sick." I peer at her out of the corner of my eye and see her lip twitch. She's never scolded me for cursing; it would be hypocritical as fuck.

"I guess I have missed it a little," she concedes, putting on a brave face before opening her door and stepping out. I do the same, eager to see my new home.

The wind is cool and crisp, refreshing compared to the usual exhaust fumes and general *garbage* smell of the inner city. I take a deep breath, letting the fresh mountain air flow through my system and wash away my annoyance at this secret fucking *wealth* she's been hiding when we've lived in near poverty my entire life. I've never even had my own bedroom, for fuck's sake. I literally went from the crib to a pull-out sofa bed.

We don't have much—two suitcases each, six boxes, and no furniture. It was all second-hand junk, and now I know why Mom didn't give a shit about throwing anything away.

I reach out and grab the giant, brass lion door knocker. I don't know if you're actually supposed to use it, but it's there, so here we fucking go. The metallic clang sounds like a gong from the outside, so I can't imagine what it sounds like echoing on the inside. We wait for a minute, and nothing happens, but this house is huge, so I cut the old man some slack.

When no one answers after another couple of minutes, I bang on the door with my fist, leaning in to put my weight into it. I need to make sure whoever the fuck is in there can hear me this time. I'm tired and want a shower and a quick jerk off. I need to release some tension.

The thick, wooden door swings inward unexpectedly, and I fall forward, smacking my face into the chest of a giant. I stumble back and peer up. . . and up. I'm pretty sure my mouth is hanging wide open with how far back my head is craned to look this massive man in the face. Dressed in a full penguin suit, he has neatly styled short brown hair and dark eyes. He stares down at me, unblinking and unimpressed.

"Lurch?" I ask, smirking like the smartass I am. He grunts and turns to stroll down a dim hallway while we wait in the foyer.

Guess this dude is the butler or some shit.

"I see Clifford is still around. Never did like him," Mom says, muttering the last part. But I'm distracted by the five-star ski lodge I'm currently standing in. How the fuck is this my new *home*? How the fuck did Mom *grow up* here? My mind is completely blown right now.

Oversized wooden beams crisscross the twenty-foot-tall ceiling, and a natural stone fireplace taller than me is off to the side in what appears to be a formal living room. Rustic, cabin-themed décor—including little wooden ducks and deer-print throw pillows—fills the entire space, causing my attention to bounce around uncontrollably.

My eyes catch on an interesting cuckoo clock hanging on the board and batten paneling—complete with pine trees, a lumberjack, and what appears to be tiny drunk people in lederhosen at a pub—and then immediately dart to several others.

There are also seven-foot-tall grandfather clocks, with swinging gold pendulums and ornate carvings that quite possibly cost the same as someone's annual salary. Does the old man have a hard-on for telling time or some shit? Because this is like *crazy old cat lady* shit, but with clocks.

A loud, raspy gasp echoes from the dark hallway that *Lurch* just disappeared down. "Raina?" an older man, probably in his sixties, asks as he appears from the shadows, bringing a shaky hand to his forehead and rubbing nervously. He has dark hair that's graying on the sides and kind brown eyes. I can see the family resemblance between us as we stand here, staring at each other in the foyer.

I clear my throat and break the awkward silence first. "Yep. Sure is, Gramps. And I'm Remington, but Remi will do just fine." I hold out my hand and give him my best good boy grin, even though I'm sure he knows I've been up to none. He chuckles and grasps my hand, pulling me into an unexpected hug. I'm frozen for a moment, unsure how to react to such a fatherly embrace.

"My boy! Let me take a look at you." He holds me at

arm's length, and I allow him to. The pure happiness on his face is a little heartbreaking. He's probably been so lonely in this giant house. "You sure are a Keller! You must be a heartthrob with all the girls."

I don't tell him I like boys, too. Best to not give the old man a heart attack on the first day of meeting him. Instead, I give him my signature grin and shrug, causing his hearty chuckle to reappear.

Mom finally breaks out of her trance and hesitantly steps forward. "Hi, Daddy."

"Rainy," he replies, voice shaky. He pulls her into an equally tight embrace, and I'm surprised she lets him. Mom isn't really a hugger.

He steps back after a few moments, eyes shining. "I'm so, *so* happy to have you both home. You have no idea."

I feel a little uncomfortable being around such a strong display of emotion from another man. I'm just not used to it. Unless it's negative and involves violence. *That* I'm very familiar with.

I glance at Mom, who looks even younger than usual, as she peers down at her simple black leggings and Chucks. She seems shy and unsure and so very unlike her normal spunky self.

"Eighteen years was far too long, baby girl." At his slightly accusing words, her dark gaze flicks up and hardens.

"Richard. Let's not get into all that right now. I have plenty I could say, but it's been a long day, and Remi and I are exhausted. Can you show us to our rooms, please?"

"Of course, Rainy. Please excuse my forwardness. I've missed you so much, and I'm so elated that you're both here. You can leave your things in the car, and Clifford will collect them. Follow me." His kind, wrinkled face has fallen slightly, and I can't understand what Mom was thinking to cut this seemingly gentle old man out of our lives. Never even gave me a fucking chance to know him. It pisses me off.

There will be plenty of time for us to clear the air later, and I'm ready to crash, so I keep my mouth shut and follow behind as I trail my hand up the polished oak banister. Rustic logs make up the railing, adding to the cabin-like charm of the oversized home. Somehow making it cozy.

When we get to the second floor, we veer left, and Richard shows Mom to her oversized bedroom suite. "As you know, Rainy, my room is at the end of the hall. I've put Remi in your old bedroom, in the opposite wing."

Oh, fuck yeah. My own wing.

I act cool and don't say anything, even though all possible ways I could sneak out are playing like an action movie in my head right now.

"Okay. . ." Mom says slowly, dark eyes searching my face, checking how I feel about things.

"Night, Ma." I smile so she knows I'm genuinely happy to be here. "I'll see you in the morning? I'm just gonna shower and crash."

"Same here. Goodnight, honey." She starts to shut the door, then pauses, remembering something. "Oh! Don't forget. Orientation is first thing in the morning. Don't be late, and you can take the car."

Dammit. I did forget. "Got it," I say instead.

"Actually, you can take any of the cars in the garage, Remi. Any at all. There are a lot to choose from. I don't drive much anymore, but Clifford keeps them all in running order." My pulse spikes at the thought of what cars could be parked inside those four garage doors. "And I know it's a little soon, but I also wanted to discuss purchasing a new vehicle for each of you."

Mom opens her mouth to protest, but Gramps halts her with a gentle hand on the shoulder. "Rainy, before you say no, just think about it. I never got to do this for you, and I'm making up for lost time with my grandson. And it would make an old man happy. So, just think about it?"

"She will. We will." I interrupt before Mom can veto me getting a new car. Fuck that. After all the bullshit she made me live through in my adolescence, I deserve this. For no fucking reason, apparently. We could have been happy, healthy, well-fed, and *safe*. Here, in Hunter Springs.

"Perfect. Thank you." Richard smiles kindly, his brown eyes soft, warm, and glowing with an inner light and happiness. I mean, *fuck*, if buying me a new car makes him this happy, I'll take a motorcycle, too. I'll bring that up later, though, once I've secured the car.

"Belinda's still here. If you're hungry, just wander down to the kitchen, and she'll reheat some of her delicious lasagna and garlic toast for you."

"I'm good. We stopped for fast food about an hour ago," I say, and Mom agrees, hastily saying goodnight before shutting her bedroom door. I think she just needs some alone time. I can't imagine the feelings coursing through her right now, being back in this house. She acts like it's all negative, but I'm sure she has some good memories warring with the bad.

"Well, I'll show you to your new room, then." I follow my grandfather down the hallway, excited to see my new space. My *own* space.

"Oh. One other thing for tomorrow, Remi. The tailor will be here later in the day to adjust your school uniforms as needed."

"Uniforms?" I blurt because *fuck*, I'll die before I wear khakis.

Richard just chuckles at my outburst. "Yes, dear boy. Did your mother not tell you about your new school? She went there as well."

"She didn't tell me shit, Gramps," I say, being completely honest with him. I'm feeling salty as hell about the secrets she's kept from me my entire shitty life. She needs a better explanation for her lies because her reasoning in the car was complete bullshit.

Richard startles at my words, stopping in the middle of the hallway and turning toward me. His dark eyes, so like my own, shine dangerously close to an emotion I don't know how to handle.

"Nothing? Nothing at all?"

"Nope," I say, popping the "p" as I lean against the wall and fold my arms across my chest. "I've never even seen a photo of you or anyone else from her past. Didn't know your name. Didn't know Mom came from money. And didn't know we were poor by choice, apparently," I scoff and roll my eyes. "Fucking ridiculous, if you ask me."

He doesn't tell me not to curse or that it's not true. He knows it is. He's lived with the loneliness and pain of having his only daughter, his only child, leave and never look back, blocking contact for eighteen fucking years. I know she says her mother was awful, but there would have been opportunities to reconcile. I honestly don't know if I can forgive her for this. At least not yet. I close my eyes and breathe slowly, opening them when a firm grip gives my shoulder a reassuring squeeze.

"You're here now. That's what's important. And I'm ready to make up for the last eighteen years and get to know you if you'll let me." His eyes shimmer with hope and, dare I even say, *love*. I've never really had anyone love me. I mean, Mom does in her own way, but she never really says it. I've been a burden to her my entire life. I know this.

"Looking forward to it," I assure him, smiling back because how can I do anything else when he's being so fucking genuine and welcoming. We continue our journey to the other wing of the house and stop in front of another oversized wooden door.

"This was your mother's room. It offers more privacy being on the other side of the house from us, so I figured that's exactly what an eighteen-year-old needs. I know I did at your age," he chuckles warm-heartedly, and I find myself laughing with him.

"Thanks, Gramps. That sounds perfect."

Privacy and seclusion are exactly what I need. I may be pissed at Mom, but I plan to pay her back for every penny she spent to bail my dumbass out and clear my record.

Because I don't plan to stop fighting.

I never did.

I just won't get caught this time.

CHAPTER THREE

LINC

I'm running late.

Crap.

I'm never late. Always on time. Mom and Dad have drilled punctuality into me since I could first tell time —at three, maybe? I don't know. Seems about right. *If you're not fifteen minutes early, you're late,* Dad always says. Well, I'm definitely late. Like it's actually past the time I'm supposed to be at the academy, and I haven't even left the house. It takes me about fifteen minutes on my moped to get there, too. And I refuse to rush these mountain roads— safety is just as important as punctuality.

It's Sunday, but I agreed to be the advisor for a new student starting in the middle of the semester. For extra credit, of course. I don't know anything about him other than his name, Remington Michaels, and that he's Mr. Keller's grandson. I only vaguely knew he had a daughter who moved away when she was young, but I had no idea her son was my age.

I rush into my en-suite to put the finishing touches on my dark auburn hair. It's cropped short on the sides, with some length on top that I smooth back and to the side with a little hair wax.

My complete heterochromia—one eye a bright green, the other a dark brown—is startling, even to me, because I look paler than normal. The freckles dusting my cheekbones stand out more, and the shadows under my eyes become more noticeable each day.

I lean down and splash some cool water on my face. My hands on either side of the sink and face dripping, I peer up to confront the boy in the mirror.

You're late. Not so perfect now, are you?

I grab the hand towel on top of the pristine white marble countertop and dry my face harshly. The pressure is starting to build, and I'm just trying to fulfill every expectation my parents have placed on me. I have the Anderson legacy to live up to and. . . *blah, blah, blah.*

I quickly finish in the bathroom and pull an oversized, cream cable knit sweater over my fitted white tee. I would normally wear a button-up, but I didn't have time to iron one last night. And I certainly don't this morning, so a T-shirt and sweater will have to do.

I adjust my silver wire-framed glasses and check the time on my phone. It's already eight-forty-five. *Crap.* I dig through my dresser and find my favorite pair of light-wash skinny jeans with the knees worn out. I hop around to get them on and rummage around the bottom of my closet for my boat shoes, slip them on with no socks, and jog down the stairs in a frantic hurry.

The kitchen is empty and spotless, like always. Not a crumb or intelligent lifeform in sight. I quickly eat a banana and grab my moped keys, rushing for the garage door. If I go a little faster than normal, I should get there by nine, but

I still won't speed. I can't, actually. I'm topped out at about forty-five miles per hour.

The retro-style moped is a hybrid, so it gets amazing mileage and leaves virtually no pollution behind. I slip my open-face helmet on, careful not to mess my hair up too much, and walk my moped out of the garage. I sling my leg over and start her up.

Betsy Anne was a gift from Mr. Keller when I turned eighteen at the beginning of the month. He has a thing for buying people he cares about vehicles, even though I really didn't want him to. But he twisted my leg, and I ultimately gave in and let him purchase Betsy as my one and only birthday present. He really is the kindest person I know, so I'm curious to meet his grandson. I haven't heard anything about him, although it's the weekend and I have no real friends, so I wouldn't exactly expect to. We'll see what people say Monday morning.

I cruise down the small hill that my house sits on. The freshly paved path is surrounded by a forest of beautifully colored oak trees. I make it to the main road in a couple minutes and turn right for my usual route to town and Blue Ridge Prep. People call it a 'hidden gem,' but really, it's a hidden horror tucked deep in the same valley Hunter Springs is nestled in.

I've never meshed well with the other kids here. Although, Mom and Dad have never really allowed me to. They've ostracized me, controlling almost everything about my life. I'm expected to study hard, participate in student council and other approved extracurriculars, and practice the piano in my spare time. That's it. That's all they *allow* me to do. All in a bid to continue the family legacy—go to Columbia, graduate with a degree in business, and run

Anderson Holdings, Inc. Everything I *don't* want for my life and future.

But maybe that can change now that I'm eighteen. I'm ready to start living for myself and not for the appearances my parents want to uphold, but that is much easier said than done. Because here I am, once again doing something to make *them* happy. Not me.

The B I got on my last Chemistry exam will drop my overall grade to an A minus if I don't get this extra credit. And my parents would not be okay with that. Our guidance counselor Mrs. Lewis specifically asked me to give a campus tour and be an advisor for the new kid. She knows I'll do what I'm supposed to and not blow it off like most of these other jerks would. So, just like the model student that I *always* am, I agreed. I didn't really have a choice. Like I said, I *need* that extra credit.

And that's why I'm currently on my way to school early on a Sunday morning. I hope this new kid will cut me some slack for being late. Maybe I could explain that his grandfather and I are friends. Anyone who meets Mr. Keller automatically loves him, so it's not a far stretch to think that fact might hold sway. And also, there are only a dozen acres of forest separating our backyards. In terms of Hunter Springs, we're practically neighbors.

I flip my blinker on and give the coordinating hand signal before making sure no one's coming around the bend to turn onto the road marked with the massive Blue Ridge Preparatory Academy sign. The hideously painted spirit rock announces that it's Ashley's seventeenth birthday, and Lindsay and Sylvie love her.

I turn into the parking lot, and as I get closer to the main building, I spot a kid with dark tousled hair, black clothes, and tattoos snaking up his exposed forearms. He's lounging on the brick half-wall separating the student lot from the rest of campus. With one leg bent and his knee poking out of the hole in his tight black jeans, he looks relaxed and completely unconcerned that it's early Sunday morning, and he's had to wait for me for at least half an hour.

I park in a guest spot and swing my leg over Betsy Anne. My palms are sweating as I attempt to tug my helmet off. I can feel his eyes on me—watching, analyzing, *judging*. Just like everyone else in this town. I ignore the prickling sensation that skitters down my spine and smooth my auburn locks back, walking over to him.

"Y-you must be Remington Michaels? I apologize for bein' so late. I'm never late, honestly. Although I'm sure that's what everyone who's thirty minutes late would say, isn't it? Um. . . please don't tell Mrs. Lewis?" I swallow roughly after that awkward bout of word vomit.

Oh, God. Now that I have a better picture of him, he looks like he could kill me and enjoy it, too. Not because he's bigger than me, but he has this aura that practically radiates trouble. His silver eyebrow stud glints in the morning sun, and he chomps on his gum, continuing to eye me up and down with a grin that pulls at one side of his mouth.

What the heck is his problem?

I clear my throat and hold one hand out to move this interaction along while I block the sun with my other so I can peer up at him, still perched atop the half-wall. "It's nice to meet you."

He abruptly hops down and lands with a thump and a

clank in combat boots that have a ridiculous amount of straps and buckles. I look down at my skinny boat shoes, bare feet and freckles visible from the top. I hesitantly glance back up, and intense dark brown eyes lock onto mine. I'm frozen in place, hand outstretched and waiting.

Without taking his eyes from mine, he reaches out and clasps his warm, rough hand around my cold, clammy one. He doesn't seem to mind though. Instead, he just squeezes tight and shakes it. And he doesn't even mention my peculiar eyes.

"The name's Remi," he says in a deep and slightly raspy voice, causing my stomach to flutter unusually. I push my glasses up with my free hand, still shaking his with my right, which has now gone on for an awkwardly long amount of time. I'm not even sure how to break contact at this point. When I shake hands with Dad's acquaintances, it typically only lasts two point five seconds.

My internal freak out is halted when Remi lets go and strolls over to Betsy, ghosting his hand over her shiny teal exterior. "Nice scooter."

I stiffen. I really, really hate that word. "She's a hybrid moped, actually. Takes very little gas and has a low carbon footprint."

"Oh, okay. Excuse me, Preppy."

I wrinkle my nose at the nickname, not exactly sure if it's a compliment, insult, or a general observation compared to his *grunge* style.

"Preppy?"

"Yeah. You didn't tell me your name," he says, smirking. "I think it fits, though, no?" He licks his bottom lip, then bites it, eyeing me from the meticulous swoop of my hair down to my feet. "But I'm into it."

I blush at his bold statement, unsure how to react. I like

boys, but I've never had anyone flirt with me if that's what this is. I'm not sure there's even another gay person in Hunter Springs, so I deflect.

"Um. Sorry. I'm Lincoln Anderson. Your student guide and advisor. Are you ready to head to the office for registration and your tour?"

His deep chuckle makes me think I don't fool him, but he just agrees, and we begin our climb up the steep brick steps leading to the main administration building, Caldwell Hall.

Every structure on campus is made out of traditional red brick and tall white Colonial columns, with a splash of natural wood and stone thrown in. The gentle slopes of the Appalachian mountains surround us with thick canopies and fall foliage. It really is a picturesque campus, but the people ruin it for me.

We check in with Ms. Nancy at the front office, and I let her know we'll be in the extra computer room. Remi's been quiet the whole time, hands stuffed into the black leather jacket he threw on over his Henley as we made our way up here.

And that's where we are now—in the spare room next to the guidance counselor's office, where students can go for private tutoring, to talk, or, in our case, register for classes halfway into the semester.

Remi is in front of the iMac, chewing on the end of his pen and flipping idly through the senior class choice brochure. He's not reading anything or even really looking at the pictures.

"What classes do you think I should take, Mr. Advisor? Actually, what do *you* take? I think I'd like to be in those," he declares with a slow, easy smile.

"Y-You'd like to be in mine?" I sputter in shock. "We

met ten minutes ago. You don't even know what classes I'm takin'. I could be in Interpretive Dance and Advanced Physics."

"Are you?"

"No. But that's beside the point. You don't know me *or* what I'm into. You need to choose classes based on your own interests. I'm just here to help if you need or want it."

"Okay. Well, I'm telling you, I need it. And I definitely *want* it." The way he emphasizes the word "want" has my abs tightening and heat filling my cheeks. "I'm feeling a little nervous about starting a new school, and I'd like to have a friendly face in my classes. So, can you sign me up for yours, or what, Preppy?"

CHAPTER FOUR
REMI

I planned to convince my student advisor to just sign off on today's tasks, but now I'm trying to convince him to sign me up for his classes instead. Not only does he look super fucking smart and nice enough to help me, but something else is there too. Something intriguing about him, hiding under a perfect, preppy exterior.

Not to mention he is seriously hot as fuck, in an innocent, I-have-no-clue kind of way. And *fuck,* his eyes. I've never seen anything like them in my entire life. One is a shocking emerald green, sparkling with life and happiness. And the other is nearly as dark as my own, swimming in shadows and depth.

They're fucking hypnotizing.

"Why do you wanna be friends with me so bad?" he blurts out unexpectedly but with suspicion. His southern drawl is sexy and understated, which I'm not used to. Everyone speaks so. . . *harshly* in Detroit. He sounds soft and musical, although I definitely don't tell him that.

"Why not?" I counter.

"We probably have nothin' in common."

"Sure, we do. We both live in Hunter Springs, and we both go to Blue Ridge Prep. I'm sure there's more; we just haven't had a chance to explore that yet. Maybe we can now. Since we'll have the same schedule."

"Explore?"

"Yeah. Our budding friendship. Can't you feel it? I think we're gonna be best buds," I tease because I already like making him flustered. He doesn't disappoint as pink settles on his cheeks, making the light spattering of freckles disappear.

"You on Insta?" I ask, ready to make a new account and check this kid out later. I'm kind of fascinated.

"Um. No."

"No?"

He just shakes his head swiftly. "Are you?"

"I used to be," I reply automatically. "I deleted it when —" I cut myself off before I reveal too much. Lincoln doesn't look like the type of guy to get into any trouble, and I don't want to deter this friendship before it even has a chance to begin.

I've known I was bi for a few years now, but I've never been with a guy or even crushed on one. Girls have always been more. . . *available* to me, but I'm much pickier when it comes to the male species. But now. . . This boy. . . this boy has me all twisted up inside, and I'm ready to fucking unravel for him.

"I just deleted it when we moved away," I go with instead of spilling one of my worst secrets on day one.

"You didn't want to keep in touch with anyone?" he questions. When I don't answer right away, he immediately backpedals and apologizes. Twice. "Sorry. You don't have to answer. That was rude and nosy. I apologize."

"Linc. Chill, dude. It's fine." This kid is way too fucking

uptight. It makes me want to rumple his hair, take him out drinking, maybe even to a fight—if they exist here. He needs to let loose and live a little. Trade the sweater and loafers for a leather jacket and some ass-kicking boots. I'll even settle for a denim jacket.

"The answer is no; I didn't want to keep in touch. I left a pretty shitty neighborhood, and the point of leaving was to get away from a bad place full of bad people and never look back."

I'm vague enough that he doesn't get any details of my past, but also clear enough to understand that I'm cool with what he asked, and I really am looking for a new friend. It's just a bonus that he's fucking hot as hell, and I'm pretty sure at least bi judging by how many times he's already blushed. God, I *really* fucking hope he is.

"Oh, okay. I can understand that. Well, we could at least trade phone numbers then since neither of us is on Insta, right?"

Ho-ly shit. Did shy boy just ask me for my phone number?

"I-if you want," he adds when I don't answer right away.

"Hell yeah, dude." I slip my phone out of my back pocket and add a contact called "Preppy," then hand it over for him to type his number in.

"Seriously?" he mumbles.

"Yeah, Linc. We've already been over this. You're preppy, and I dig it, okay?"

"Okay," he agrees, ducking his head and blushing while he types in his digits. He hands it back, and I send him a quick text so he has mine. And then I just stare at him while I wait for his response. It's gonna be good.

His phone chimes, and he checks it. His mismatched

eyes quickly flick up to mine, back down to his screen, and then up again. He holds his phone out, showing me what I already know is there because I just texted it to him.

"This is you?" he asks with pink cheeks and red ears. It's really fucking adorable. There are so many other ways I could make him blush, and I suddenly want to experience those things with him. But for now, I nod my head slowly and bite my lip, eyes darting to the two purple eggplants I sent as a friendly hello.

He chuckles softly, not even acknowledging what I'm insinuating. . . not even in the slightest. "Well, scoot on over, and I'll see if I can get you into my classes."

"Yeah?" I ask, a little surprised. I guess it wasn't too hard to win him over when we just sort of *clicked*, even if we are polar opposites. And now I can't stop the giant grin from spreading across my face as I slide over in the desk chair, half my ass hanging off the seat. There's only one chair in here; the other seating is an ugly, upholstered armchair and a well-worn couch.

"Yeah. I mean, why not? We're friends now, right?" he asks skeptically, almost like he thinks this could all be a cruel joke. And it makes me wonder what's happened to him.

"Definitely," I agree. He slips into the vacant half of the chair, pressing our sides together and brushing his soft hand against mine as he takes control of the computer mouse.

I could tell he has a sensual touch from his earlier hand-shake. It's part of the reason why I couldn't let go. His feather-soft caress felt too good against callused hands that have seen way too many fights.

He's too good for me, of that I'm certain. It doesn't take

a genius to figure it out. Regardless, I'm still going for him, even if I have to be his *friend* first.

Lincoln gazes intently at the computer screen while I shamelessly stare at his profile, practically an inch away from his handsome face. From this close, I map every little freckle dotting his sharp cheekbones and the bridge of his nose. His thin, wire-framed glasses are oversized and way more trendy than I could ever manage, but Linc pulls it off effortlessly. I don't think he even tries to be fashionable. He must be going for classy comfort with a dash of my-parents-made-me-wear-this.

"Um, could you not do that? I'm tryin' to concentrate on your—" He turns his head to finish the sentence, and his words die in his throat when he realizes my face is an inch away from his, our lips hovering a breath apart. I can smell mint toothpaste on his breath, and I'm fucking dying for a taste. I've never kissed a boy before, but the thought gets me so excited, so fucking *horny*.

His eyes zero in on my mouth, and I purposefully lick my lips, teasing him.

"Do what?" I whisper, my words ghosting over his lips, caressing them, *provoking* them.

An intense chemistry crackles in the air between us. Sizzling attraction mixed with a healthy dose of intrigue. And I'm pretty sure it's mutual.

He whips his head forward fast, breaking the potent spell we were under. "Stare at me. I'm tryin' to arrange your class schedule. I need to concentrate." He pushes the bottom of his glasses up and clicks around on the computer, but I don't take my eyes off him. Even though he asked me to.

"So, I have you down for the standard courses— English Lit, Calculus, US History, and Study Hall. Have you taken any AP classes before?" he asks, continuing his clicking.

"Uh. No. Wasn't exactly encouraged at my old school."

He furrows his brows, clearly not understanding where I come from. "Okay. Well, um, in addition to AP Chemistry, I'm also takin' AP Environmental Science. And then my two electives are also science courses—Oceanography and Astronomy. But honestly, they're fun and easy."

"Shit. You really like science, huh?" *Fuck.* Why couldn't he be into pottery or photography? Anything but *four* fucking science classes. And no Gym? What the hell is that about?

He chuckles and blushes slightly, smoothing his already perfect hair back and peering at me from the corner of his eye. "I told you that you should pick your own classes. What you're actually interested in."

But then I would have no one to help me pass those classes, dear Lincoln.

Really though, it's not just that. I want to see him tomorrow, the day after that, and every day for the foreseeable future. I've set my sights on him, and there's no stopping these new and exhilarating feelings fluttering through me.

But I have to ask, "Why no Gym? And dude, those aren't even electives."

He finally turns to me, our lips once again inches apart. "They are to me. Science is what I'm interested in. And for now, I'm allowed to embrace that and choose my own courses."

Allowed? What the fuck does that mean?

I don't ask, of course. I think I've invaded his life enough for our first meeting. There will be plenty of opportunities to dig a little deeper later.

"As for Gym, it's only a two-year requirement," he states matter of factly.

"But it's easy and fun."

"Not for me. It was torture, and I won't put myself through that when it's not needed. I got my credits and moved on." His bewitching eyes glow with an emotion I can't quite name as they bore directly into mine—intense as fuck.

I open my mouth to ask, but he cuts me off. "Don't. Please."

That's all he says. Two words. But the feeling behind them stops me in my tracks. I nod, mentally adding that comment to the growing list of questions I have about what the fuck is going on under his perfectly put-together, hand-some-as-fuck exterior.

I face the computer again. "Sign me up, Preppy."

You'd think four science classes would stop my crazy plan to win Lincoln Anderson over. To bring him out of his shell. Shake him up a bit. Do something a little reckless and fun. But it won't—I'm determined. And I'm going to flip his life upside down.

I think I have my first boy crush.

CHAPTER FIVE

LINC

"Registration complete," I say, shutting the computer down and standing up. I arch my back after sitting hunched over on half a chair for the past thirty minutes. I reach back and massage my sore shoulders with one hand.

"Here. Let me." Remi stands up and approaches me from behind, his combat boots rattling with each step. He gently brushes my hand aside, and I freeze at the feel of his strong hands on my shoulders, squeezing and kneading.

He's not much taller than my five-foot-eleven height— maybe just an inch or two. But he *is* a lot broader and stronger. And his fingers are loosening the knots that have been bothering me lately. I'm too stressed, but there's nothing I can do to change that.

Remi hits a particularly good spot, and I can't help the groan that escapes my lips. I close my eyes and drop my head forward, lost in the moment, as he continues to rub my shoulders. I'm putty in his hands while he gives me the best massage of my life here in the guidance counselor's spare room.

"You're really tense. You need to relax, loosen up a bit."

Impossible, but I don't tell him that.

He digs his thumbs into the space between my spine and shoulder blades, and I moan again, practically going limp. It feels incredible.

Remi's raspy laugh pulls me back to the present, and I clear my throat, stepping away from him and feeling a little embarrassed that I let my new friend give me a back massage.

"Um. Are you ready for your tour now?" I don't turn around. I can't look at him. I'm sure my cheeks are bright red. And there's also the minor inconvenience of a boner currently tenting the front of my pants.

"Sure thing, Preppy."

I still don't move.

"You ready then, or what?" he asks, and I try desperately to will this ill-timed erection away.

"Yep. Just thinkin' of what I should show you first," I lie.

I squeeze my eyes shut tightly, thinking of anything unpleasant.

Running late.

My to-do list.

Corn on the cob.

Gym class.

And erection deflated.

I finally turn around and paste on what I think is a confident smile. "I'll show you the science building first since you'll be spendin' a lot of time there—"

"With you," he interjects.

"Yes. With me, I suppose," I concede. Guess he's kind of forced me to adopt him or something. He has those big puppy dog eyes, and they are working.

"Definitely with you," he teases, and I can't help the small smile pulling at my lips. It feels good to have someone actually interested. . . in *me*. My parents only care that I live up to their every standard. They have no regard for me as an actual person.

"Follow me, then." I pass him by, and his woodsy, pine scent seeps into my senses, attempting to corrupt my now-behaving dick.

I hurry out the door, hoping the cool air will filter the lust from my brain.

He's my new *friend*.

At least, that's what I tell myself as I hear his heavy steps stomping down the hall right behind me. His deep voice sends a chill down my spine.

"So, where do you want to meet up in the morning? We should go ahead and pick a spot."

We push through the front doors of Caldwell Hall, and I blurt out the first thing I see. "The flagpole?"

"Meet at the flagpole?" His eyes are sparkling like he's teasing me, but I don't know why.

"Yeah?" It comes out as a question, not an answer.

"Okay. I like it. Flagpole it is. Just don't pull my pants down and tie me to it."

"Wh-what?" I sputter, confused. "I wouldn't do that to you, Remi. I wouldn't even be able to if I tried."

Remi tips his head back and barks out a loud laugh. "I was just joking, but that's good to know. Thanks, Lincoln. I wouldn't do that to you either," he says, winking at me again. I stare down at my feet and the spidering cracks in the cement—anywhere but his handsome face.

"Now, where's this science building?" He bumps my shoulder with his bigger one, making me peer into his dark eyes. A big, genuine smile graces his features, causing my lips to quirk, even though I can feel the heat burning in my cheeks.

Why does my new friend have to be so *hot*?

———————— ⟨∞⟩ ————————

"Okay, that's probably good enough, Linc," Remi says as he balances on the tall brick wall next to me, with his arms stuck out on either side for balance.

We walked to the main buildings he needs to know, as well as the cafeteria. But it wasn't really necessary. He has a map, and we also have an identical schedule now. His locker is even down the same hallway as mine.

I'm hopeful that he really does want to be friends. He's not from here. He doesn't know anything about me. And he doesn't know that no one likes me. Well, except for Grady and Sierra, but it doesn't really count since our parents are best friends. They're a year younger, so we really only see each other at lunch sometimes. But unlike me, they actually have friends.

Come Monday, Remi will figure that out. But for now, he doesn't know. I don't get the sense that this is some master plan to hurt me. Not with how he constantly brushes his arm or hand against mine or how close he stands to me while we speak. It's both confusing and exciting.

"Wanna get out of here and hang out more? What's there to do for fun?"

I lick my dry lips, still trailing next to the perimeter wall where Remi is apparently practicing his balance beam skills. He wanted to see the gym, which is at the very back of campus, next to the football and baseball fields, and right by the wall. An imposing brick structure that I've *always* hated. I've been shoved into it too many times to count.

"Um. Not much. We could go see a movie?" That's not entirely true. There is definitely stuff to do here; I'm just never invited.

"Nah. I don't wanna sit in silence. I want to get to know you more."

I swallow thickly at his words. "Probably not my place, then."

I stare up at him, blinking against the sun, as he peers down at me instead of watching where he's walking. "Remi, you should be more careful. That's really high up." I bite my tongue. Why did I just say that?

A cocky grin tugs at his lips. "Aw, you worried about me, Preppy?"

"You could fall. There's a high probability you'd break a bone from that height." I roll my lips inward to stop more unnecessary comments from pouring out of them.

It's like a shutter is drawn, and his face steels over. "I won't be falling or breaking any bones. . ." He mumbles something else, and I swear it sounds like "ever again." But I don't miss his change in mood, so I don't ask him to repeat himself.

Before I can steer the conversation back to hanging out, Remi abruptly stops and turns away from me. I open my mouth to ask what he's doing but just stand here gaping as he launches himself off the edge of the wall with a powerful thrust of his legs, curving his body and doing an impressive-as-heck back flip. He lands perfectly, with a loud thump of his boots, surprisingly graceful and nimble.

I finally gain use of my jaw muscles, and I can't stop the exclamation from pouring out of my mouth. "Holy freakin' crap, Remi! That was so cool!"

He brushes his dark locks out of his eyes and snorts. "Thanks. You don't curse, do you, Preppy?"

I push my glasses up but don't break eye contact. "Oh. Um. No. Not out loud, I guess. My parents have never really tolerated any kind of bad language."

"Side quest. Make Lincoln say *fuck*." His eyes twinkle, and I know he's teasing me.

"I won't."

"Oh, I bet you will. Bet I'll make you." His voice is deep and sultry.

My eyebrows scrunch together. "What does that mean?"

"Nothing, Linc. Don't worry about it, dude." A friendly smile replaces the more predatory one, and I swallow thickly, wondering if I'm reading this right.

Is he insinuating what I think he is?

No.

There's no possible way a guy like Remi could be gay.

I would never be that lucky.

He probably just wants to use me to pass all his classes. And I'll probably just let him.

A random thought about what we can do pops into my head. Somewhere fun from my childhood that Mr. Keller used to take me to. "Oh. We could go to the arcade. Do you like video games?" I ask casually. We're back at eye level again.

"Sure, dude. That sounds like fun. I'll drive us, though. I don't think I'll fit on the back of your moped," he says, and I chuckle.

He definitely wouldn't.

CHAPTER SIX

LINC

Remi pulls up to a partially dilapidated, free-standing building. The red and blue neon sign reading 'The Co-Op Arcade' looks straight out of the eighties. I haven't been here in a long time, so I hope the inside is better.

Remi puts his bright green Camaro into park, or I should probably say *Mr. Keller's bright green Camaro*. Although, I'm sure he'll offer to buy his grandson whatever he wants if he hasn't already. Like I said, it's his thing. It makes him happy, and it's hard to say no to the kind old man.

"So this is the arcade, huh? Kinda looks like I'm still in my old neighborhood."

"You had an arcade like this one?" I ask. I'm not sure where he's from, only that he called it a *crappy* place earlier.

"No. I just mean it looks kind of old and. . . possibly vacant. Which reminds me of home. Of Detroit."

"I didn't know where you were from. That's really neat."

"Neat?"

"Yeah? Cool?"

"No, Preppy. My old neighborhood was an absolute shithole, crawling with scumbags and lowlifes. Nothing neat about that, trust me."

"Sorry. I didn't mean anything by it."

Is he mad at me?

I gaze down at my hands in my lap. I don't really understand what I said wrong. I was just being polite. This is one of the reasons why I have no friends. I never know what to say or say the wrong thing. Another reason is that my parents don't let me go to any parties or hang out with anyone from school, and they never have. Not that I even want to anymore.

I was homeschooled by a tutor for elementary, but I went to middle and now high school with these kids, yet I've never seen them outside of class. They stopped asking long ago. Now they just like to harass me constantly. Some more than others.

Cool, rough skin grazes the back of my neck and squeezes gently. I slowly turn my head to peer at the boy who's once again touching me tenderly, like he actually cares.

"There's nothing to apologize for, Linc. Just explaining that I didn't come from a good place. We didn't live on the nice side of town. But don't worry about it. Hunter Springs is my home now." He smiles with all his teeth, and it's so entrancing that I swallow thickly and look away, staring at the run-down arcade I once loved. His hand is still on the nape of my neck, and it feels too good.

"Remi," I whisper breathlessly. How can I control my reaction when his hands are so strong and skilled? Even if this is so, so embarrassing.

He's not gay. He just wants to be friends.

I can't let the fact that I'm awkwardly starved for attention and touch ruin my chance at this friendship just because I'm reading more into his charismatic personality than I should.

I lean forward, pulling away from his commanding grasp. "Ready?" I ask, peeking over at him from the corner of my eye. "Sorry it's so crappy lookin', but we should at least check out the inside since we're here. Right?"

"Linc. Dude, stop apologizing for shit. I bet it's awesome inside. Let's go." And then he's climbing out of the driver's side, and I'm scrambling after him.

When Remi pushes the heavy metal door in, he holds it open with one arm, allowing me to slip through first. I brush against his hard body and once again have to tell myself we're just two new friends hanging out. Getting to know each other. This is definitely *not* a date. And he is definitely *not* gay.

The entire arcade is exactly as I remembered it. The dark interior is highlighted by colorful neon strip lights lining the perimeter of the floor and ceiling and an old black carpet with glow-in-the-dark planets and stars dotting it. Two bowling lanes are tucked into the left corner, and the rest of the space is filled with every arcade game imaginable, from Pac-Man to Skee-Ball. There's a small seating area in front of a counter where you can order basic food like pizza and hot dogs. All in all, it's pretty nice compared to how the run-down outside looks.

"Oh. Nice, Preppy. No one's even here. We have the place to ourselves."

I can't help the smile pulling at my lips. "We do." My eyes scan the room, searching for what I want to play first. "Air hockey?"

"Fuck, yeah. I bet you twenty bucks I'll whoop your ass."

"Um. Pass. You're probably right."

Remi tilts his head back, belting out a loud laugh, causing the little old lady behind the counter to glance our way. I give her a small wave and a hesitant smile. Hopefully, she's happy to have some customers. I'm surprised they've stayed in business so long.

"Let's get some coins," Remi declares, striding confidently over to the booth.

"Good afternoon, ma'am. Can I get forty dollars in tokens, please?" He reaches into his back pocket and pulls out a leather wallet attached to a shiny silver chain hooked to his front belt loop. He slips two twenties from it, sees me watching, and winks.

"I can buy my own tokens," I mutter shyly, peering down at my feet. This whole situation keeps feeling more and more like a date, though I have nothing for comparison. Again, no one likes me.

"Nah. It's cool. I'm the one who asked you to hang out."

"Here you go, boys. And please, call me Barb. This little old lady isn't quite ready to settle down and be a *ma'am*," she chuckles, even though she definitely *is* a ma'am. I don't think my mother would approve of me calling her anything else. She must have been listening to our whole exchange because she hands each of us a cup of tokens.

"Thanks, Barb." I guess Remi has no issue calling her by name.

"Thank you, ma'am," I reply automatically, unable to stop the "Southern gentleman" from pouring out of my mouth unbidden. I roll my lips inward, heat tickling my cheeks.

Remi and Barb laugh, but I know they're not laughing *at* me. "I can't help it. I'm not sure I can call you by your first name, to be honest," I admit truthfully.

"How about Ms. Barb? Fair compromise?" she asks, and I immediately nod.

"Yes, ma'am. I mean. . . um. . . Ms. Barb. I'm Lincoln, and this is Remi."

"It's so good to have you boys here. Now, go have fun." She shoos us away, and we jog over to our first game. Remi seems pretty competitive. Me, not so much. I'd just prefer to have a friendly, low-key match.

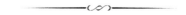

After Remi wins at air hockey, basketball, racing, *Street Fighter*, and *everything* else, I give up. We take a break and get drinks at the counter, then choose a table, pulling out two white plastic chairs you would normally find on an outside patio. We plop down, ready to enjoy our cold beverages.

"So, tell me more about yourself, Lincoln. What do you like besides science, mopeds, and arcade games?" His smile ticks up on one side, crooked and teasing.

"Um. I mainly like to read and play video games. And I guess swimmin' sometimes, too." I think about whether I should count piano and student council, but then I tell myself it's what my parents want, not what I want.

"Let me guess, science fiction?"

I lean forward and take another sip of my sweet iced tea, lowering my gaze. "And some fantasy, too," I mumble around the straw.

"What about you?" I ask in return.

"Working out, boxing, MMA, racing cars."

I choke on my tea, the ice-cold liquid going down the wrong pipe. I'm lucky it doesn't spew out of my mouth and all over Remi's face. That would be mortifying.

Everything he just listed is so. . . *dangerous*. So risky.

Remi gets out of his seat and squats next to me, patting my back gently. "You okay, Linc?"

I gain use of my lungs again and clear my throat. "Yes. Sorry. You just caught me off guard. That's all so reckless. Don't you have any low-key hobbies?"

He squints his eyes and looks off to the side, thinking hard about it. "I guess probably science for me now, too. And I'd be down to game with you. Or go swimming, as long as the water's warm."

"I have a PS5 and a heated pool," I blurt out. Not thinking about the fact that he may have to meet my parents if he comes over. Now that I'm eighteen, I should be able to hang out with whomever I want. And I really, really want to hang out with Remi more.

"Oh nice, Preppy. You inviting me sometime?"

"Yes?" I'll figure out my parents later.

"Fuck, yeah."

I distract him from the conversation when my eyes catch on something. "Oh, look. They have a photo booth." I point behind Remi. "I've always wanted to do one of those," I whisper longingly, not even considering how pathetic that might sound.

He turns in his seat, peering back at the old machine. "Yeah? Okay. Let's do it."

Remi slurps the rest of his soda and tosses it into the trash can. I follow suit with my drink, and then he's holding his hand out. I automatically place mine in his.

Do guy friends do this? Hold hands? I feel like maybe they don't.

Remi gently tugs me over to the brightly lit photo booth. He slides the curtain open and lets go of my hand.

"After you."

I crawl into the booth and plop down on the seat, Remi sitting right beside me. I'm a little nervous now that we're in such a tiny space together.

I lean forward, insert two tokens, and awkwardly press the start button, sitting back as the machine whirs to life.

Remi slings a heavy arm over my shoulder and leans into me, pressing the sides of our faces together and smiling wide. His soft stubble grazes my bare cheek, and goosebumps erupt, traveling down my neck and spreading to the tips of my toes.

I'm frozen for a second as the photo countdown commences.

Three. Two. One.

Flash.

I snap out of it and smile for the next four pictures, grabbing the photo strip as it prints out.

Dang it.

That first one is so embarrassing. I hold it away so Remi can't see it. I look all discombobulated—awkward and weird—while Remi is so good-looking it doesn't seem real.

"Lemme see."

"Let's redo them."

"Uh-uh. Hand it over, Preppy." He holds his hand out and taps his fingers against his open palm. I reluctantly place the strip of photos into his waiting grasp.

He chuckles, not unkindly. "These are good. Just looks like the flash caught you off guard in that first one," he says, giving me a wink that makes me think he knows I was flustered.

We take another round of friendly, smiling photos. Then Remi reaches over and gently slips my glasses off, folding and setting them on the little ledge in front of us.

"You don't like them?" I ask self-consciously. I can't do

contacts. The thought of touching my eyeball twice a day, every day, makes me shutter.

"They're awesome, Linc. Just wanted to try some pics without them, too. So I can decide which look is hotter. But I think it'll be a tie." His smile is wolfish, full of mischief, and his eyes sparkle as he awaits my reaction.

"H-hotter? Me? Y-you like guys?" I hate that I'm stuttering around him, barely making sense, because he keeps tossing every expectation I have out the window. And it's throwing me for a loop.

I've had limited positive social interactions my whole life, and now I feel like I've been cast into the deep end. His presence is magnetic, all-consuming, *devouring*. There's no other way to put it. He's a force of nature. And I've known him all of two hours.

"Yup. Girls, too." Then he smirks and winks at me, and I know my face is on *fire* right now.

"I'm bi," he clarifies.

"You are?" I ask in an incredulous tone. My heart's starting to race, and my stomach flutters wildly.

"Uh-huh. And you are. . .?" he trails off, waiting for me to fill in the blank.

"Um. . ." I tug at the collar of my sweater with trembling fingers.

Good grief. Why is it so freakin' hot in here?

I've never told anyone my truth before. The truth that I've known since I was thirteen.

"Linc. It's okay—"

"I'm gay!" I shout unceremoniously, tactlessly. My mother would be appalled, probably more about the shouting than the fact that I'm gay. Although, trust me. She'll hate that, too.

"I've never told anyone that before. Ever," I admit, tucking my hands under my thighs so they'll stop shaking.

"Wow. Dude, I'm honored to be the first person you came out to. And don't worry, your secret's safe with me." He slings his arm around my shoulders again and gives me a side hug. I melt into him a little, needing the comfort. I wasn't expecting to come out to anyone today. But I actually feel lighter now, freer.

"Let's take some more pics." Remi leans forward and presses the countdown button again, and the giant smile splitting my face has never felt more genuine.

I appreciate that Remi isn't focusing on how we just came out to each other. He's acting like it's no big deal, which makes me feel like maybe it actually isn't. But then I think about telling my father or mother, and I'm not so sure. My smile falters.

"Linc, you need to let loose; be yourself more." He stretches his legs out, propping one boot against the wall in front of us.

"I am myself. See." I grab the next photo strip from the cubby hole and hold it out in front of us. I'm smiling. I look relatively happy.

He snorts and rolls his eyes. "Make a funny face or something, for fuck's sake. Or we could kiss."

"K-kiss?" I stutter, and I really don't know why. I've never had a problem speaking articulately before.

"Have you ever kissed anyone, Linc?"

"Yes. A girl. Once." I wrinkle my nose in distaste, thinking about the awkward and messy thirteen-year-old kiss that finally convinced me I was gay. Remi barks out another raspy laugh.

"Not your preference, got it." He puts his foot back down with a heavy thud.

"Well, if you're down, we could kiss now? As friends, of course. You can make sure you like it, and I can get one of those classic kissing booth photos." His smile is crooked, and I can't say no.

An intense magnetism hums between us. His confidence and authenticity pull me in, drawing me to him like opposite poles attracting.

There's no stopping it.

"Okay," I whisper, our faces inches apart for the second time in only a few hours. My glasses are off, but I can see him perfectly from this close. His eyes smolder like this is more than a friendly kiss for some practice and a cool photo.

He leans in and presses his lips to mine just as the first flash goes off.

I close my eyes and relish in the feel of his soft yet firm lips on mine. His gentle hands skim up my neck and cup my jaw, the coarse pads of his thumbs stroking the sensitive skin in front of my ears, and I gasp, opening for him. He doesn't miss the opportunity and plunges his tongue into my mouth, tangling it with my own. He cradles my face reverently and kisses me with such passionate affection.

Ten seconds or two hours later—I couldn't tell you which—the camera stops taking photos, and Remi pulls his lips from mine. I lean forward, chasing after them and wanting more but unable to voice it.

He reaches forward and grabs the new photos. "Holy shit. These are hot as fuck. Damn, Preppy. You can kiss."

I blush at his praise, biting my lip. I really want to do that again.

"Check them out."

I take the photos from his grasp, and *whoa*. They *are* hot. I kind of want them for myself.

Before I can work up the courage, Remi asks, "Wanna do that again?"

I stop focusing on the photos in my hand and stare at him instead.

"So we can both have a set, of course," he says casually. And he winks. . . again. And I blush. . . again.

Did he just read my mind?

CHAPTER SEVEN

REMI

oly shit.

Ho-ly shit.

I didn't tell Lincoln this, but that was my first time kissing a guy, too. And I really want to do it again, so the moment he says "Yes," I grab his face and crush my lips to his. My thumb slips to his chin, tugging it down so I can slide my tongue inside. This time he's less hesitant, and I'm less soft. I kiss him deeper and more urgently, spearing my tongue into his mouth and licking *everywhere*. Even his fucking teeth. *I want to taste him. Consume him from the inside out.*

I run my fingers through his thick, auburn hair and grab on, causing him to let out a yelp, followed by a small groan.

I grin against his lips. He likes it. *Fuck*. I'm so turned on.

I use my grip on his hair to tilt his head just how I want it and cradle his face with my other palm, ensuring the camera can still capture every hot-as-fuck moment unfolding between us.

I can't stop. *Fuck, I can't stop.* I have to fight against the urge to pull him onto my lap and grind my dick against him.

I lean back instead, and he doesn't disappoint, once again chasing after me with an open mouth and swollen lips. I stick my tongue out, and he follows suit. We tangle them together in front of the camera for a filthy, messy kiss. I don't give a shit if I'm sitting in a photo booth in the middle of an old-ass arcade making out with my student advisor. This is the hottest kiss of my life. And my dick sure as fuck agrees.

I grab Lincoln's face with both hands, well aware this is turning into something more than just a friendly, explorative kiss. I don't give a single fuck about it and seal our lips together once again.

I'm so hard. So horny. My dick is fucking throbbing.

A throat clears from the other side of the dark curtain, and we abruptly pull apart. "Knock knock, boys. I know there's no one else here except this little old lady, but let's keep it PG, please," she chuckles, her footsteps telling me she's not waiting for a response.

I stick my head out of the curtain anyway. "Sorry, Barb!" I shout after her and then pop my head back in. I glance at Lincoln and burst out laughing. I haven't had this much fun in. . . I don't even know how long.

Lincoln is laughing, too, a blush gracing his cheeks, and I reach for our new, more R-rated photos.

Fuck me. Now *I'm* blushing.

"Whoa, Preppy. These are. . ." I clear my throat and shift in my seat, hoping my black jeans hide the raging boner in my pants. Wishful thinking maybe, but I'm going with it.

"Let me see." He holds his hand out expectantly, and I place the photo strip in it, watching his face for every micro-reaction. I eat that shit up, and I'm not disappointed.

His blush deepens, and his mismatched eyes dart up to mine, freezing me in place and searing me with intensity —*heat*. The fucking desire swirling inside them has my baser instincts wanting to take over. My amygdala or some shit.

He wants me.

He may be shy and reserved, but he likes guys, and I know he likes me.

I just don't want to scare him away. I recognize skittishness when I see it. And every bone in my body screams at me to figure out why.

What's going on with him?

I don't ask, of course. Instead, I tease him with a different question. One I damn well know the answer to.

"So, did you like it? Kissing a boy? You gay, for sure then?" I can't help it when my lip quirks, and his eyes zero in on the movement before they flick back to meet mine. I see a moment of panic flash across them.

Please don't run away, little mouse.

"Lincoln. Chill, dude." As soon as the words leave my mouth, I wonder if it will become a regular thing. Me reassuring him. And I think I'd be okay with that. "This is a safe space with me. We're friends, and we're just exploring things together, right?" I decide to open up to him and hopefully ease his nerves.

"That was my first time kissing a boy, too. And honestly, it blew my fucking mind. To the point where I'm questioning if I'm even still bi, or maybe I'm just gay now. Because damn, Linc." I grab the photos from his hand and flutter them in the space between us. "Can I keep these?" I ramble, but it does its job, and his shoulders relax as he lets out a surprised giggle. It's melodic and twangy, and the pleasant sound makes me wonder if maybe he sings.

He peers at me out of the corner of his eye and sinks his teeth into his bottom lip before whispering, "I did like it. A lot. I'm definitely gay, Remi." And then he smiles, and it's crooked and so fucking alluring—just like his eyes—that I have a hard time not staring. He seems self-conscious, and I have no idea why.

I bump my shoulder into his. "Nice, bro. Glad to be of service," I say, just messing with him, knowing these photos will be *of service* to me later tonight. I stand and slip them into my back pocket, making sure they don't get wrinkled. Definitely going to enjoy these later, in the privacy of my new bedroom suite. And maybe again in the shower, if I can find a plastic baggie to put them in.

Before my softie turns into a half-chub, I change the subject. "Let's grab something to eat, then head out." I pull the curtain back and blink rapidly as the bright lights of too many arcade games assault my darkened senses.

I hold my hand out, and a surge of pride rushes through me when Lincoln doesn't hesitate to place his in mine and allows me to pull him to his feet and out of the booth. I sling my arm around his shoulder, as friends, of course, and steer us toward the food counter, where we order lunch and grab the same plastic seats from earlier. We dig into our food in silence, and it doesn't take me more than five minutes to nearly finish mine.

"Every hot dog you eat could take thirty-six minutes off your life," Linc morbidly informs me as I stuff the last bite of my second dog into my mouth. There goes an hour. He chose a grilled chicken sandwich. It's their healthiest option, although it still looks a little greasy.

"I live recklessly, Preppy," I mumble around a mouthful.

"Seems that way," he replies under his breath. He really has no idea, but I'm hoping to show him. He needs to lighten up more. I liked seeing him like that in the photo booth when it was just the two of us. I need more alone time with him.

We've already been here a few hours, so it's about time to leave. "Ready for me to drop you back at school?"

He delicately dabs the corners of his mouth with the paper napkin on his lap and stands. "Yes. Please." So fucking proper and polite. And it does something for me.

I grab our trash, standing as well. "Wanna hang out after school this week? Study and work on shit?"

His mismatched eyes dart to mine, and he pauses, staring back at me strangely. He blinks rapidly and runs a hand through his auburn hair.

Lincoln breaks eye contact and stuffs his hands into his tight-as-fuck front pockets. "Yes. I can help you with your homework—"

I cut him off right there. "That's not why I want to hang out, though. You get that, right?"

He shuffles his feet and then peers back at me, speaking softly. "I guess so."

"Well, know so, Preppy." I sling my arm around his shoulder again and steer us toward the exit. We pass Barb, who gives me a knowing grin, at the counter again, and I can't help but wink back. "See ya later, Barb!"

"Looking forward to it, boys!" she says, smiling kindly at us. I peek over at Lincoln. His cheeks are so adorably red, and he has the most genuine smile gracing his lips. *Fuck*, I really want to lean in and kiss them again. So I remind my horny brain and semi-hard cock that we're just friends. . . *for now.*

By the time I pull into the garage and turn the Camaro off, my blue balls are nearly killing me. I was brought to the edge in that fucking photo booth, then cockblocked by a little old lady. I swear I was about to come in my pants before Barb interrupted.

The entire ride back to school, I couldn't help myself. I glanced at him at least five times per red light. And I swear to God, he blushed every single time. There's just something about him, and I *have* to know more.

I need to get to my room stat. I rush through the garage and past the kitchen, which, luckily, no one is in. I don't feel like getting the third degree from Mom. I practically run up the stairs and down the hallway to my wing of the house.

Can your balls explode? Is that possible? There's gotta be at least a gallon of jizz in there.

I shut my bedroom door quietly behind me and lock it, nearly tripping over my boots as I toe them off and desperately shed my clothes like there's a naked girl—or boy—on my bed, waiting for me. But no, it's just me and my hand and some lotion.

I grab the photo strip before I jog—butt-ass naked and hard cock bobbing—to my en-suite and rummage for the lotion I know I have in my toiletry bag.

I uncap it and squirt a good amount into my hand, grasping my cock and groaning at the cool, slick sensation. I drop my head and brace my arm against the counter, closing my eyes as I stroke myself faster. The lotion makes sloppy noises that remind me of our kiss, and I pick up my pace.

I need to come so fucking bad.

I open my eyes, and the images of Lincoln and I making out are on the counter, staring back at me like my own personal porno as I imagine all the filthy things we could do beyond kissing.

He seemed so into it—so enthusiastic, fucking raring to go—and that thought has my mind flipping to what he might be like in bed.

I zero in on the photo of us tongue-kissing for the camera, and I imagine that tongue on my dick. I picture him in my mind. He's on his knees in front of me, licking my cock and sucking my balls into his mouth with vigor.

And that's all it takes. Literally, all it takes.

I grip myself tighter and squeeze my eyes shut as I nut all over the bathroom counter with a quiet groan. I'm out of breath as I come down from the orgasm high, my dick softening in my hand.

Wow.

First time I've jacked off to thoughts of a real guy.

Definitely a fan.

CHAPTER EIGHT

LINC

It's Monday morning, and I'm standing by the flagpole waiting for Remi to get here. There are only five minutes left until the first bell rings, and I'm getting anxious that he'll make us both late. I can't get a tardy if I want to maintain my perfect attendance.

I adjust my navy blazer and smooth my hair back as the brisk autumn wind continues to assault me and my wardrobe, causing a chill to seep into my bones. Maybe we should meet somewhere inside from now on. Or maybe even carpool; it's almost time to retire Betsy Anne for the season.

I didn't tell him we're practically neighbors. And I don't really know why either. I froze when he mentioned hanging out after school this week. I'm not sure what my parents will think of him. Will they like him because he's technically a Keller? Or will they take one look at the dark clothes, tattoos, and eyebrow piercing and tell him to leave? It could go either way. My hands start to clam up just thinking about it.

As I slip my phone out of my messenger bag to text him

for the first time, a black Range Rover pulls into an empty spot near the front. The driver's side opens, and Remi hops out. I smile because Mr. Keller must have already gotten to him about the cars, and Remi must be giving them all a test drive.

I adjust the strap of my bag and bite my lip as I take him in, thinking about how we made out at the arcade yesterday. If I think about it too hard, I'll *get* hard, which cannot happen now.

He slings his backpack over his shoulder and slams his door shut, shaking his head and attempting to brush the unruly strands away from his forehead. His black hair is short on the sides but long and messy on top. And his jaw is so sharp, so angled, it looks cut from stone.

His uniform fits him impeccably—the school blazer stretches tightly across his broad shoulders, and his forest green and navy blue plaid pants are definitely tailored professionally. He's wearing the same combat boots as yesterday, and his silver wallet chain hangs from his front belt loop to his back pocket. Rings and the eyebrow stud complete the punk rock vibe, and I don't think anyone in the history of the academy has ever looked so freakin' good in this uniform. Although I can't help but wonder how many dress codes he's violating. I really hope he doesn't get detention.

As Remi approaches, he smiles wide, and I give him a half-grin and an awkward little wave in return. The girls will be into him for sure. My stomach plummets at the thought. He said he likes them, too.

I heard a few whispers about the new kid as people walked by this morning. Word is that Remi is an illegal street fighter who killed a guy at his old school—with his bare hands—and that's why he had to move all the way to

North Carolina. I don't believe it. Not with how easygoing he seems to be and how fun and completely charismatic he is. There's just no way. Gossip can really get out of hand around here.

"Looking good in that uniform, Preppy," Remi says as he stops right in front of me. The tips of his combat boots touch my loafers, and I stare down at them.

I don't know why I feel shy after yesterday, but I do. "Good mornin'."

I nudge my glasses up and anxiously clutch at the strap across my chest as I flick my gaze to meet his again. "The first bell's about to ring. We can't be late. Follow me." I turn on my heel and scurry away, listening to his deep chuckle as he stomps down the path behind me.

He catches up in no time, slinging a heavy arm around my shoulder, just like he did yesterday. Except we're at school now. I dart a nervous glance around the front entrance to Caldwell Hall. A few people take notice of us and stare, but most of the kids are probably at their lockers, sorting their books for the day like I should be doing.

I allow myself to lean into his warm, strong body for a moment, pulling from his strength and not worrying about the eyes on us.

We're just two guy friends.

Who kissed yesterday.

When we get to the front double doors, Remi takes his arm off me, and I instantly miss the weight and reassuring contact. But I don't dare ask him to place it back; we're about to walk into the lion's den.

He pushes the heavy metal door in and stretches his arm out, bracing it open. I slip in first, Remi right behind me.

The entire place goes silent, like someone pressed pause

on a TV. I freeze as well, like a deer in headlights, unable to look away from an inevitable impact.

Remi strolls to my side, confident as always. He's standing so close our hands graze, and his middle finger traces a line down the center of my palm. I try not to shiver.

I turn my head to the side, giving him a questioning stare even though we have quite the audience.

What the heck do we do now?

I hope my slightly panicking eyes convey this question as he looks back and forth between them. I don't like this much attention on me. *Ever.*

Remi must make a decision because he faces the crowd of gawking bystanders and clears his throat, loudly projecting his deep voice. "Blue Ridge! Sup, my peeps? Name's Remington Michaels. But if you don't wanna be an asshole, just call me Remi." And then he gives them his megawatt smile.

That seems to snap everyone back into motion, and a few of the guys and girls that aren't jerks to me come over and introduce themselves, being surprisingly welcoming. To Remi. Not me. They still ignore me.

However, I listen to their conversations, and it doesn't take a genius to figure out the dynamic that's developing here. The guys want to be him, and the girls want to date him.

These realizations make me cringe, but at least everyone automatically respects him. Partly because they might be afraid, or at least intimidated, and partly because he's actually a Keller by blood. And that is a *big* family name around here. Not to mention Remi's style, charisma, and the way he carries himself so smoothly and confidently—it just draws people in.

I wish I could do that.

A few of my normal tormentors watch with rapt attention, making me nervous. I quickly look away, focusing back on the conversation in front of me as Remi deflects questions like a seasoned pro, excusing us so we can make our first class on time. We'll have to skip our lockers this morning because the first bell rings just then, and we need to make it to the science building in five minutes.

"Let's go," I mumble as we finally leave the group of overzealous sycophants and head for the back exit. "If you remember from yesterday, it takes approximately three and a half minutes to make it to Holston Hall from here, and that's if we walk briskly and don't stop. Environmental Science isn't too hard, and I'll help you, of course, but Dr. Benson hates it when anyone shows up late."

Remi just chuckles, "Got it. Brisk pace." We power walk side-by-side, making it to class well before the two-minute warning bell.

"Ah, you must be our new student. Remington Michaels?" Dr. Benson eyes him up and down. Not in an unkind way—more curiously—but Remi stiffens nonetheless.

"Yeah. I am," he replies tersely, gripping the straps of his backpack until his knuckles go white. I really hope Remi doesn't start out on the wrong foot. Dr. Benson is a great teacher, and I'm not sure why Remi's acting so defensive around him.

But I just stand here with him anyway.

Why?

I'm not so sure, either.

Guess I feel a little protective over him. And I definitely don't want him to get into trouble. He didn't tell me what happened back in Detroit, but I think it was something bad.

Luckily, Dr. Benson brushes off Remi's prickly attitude.

"Great." He grabs a stack of papers from his desk and hands them to Remi with a genuine smile. With short chestnut hair, kind brown eyes, and a trendy suit, Dr. Benson is a student favorite, especially because he's only thirty-two. "Here's your syllabus, last week's homework assignments I'd like you to get caught up on—which I'm sure Lincoln will help you with—and finally, a permission slip and payment link to sign up for the field trip to Pisgah National Forest this weekend. You won't want to miss it. Saturday and Sunday are peak days for the leaves to show-case their fall colors. You'll work in pairs to catalog the different types and create a leaf morphology chart. And those pairs will be sharing a cabin. It's a really great experience."

Then he turns to me, "You too, Lincoln. Please try to get an answer from your parents before tomorrow. It's the deadline, and I'd really like you to go. I know you would enjoy it."

He doesn't know that this isn't even Mom and Dad's doing. I've never wanted to go on a weekend trip with my classmates, but now that Remi's here, I think I do.

"Can we pick our own partners—who we share a cabin with?" I blurt.

Why did I just ask that out loud? It's not even eight in the morning, and the class is filling up behind us.

He just smiles and informs us that we can fill out our choice of bunkmate on the form and any other special requests needed.

Remi takes the papers and grunts, "Thanks." I side-eye him, unsure of what his problem with Dr. Benson is.

We shuffle down the far row by the window and take two seats halfway down. I turn to whisper to him before the final bell rings. "I'll go if you go. It should be fun, and we could share a cabin together if you want. Dr. Benson is really nice," I add, wanting them to get along.

He flicks his dark gaze to the front of the class, then back. "Yeah, okay. Guess he doesn't seem so bad. And a weekend getaway with you, Linc? Sign me the fuck up. I'll happily take the science right along with it."

My lip twitches, and my smile blooms. "It's goin' to be beautiful, Remi. The leaves. Their colors." I lean forward over the back of my chair and whisper more softly. "The pigments change as the leaves gradually lose chlorophyll, and like Dr. Benson said, this weekend is peak season. I've never been to Pisgah during that time, but I've seen photos. It's spectacular."

"Damn, Preppy. You got stars in your eyes," he teases, gracing me with a crooked smile that I return just as the final bell rings. I turn around in my seat, continuing to smile as class starts and discussions of chlorophyll and hydrocarbons attempt and fail to push thoughts of this weekend out.

Because. . . All weekend in a mountain cabin with Remi?

I don't think I'll be able to concentrate for the rest of the week.

CHAPTER NINE
REMI

After Study Hall—our last class before lunch—I tell Lincoln I'm going to the gym to see if anyone knows of a nearby boxing or MMA training facility. He looks at me with those intense-as-fuck eyes like he wants to object but doesn't. Instead, he pushes his glasses up his nose and nods a few times. "Okay. I'll save us a table?"

"Thanks, Preppy." I lightly brush his hand with my own, unable to keep from touching him. "See you in a few."

We split up, and I follow the brick path toward the back of campus, thumbs looped into the bottom straps of my backpack. The sharp scent of freshly-cut grass tickles my nose. Vibrant greens and warm fall colors bombard me from all directions. It's almost an assault to the senses when I'm so assimilated to the harsh and unforgiving environment of city life and surrounded by concrete and steel.

I continue on, intending to introduce myself to the coaches and any student who might know about the underground fight leagues around here. But I have to feel it out first. Test the waters. Not only do I need to pay Mom back, but I'm itching to get back into the ring again. It's been too long. I'll just be more careful this time.

I push through the heavy metal doors, in a hurry to get back to lunch and to Lincoln, and jog down the steps to the locker rooms, where I know the coaches' offices are.

When I round the corner, I see a middle-aged man with slicked-back dark hair starting to gray at the temples. He's sitting behind a large mahogany desk, sorting files and eating his lunch. I knock at the open door before entering.

His head pops up immediately, greeting me with a polite smile. "Hello. How can I help you?"

I glance at the nameplate on his desk. "Hey, Coach De Luca. Name's Remi. I'm not in any of your classes, but I wanted to talk for a second."

"Of course, Remi. Come on in and shut the door."

I do that and sit in front of his desk, dropping my tattered backpack on the floor by my boots.

"You're Richard Keller's grandson, aren't you?"

I shift in my seat, suddenly uncomfortable that this man knows my grandfather, which also means he probably knows my entire fucked up family history.

"Yeah. I guess."

"You guess?" His bushy caterpillar eyebrows rise comically high.

"I'm sure you've heard the gossip, Coach. This town isn't very big. I only got here two days ago, but I've never met the man before then."

He steeples his hands in front of his chin, looking like a fucking psychologist—analyzing me or some shit—and I bristle, straightening my spine.

"Richard is a good friend of mine. So yes, Remington. I am aware of your. . . unfortunate past."

I scoff at that and stand, rolling my eyes. "*Unfortunate?* What a joke—"

"Sit down for a minute, Remi. Hear me out, please." He holds his hand out, imploring me. I huff out an annoyed breath but plop back down unceremoniously.

"I'm actually really glad you came to see me today. Your grandfather wanted me to check in with you. See how your first day is going. But let's talk about why you stopped by. What's going on?"

"Just wanted to see if you knew of any boxing or MMA gyms taking new members? Or any recommendations?"

His ridiculous eyebrows jump up again, and I can't suppress the smirk tugging at my lips.

"Actually, I do. My younger brother has a place in Asheville, about thirty minutes east of here. Otto's Boxing Club. But, son. Are you sure that's the best idea considering your track record?"

I stiffen at his words. "Okay, whoa. No one asked you, *sir*. It's none of your business. I don't care if you've known my grandfather your whole life. I've known him all of two days and you for two minutes so that doesn't mean shit to me." I lean down and snatch my backpack up. "Thanks for the info, though. Maybe I'll let your brother train me." And then I give him my signature grin, leaving him gaping after me.

He's probably never had a student speak to him like that. But he doesn't know me, and I'll be damned if I let him judge me. I'll go to his brother's gym out of fucking spite. Hopefully this Otto guy won't be as big of a know-it-all prick as his big bro.

What-fucking-ever.

When I step out of the cafeteria line with my steaming meatloaf and mashed potatoes, I spot Lincoln sitting alone in the corner by the wall of windows. It has an incredible view of the sprawling mountains, and I'm not sure I'll ever get used to all this. . . *nature*.

Lincoln has his head buried in a textbook—a science one, I'm sure—as he munches on a bag of baby carrots. I arrive two seconds behind a group of douchey-looking guys who stroll up to the table and stand right next to him.

What's-his-face and his cronies.

Oh yeah. *Brandon*.

I knew I didn't like him in Calculus earlier, and I definitely didn't miss the way he stared Lincoln down like a fucking psycho this morning. I'm always aware of my environment and looking for threats. I didn't survive for almost eighteen years running the streets without being hyper-vigilant.

"Beat it, Scooter. We're sitting here today," he sneers at Linc, his thin lips peeling back and showing way too much teeth. He's a couple of inches taller than me, but that doesn't mean shit. I've beaten bigger guys.

He's average-looking, with dirty blond hair tied into a messy topknot. His dark blue eyes shine with unnecessary malice that has me stepping closer.

"What's up, Brandon?" I ask in an even tone. "Is there a problem?"

"Yeah. This loser *freak* is sitting at the table *we* want to sit at today. You can join us, though, Rem." He nods to me, then turns to the table. "Move, Scooter Boy."

Linc peers up at all of us, mismatched eyes nervously bouncing back and forth between Brandon and me. I *hate* that he seems scared of these assholes, but I'm glad he doesn't move for them.

I reign in the urge to pummel this fucker's face in. I've gone off for far less in the past.

I casually set my tray down in front of Lincoln, spinning to face Brandon again. "First of all, it's Remi—we aren't friends. Second, if I hear you call him a freak or anything else again, I will risk expulsion to make sure you physically can't speak. For at least three months. Ever had your jaw wired shut?" I threaten in a calm, even tone. "And third, fuck *all* the way off. I'm sitting *here*. With my *friend*. He's more fun to hang out with than any of you pricks. There's no comparison." I raise a single brow in challenge and dare him to provoke me more. I'd love nothing more than to lay this tool out in front of the entire cafeteria. All consequences be damned.

I hate bullies.

Brandon and his lame-ass friends just stand there with their mouths open, which is fucking hilarious to me because I literally just left Coach De Luca like that ten minutes ago.

"I said. . . Fuck. Off." I step into his face, letting him know to stay away from me and my friend.

He sputters, clearly not knowing how to respond to my unexpected defense of Lincoln and probably not used to it. I roll my eyes. Pathetic. A bully with no backbone.

I turn away from the sheep, effectively dismissing them, and smile at Lincoln. "Chocolate milk?" I ask, nodding to the plastic bottle on his tray and slipping into the seat in front of him.

Brandon and his posse practically tuck tail and run to the other side of the cafeteria, where it looks like most of the popular kids are sitting at a cluster of tables. I make eye contact with a few of the girls sitting there and wink. They wave, then giggle and whisper to each other.

Sorry, ladies. I'm going after a boy this time.

"It's good for your bones. I don't want osteoporosis."

My lip quirks at said boy's answer. "Good point, Preppy." I glance back at the lunch line I just got out of. It's dwindled down now. "I'll be right back. Guard my lunch." He nods, taking another sip of his milk. . . with a straw.

I march to the large, glass-door refrigerators full of assorted bottled drinks. I reach in and grab myself a strawberry milk, quickly going through the checkout line again.

What? I don't want osteoporosis, either.

I slide back into my seat across from Lincoln and break the seal on my bright pink beverage, taking a big gulp and nearly choking. "Okay, that is sweet as fuck. I think I'll go with plain next time."

Lincoln peeks at me from under his lashes and smiles softly, taking a small bite of his fancy-ass sandwich. I saw off a big chunk of meatloaf and shove it in my mouth to offset the sweetness of the strawberry milk.

"Excuse me. Hi, Lincoln. Um. . ."

A tall, lanky kid with light brown skin and curly black hair that's faded on the sides stands awkwardly at the end of our table. I take a loud slurp of my disgustingly sweet beverage and spread my legs as much as these stupid fucking plaid slacks will allow. I lean back in my chair and wait to see what this new guy has to say. He better be nice. I've dealt with enough dicks for the day.

He licks his lips, regroups, and tries again. I continue to stare at him, amused. "Um, could I sit with you guys today?"

Before I can answer, Lincoln speaks up, putting the kid out of his misery. "Of course, Grady."

He moves his messenger bag off the seat next to him. This Grady kid walks around, gracefully folding himself into the chair next to Lincoln, and sits there with perfect fucking posture to eat his lunch. I watch intently from the opposite side of the table, slouched in my seat. I have to remind myself we're just friends. And this must be one of his *other* friends.

"Hey, Grady. I'm Remi. Lincoln's new best friend."

Fuck, I just can't help myself. Impulse control is not my strong suit.

"You a senior?" I add casually.

He looks at Lincoln nervously, then darts his gaze back to me. "It's nice to meet you. And no, I'm a junior."

I nod in acknowledgment. I'm too hungry to carry much of a conversation, so I eat the decently flavored chunk of meat instead.

"Were Brandon and his friends givin' you crap, too?" Lincoln asks, and Grady shifts in his seat, looking agitated. He pushes his curls off his forehead, but they flop right back. His golden brown eyes meet Linc's, then flash to mine for a brief second.

"Um, yeah. They tried to grab my violin case again. Same juvenile games as usual."

"Where is it now?" He doesn't have anything with him except a backpack, so if those fuckers took it, I'm ready to start some shit. If he's Linc's friend, he's mine now, too.

"Locked up in the orchestra room." He gives me a small fleeting smile. I think he realizes I was ready to hunt down whichever asshole took it. I don't fuck around with bullies who think they're bigger or stronger or better than others.

"Okay, good. Tell me if that prick tries to take it again." I scoop a giant heap of garlic-mashed potatoes into my mouth. This shit is good. Much better than the half-burnt frozen pizza and greasy fries at my old public school.

"Where's Sierra?"

Before Grady can respond, a pretty girl with a sleek dark ponytail walks over, and they must be related. A very skilled swoop of black eyeliner highlights her amber eyes, enhancing their cat-like appearance. Her full lips are painted a pale pink, and a soft shimmer highlights her sharp cheekbones. She wears her school uniform with a dignified grace, the skirt sitting just above her knees.

"Here," she says softly, glancing over and smiling before sitting next to me.

"Twins?" I nod my head to both of them.

"Yep," Grady answers. "My baby sister by five minutes —Sierra Marie."

She rolls her eyes but can't stop a sweet little smile from blooming. "Grady, you don't need to introduce me like that to every new person we come across."

"But it worked this time. He just asked if we were twins."

"I apologize for my brother, Remi. I'm Sierra." She holds a dainty hand out that I shake gently. If I wasn't into the shy, intriguing boy across the table from me, I might be interested in this new arrival.

"Nice to meet you," I say with a genuine smile, glad to see Lincoln has some nice friends. I was starting to wonder if there were any. Not that it would matter to me. I'm still going to be his best friend. . . and more.

So much more.

"I saw Brandon stalkin' away from here. Was he givin' you both trouble? I swear he's delusional if he thinks he ever had a chance with me when he treats my brother and friend like crap."

"He bothers you, too?" I ask, concerned that I now have three friends targeted by the same bully.

She rolls her eyes again like it's of no consequence to her. Just a minor inconvenience. "Yes. Since middle school. He just can't take no for an answer lately."

"What does that mean, Sierra?" Grady questions from across the table, eyes suddenly hard.

"Yeah, Sierra. What the heck does that mean?" Linc parrots. I turn to the beautiful girl in question, who busies herself by opening various lunch containers without making eye contact with anyone.

"Relax, you guys. I just mean he's always askin' me out, beggin' me to come over and chill." She makes eye contact with her brother and then Linc. "You know Mom and Dad would never let me date him, even if I wanted to. And just to clarify, I definitely do not." She takes a small bite of some kind of chicken salad wrap.

My eyes flick to each of them, eating with perfect fucking manners, while I stab another oversized chunk of meatloaf and shove it into my mouth. I finish chewing before I speak so I don't look like a complete heathen in comparison.

"Tell me when he doesn't back off. I'll have a chat with him, 'kay? Any friend of Lincoln's is a friend of mine because. . . Well, did you hear, Sierra?" I face the boy that's occupied my every thought since I met him yesterday morning. Attraction isn't a strong enough word for what I'm feeling. I can barely stop myself from reaching across the table and touching him. My fingers twitch just thinking about it. "Linc and I are best friends now."

His face burns bright, just as I expected. I take a large gulp of strawberry milk, hiding my smile and feeling supremely satisfied by my claim.

"Oh, reeeally," she says, drawing the word out. "No. I did not hear this. Lincoln, you could have texted me if I was bein' replaced," she teases warm-heartedly, and I bite back another grin. I really like her.

Linc once again misconstrues her words and takes them literally. It's fucking endearing as hell, and I'm sure she thinks the same, judging by the twinkle in her golden eyes. "Sierra, I'm not replacin' you. Or Grady. I would never. You know me better than that. Remi and I. . ." He trails off and runs his long, slender fingers through the front of his hair, smoothing the already perfect strands back. I'm completely distracted by the movement.

"We met yesterday. But yes, we're friends now."

Sierra covers her mouth and giggles softly. "I was just teasin', Linc. I'm glad you found a new friend." She bumps her knee into my leg, conveying a world of meaning in one small gesture, but I hear her loud and clear.

Take care of him.

Don't hurt him.

This is important, and I don't take my earlier declaration lightly.

Start as friends, then make him *more*. Make him *mine*.

CHAPTER TEN

LINC

Fog hovers above the slightly damp pavement, and the distant mountain peaks hide in the clouds as the cool October wind whips me in the face. I'm traveling at an easy twenty miles per hour along the outer edge of the main road leading from school to home. Early afternoon showers left behind a mist that disperses around me as I cut through it on my moped.

Today was a pretty good day. Having Remi in my classes is going to be. . . interesting, to say the least. And I so desperately need something *interesting* in my life. A small smile pulls at my lips as I remember him standing up for me at lunch, ready to fight for Grady and Sierra.

I continue down the road, my head in the clouds and my heart fluttering with excited nerves. My smile grows wider, thinking about the weekend overnight field trip to Pisgah. Since Grady and Sierra are juniors, we've never had the same classes or opportunities. So I've never even asked my parents about a trip before. They'd definitely say no to parties or sleepovers, but since it's for school, I'm hoping they'll agree. Technically, I'm eighteen and don't need their permission, but the academy doesn't like to discriminate against those who are still seventeen, so we all have to get parental signatures.

An engine revs, and I'm torn from my thoughts when a familiar, nasally voice shouts, "Thirsty?!"

Before I can comprehend what's happening, something hard slams into my helmet, jerking my head to the side and exploding into a mess of pink liquid that coats my face and glasses, essentially blinding me. I lose control of my moped, swerving back and forth, and the force of the impact throws me off balance as I struggle to right myself again.

I fail miserably.

Every molecule of oxygen in my lungs is expelled when I hit the ground and roll down the embankment like a rag doll with no control over its body. Pain lances across my chin and slices my torso, my shirt riding up as I roll across stones, twigs, and sticks.

When I finally come to a stop, I stare unseeing at the sky —chest heaving, tears and strawberry milk blurring my vision. I take a mental inventory of my body. Nothing feels broken, but my chin throbs and my stomach stings from what feels like hundreds of tiny paper cuts. And I think I might be in shock because I'm stuck on the ground, unable to move.

Tires screech and squeal on the road above me. My heart races frantically, banging against my rib cage like a mallet, thinking they've come back to finish me off.

"Lincoln!"

It's Remi.

The panic in his voice is clear, but I just feel. . . numb.

"Oh fuck! *Oh, God.* Are you okay?" I hear him slide down

the embankment, and then he sinks to his knees beside me. Breaking out of my shock-induced paralysis, I groan and lift my head an inch, attempting to sit up.

"No! Don't move! Fuck! You're not supposed to move," he pleads, trying to brace my neck and keep me flat on the ground at the same time.

"Remi. Just help me up, please," I rasp out.

Soft fabric gently wipes my eyes, allowing me to blink them open more clearly, but I still can't see very well. I have no idea where my glasses are.

"Are you sure you should move? That was a pretty epic fall."

"You saw?" I groan, completely humiliated. "And yes. I'm fine. That's not the first time they've done that. Well, actually, it was chocolate milk the other time, and I was walkin', but still." Remi growls—literally growls—and I realize I probably shouldn't have admitted that out loud.

"Who's *they*? Because I'll make sure *they* never do it again."

"I don't know who it was. Just help me up, please. I need to check on Betsy."

Lie.

I'd know that horrible, nasally voice anywhere.

Connor.

I don't know where he was this morning or at lunch, but Remi has yet to meet my main tormentor. And I wouldn't be surprised if Brandon was with him just now, either.

Remi slips one hand behind my neck and one behind my back, slowly lifting me to a seated position. Continuing his momentum, he pulls me into a loose embrace. His lips touch the shell of my ear, causing goosebumps to skitter down my neck, even though I'm hurting.

"I don't believe you, Linc. I know you know who that was, and I *will* get my answer." He pulls back, eyes hard but still worried. *Concerned.* And my stomach twists at seeing the contrasting emotions in his normally playful gaze. Both are equally as intense.

"But right now, I need to make sure you're okay. I'm taking you to the hospital. And also, sorry, but fuck your moped right now. We can call a tow truck later."

I really don't need or want to go to the hospital.

All the germs?

Everyone touching me?

My parents finding out?

No thanks.

"No hospital. I hate hospitals. I just have a few scrapes. I'm fine."

"You could have internal bleeding," he counters, sounding just like I would if our roles were reversed.

"I don't."

"You could have a concussion."

"I'm wearin' a helmet."

"Fine. But I'm taking you home and cleaning you up. It's non-negotiable."

I don't argue. Instead, I let him help me to my feet, hissing in pain as the tiny cuts on my abdomen pull and sting. My chin aches, and I can feel the blood trickling down my neck. The pain is almost enough to make me curse. *Almost.*

"Preppy. . ." The whispered endearment is low and urgent.

"I'll be fine. Really. Just take me home, please."

I suppose I need to tell him now.

"There's somethin' you should know. . ."

He stares at me expectantly.

"We're sorta neighbors."

"You're the boy next door?" he asks, his deep voice full of disbelief and. . . *excitement?* A slow grin pulls at his lips until a full-blown smile is on display.

"Oh, this is fucking gold."

"Turn here," I inform Remi from my seat in the passenger side of his Range Rover.

"I thought you said we were neighbors? I don't live on this street."

"*Neighbors* is a relative term out here. My house is the closest home to yours, but it's still a forest apart. I can show you sometime." I just want to get clean and curl up in bed with a good book or maybe watch *Heartstoppers* again. Anything to distract me from what just happened.

"Keep goin' to the end of the road. It's the only driveway on the left."

Remi turns in, and we ascend the small hill my house is on. He pulls right up front, ignoring all reason and blocking the roundabout. He jumps out before I can say anything and runs around to my side, opening the door and leaning in to unbuckle me.

His blazer is gone, ruined when he wiped the sticky mess from my face. With his tie loose and the top few buttons of his dress shirt undone, his tattoos peek out. I idly wonder what they are. I can't quite tell.

"Linc. Let's go get you cleaned up."

He's standing there, door ajar, with his hand held out. And I'm still just sitting here. Staring.

Oops.

I try to snap out of my weird daze and place my hand in his. Remi pulls me up, and then he's digging my keys from his own pocket as we walk up the steep steps to the front door. He must have taken them from the ignition when I wasn't paying attention.

I didn't even think of the keys. I hope he found my glasses, too.

Remi grips my elbow lightly, guiding me so I don't fall. When he unlocks the door, I quickly turn the alarm off, and we head straight upstairs.

My parents aren't home yet. We have a condo in Asheville where they stay whenever they have too many meetings in one day. I'm not sure if today is one of those days, but cheers to hoping it is.

I point to my room, and Remi tugs on my hand gently, leading me straight to my en-suite and the sink.

"Up," he commands softly, and I lift myself until I'm sitting on the counter, leaning back against the mirror.

My eyes track Remi while he busies himself, turning on the shower and gathering items around the bathroom—a first aid kit, washcloth, and a towel. He sets his supplies down and just stands there, staring up at me.

"Take your shirt off. Let's see the damage," he states matter-of-factly. Clinically almost.

"O-okay." With fumbling, shaking fingers, I undo the buttons on my now-pink school dress shirt. I slip it off, letting Remi take it from my grasp and toss it to the floor.

He reaches out slowly, as if he's afraid he'll spook a wild animal, and grazes his fingertips near some of the scrapes on my stomach. My abs twitch under his touch, and even though I'm in pain, my dick can still appreciate the soft caress. I close my eyes and swallow thickly as I start to harden. I keep them squeezed shut until his touch disappears.

"The water's lukewarm. It'll still hurt, but you don't want it too hot. You need to get those cuts and scrapes cleaned out. You're covered in dirt and strawberry milk." His sharp jaw clenches, and I know he's angry at what happened. Even though we just met yesterday, it's clear he's a fiercely loyal person—maybe to his detriment.

"Thanks," I murmur.

"I'm gonna leave the door cracked open. Holler if you need me. Maybe leave your underwear on just in case," he says, eyeing me like he doesn't think I'll be able to shower on my own.

Then he slips out of the bathroom, and I slip out of my pants *and* boxers. Not even thinking about what he said or what I did.

At all.

In one ear and out the other.

I decide to just rip the Band-Aid off and step right into the water flow.

"Son of a—!" I shout, stopping before the actual curse word leaves my lips.

Remi bursts in, and I immediately cover my junk, stumbling backward out of the spray of water until my back bumps into the cold tile. Goosebumps erupt across my entire body, and I shiver.

It's a walk-in shower.

Goodness, gracious.

There *is* no door.

Remi just stands there, stunned. As if he didn't realize I'd actually be naked when he rushed in here. It's my fault, though. I screamed—literally screamed.

"Remi," I whisper over the water splashing against the tile floor between us.

He clears his throat and glances off to the side, speaking roughly. "Linc. . . I heard you shout. And I just wanted to make sure. . ." He runs his hand through his messy dark hair. "I didn't think you'd be *naked*, Preppy. *Fuck—*"

"It hurts," I interrupt, whimpering pitifully, still huddled in the corner away from the water. I know I'm being a baby, but I've never been good with pain.

He sighs. "I know it does, but you gotta do it. I'll wait out here, away from the shower, so I can't see you. But you need to wash those cuts out."

"Okay," I agree, stepping back into the warm spray on the gentlest pressure setting.

"It stings!" I cry out as the water runs over me, not soothing in the slightest.

"Okay, I'm coming in."

I don't even care at this point. I drop my hands from my junk and let the water drip down my face and lips as I breathe heavily for entirely different reasons.

Remi undresses in front of me, leaving his gray boxer briefs on. I glance down and gulp, my stomach tightening with arousal. They're already clinging to *everything*, and he's not even wet yet.

The tattoos decorating his body accentuate every sculpted muscle, and the koi fish on his bicep are especially beautiful. I can't help but let my eyes wander all over him. It's not my fault they end up lingering on his impressive bulge like an absolute creep.

Unlike me, Remi's a gentleman and doesn't look down. Instead, he takes the body wash and squeezes some onto a washcloth, lightly rubbing it against my abraded skin.

I suck in a sharp breath, biting my lip to keep from crying out *again*. The soap burns, and the fabric is rough.

Remi frees the tender flesh with his thumb. "Stop that. You're hurt enough."

"The washcloth hurts—" I complain. He stills, then tosses the offending item to the corner with a wet plop.

Remi squirts some body wash into his hand and looks me in the eye, waiting for my answer. I nod, knowing my face is crimson.

I'll get a boner if he touches me with his bare hands. There's no stopping it. Like the leaves change and snow falls, this is inevitable. It's going to happen.

One glance down, and he'll see *everything*.

Do I want him to?

Oh, God. I think I want him to.

His touch causes a dual sensation—pleasure and pain warring within me. And the feeling is. . . *euphoric*.

He moves his hand in a circular motion all over my chest, brushing against my nipples before moving south to my stomach. All the while maintaining eye contact with me.

I forget every cut, scrape, and abrasion while he takes care of me. I forget the bullies. I forget the pain—mental and physical—and just feel his touch instead. *Relish it.* I close my eyes, my raging hard-on pulsing with need.

All too soon, his hand disappears, and then I'm gritting my teeth as the water washes away this afternoon's unsavory events.

"Turn around. I'll wash your back."

I spin around automatically, not caring if he decides to check out my butt. Remi repeats the process, cleaning my back but never going lower. And then his fingers are massaging my scalp and washing my hair. It feels incredible; the moans slipping from my lips are mortifying yet involuntary.

My breathing picks up. "Remi—" I whine, not a clue as to what I'm saying, what I'm asking. All I know is that I've never been so hard in my life. And there's an amazing, kind, sexy boy standing in his underwear behind me. Taking such gentle care of me. Like no one ever has.

"Remi." The whispering echo escapes my lips before I can even think twice.

He finishes rinsing my hair and grips my shoulders, turning me to face him. His dark eyes, so deep and mysterious, flit back and forth between mine. "What are you asking for, Preppy?" His voice is low and seductive.

I swallow hard and gather the courage to purposefully look from my aching erection to his. He's hard, too. The wet fabric clings to him, showing off every bulge and ridge. And. . .

His *length*.

I'm so horny, and I just need to feel something else. *Anything else.*

"Yeah?" he asks, sounding a little unsure.

My tongue darts out to lick the water droplets from my bottom lip, and his half-lidded eyes track the movement.

I nod quickly, becoming impatient. I so desperately need to come. I want him to touch me more. *Lower.* I need to forget about everything that happened this afternoon. I need to focus on this new, *good* thing in my life. This whirlwind. This boy.

Remington Michaels.

"*Fuuuck.* You are so goddamn hot." He sinks his teeth into his bottom lip and peruses my naked body, eyes lingering on my cock, which jumps from the attention. His heated gaze darts back to mine. "I am definitely one hundred percent here to experiment with you, Preppy. But you're injured and. . .”

I have no idea where this newfound bravery has come from, but I silence his concerns when I step forward and press my lips to his. Remi wastes no time and reaches down, grasping my hard length and squeezing tightly.

Every single nerve ending in my brain fires. Electrical impulses travel through my body, alighting me in ways I've never felt before. He licks into my mouth, owning me with his kisses, and alternates between stroking me fast and torturously slow.

Remi peels his lips from mine, lightly trailing his fingers up and down my shaft and around my swollen head, teasing me. My breathing is embarrassingly loud—these new sensations and emotions blotting out the bad.

“I jerked off to you last night in my bathroom,” Remi whispers. “Came all over my sink to the filthiest thoughts of everything I wanna do to you, Preppy. Look down. Watch my hand stroke your cock. You need to come, don't you? You look like you're about to explode.”

Good grief.

His dirty words tip me over the edge, and I squeeze my eyes shut, coming with a strangled shout as my orgasm tears through me. Load after load of jizz spurts out of my dick, landing all over Remi's hand and boxers.

I drop my head to his shoulder, panting heavily.

Holy cow. Remi just made me come.

My brain short-circuits.

“You mind?” His hand is full of my cum as his other thumb hooks the waistband of his underwear. There's a sparkle in his eyes, and the eyebrow with the piercing rises with his question.

I shake my head *no* frantically. I'm so ready to see him.

He yanks his boxers down, steps out of them, and stands proudly, slinging them into the corner of the shower with his foot. My eyes immediately dart down to the impressive cock at full attention between his legs.

Well, that just exceeds the balance of decency.

He's bigger than me—in both length and girth.

By a lot.

I tear my eyes away from the first cock I've ever seen and brave his gaze instead. He must see the panic racing through them because he lets out a raspy laugh.

"Don't let your mind go there today, Preppy. We'll figure things out when we need to." And then he winks before reaching down with his hand full of my cum, stroking himself right in front of me, the shower still running idly behind us.

With hooded eyes, he stands there jerking himself slowly, leisurely. As if there's no rush in the world. No threat of parents or housekeepers walking in.

His stare is hungry with pure desire aimed at me. It's a heady feeling and has my own dick perking up again. Remi doesn't miss it.

"Touch yourself. I wanna see how you make yourself come. I need a visual of what you do in this shower by yourself. Show me, Preppy."

I grab the body wash, squirt a small amount into my hand, and start to jack off with Remi doing the same two steps in front of me. I widen my stance, squeezing and tugging on my balls just the way I like it.

"Oh fuck, that's hot. I'm gonna come. . ." he says, teeth clenched tightly, jaw popping. And then cum is shooting from his angry red tip, and the new, filthy sight triggers my release. My dick pulses as I come for the second time in five minutes, wringing me dry.

I close my eyes and slouch against the cool tile, trying to catch my breath as I start to crash from too many endorphins running through my body in one afternoon.

"You can tell me how amazing that was while I tuck you into bed," Remi says, and I can hear the teasing in his voice. "You're exhausted, Preppy."

I smile because I think I might just enjoy being tucked in by Remi.

CHAPTER ELEVEN

LINC

"Who the hell are you?!"

I wake groggy and disoriented, sitting up and groaning at the stiffness in my limbs. I barely remember Remi guiding me back to bed, where I lay down in my birthday suit while he applied antiseptic cream to the small cuts on my torso and chin.

Is it possible to be so uptight around everyone else in your life yet completely open and free with one specific person? And with someone you just met, no less. I don't have time to ponder the vastly changing tide of my life because more angry voices filter through my open door.

"Robert! Call the police!" My mother's threat snaps me into motion, and I whip the covers back. My face heats at the fact that I'm still completely naked. I grab my spare glasses, throw on some gray joggers and a dirty T-shirt from my hamper, and run downstairs to intercept this trainwreck.

"Listen, ma'am—"

"Excuse me, young man! I will have you arrested!"

Oh God, Remi.

I panic at what is happening as I hop down the last two steps and grab hold of the banister, swinging around and propelling myself toward the foyer.

"Dad! Stop!" Both of my parents stand just inside the front door, my father's thumbs poised to dial nine-one-one.

I scurry past them and down the hall to stand next to Remi, who has a water bottle in one hand and a plate in the other.

"This is my new friend. Everything is fine."

My dad eyes Remi up and down, likely judging the messy hair, tattoos, and borrowed sweats. If he was still in his school uniform, this would have gone a little smoother, but probably not much.

"Lincoln James. What on earth are you wearing?" Mom furrows her brow, and I peer down at my wrinkled clothes.

"Who is this boy, Lincoln? And what is he doing in our house, eating our food?" Questions on top of questions, per usual.

Remi snorts at that. I turn to him, widening my eyes and silently begging him to be *nice*.

"I was hungry." He tucks the water bottle under his arm and picks up half the sandwich. He hands it to me, then takes a massive bite of the other half, chewing with his mouth open.

I'm starving too, so I take a bite. We both stand in wrinkled, dirty sweats, eating ham sandwiches in front of my flabbergasted parents.

Mom's mouth is gaping comically, and Dad's face is starting to turn a vibrant shade of red.

An inappropriate giggle bubbles up from that awkward place inside me that misinterprets social cues and laughs at inopportune times. It escapes my mouth, along with some bread crumbs, and Mom's shock turns into a horrified sneer.

Remi bursts out laughing, his deep chuckles rolling through me. He actually seems to like me this way, and I couldn't even tell you why.

"I don't know who this boy is or what's gotten into you, Lincoln, but you need to cut it out this instant. We have a charity dinner to attend tonight." She glances at Remi dismissively. "As a family."

After the day I had, I just can't.

"No," Remi declares, speaking up for me and voicing what I can't say for myself. "He's not going anywhere tonight."

"Alright, that is enough. You will not disrespect my wife or me in our own home." Dad's nostrils flare as he stalks toward us with a determined look. He's a couple of inches taller than Remi but not nearly as muscular. He looks like a forty-something version of me with his auburn hair, glasses, and fair skin.

I need to stop this before it gets any worse.

"This is Mr. Keller's grandson, Remi, who just moved here two days ago and started at my school!" I shout in a single breath.

It gets the job done and halts Dad's progress, making him change his tune instantaneously. He's always wanted to acquire some of Richard's businesses and bring them into Anderson Holdings. He's never been able to achieve that, but I know exactly what he's thinking. I can practically see the wheels turning in his head.

Remi's his way in.

I'm his way in.

Dad clears his throat and adjusts his tie, loosening it slightly. "I'm disappointed you kept this from us, Lincoln."

Then he turns to Remi with his usual insincere smile fixed in place. "Please excuse my son—"

"I'll excuse *you* for nearly calling the cops on me for making a fucking sandwich," Remi snaps back before taking an obnoxiously large bite of said sandwich. I roll my lips inward and push my glasses up, waiting for Dad's response.

He sputters, cheeks turning pink. He doesn't know how to handle Remi. I mean, *I* barely know how to handle Remi.

Dad won't apologize to anyone. *Ever.* So he changes the subject instead.

And per usual, he presents an objective *he* desires in a way that seems like a favor or special invitation, always ensuring he gets what he wants. It's part of the reason Anderson Holdings has doubled its annual acquisitions for five years straight.

"Well, Remi. I'd like to get over this little mix-up and invite you to the charity dinner tonight. It's just your luck, we have an extra seat at the table, and you can keep Lincoln company."

Remi's still chewing when he answers casually. "No, thanks."

Dad tries to play it cool, but the vein in his forehead belies his frustration.

I've only known Remi for two days now—granted, we've spent nearly every moment together and done *things* —but I already know he won't do anything he doesn't want to.

"Well, I suppose it's a school night and late notice," Dad reasons to himself. "But I'd like to reach out to your grand-father and set up dinner. It's been a while since I've seen Richard and years since anyone has seen your mother. It would be great to catch up. Have you met Grady and Sierra? I'll invite their family as well."

"The Forsythes, too," Mom adds in, and I stop this before it becomes an event planning session.

"We're goin' back upstairs now. We need to study."

"Of course, Lincoln. We can discuss this later. Your studies come first."

It always works. Mention studying, and I can usually slip out of any unwanted social interaction.

My dad sticks his hand out and approaches Remi on our way back upstairs. "It was great to meet you, Remi. Snafus aside."

I internally groan.

Snafus?

Remi grasps his hand and shakes it, squeezing a little too hard if I go by the grimace on my father's face.

"Sure thing, Bobby," Remi responds with a straight face.

I know for a fact that my father hates being called Bob, so I can't imagine how he feels about *Bobby*. We don't wait around to find out and head upstairs.

———— ⟨⟩ ————

"I'm thirsty, but I don't wanna go back down there. My parents are drainin', and I don't have the energy right now," I say with a whine.

Remi uncaps his water bottle and takes a huge swig, then passes it over.

I stare at the top, unsure.

"We made out yesterday. And I jerked off with your cum today," Remi deadpans. "I think you can manage drinking after me, Preppy."

My face heats, feeling impossibly hot.

He's not wrong.

I grab the water bottle from his outstretched hand and seal my lips to it, downing half of what's left before placing it on my nightstand.

I glance over at Remi, lounging against my headboard and grinning.

"Not too gross? Better than dehydration, at least. Right?" he teases, with that dazzling smile of his. And without thinking, I grab the pillow from my lap and smack him with it. He grabs on and tries to wrestle it from my grasp, taking me down. A carefree laugh bursts from my mouth.

Remi pries the pillow from my grip and tosses it to the ground, pinning my wrists above my head, avoiding my torso and the scrapes. He stares down at me, dark eyes intense as always.

"About what happened earlier in the shower."

I swallow thickly. My tongue feels too big for my mouth.

Does he regret it?

"I really fucking liked it, and I wanna do it more. So, I was thinking. . . *friends with benefits?*"

My heart starts to beat faster, my chest visibly rising, and I quickly respond before I can change my mind.

"O-okay. Yes."

"We can experiment. Try different things. It'll help us figure out what we like. What we don't. But I doubt there's anything I wouldn't like to do with you, Preppy."

His eyes look between mine, and he whispers, "Can I kiss you?"

I can only nod and allow him to lean down and press his plush lips to mine. He lets go of my wrists and cradles my face between his rough palms as if I'm something precious to him. Careful not to bump the little bandage under my chin, the tender touch causes a flutter in my heart that travels south to my dick, plumping it up. I thrust my hips into the air. Horny *again*.

Remi kisses me harder, angling his head and plunging his tongue deep into my mouth. His kisses are so possessive, so powerful, owning my entire mouth.

He pulls back before we get carried away, which is something we seem to do judging by the shower scene not even two hours ago. I honestly don't know what's come over me. Maybe I've just been so repressed, and now that I finally have someone to break me out of my shell, or my *cage*, I'm just all in.

No holding back.

One hundred and ten percent.

If he wants friends with benefits, I'll give it to him.

My cock pulses, tenting my sweats with a full-on erection.

"Again?" Remi asks in mock disbelief. "You said you've never done anything before, right?"

"That's why I'm so horny, Remi. Simple cause and effect," I state matter-of-factly.

Remi chuckles lightly before turning serious. He brushes the hair from my forehead, running his fingers through the length on top. "We should probably slow down before we go any further, Preppy." He scratches my scalp, and I close my eyes, a shiver running down the length of my body.

"There's plenty of time for more later. You had a really stressful day."

He leans down and gives me a quick peck on the lips. "You feeling okay?" he whispers, even though we're the only two people in my room.

No one ever asks me if I'm okay. Even when I'm sick. For Remi to care so soon. . . A lump of emotion clogs my throat, and I swallow thickly.

When he gazes at me with those impossibly dark eyes, so earnest and compelling, I want so badly to open up to him. I want to tell him everything. That I'm not okay. I'm really, really not okay. But I don't. It's too soon, even though we've seen each other's dicks and watched each other come. This afternoon was full of enough pain and humiliation; he doesn't need to know anything more. I can't handle it.

But these past two days, I've never felt so free in my entire life. So happy and, dare I say, hopeful. Hopeful for the future. For more opportunities to make my own decisions and do what I want with my life. Not what *they* want. And it's all thanks to Remi.

My new friend.

With benefits.

So instead of the full truth, I just smile and reassure him. "I'll be fine. Probably by the weekend, even. The scrapes are superficial. The chin will take a little longer, though." I reach up and run my fingers along the small bandage Remi applied, but he gently pulls my hand away.

"That didn't answer my question, Lincoln." His brows draw together, and I absent-mindedly reach up to trace the crease with my fingers.

"How are you *feeling*?" he asks again, emphasizing the last word.

"I feel. . ." I trail off, my gaze veering to the side as I break eye contact, unsure how to voice this to Remi without sounding desperate or pathetic. But he's already seen me at my worst today, and he still wanted to give me a handy, so I give him a little more. "I'm feelin' conflictin' and confusin' emotions right now. I'm upset, humiliated, happy, hopeful, *alive*." I return my gaze to him, the last word a vulnerable whisper that escapes of its own accord. "Any of the good is because of you, Remi."

He leans down and presses his lips to mine again, kissing me passionately. So unfriend-like that my head spins. Pulling back, he cradles my face with both hands, fathomless eyes searing my soul. "You're alive, baby, trust me. *You're so fucking alive.*" His declaration is so impassioned and urgent that my stomach bottoms out. And the fact that he just called me *baby* does not escape my notice.

We continue to stare at each other, trapped in this intimate moment. And for once, the strong emotions flowing between us don't scare me. They excite me. Even if we are *just friends*. It's more than I've ever had.

"Thank you, Remi," I murmur, and my eyes dart to his mouth. He gets the hint, lowering his lips for yet another tender kiss—so soft and completely opposite to his rough exterior.

The fact that people at school think he killed someone. . . An awkward laugh bubbles out of me and into Remi's face. I quickly slip my hand between us and cover my mouth. I feel an embarrassing giggle-fit coming on.

Remi sits up, giving me space. "What are you laughing at?" he asks, chuckling. It's contagious.

I remove my hand and take a deep breath. "I-I was just thinkin' about—" I'm cut off by my own laughter, and I can feel my face heating up, but I try again. "Did you know kids at school think you killed someone, and that's why y'all moved back here?"

Remi's deep laugh joins mine, and I like how we sound together.

"I did hear that. I didn't bother to correct anyone. I

kinda like it. Lets them know to fuck off. And I didn't, by the way—kill anyone." He grins savagely. "Might have come close a few times, though."

My mouth drops open. "W-what?"

"Only joking, Preppy." He smirks, shaking his head, but I'm not really sure if he *is* joking.

A phone buzzes, and Remi goes to check his bag. "That's my mom. Guess she's trying to check in or some shit. I better get going."

He gets up to gather his things. "I called a tow truck while you were sleeping, and they took your moped to my place. We'll get it fixed up, and your parents will never know. I'll pick you up in the morning, so just tell them we're carpooling. They fucking love me now, right?" He wiggles his eyebrows, and it makes me smile.

How is he so amazing?

"You didn't have to do all that, but I really appreciate it. Thank you, Remi."

"What are friends with benefits for?" He grins wide, showing off his brilliant smile, and I wonder how I got so lucky.

CHAPTER TWELVE

REMI

Monday was a fucking disaster and a blessing at the same time. What Linc and I did was mind-blowing, but what those fuckers did to him has me visualizing some pretty horrendous shit. Things I'll do to whoever was in that vehicle.

I mean, who the fuck does something like that?

Linc still won't tell me who it was, but I have no doubt I'll figure it out. I'll find the opportune moment to strike, and it will be vicious and without mercy. Because no one should be able to get away with shit like that. Especially to someone that I'm starting to care so much about.

Speaking of fuckboys, another one showed up on Tuesday. *Connor.* Bright blond hair and dull brown eyes. He's a football player and thinks he's God's gift to all women. The prick eyes me whenever one of the girls giggles at something I say. And to top it off, he's also friends with Brandon *and* in our Environmental Science class. So that means he's going on the field trip this weekend.

I've kept my distance, only introducing myself when he approached me in class. I was cordial, but there's some-

thing about him throwing off major red flags. And I definitely haven't missed the nasty looks he throws Lincoln's
way. I've got my eye on him for sure.

The field trip wasn't a hard sell for Linc's parents when
they found out we'd be partners. I know they love my
grandfather, and I'm pretty sure they just want to kiss my
ass to get in good with him.

Linc and I didn't hang out Tuesday after school. He had
piano practice and texted that he was crashing early.
Understandably so after what he went through the day
before. I would normally be worried he's pulling away after
our hookup, but with the way he came twice in a matter of
minutes, I know he's doing anything but. He seemed pretty
into this whole friends-with-benefits idea that popped into
my head. I mean, both of us are so new to this that I think
it's what we need.

A safe space to explore and experiment and come.

A lot.

Definitely come a lot.

Now it's Wednesday afternoon, another day of school
passing by smoothly. I dropped Linc off at his house, and
I'm on my way to Otto's Boxing Club in Asheville, as recom-
mended by our dear old gym coach.

I need that outlet again. And I need a way to make some
quick cash to pay my mom back. Even though her family
—*our family*—has money, I take responsibility for my own
actions.

It's a quick drive, and I'm pulling into the small parking
lot in front of the old gray building in just over thirty
minutes. A big black and white sign with boxing gloves as
the logo announces the place as Otto's.

I park out front and head to the large, double-glass
doors, giving me a good view of the space inside. The little

bell above the door chimes as I walk in and over to the young woman at the reception desk. She has short purple locs pulled into a spiky ponytail, deep brown skin, and a septum piercing with elaborate jewels. A single lightning bolt tattoo lines her high cheekbone, just under the corner of her eye. She looks badass, and I wonder if maybe she fights, too.

"Hey there. I'm Sasha. How can I help you?" she asks, smiling kindly.

"I'm here to see Otto De Luca. Recommendation from his brother." I smirk, knowing I'm purposefully stirring shit up and not giving a single fuck about it.

"Of course. Let me buzz him." Her fingers fly across the keyboard, pause, and continue moving at an almost unnatural pace, the rapid tapping noises weirdly satisfying.

She stands up, impressive at nearly my height of six feet even. "You can follow me, hun. He's in his office." I stare at the designs on the back of her employee tank top as I trail after her to meet Coach De Luca's brother.

We pass through the main gym area, and I take in all the equipment: treadmills, weight benches, rowing machines, speed bags, heavy bags, and three rings where guys are currently sparring. I follow Sasha down a hallway marked *Employees Only* until we reach a closed door with a gold nameplate on the outside that reads *Otto De Luca*.

"Okay, here we are. Good luck," she teases, giving me a little wink.

"Thanks, Sasha." I smile back at her.

I knock firmly as she retreats down the hallway. "Come in," a deep voice calls out. I turn the knob, walking in and peering around at the neat, brightly lit office with minimal furniture and zero clutter.

My eyes land on a man who appears to be in his mid-thirties. He looks like a younger, more in-shape version of Coach, and I know this is Otto. His dark brown hair is shaved on the sides and short on top. He has the same olive skin and thick eyebrows as his brother, although Otto's are more groomed. His chiseled jaw is dusted with a five-o-clock shadow, but I can see the dimple in his chin. Overall, he's a pretty good-looking man.

I came straight from school, so his inquisitive gaze tracks over my uniform, dark gray eyes sparking with recognition. "Ahh. A Blue Ridge boy."

I bristle because what the fuck is that supposed to mean? I glance down at my body like I don't remember what I'm wearing today. "Nah. Not really. Just started on Monday."

He sits there digesting everything, not unlike his brother, except it doesn't feel so probing or judging.

"And you know Sterling?"

"Know what?"

He chuckles. "Coach De Luca, my brother."

"Oh yeah, I guess. Enough to know he's a nosey prick and a know-it-all."

His eyebrows shoot up his forehead, just like his brother, but his grin also starts to widen, so I don't hold back.

"Not a fan of your brother, to be honest. Hope you're not an asshole like him," I rib, testing Otto to see if he can handle a little roasting. If he can't, this isn't the place for me.

"Oh, trust me, kid. I know. He's the biggest prick of them all, but I'll also tell you this. He has the biggest heart I've ever known, too. And if he wants to help you, I suggest you think long and hard about it and take him up on whatever his offer is."

"He didn't offer me shit, except the accidental recommendation of your gym. So, are you accepting new members or what? I need to start training again."

"Take a seat." He nods to the black leather chair in front of his desk. I walk over and plop down, sinking into the plush cushion.

He rubs his chin, making a noise like sandpaper as he scratches at the stubble there. "I can see your fire—your drive. But I also see volatility and aggression. And that instability, kid, will get you hurt."

"Look, Otto. I appreciate the warning, but I've been fighting for a while now. I don't need the safety *or* the mental health lectures. I just need your answer. Can you train me or what?"

He stares at me for a minute, and I hold eye contact, not looking away or even blinking.

I must pass some kind of silent test.

"Alright, kid. I have a spot for you. What's your name?"

"Remington Michaels. But I go by Remi." I lean back further in my seat and wait. If his brother knows my family, chances are he does, too.

He has a good poker face, I'll give him that. He doesn't even flinch.

"Raina's son. . ." he trails off, sounding kind of strange.

"My mom?" I question, the surprise in my voice evident. Why is he bringing her up instead of my grandfather? She was only sixteen when she left and never looked back. But I guess Otto is just as young.

"Yes. Your mother and I were in the same grade at Blue Ridge Prep." He smiles sadly, fucking reminiscing or some shit. "We were friends. I was just the scholarship kid, but she was always kind to me. Always stood up for me. Sterling is ten years older. He looked up to your grandfather, and now they're good friends."

He clears his throat, realizing he just took an unintentional trip down memory lane.

"How's she doing?" Otto inquires.

"Fine." I fold my arms across my chest, suddenly feeling defensive of my mom, and I think Otto can tell.

"Okay, kid. Tell her I asked about her?"

"Yeah, sure," I lie. I won't be telling her shit. She'd know I was training again and maybe fighting again, too. I can't have that.

Once I settle in here, I'll find the underground fight scene. Most cities have one. I'm sure Asheville is no different. I definitely don't tell Otto this, though. He doesn't seem like he'd go along with the idea, especially if he's possibly still pining after my fucking mom. And I'll be damned if I ever let another man control me. My asshole father is gone, and I won't be told what to do anymore. If I want to fight, I'll fucking fight.

"Let me show you around the gym before you sign the membership papers." Otto stands from behind his desk, and I follow suit. He's a good four inches taller and looks like he could bench-press me, too. He's wearing an employee tank like everyone else and tight black joggers that hug his muscled thighs.

We leave his office and enter the main part of the gym, where Otto shows me around and introduces me to some of the guys. A couple of them eye me up and down, mean-mugging me like my preppy-ass uniform personally offends them.

It's all good, though. They'll see what I can do soon enough. I always surprise people the first time they watch me fight. I didn't earn the nickname *Ruthless Remi* at my first fight for nothing. I knocked Beau Godfrey out in the first round and then continued to punch his fucking face in until Hydro pulled me off.

Beau made an inappropriate MILF joke that week at school, so I had to send an important message. I delivered it with a broken nose and a concussion. Hydro and the entire crowd chanted "Ruthless" over and over while Beau was laid out, his face a shiny vermilion.

I may have been a little reckless, a little out of control, but I was only seventeen. And I made three hundred bucks that first night. It gave me a taste of the money I could win, and that, combined with the adrenaline rush of the fight and the high of everyone jocking me, I couldn't stop. By the time I got arrested nearly a year later, each win was worth over three times the initial amount. Minimum. Too bad I never got to enjoy much of that money since Dad couldn't hold a job down and left everything up to Mom and me.

We continue our brief tour, and by the time we're done, I'm itching to get back in the ring again. Even if it is just working out and training to start with.

As we're heading back toward the employee hallway, my phone vibrates twice in my pocket, and I pause to check my notifications.

Two texts from an unknown number.

I know where you went.

And I know you have money.

My eyes snap up, darting around the gym—searching, scanning, cataloging everything and everyone. Looking for the threat.

It could be anyone. Someone from Detroit, no doubt, but it could be someone who lost money betting against me, whose ass I kicked, or maybe even whose girl I fucked.

Yeah, I've hooked up with a few chicks in the past, not

always knowing whether they were single or if they just really wanted to fuck the champion.

Or maybe it's my fucking dad, and he finally went home to the apartment to find us gone.

"Something wrong, kid?" Otto asks, and I realize I look sketchy as hell right now, and it's probably not the best first impression to be making for my new boxing coach.

"Um. Just thought I saw someone I know," I lie once again. He eyes me suspiciously but doesn't comment.

We continue to the breakroom, where there's a small kitchen with a few tables and chairs and a decent-sized area with two comfortable-looking sofas. Some college basketball game plays on the seventy-inch TV, unwatched.

We sit at one of the tables, and Otto hands me a new member packet. I set my phone down and start to read the papers, although my mind is reeling from the texts. I'm having trouble concentrating on the words.

"Here's my business card. It has my personal cell and my direct office line on it." I glance up, distracted, and take it from his outstretched hand.

"Thanks," I mumble automatically before attempting to focus back on the contract in front of me.

My phone vibrates on the table, buzzing loudly, and I blanch at the next text.

I'm coming.

I snatch it up from the tabletop and stand abruptly, the metal chair screeching against the ugly vinyl floor.

Otto shoots to his feet, looking just as alarmed as me. "You running from someone, kid?"

"What? No. Nothing like that. Just realized I need to be somewhere, and I'm late for an appointment," I lie for the millionth fucking time.

Shit. Shit. Shit.

I'll be surprised if I don't get a voicemail later declining my gym membership. Nothing usually spooks me, but this is an outright threat.

I lean down and quickly scribble my name on the paper before stuffing his business card in my front pocket. "I'll be here tomorrow night for your class," I say with a reassuring smile, or at least what I hope is one. Judging by his frown and the deep creases between his thick brows, I'm not sure I nailed it.

"Remi, hold on—"

I cut him off instead. "Gotta go, but I'll see ya, Otto!" I hold my hand up in a silent goodbye and don't look back as I rush out of the room toward the double-glass doors. I wave to Sasha before pushing through the exit and jogging to my car. My eyes dart around wildly, and my body is tense in anticipation of someone trying to jump me.

Who the fuck is coming?

The drive home was a manic shitstorm. Any car that followed me for longer than two miles, I took an unnecessary turn and looped back around, just to make sure I lost them. I may be paranoid, but I'm not an idiot. If anyone from my old neighborhood knew I came from money—*big money*—it wouldn't have gone well for me.

As soon as I get inside and take a piss, I make a beeline to the kitchen—starving, jittery, and completely on edge. Opening the massive fridge hidden in the wooden cabinetry, I grab a cold beer, popping the top off against the marble countertop and guzzling it down. I grab another and chug that as well, leaving them lined up on the counter as I reach for my third. I need to calm these nerves before I do something reckless, like text this fucker back and tell them to come and fucking get me.

I pace back and forth, sipping my beer slowly this time. I slip my loose tie over my head and toss it on the counter before unbuttoning my dress shirt and doing the same.

Who the fuck could it be?

I rack my brain and come up completely blank. I can't pinpoint one specific person with the skills needed to track me here, let alone have a big enough vendetta to try. It makes no sense. There's no way it's my deadbeat loser of a dad. He's too lazy for games and anything involving too much effort. Besides, he wouldn't beat around the bush; he would make his demands known. Loudly and violently. *The prick.*

I'm startled when my pacing is interrupted by a giant standing sentry in my path. *"Jesus Christ, Lurch!* How are you so big yet so fucking quiet?" I place my hand over my already racing heart.

Seriously though, how did this giant fucker just sneak up on me?

I need to get my shit together. Quick.

His dead eyes glance from the bottle in my hand to the two on the counter and my crumpled ball of clothing. He just grunts and retreats back to wherever he came from.

Fucking weirdo. No wonder Mom doesn't like him.

Not even two minutes later, I open my fourth beer and a bag of Doritos. I've stopped pacing and am perched on a rustic wooden barstool at the kitchen island.

Richard wanders in, his gaze zeroing in on the four beer bottles, and I get it now. Lurch is a snitch. *That's* why Mom doesn't like him.

"Sup, Gramps?" I ask casually, like I'm not starting to

get a major buzz. All thoughts of the threatening text messages easily float away.

I wish I had some weed. I need to find a guy ASAP.

"Remi, my boy. How was school?"

"It was good," I answer honestly. I get to spend every moment with Lincoln, so I actually fucking like school now. It's wild.

"Well, then. Is there a particular reason you're on your fourth beer on a Wednesday evening?"

"So, you're saying if it was a Saturday or something, it'd be cool? Just not Wednesdays? Is that a family rule? Or a house rule?" I smirk, the alcohol loosening my already smart mouth.

Good thing Gramps can take a joke, just like Mom. He ambles over, chuckling in that bowl-full-of-jelly way—warm and kind, like Santa Claus.

What the fuck?

I must be drunker than I thought.

He grabs the empty bottles and walks them to the recycling bin under the sink. I chug the fourth before he can take it away, setting it down on the counter too loudly, misjudging the distance. I blink a few times—the beers hitting me harder than normal with no real food in my system.

"What does your mother allow? I don't feel it's my place to tell you whether you can or can't drink. I don't think Rainy would appreciate that. And I'd rather you do it safely if you're going to. Here at home."

My grandfather is literally the nicest old person on the planet and fucking reasonable, too. Mom would probably chew his ass out if he tried to *parent* me. "She lets me have a couple of beers every now and then, ever since Dad left. . ." I trail off, unsure if he knows about my dad being a deadbeat and if Mom would want him to or not.

He nods sagely. "Ah, yes. Your mother opened up to me on the phone a little when she called to explain your *circumstances*. I know about Logan and his problems."

I snort, the stupid alcohol lowering my inhibitions. "You don't *really* know about him. Neither does Mom." I hop off the barstool and stroll over to the fridge, my vision wavering slightly. Four beers in less than thirty minutes on an empty stomach will *fuck* you up, apparently. Hydro would get his jollies off over this—I'm not usually a lightweight.

I reach in and grab a fifth because talking about my old man really pisses me off. All the shit I've let him get away with has been festering and rotting inside me. And there will come a time, probably soon, when I'll need to let it out before it poisons me. But it sure as shit won't be around my new grandfather. Or even my mom.

"And what don't we know, dear boy?" he enquires, pinching his chin and studying me intently. It would normally put me on edge, but I'm either too drunk or he's just too nice. Probably both.

"He's a prick," I mumble, guzzling my fifth beer while Richard observes me like some kind of wild animal in its natural habitat.

"I'm starving. I need cheesy eggs."

I open the fridge again and grab the necessary ingredients, nearly dropping the carton of eggs and ruining what's bound to be the nicest drunk food I've ever had. I think I even saw fucking gouda in here. I set everything on the counter and look for a mixing bowl and skillet.

I find everything I need, but Richard grabs the whisk

from my hand and slides the eggs away from my reach. "Let me whip this up for you, Remi. You just take a seat."

"Make sure you use the gouda," I instruct him before slinking off to the living room. "I'm gonna lie down for a second."

"I'll let you know when it's ready. I'll make enough for all three of us."

And that's how my Wednesday night ends—wasted off my ass, full of the fanciest cheesy eggs I've ever had, and watching a movie. . . as a *family*. In my new home.

It all just feels so normal that I almost forget about the threatening text messages and Lincoln's psycho bullies. . . *Almost.*

CHAPTER THIRTEEN
REMI

A loud beeping noise pulls me from the alcohol-induced slumber I was pleasantly suspended in. I reach out and slap my hand around until I find the old-fashioned digital alarm clock on my nightstand. I mash the buttons repeatedly, but it continues to beep obnoxiously.

My head is fucking pounding. Why won't this piece of shit stop?

I grab the old black box and yank it from the wall, throwing it to the hardwood floor with a loud clatter.

Who even set that?

Thoughts of Lurch sneaking into my room in the middle of the night to set my alarm clock send little prickles of unease skittering up my spine.

And with that, more memories flood in as my brain starts to wake up—mainly the attack on Lincoln and the threatening texts from yesterday. My stomach churns, and I rush for the bathroom. I turn the faucet on and splash cold water against my face, ignoring the headache pulsing behind my eyes until I can fight this nausea.

I've been here five days. *Five. Fucking. Days.*

I should be focused on my next Chem exam, not whether someone's after Lincoln or coming for me.

Fuck.

We need to get out of town, and this weekend couldn't be more perfectly timed. I'll take one of the blacked-out SUVs, and we'll stay inconspicuous and under the radar.

Once the nausea passes, I jump in the shower and wash quickly so I don't make Lincoln late. I grab one of the neatly-pressed uniforms hanging in my closet and throw it on, combing my wet hair with my fingers.

When I rush into the kitchen, Richard and Mom are both there, sitting in front of a full fucking breakfast spread on the island. I'm talking eggs, bacon, sausage, hash browns, pancakes, and fruit. And I think I see biscuits and gravy.

Yep, I sure as fuck do.

I head straight for the food, not even saying good morning to anyone. I need to beat this hangover before I leave for school, and I'm pretty sure biscuits and gravy are exactly what'll do it. I load my plate high and skip the fruit.

There's an empty seat between them, so I take it, plopping down unceremoniously. "Morning, Ma. Gramps," I say nonchalantly, like I'm not hungover as fuck on a Thursday morning. I set my full plate down and dig in, enjoying the flakey, buttery biscuits and the savory white gravy with little chunks of sausage in it. "This is fucking amazing stuff right here," I mumble around a mouthful.

"Thank you very much," Richard says proudly, his kind eyes crinkling in the corners.

"You made this?" I ask rudely, waving my fork in the air toward all the food in front of us.

"I sure did. I've always loved to cook. I just don't do it

enough lately, but I hope to change that now that you and Rainy are home."

"Fuck yeah, I'm down with that," I agree, shoveling more food in. Mom doesn't cook; the best we ever did were leftovers from the different diners and restaurants she worked at over the years.

"Remi."

Uh-oh. She's using her stern voice.

"Mom," I mimic her tone.

She huffs at my response. "Please explain to me why you decided to get drunk last night. And also why you decided to do it so openly. I mean, really, Remington. You could have just snuck a few beers to your room like a normal teenager. Are you trying to make me look like a bad mother?"

I roll my eyes just as Richard sets two pills in front of me. I'm not telling them the truth; they don't need to worry. Mom's trying to settle in here just as much as I am. I'm not willing to saddle her with this extra weight. And Gramps, *fuck*. His eyes light up every time he glances at Mom or me. Now is not the time to stress either of them out. I can handle this one on my own. I just need to figure out who the texts are from first.

"Gramps don't care, Ma. See?" I grab the ibuprofen that Richard gave me, swallowing the little pills dry. "I'm eighteen anyway. You can't ground me."

"Remington, you're still in high school, and you are still under my care. So yes, you will listen to me." I bristle at her words, confused as to why she's suddenly trying to parent me. It's too little, too late. She can't start when I'm fucking eighteen.

"Look, Mom. I'm not trying to argue right now. I just woke up, and I already have a headache. I won't get drunk in front of Gramps anymore. Okay?" I shovel the last bite of biscuits and gravy into my mouth and slip off the barstool.

"What time is it?" I ask, and there's a brief pause before I burst out laughing as I glance around at the half-dozen clocks in the kitchen alone. My favorite is the classic black cat, with its swiveling eyes and swinging tail.

Always the smartass.

"For real, though, I need to go get Lincoln. He hates being late. Oh, and he's coming over after school to study, by the way."

"Lincoln is a wonderful boy. I'm glad you two are friends. He'll be able to help you catch up in no time," Richard says, placing another pancake on his plate, adding strawberries and whipped cream instead of syrup. Just like Mom and me.

I set my plate in the overflowing sink and turn around, leaning against the counter. I cross my arms, testing the integrity of this fancy-ass school button-up, and face both my mother and grandfather.

"He's a great advisor. We've been teaching each other things. Experimenting," I say with a big grin. Mom looks a little suspicious, narrowing her eyes at me. She knows I like boys, and she also knows when I'm up to no good.

"Science stuff. Lots of science stuff. Like the field trip you signed for, Ma. I'm going with Linc," I add, hoping to cool the fire I may have just started.

"This is the neighbor boy who crashed his scooter?" Mom asks. She was home when the tow truck dropped Linc's moped off, and I wheeled it into the garage. I just haven't had a chance to mention it to Richard yet.

"Moped," I correct automatically. "And it just tipped over and got a little scratched, is all." I'm no snitch. If he doesn't want people to know, he doesn't want people to know.

"Oh, that's terrible, but I'm glad it was nothing worse," Richard says. "I can have Clifford fix the exterior up in no time."

Speak of the devil.

Lurch slowly walks into the kitchen, like a seven-foot-tall mummy, eyeing the mess of pots, pans, and dishes that Gramps made while cooking this delicious meal. His lips purse and I don't like it.

"Did you set my alarm?" I narrow my eyes at him, but his dark stare doesn't waver.

He's dead inside. I'm convinced.

I heard him whispering to Richard earlier, so I know he speaks. He just doesn't lower himself to speak to *me*.

"I did, young sir. You would be late for your studies otherwise." The most posh-sounding British accent flows freely from his lips, and I'm completely taken aback. From all the grunts he's been giving me, I was not expecting *that*.

I school my features and don't let my surprise show. He needs to know I have boundaries, and he needs to learn them quickly.

"Well, don't. For future reference. I don't care if I'm blackout drunk and sleeping it off on the bathroom floor in a pool of vomit. Don't come into my room when I'm sleeping or ever again—"

"Remington!" Mom cuts me off, even though I know she doesn't want this fucker snooping through her shit, either. "That's enough."

I give Lurch another glare and mouth the word "boundaries" before pushing off the counter and storming from the room. I grab my backpack and blazer and head for the garage, contemplating which car to test drive today.

———— ⟨∽⟩ ————

Five minutes later, I'm coasting down the rural mountain road that I now live off. I won't lie; it's scenic-as-fuck. Maybe because this is all still new to me, but it's almost distracting. Not to mention I'm on my way to pick up the boy that's been on my mind since the moment I met him.

I glance at the clock on the dash, excited that I'm right on time and that my hangover is finally starting to fade. One more day of school, and I'll get Linc all to myself for the entire weekend. In a mountain cabin. My dick plumps up just thinking about it and all the fucking possibilities it comes with.

I pull into the roundabout and put the cherry red Jeep in park. It's definitely a contender, but my eye hasn't strayed too far from the neon green Camaro. Tapping the horn twice quickly, I wait for my carpool buddy to come out.

Three days of picking him up, and it still hasn't gotten old.

The giant oak door swings inward, and Lincoln steps out into the morning sunlight. His auburn hair shines, revealing lighter shades woven into the perfectly-styled tresses. His eyes are so startling that I can notice the color difference from here. His green eye practically glows right along with his hair, and his dark eye holds so much depth. I'll never get tired of staring into them. I continue my perusal, appreciating his lean swimmer's build, knowing exactly what's underneath, and wanting more. He's slim, and his smaller muscles are so toned. It's sexy as hell.

I roll down the passenger window and lean forward, tipping my aviators to look over them. "Morning, Lincoln. Looking good as usual."

"Good mornin'," he replies, opening the door and

climbing in. "And thanks, you look nice, too." He glances at me and smiles warmly, cheeks slightly pink.

I chuckle and take off down the hill, probably going faster than I should. "Just one more day of school to get through, and it's you, me, a cabin, and a bunch of fucking leaves. You excited or what, Preppy?"

"I really am. My parents didn't even make a fuss about it. I guess because I'm goin' with you."

"They like my grandfather so much that I get some kind of automatic pass? Just for being the neighbor boy?" I'm not one hundred percent sure why Lincoln's parents changed their attitudes so quickly once they found out who I was.

"Um. Well." I see him fidgeting and rubbing the back of his neck in my peripheral. "There's a little more to it. Less honorable intentions on their part."

"Okay. . ." I trail off, gripping the steering wheel a little tighter until the leather creaks. I really don't need any more trouble.

"My family's company is Anderson Holdings. Father owns half the businesses in town and a handful in Asheville, with percentages in dozens of other businesses throughout the southeast. Your grandfather has his own companies—long-standing, profitable enterprises across the country that my parents have been dyin' to get their greedy, manipulative hands on."

Well, that definitely answers some things.

He doesn't like his parents. They're obviously controlling assholes. Richard owns a shitload of businesses which is why I'm living on a fucking estate. And Linc's asshole parents want a piece of the pie. *My family's pie.*

I pull up to the first red light in five miles, turning to stare at Linc. "So, they want to use me to get to my family's businesses. And what? Buy them out? How do they expect me to influence something like that? I just got here."

"It's the long game with them, Remi. Always the long game. They're thinkin' of the near future when Richard is too old and passes the reins to his grandson. To you."

"To me?" I parrot.

Oh shit.

No fucking way.

"You don't know anything about your family's businesses? They're everywhere, Remi. New York. Boston. Miami." He squints his eyes, almost like he doesn't believe me.

"Nope. I thought I was poor last week. I had no clue any of this existed. My mom fucking lied to me my entire life."

"Remi—"

"It's fine, Preppy. I don't want to get into my feelings this morning," I interrupt.

"Do you at least know what they *are*?"

"What what are?" I ask unnecessarily, still waiting for this red light to turn green. I glance in the rearview mirror. A car finally pulls up behind us.

"Your family businesses."

"Uh. . ." I hesitate, sort of embarrassed that I haven't asked *why* or *how* Gramps is so rich.

"Jewelry—Keller and Sons. Watches are their specialty, high-demand item. Then there's the uber-successful clock-smith business, which explains the main décor of your home, in case you were wonderin' what all that was about," he giggles. "Mr. Keller, his father, and his father's father have always been horologists—collectin' and makin' clocks. And then there are also hardware stores, restaurants, and all the investments."

I stare at Lincoln, eyes wide. "Gramps runs all that?" I

ask in disbelief, imagining the gentle and slow-moving old man sitting in a boardroom all day in his soft cardigans and suspenders. I know for a fact he was home all week, doing what I thought was, well, nothing.

Also, I am once again pissed that no one in my family tells me shit. I mean, this is a big fucking deal.

A car horn blares behind us, really laying on it. My head automatically whips forward, and I see that the red light has turned green. I press my foot to the gas, tires squealing as we speed away.

Lincoln's melodic laugh filters into my senses, causing my abs to tighten.

Fuck, I like hearing that.

He grabs onto the door handle as we speed down the winding road and answers my earlier question.

"Your grandfather doesn't run it per se. He oversees major decisions, yes, but he has a lot of people working for him. These teams—all with various managers and levels— run different areas of the country and the businesses within that region. It's honestly a complicated web, from what Mr. Keller has tried to explain to me. And I'm not so sure he quite gets it himself, really. Especially after his wife, Ms. Margaret, passed away. That's when he and I got close. I think he was lonely, and he just kinda gave up. He left all the day-to-day stuff to his teams and advisors."

I clear my throat, wanting to change the subject. I'm not ready to discuss the dead-grandmother-that-my-mom-hates thing. I know whatever actually happened is an extremely sensitive and fucked up situation. And I know I need to have that discussion with Mom and Gramps. *Eventually.*

"Hmm," I say distractedly, thinking about all the shady shit people on these teams could be getting away with if

Richard isn't monitoring his companies properly. "I might have to look into this more. Make sure they're all legit and no one's taking advantage of Richard."

"I completely agree. He's too nice for his own good. I'll help you, Remi. Mr. Keller wouldn't let me last time I tried to look into things for him. Doesn't want to be a burden, even though he never would be. I care about him like he's my own grandfather."

"Thanks, Preppy." I glance over at him and smile, an odd warmth blooming in my chest. "You're pretty awesome, you know that, right?" He ducks his head with a shy grin and red ears.

But my good mood is instantly soured with a single vibration. My stomach drops to my feet.

CHAPTER FOURTEEN
REMI

I park today's ride in my normal spot and leave the engine running while I grab my phone from the center console. It buzzed two more times before we even got to school.

I hold it in my hands, staring at the black screen and hesitating to unlock it.

Three texts.

That's all.

Maybe it's just Hydro seeing how the weed is down in North Carolina.

"You okay, Remi?"

I glance at Linc with a forced smile. "Yep. Just gotta check something."

I angle my body, ensuring he can't see the screen, forcing myself to open my texts. They're from the same unknown number. My mouth instantly goes dry. I try to swallow, but my throat makes a weird clicking noise instead. I tap the thread, and my stomach bottoms out at the ominous words staring back at me.

Unknown: I've been waiting for your response.

Unknown: Don't think I've forgotten.

Unknown: I expect some acknowledgment soon.

My hands tremble, but I quickly type out my reply before I think too hard about it.

Me: Who the fuck is this?

Me: No need for vague threats. Come at me bro if you know where I am.

Unknown: What a riot. You'll regret that soon enough, boy.

My heart rate picks up. This Unknown fucker sounds like the type to try and catch me unaware. I'm confident in my ability to defend myself, but if guns or knives are brought into the equation, it's a completely different story. I didn't bring my switchblade with me when we moved. Didn't think I'd need it in Tiny Town, North Carolina. And it's a slightly vulnerable feeling.

I block the number and toss it to the bottom of my school bag, zipping it up quickly. I turn to Linc, who has a peculiar expression on his face. Concerned? Confused? Maybe a little of both, which won't do, so I distract him with a big smile.

"Hey. You wanna go a night early?"

"W-what? Tonight?"

"Yeah. Let's get out of town early and go after school. We don't have to meet up with the rest of the class until Friday morning. We can already be there, well-rested and ready."

He pushes his glasses up and grins crookedly. "Okay. Yeah. Let's do it. I'm sure my parents won't mind since it's you. Remington Michaels," he says teasingly. "You can do no wrong." The flirty banter takes my mind off the lead weight currently settled in the pit of my stomach.

"Damn, straight." I tug on the lapels of my blazer,

giving him a cocky smile and a head nod, eliciting my favorite shy little giggle from him.

The pack of gum in the cup holder calls my name, and I grab it, unwrapping a piece and popping it into my mouth. The sweet mint flavor explodes on my tongue. I really need a cigarette or, better yet, a joint, but this will have to do for now. I hold the pack out to Linc, but he shakes his head no.

"I'll call the cabin and make sure we can extend the reservation. This is a really popular weekend," he explains.

"How do you wanna split the extra cost?" I ask, chewing my gum in what I know to be a pretty obnoxious way.

"I'll just tell them to charge my parent's card. A business expense," Linc answers with a mischievous glint in his eyes. I love this side of him. The flirty, carefree side. And I vow here and now to make sure I bring it out more.

"Niiice," I say, drawing the word out as a sly grin overtakes my face. "You gonna wine and dine me, Preppy?"

Lincoln's ears turn red, and the most beautiful laugh bubbles out of him.

God. I want to kiss him so bad.

I glance around. The Jeep is mostly tinted, and I doubt anyone is looking.

Leaning forward, I press my lips to his still-laughing ones, catching him off guard. He freezes for a second, then lets out the most tempting moan. My dick instantly jumps to life.

Lincoln slips his tongue into my mouth, taking what he wants and not thinking twice about it. He's loosened up so much in a matter of days. And I can't wait to loosen him up even more this weekend.

Starting with tonight.

I let him think he's in control for a moment longer before I grab his tie and pull, forcing him to lean into me across the center console. He follows like a puppy on a leash, and all the blood in my brain immediately rushes south to my dick. It's the only explanation for what happens next. I keep pulling, and he keeps coming until he's on my lap, straddling me in the front seat of my grandfather's Jeep. In the school parking lot.

Neither of us gives a single fuck right now. We're lost in the moment, lost in each other. I keep my grip on his tie and kiss him deeper, flexing my hips to show him how much I want him. He grinds down against me, just as horny and just as fucking hard.

He smells like fresh soap and citrus, and it's fucking intoxicating. I trail reverent kisses from the corner of his mouth, across his jaw, and down to the crook of his neck, where I bury my face. I inhale him, groaning at how fucking hard he makes me.

We continue to grind against each other in our tight-as-fuck uniform pants, erections straining to be free. I bite down on his neck and growl, still damn near humping him. Lincoln's whimpers and moans have me returning my lips to his so I can swallow them down. I lick into his mouth, tangling our tongues together. His thick, auburn hair is begging for my fingers, so I run my hands through it, messing up his perfect appearance and leaving my mark.

I reluctantly peel my lips from his, breaths ragged, and my gum is now in *his* mouth. "Fuck. I'm gonna come in my pants, Preppy."

Just as I say that, the first bell rings. The shrill sound blares from the outside speakers to ensure the slackers and stragglers hear.

"Crap!" Linc jumps up and smacks his head on the ceiling, his already tousled hair turning into a sexy, just-woke-up style. He ducks slightly, still on my lap, and rubs the back of his head. "Double crap."

I burst out laughing, smiling wide as he clambers back to the passenger side, grabbing his school bag from the footwell. It's a good thing we were forced to stop this impromptu makeout session because I'm not sure either of us would have had the strength to pull away. And that would have made for a really sticky, really uncomfortable day at school.

I'm on edge the entire day, constantly looking over my shoulder. And the blue balls sure as fuck didn't help. Not knowing my way around this town adds to my unease. In Detroit, I knew every hole in the wall, every abandoned warehouse, and which ones were safe. Here, in Hunter Springs, I don't know shit. Not a single path through the woods. No shortcuts. No hideouts. No escape routes. Nothing.

Linc and I split up after last period. He went to speak to our Environmental Science teacher, and I went to find a fucking cigarette. I wandered over to the art building in the center of campus, where I heard all the stoners hang out. And sure enough, someone was smoking in a stall, the harsh smell of burning tobacco filling the enclosed space. Complete moron if you ask me, but I walked right up and knocked anyway. I bought a pack of cigarettes and told the blue-haired kid to meet me at my Jeep in five and bring the weed and alcohol. I plan to be fully stocked and completely prepared for this weekend getaway.

I flick my silver lighter engraved with "Ruthless" and lean forward, cupping my hand to block the wind and lighting my cigarette. Breathing deeply, I release the tension and lean back against my Jeep while I wait for Lincoln to finish speaking to Dr. Benson.

After confirming the extra night with the cabin rental agency, he wanted to inform our teacher that we're going up a day early—always the model student. We received the papers for our project today in class, so we can get started early if we want. But fuck that. I have much more interesting things planned. And they don't involve leaving the cabin. At all.

"Yo, Remi! My guy. I got what you need." Ivan walks up to me, his black backpack bulging and clanking with the sounds of glass bottles rattling. He unzips it and holds it open for me to peer into.

Vodka, rum, and maybe an eighth.

"Ivan, bro. You're a lifesaver. Put it in the back, under the seat, if you can."

"On it."

Ivan comes back thirty seconds later. "Alright, my dude. The goods are secured."

Richard gave me two hundred bucks for the trip for gas, food, and snacks. I won't need that much. I hold my cigarette between my lips while I slip three twenties from my chain wallet. We discreetly shake hands, transferring the money from my palm to his. Ivan zips his now-empty backpack up and slinks away. Off to push more product to all the rich, spoiled brats looking to numb their feelings this weekend.

My new plug is long gone by the time Lincoln comes hustling down the sidewalk and over to the Jeep. His smile is so wide and genuine. He's fucking breathtaking like this.

"How'd it go?" I ask when he finally reaches me, holding my cigarette low and away from him. His cheeks are flushed pink, and he's a little out of breath from his excitement and the jog over here. It's endearing as fuck, and I can't fight the crooked smile tugging at my lips.

"Dr. Benson is cool with us goin' early. I told him I was excited to get a head start since it's my first class trip."

Lincoln notices the cigarette in my hand, and his smile drops, brows furrowing. "I didn't know you smoked cigarettes, Remi. That's. . . really bad for you. Did you know—"

"I don't," I blurt, quick to defend myself before he can supply me with some morbid scientific fact. I drop the cigarette and step on it with my boot. "Not really. Just sometimes when I'm too stressed."

"You're stressed? Are the classes too much? Am I not helpin' you study enough? I knew I shouldn't have signed you up for my schedule. I'm so sorry, Remi. It's my fault." He voices his concerns in a single breath, rolling his lips inward when he's done. He peers back at me with big, owlish eyes behind his wire-framed glasses that I found unharmed on the side of the road and cleaned up for him. His hair is still messy from this morning and hanging over his forehead in disarray. I reach out and comb it back from his eyes without even thinking.

"Whoa. Whoa. Just breathe, Preppy. I'll be fine. I have everything under control. It's not school, and it's definitely not you." I quickly change the subject from my bad habits and nerves to something more positive—our road trip.

"I'll drop you off at your house, and we can take an hour to pack or whatever. Then I'll be back to get you." My eyes dart to the dark woods lining the parking lot as Lincoln circles the Jeep for the passenger side. I scan the shadows, looking for any movement or threat.

Are you out there, Unknown?

I pull into the garage and jump out, my black combat boots squeaking against the high-gloss floor. I grab my stash of contraband from under the back seat and stuff it into my backpack, adding my school blazer so no one hears the bottles clinking against each other.

I jog up the steps to the door that leads into the house and swing it open. "Ma! You home?" I shout.

"In the kitchen, Rem!" she hollers back, and I wander down the hall to speak to her. She's sitting at the island with a cup of hot tea in one hand and her phone in the other. "How was school today?" she asks like she's about to pull a tray of cookies from the oven and pour me a glass of whole milk. Something she's literally *never* done. But maybe she will now that she's taking a break from working. Figuring herself out a little.

I just roll with it. "Really good. Lincoln and I are actually leaving for Pisgah a little early. As in right now. Don't worry about paying for anything, though. Linc's parents are covering the extra night, and Gramps gave me two hundred for food." I hate accepting money from Richard, but he has so much, and it would only hurt his feelings if I didn't.

Besides, I'll make my own money soon enough. I'm going to pay Mom back every penny she spent to bail me out of the bullshit mess I got into.

This weekend is my break from reality. Time to enjoy myself. *Enjoy Lincoln.* Next week I'll get back on track with my plan to train and find a fight league.

Quick cash is always best, and fighting provides that. I know I have to be extremely careful, but I won't be caught slippin'. Last time was a fluke, an accident. It won't happen again.

"Oh, that sounds like fuuun," she says teasingly, drawing the last word out. "And is there something going on between you and the neighbor boy?" I swear it's like having a sister rather than a mom half the time.

I roll my eyes. "No, Ma. We're just friends," I tell her truthfully. We *are* just friends, even though I'm not looking at anyone else—boy or girl—and I don't think he is either. It's just. . . We only met on Sunday. We can't jump into a relationship. That's too soon. I've never been in one, and I don't even know if I'd be any good at it. What I *am* good at is sex, and even though I've never had it with a guy before, I know I can make him feel good. And it's not too soon for that.

While I'm stuck in my head, reasoning with myself, Mom's sweet smile grows into a full-on Cheshire grin. I narrow my eyes at her, convinced she's about to be an asshole.

"Then why did a mini-life crisis just pass over your adorable little face? Are you crushing on your new friend, baby?" she teases, being the asshole I knew she would be.

"Ha. Ha. Very funny, Ma. We're going on a school field trip; lay off."

"Yes, and you're going up there a day early."

"So? There's no reason why we can't. We're excused from all of our classes tomorrow." I hate that she's making me defensive, but I know Linc hasn't come out to anyone, so it's none of her business whether I'm crushing on the neighbor boy or not.

Which. . . I am. I most definitely am.

I'm ready to move this conversation along and get packed up. The sooner we get on the road, the sooner we can get settled into the cabin. And from what I've seen online, it's pretty fucking cozy for a school field trip.

"I'm just teasing you, honey. Did you want me to make sandwiches for the road?"

"That would be awesome, Ma." I walk over and kiss her on the forehead.

"I'm gonna pack, and then I'll be back to grab the food and say goodbye. Let Gramps know if you see him? I wanted to thank him for the money and for letting me take one of his cars."

She agrees, and then I'm jogging up the stairs two at a time, excited to get on the road.

———————— ⟡ ————————

Less than an hour later, we're at the gas station on the outskirts of town, filling up and making a snack run. When the tank of the blacked-out SUV is topped off, Linc and I wander into the convenience store to pick out some candy.

"What kinda road trip snacks do you like, Preppy? I think I'm gonna get a Mountain Dew and some Skittles."

"Um. I'm not sure. I've never been on one."

"You've never been on a road trip?" I ask in disbelief.

"Nope," he says, popping the "p." "You met my parents. They're more the fly-directly-there-and-back type of vacationers. Not that we've really had many of those. And I've never been on a trip with friends. Or even a school trip. Until now." He rolls his lips inward like he's embarrassed he let all of that slip out. But I love hearing anything and everything he says in that slight drawl.

I chuckle at how fucking cute and sexy he is. He has no idea, either. Everything he's self-conscious about, I'm completely and unhealthily obsessed with. His mismatched eyes, his quirky personality, his intelligence, his kindness, his fucking innocence. *Gah*, I want to wreck that innocence.

Teach him and show him everything we've never done before. Because even though I've been with plenty of girls and watched plenty of gay porn, I've never been with a guy until the other day. With Lincoln.

"Okay. We'll just get a bit of everything, then." I grab chips, popcorn, two chocolate bars, and a bag of Blow Pops —because anything with bubblegum inside is fucking amazing. Especially ice cream.

Linc stands in front of the glass refrigerator pondering his drink decision like it's his last.

While he's distracted, I wander down the personal care aisle until I spot what I'm looking for. I grab a small bottle of lube and a pack of condoms. I'm not sure we'll use either this weekend, but it doesn't hurt to be prepared. I add a few more snacks to my basket, a two-liter of Coke, and cranberry juice for mixed drinks and chasers.

I noticed the big, burly gas station attendant sneering at us the second we walked in. Maybe he saw the quick peck on the cheek I gave Lincoln outside after he stumbled over a crack in the pavement. Or maybe he's just repressed and mad at how hot we are. Because honestly, no one should care that much what someone else does. Either way, I don't want Lincoln to see and have it affect our plans. Because I know it would upset him. So, I sidle up next to him and take the Snapple from his hands.

"Go wait in the car. I'll check out," I whisper into his ear, allowing my lips to ghost over the skin. And sure enough, a small shiver runs down Lincoln's body. I glance up at the lumberjack cunt and wink. His face turns bright red. Linc and I break apart, and I strut toward the counter, ready to check out.

I wait until the bells above the door chime then set my basket on the counter.

"Beautiful afternoon, isn't it. . .?" I glance down at his name tag. "Jimbo."

He curls his lip in disgust while he checks out every single item with an unnecessary and uncalled-for rage. Jimbo grumbles under his breath as he scans the condoms and lube. He shoves my change and my bags at me forcefully.

"My Doritos better not be crushed, or I'll be back for a refund, Jimmy!" I call over my shoulder with a wild cackle.

Homophobic prick.

At least he knew to keep his mouth shut.

CHAPTER FIFTEEN

LINC

A n hour and a half into our journey, the GPS lets us
know we're almost there. "I Like You" by Post
Malone and Doja Cat ends, and Remi pauses his
new road trip playlist with the steering wheel controls.

"Love me some Posty," he chuckles, knowing I do, too.
We haven't chatted that much, more so just enjoyed the
music and snacks while I've been glued to my latest book.
We did, however, discover we have the same eclectic taste
in music, loving everything from hip-hop to indie rock.

Remi has his left hand on top of the wheel and holds
out his right, waiting for mine. I don't even hesitate before
placing my hand in his, threading our fingers together. He
darts his dark gaze over to me and bites his bottom lip,
giving me his signature wink, and my stomach flips low.

Crap. Don't get hard. Please don't get hard.

I'm too horny. Maybe I need to jerk off more. I can't get
an erection from a simple handhold. It's embarrassing.

We rest our entwined fingers on the center console, and
Remi gives me a reassuring squeeze. "Having fun on your
first official road trip?" he asks, glancing at me again. I've

noticed he does that a lot—look at me. Watch me. Like he's fascinated by my every reaction. It's overwhelming in the best possible way. I close the Kindle app and set my phone down, giving him my full attention.

"Oh. Um. Yes. It's been really fun." I pour some Skittles into my hand and tip my head back, dumping them into my mouth and chewing a few times. "I like snackin' and readin' while you drive," I mumble around my mouthful of candy. Something I wouldn't normally do. But I'm basically on vacation right now, so screw it. "It's relaxin'."

"And I like driving and snacking while you read," he replies with a smoky chuckle that curls my toes. "I like seeing you relaxed and happy, Preppy."

Warmth unfurls in my gut, butterflies taking flight. I set the bag of Skittles down in the cupholder and stick my hands into my front hoodie pocket, unsure how to respond to something like that. Remi told me to dress comfortably and not bring any button-ups or slacks. So instead, I'm sitting here in one of the few hoodies I own, with Blue Ridge Prep Treasurer stamped across the chest. And I'm wearing the same soft, light-wash jeans I wore the first day we met, along with my Chucks. I brought hiking boots that look similar to the ones that Remi likes to wear, although they have fewer buckles. A lot fewer buckles.

Remi is as dark and mysterious as ever, his black Henley sleeves pushed up to his elbows, showing off the intricately shaded tattoos snaking his muscular forearms. I've been trying not to stare, but he's usually covered up by his school uniform. From what I can see now, there are flowers and sparrows and skulls. A jungle full of hidden mementos, with space for more. It's beautiful. *He's* beautiful.

Continuing my perusal, my gaze trails down to his skinny black jeans that have rips from thigh to ankle, letting his pale skin show through. My eyes dart back to his face, admiring his sharp cheekbones and strong brow just a little while longer.

He peeks at me and smirks.

Caught.

I blush and stare out of the front window instead of at him.

Remi's phone tells us to turn right in half a mile, and he slows down so we don't miss it. These street signs are hard to see, hidden in the thick tree branches that overhang the winding dirt road. It's so narrow it's barely even two lanes.

"We're almost there!" Remi says excitedly before making our last turn. I smile at him. His playful enthusiasm is so charming. It's infectious.

As we round a copse of trees, our weekend lodging finally comes into view, and I sit up a little straighter in my seat.

Half-hanging off the mountain and built on stilts, it's cozy, quaint, and adorable. The tiny log cabin has a wrap-around porch with a small hot tub already bubbling, thick steam radiating from the surface.

A twisted, natural wood arch welcomes us with a hand-painted sign reading, *The Buffalo Bungalow.* I look to my right and squint. The next cabin isn't too far away, and I can see it's named *Hummingbird Hill.* Hopefully, Connor isn't in that one. It would be my luck. I can see more small cabins further down the road, nestled in the beautiful fall foliage surrounding us. Daylight is waning, casting everything in a golden glow and elongating the shadows.

Remi pulls the SUV into the gravel driveway, the tiny stones crunching underneath the tires. He parks, and we immediately hop out, needing to stretch after sitting for so long. I arch my back and reach my hands above my head before bending over to touch my toes.

When I stand back up and look around for Remi, I spot him at the back of the SUV, watching me while he chews on his bottom lip. And then I realize I just bent over right in front of him. I blush at how his eyes devour me, excited nerves fluttering low in my belly at the thought of trying more *things* together. *Soon.*

It's been a few days since the incident on the side of the road. The gash tucked under my chin has scabbed over and is barely noticeable, and the tiny cuts and scrapes on my torso are also nearly healed. All in all, I'm feeling good and ready for whatever Remi has in store for us. Because I definitely don't think I could make the first move. At least not yet.

"Ready to go in?" I ask in an embarrassed rush. I have no idea why I'm still so shy around him when he literally jerked me off a few days ago and asked to be friends with benefits.

"After you, Preppy." He holds his hand out, indicating that I go first. I grab my backpack from the backseat and sling it over my shoulder while Remi carries our suitcases.

I bounce over to the wooden arch and trail my hand over the smooth, intricately woven branches. "This is so cool," I whisper in awe, pushing my glasses up my nose and inspecting the craftsmanship. Definitely hand-made. I've never stayed in such a small, rustic cabin before. My parents would never lower themselves to anything that doesn't come with five-star service.

Remi's deep chuckle hits me low in my gut, and my abs tighten. I glance at him over my shoulder with a soft smile. And—who am I kidding—probably pink cheeks. His dark eyes dance in the growing twilight.

Continuing to the front door, I use the key Dr. Benson passed out in class today and push the door open. I'm greeted by a cozy living room with plush, mismatched couches accented with quilted throw pillows. An old wood-burning stove is tucked into the far corner with a basket of small logs next to it. The oversized windows show off the spectacular mountain view and the ravine below, giving the small space an open feeling. I absolutely love it. Even the creepy chandelier made from antlers.

There's a modest kitchen equipped with the essentials and a hallway leading to what I'm assuming are the bedrooms. I flip the light on and wander down, only finding a storage closet and a small bathroom.

"There aren't any bedrooms down here, just a bathroom!" I shout toward the kitchen.

"They must be upstairs!" he yells back.

I do my business while I'm here and head toward the stairs. As I pass Remi in the kitchen, I see him loading two very large bottles of alcohol into the fridge along with the other drinks we bought. We saved the sandwiches that Remi's mom made, deciding to keep them for dinner. There won't be any meals provided until tomorrow when Dr. Benson and the rest of the class arrive.

I pass through the small living room and climb the ladder-like steps until I'm standing in an open loft that acts as the only bedroom for this cabin. There's another issue, too.

"Um, Remi?" I holler. "There's a problem!"

I hear the thudding of feet up the stairs before he appears next to me.

"Huh," is all he manages to say, or more accurately, grunt.

"There's only one bed," I say, stating the obvious.

"Well, it *is* a pretty big bed, to be fair," Remi counters.

"Should we call Dr. Benson? Or maybe the cabin rental? Although, with it being a peak weekend, I highly doubt they have more available cabins. Hmm. I could sleep on the couch? It looks decently comfortable."

Remi's eyes sparkle with mirth by the time I finish my outburst.

"Dude. Do I really need to remind you *again*? I gave you a handy, then used your jizz to jerk off while you watched and also jerked off," he deadpans. "I'm pretty sure we can share a bed. Possibly even cuddle."

A carefree laugh escapes me because I guess he's right. But on the other hand, sleeping next to someone seems so... *intimate*.

And I am most definitely not used to intimacy.

"O-okay," I stutter again, feeling a little flustered by the predatory gaze focused on me right now. Remi has this all-consuming presence. I can't think around him. I become this inarticulate, bumbling idiot my mother would be ashamed of.

He stares at me in that intense yet playfully disarming way only Remi can achieve, and I swallow thickly.

"What should we do first?" I whisper. And only when his lips split into a wolfish grin do I realize how that may have sounded. I shuffle over to the large window and take a moment to peer down into the ravine below, gathering my wits before I face him once again. "I mean, do you want to explore the trails before it's completely dark?"

Remi stalks toward me, a feral glint in his dark irises. "Uh-uh."

"No?"

"No," he parrots. "You were driving me absolutely wild

in the car. Watching you suck on those lollipops? Fuck, Preppy. I wanna suck on *you*."

"You w-what?" I stutter again, tripping over my feet as I stumble to the bed. I plop down on the end before my legs give out from nerves, excitement, or arousal. I'm not quite sure. Probably all of the above, judging by how fast my heart is racing.

"Let me blow you."

"Right now?"

"Right now," he confirms.

I scramble off the bed quickly, fumbling with my belt buckle, eager to get my dick in his mouth.

My skin is humming with need. The need for him to touch me. Lick me. Suck me. Anything and everything. *I want it all.*

Oh God, do I want it all.

He kneels in front of me, and I nearly faint at the sight of big, bad Remi on his knees for me. Reaching up and never taking his eyes off mine, he undoes the button on my jeans, ever-so-slowly pulling the zipper down. He helps me out of my pants, leaving me standing before him in my purple briefs. I instinctively place my hands in front of myself as if I could hide from him.

Good grief. Why did I wear these?

My face heats.

Remi climbs to his feet again, cupping my cheeks tenderly and forcing my gaze to his. "Hey. Don't do that. Everything about you turns me on. You could have little pink bunnies on your underwear, and I'd still want to suck your cock right now," he smirks. "Take the hoodie off. I want to see all of you."

Even though I can still feel the heat blazing in my cheeks, I nod and pull my hoodie and T-shirt over my head, tossing them to our bedroom floor. And now I'm standing here in just my tiny purple briefs and tall white socks as Remi peruses my half-naked body. My cock starts to fill from the anticipation of what's to come.

"Mmm. Yes. I like this. All of this," Remi practically purrs and drops to his knees again. He leans forward and mouths my dick through the soft fabric. I gasp and automatically reach down, grabbing onto his messy, dark locks for purchase. Fingers slip into the elastic of my underwear and yank them down, freeing my erection.

Remi's big, rough palms tickle my skin as he runs his hands up my thighs and around my hips, squeezing my bare cheeks, slightly spreading them. I whimper at the sensation.

He whips his eyes up to mine when the little noise escapes my lips. "You like this," he growls. It's not really a question, more of a statement.

And then he does it again. Kneading and massaging and getting so close to where I really want him to touch me. I pinch my eyes shut and nod emphatically.

"Mm-hmm," I moan shamelessly, still running my fingers through his soft hair.

He releases me, and my eyes pop open, peering down at him. The lust blazing between us is powerful and uncontrolled, creating an inferno of need within me.

His mouth is an inch away from my cock, and the anticipation of what his warm, wet tongue will feel like has my dick twitching in front of his face. My breathing grows faster and louder as he slowly leans forward.

Remi sticks his tongue out and swipes at the bead of precum oozing from my slit. I tip my head back, groaning at the ceiling from just the slightest touch of his tongue.

"Lincoln," he murmurs softly, reaching his hands

around to caress my bare butt once again. "Watch me suck you. Keep your eyes open."

My eyes lock back onto his. He's so sexy right now. Taking charge, yet on his knees. I'm not going to last long. I already know it.

Ever so slowly, Remi engulfs my cock in his mouth, sucking on the tip before taking my full length into the back of his throat. My eyes instantly roll into the back of my head, disobeying what he told them to do.

Remi has my entire dick in his mouth, his nose grinding into my pelvis, as he uses his grip on my backside to push me into him forcefully. It's hot.

It's so, so hot.

My dick pulses in his mouth, and he must know I'm seconds away from nutting because he pulls off with a *pop.* I groan, even though I don't want to come yet.

Ducking his head, Remi licks a long stripe up the underside of my cock. His wicked tongue laps at my slit, placing exquisite pressure there and driving me wild.

"*Oh, God.* Remi. Keep doin' that," I moan wantonly. "Please," I whine.

He reaches back around, grasping my cheeks before slipping a finger into my crease and lightly caressing my hole. "Ohhh," I moan slowly, drawing the word out obscenely.

"Look at me." The whispered command has my eyes instantly popping open. I gaze down at him, his smoldering stare intense as ever. He licks and laps at my cock, paying special attention to the spot right under my head, and it's never felt so good. My legs start to tremble, my orgasm on the brink.

He sucks me back into his mouth, and it doesn't take more than two seconds before I'm spilling down his throat in a breathy shout. My dick pulses in his mouth, wave after wave of ecstasy coursing through me. He presses more firmly against my hole while I'm coming, and I swear a second orgasm is right behind the first. And then it's blast-off, and I'm flying to the freakin' moon. My legs nearly give out as I whimper and twitch until I'm completely and totally spent.

My too-tight grip on his hair doesn't let up until my dick starts to soften, and Remi releases me with a wet slurp, swallowing every last bit of the mess. And I can appreciate that.

Even in my blissed-out state, I appreciate him cleaning up after himself.

Another inappropriate laugh bubbles out of me.

"Okay. Not what a guy wants to hear after he gives his first blow job, Linc," Remi teases, even though he knows that just rocked my world.

He stands up and kisses me abruptly, silencing my laughter with his mouth and forcing me to taste myself on his tongue. I kiss him back, unbothered by the fact that he just swallowed my cum.

Now it's my turn to return the favor.

"Can I try?" I'm feeling brave, so I grope him through his jeans. He's got to be dying to get these off. He's so hard, and his cock is practically snaking down his thigh.

"Fuck yeah. You can try anything you want, Preppy. My body is your playground." And then he winks, reaching down to unbutton his pants. He shimmies them down, kicking them off before pulling his Henley over his head in one smooth motion. And now he's standing before me in just his underwear and socks—both black, no surprise there. His creamy skin is smooth and toned, his muscles rippling under my touch. I run my hands over his chest and abs, appreciating all the hard work he must put in to look this good. I trail my fingers down his bulging biceps and caress his toned forearms, continuing to trace the beautifully shaded tattoos there. When my hand passes over his, he grabs it and walks backward, tugging me toward our bed for the weekend.

He stops at the foot of the bed, and I get on my knees for him, just as he did for me. I peel his skin-tight boxer briefs down in one motion. His hard cock bobs out, nearly smacking me in the face, but I grab it and place a tentative peck on the swollen tip, making him groan.

"Oh fuck. Do it again, Preppy." His voice is husky and lightning jolts through my stomach, knowing I'm the one making him feel like this.

The drop of precum beading at his slit is teasing me, and I lap it up, moaning at the salty, bitter taste. I lick his shaft, dragging my tongue along the thick vein there. He stares at me with hooded eyes, sinking his teeth into the tender flesh of his bottom lip. Remi stays impossibly still as I attempt to stretch my lips over the wide girth of his cock.

I know he likes eye contact, so I peer up at him, only slightly self-conscious of my strange eyes. But I know Remi seems to be intrigued by my heterochromia. He hasn't asked me about it, and I like that he just accepts me for me.

I focus my attention on the velvety soft flesh in front of me and continue to swallow him down, enjoying the heavy weight of a cock on my tongue for the first time.

CHAPTER SIXTEEN
REMI

"Fuck. You're such an innocent person, Linc. I get hard just knowing you're looking at a dick—my dick. It's twisted," I confess. "But when you touch it? Or put your mouth on it. . ." I trail off, unable to form words to describe what I'm seeing before me.

His pink lips can barely stretch enough to accommodate my girth, and it's so fucking sexy. His alluring eyes pull me in as much as the suction of his mouth is pulling on my cock. Because holy fucking hell, is he sucking me with serious force. Like some *Star Wars*, Jedi master type of force.

I run my fingers through his silky tresses without applying any pressure. He continues to bob his head vigorously, and I lower myself to the edge of the bed before my legs give out. Lincoln adjusts to the new angle, never removing his mouth from the chokehold it has on my dick. I spread my legs wider, giving him more room to work. He pops off to catch his breath, spit hanging from his swollen red lips and trailing down to my cock.

Fuck, this is so hot.

I lean back with my arms braced behind me and watch him with half-lidded eyes and a pounding heart.

He takes a five-second breather before diving back in, licking my shaft up and down and swirling his tongue around the head.

All thoughts disappear as I focus on his passionate mouth and the way he's sucking me like a pro. He's tonging my slit with delicious pressure, nearly slipping it inside before he flattens his tongue and turns his head sideways, licking me up and down. I lift my head up and peer down at him. "Holy fuck. What are you doing, Preppy? That feels amazing."

My breathing grows uneven. He's so sloppy, so enthusiastic, and it's making me achingly hard for him. I'm about to nut right now from the wet slurping noises alone. My eyes roll into the back of my head, and I squeeze them shut, gripping the comforter tightly, trying to ground myself. If I look at him right now, I'm a goner. I'll fucking detonate. I've never had a blowjob like this in my life. And it's from a boy.

"Suck on my balls," I manage to choke out, spreading my legs even wider and attempting to give my dick a reprieve so this doesn't end too soon. He pops off, trailing little wet kisses south, where he draws one of my balls into his mouth and sucks gently. He strokes me while he does this, and I can't help but thrust into his hand.

"So good," I praise, gazing down at him in wonder. "So fucking good for me, Linc."

He preens, a soft blush staining his cheeks, before he makes his way back to my dick, sucking me down again.

I'm so close, and the dirtiest thought occurs to me. One to push his comfort zone even further.

"Open your mouth and stick your tongue out."

He obeys, releasing my cock with a wet *pop*, and quickly opening wide. And then I'm shooting my load all over his flattened tongue with a restrained grunt. "Don't swallow," I manage to grit out as I squeeze my dick until every last drop is wrung out.

His tongue darts back into his mouth, and he holds my cum there, waiting for further instruction.

"Such a good boy," I praise, running my fingers through his soft hair and making him whimper.

"C'mere." I'm slurring my words, and we haven't even started drinking yet.

He listens, and I pull him onto my lap, fusing our mouths together and swapping my cum in a filthy, nasty kiss.

"Now swallow." He does with a whimper, his cheeks and cock flushing a brilliant pink, a dopey smile on his face.

Oh. This is going to be fun.

A phone buzzing three times in rapid succession has the desire in my veins turning ice cold, halting any plans to possibly take this further than mutual blow jobs.

I wrap my arms around him and squeeze tight, pressing his still-hard cock against my abs. "That, Preppy, was an amazing fucking blowie. How the fuck are you a pro on the first try?" It's like he gets As in everything he does.

He ducks his head into the crook of my neck, his breathy laugh tickling my skin. "I think it's my new favorite thing," he admits shyly.

"Yeah?"

He nods into my neck, whispering, "Can I do it again later?"

I softly trail my fingers up and down his spine, eliciting a delicious shiver from him.

"Fuck, yeah, you can. Anytime, Preppy. Any. Fucking. Time. Day or night."

I'm rewarded with more melodic laughter before my phone buzzes two more times and then begins ringing ominously.

My heartbeat falters for a second, and my smile slips. I help Lincoln off my lap.

"I better check that," I say calmly, belying the unease rumbling under the surface.

"We should probably eat, too. I'm starvin'," Linc says. "All that strenuous activity," he adds with a mischievous glint in his eye.

I jump up, slipping my jeans back on sans underwear. "I'll show you strenuous activity," I growl, reaching for him again, even as my phone continues to be a literal buzzkill in the background. Lincoln scrambles from the bed, laughing. I'm glad he's oblivious to the inner turmoil raging inside me at the moment.

He slips his clothes back on slowly, unconcerned by his own nudity, causing a small smile to tug at my lips. He's so different when it's just us, and he seems to be letting loose more and more each day.

"I'll get the sandwiches your mom made," he says excitedly, and I chuckle even though my heart is racing and my palms are sweaty.

I blocked Unknown, but that doesn't mean they can't find another phone to use. It's not like I asked Mom to change my number. She would have been instantly suspicious and questioned me about what I was up to.

I tug my hoodie on, grab my phone from my backpack and tuck it into the front pocket, and follow Linc to the kitchen.

"Would you like to eat outside? It's really nice out. Not too cold, yet."

"Sure," I agree, hating that I'm distracted by the lead weight in my pocket. I've never been afraid of much, but here I am, unable to open my damn text messages. I wish this fucker would just show their cards and quit playing games. I'm not about this cat-and-mouse bullshit.

Linc has the sandwiches unwrapped, and we mix and match until we have three halves each. I need to relax, so I pour a rum and Coke for both of us and hand Lincoln his. He heads for the back porch, ready to enjoy our simple dinner and cold drinks.

Once he's outside, I take a deep breath and set my plate on the coffee table for a second before I join him. I slip my phone from my hoodie pocket and glance down at the lock screen, needing to know.

Sweet relief floods my veins, melting the anxiety away.

It's just Otto.

Shit, though. I guess I was a no-show on my first day, no less. And I haven't even paid. This is not a good look, but what the fuck can I do now? I'm just relieved it's not Unknown. And now that I know it's not, I really don't give a fuck to deal with this on my vacation. I don't owe him an explanation; I don't even fucking know the guy.

I toss my phone onto the couch without opening my texts or checking for a voicemail to see what he has to say.

I already texted Mom when we got here, and other than that, she knows that no news is good news when it comes to me. I pick up my plate and glass and take a big swig of my drink, enjoying the burn as the cheap rum slides down my throat and warms my belly. The sliding glass door is cracked open, and I make my way over there, joining my new friend.

Outside, he has a homemade quilt tucked around his legs, his plate of sandwiches perched atop his knees. He's back in his Blue Ridge Prep Treasurer hoodie and looking cute as ever in his wire-framed glasses and chipmunk cheeks as he chews without worrying about who's watching. I like it. I like it a lot.

Fuck anyone who makes him feel like he can't be himself. Including his parents.

I take the other wicker chair, sinking into the soft red pillows. I set my drink down and dig into my food. Mom can't cook worth shit, but she can at least make amazing sandwiches. And eggs. She makes bomb-ass eggs.

There's a deep, low rumble in the distance, and the leaves rustle in the wind. "Sounds like a storm's comin' soon," Linc comments in his sexy Southern drawl, and I hum my agreement.

I think we were messing around for longer than I realized. The moon is out now, bathing the trees in a luminous glow. The crickets continue to chirp, unconcerned with the advancing thunderstorm. It's peaceful out here, away from civilization, away from everyone but the one boy who makes me so inexplicably happy.

We finish our food before I decide to ask him how he's feeling about our special *arrangement*. I need to make sure he's still okay with it. And if he wants to go further.

Setting my plate down, I bend a knee and turn to face him. The forest-scented breeze filters into my senses, clearing some of the haze that's started to form in my mind.

"Preppy."

Lincoln turns slightly vacant eyes to me, "Hmm?" He was lost in his own thoughts, staring blankly into the distance, just like I was. And it has me wondering what he's thinking about. What troubles are weighing down his mind right now? I really hope it's not us and what we've been doing.

"You good?" I ask, realizing when he sets his empty glass down that the slightly vacant look is actually a slightly drunk look. His glassy, mismatched eyes are practically iridescent in the moonlight, reeling me in with their otherworldliness.

I made those drinks strong as fuck. And he's probably not used to alcohol, either. *Shit.* I shoulda asked.

"I'm fine, Remi. I'm just full, relaxed, and comfortable." He smiles shyly and pulls the quilt up to his neck, tucking his fists under his chin and slouching back in his seat. He gazes into the trees and the ravine below, just barely outlined by the silver moonlight.

A laugh escapes my lips at his candor. He's safe here with me, but that innocence wouldn't serve him well where I came from. Or in the real world. And it's a little concerning. I wonder if he'd be open to training at the boxing gym with me? Even a couple days a week would help.

With an unknown threat lurking out there, I don't like having anyone I care about vulnerable. And I definitely care about Lincoln. If I'm being honest with myself, the only reason I haven't asked him to be anything more than friends with benefits is that I don't want to scare him off. He's never even come out to anyone except me. And that wasn't even a week ago. He's obviously horny as fuck and more than ready to mess around, but I'm not so sure he's ready for me to publicly claim him. . . Well, at least in a romantic way. Because I have definitely already publicly claimed him as my friend. I grin at the thought and chug the rest of my rum and Coke.

I grab his glass and slip into the cabin. He doesn't even notice. Lost to his own thoughts and the alcohol.

Five minutes later, I return with two more drinks and my stash box tucked into my front hoodie pocket.

"Yo, Preppy. You awake?" I ask, sliding the glass door shut behind me and taking my seat.

"Mhm. I'm good." He smiles at me and nudges his glasses up with a quilted hand.

"You wanna smoke with me? Don't feel like you have to." I never want him to feel pressured with anything.

"Um. I never have, but I guess I'm all about tryin' new things with you, Remi." His eyes sparkle, and I lean across the table, silently asking him to meet me halfway. He sits up and leans forward until our lips touch.

I press mine more firmly against his, licking at the seam of his mouth, demanding entrance. He opens for me, and we tangle our tongues together until I pull away, both of us out of breath.

I smirk at him. "I like trying new things with you, too, Preppy. Now let me show you how we roll blunts back in Detroit."

His tinkling laughter makes my abs tighten and my dick start to fill. But we can't just fuck around like bunnies out here, so I take another swig of my drink and roll the best blunt of my life. Before I light up and we both get too fucked to talk, I make sure to cover some of the things on my mind first.

"So, you said you like trying new things with me. And I think it's safe to say that you've enjoyed yourself thus far." I tip my head back, finishing my drink before peering at the sexy, shy boy next to me. My dick plumps up just thinking about everything we've done and everything we *could* do.

"How far do you want to take things?" I ask bluntly. I'm

too tipsy to beat around the bush, and I need to make sure we're on the same page before we do anything more than blowies and handies.

"I really like spendin' my time with you, Remi. And I *really, really* like when we mess around. I want to try more. I-if you do, too, of course. I just. . . I don't know what I'm doin' or how any of it works," he says vulnerably, the alcohol lowering his inhibitions. He stares intently at me, waiting for me to take the lead, and fuck if it doesn't stroke my ego.

"Well, you coulda fooled me with the way you were trying to suck my soul outta my dick earlier," I tease.

He blushes and ducks his head, smiling softly.

"Let me tell you. It was fucking awe-inspiring."

We both burst out laughing, his higher pitch harmonizing with my deeper rasp, and the sound makes me curl my fucking toes.

"For real though. That's fucking awesome because I want more, too." I reach across the space between us and stroke his soft hair back from his forehead. He doesn't have any more of his usual product in, so it's been flopping over his forehead all night. Driving me wild with the need to run my fingers through it. He keeps eye contact with me, absorbing my words and my touch. "And don't worry about how it all works. I've never been with a guy, but I'm no virgin, and porn helps, too." I smirk at the surprised look on his face.

"You ever watched gay porn?" I ask. "Ever seen two guys fuck?"

What? I'm blunt when I'm drunk, and I'm definitely well past tipsy.

"U-um. No, I haven't."

"Ever watched straight porn?" I need to know just how innocent he is.

"No."

"Damn. You're an angel, Linc," I tease. "I'm going to corrupt the fuck outta you."

He whips the blanket over his head, hiding from me. I throw my head back and roar with laughter. He's so fucking adorable.

He pulls the blanket down to his nose, only his glassy eyes peeking out.

My smile is huge, waiting for what he's going to say.

The quilt comes down another inch, and he licks his lips.

"A-are you a top then, Remi?" he asks hesitantly yet matter-of-factly. More like it's science and less like it's dependent on actual feelings. The frank question catches me a little off guard.

"Dunno. Never been either," I answer truthfully. I honestly don't know if I'll prefer to top or bottom. Maybe I'll like both. I like to leave all my options open. Bisexual and vers. I bet that's me.

"What about you, Preppy? Think you'll top or bottom?"

"I'm not sure either. Um. Bottom, maybe?"

I take a risk and go for it since we're both so open right now. "Well, we can just go with the flow, but I'm ready to try everything with you, Preppy. *All the things,* if you catch my drift."

He sits up straighter, the blanket falling to his lap, tenting over his erection. Sneaky little shit. I wonder how long he's been hiding a boner under there.

His throat bobs as he swallows with an audible gulp. "Y-yeah. Yes," he stutters. "I want to try everything, too. If you'll show me how."

"You fucking bet," I agree, climbing to my feet and walking over to the railing. I lean over and peer down into the dark ravine below. Another rumble of thunder echoes in the distance. A warning of what's to come. "We better smoke this before the storm rolls in."

I spin around and hoist myself up to sit on the edge, leaning against one of the support beams, but still facing Lincoln.

"Remi, be careful."

"Aw. Worried again? Guess you like me for more than just my cock, huh?" I clutch my heart like a smartass.

"'Course I do," he says earnestly. Even in the darkness, I can see his face turn red.

"Don't worry, Preppy. I was practically a parkour champ back in Detroit." Okay, that may be an exaggeration. But I can't tell you how many times I've had to run and hide in the streets—to climb, jump, *evade*. Too many times to count, really.

"It's at least a hundred-foot drop, and you're drunk. And about to be high. Can you just sit back down, please?" He starts to bite his nail nervously, and I realize I'm causing him anxiety. That's the last thing I'd want to do. I hop down and sit back in my seat.

"No worries, Preppy."

Lincoln leans back in relief, and I slip the blunt from behind my ear and place it between my lips. I duck my head, cupping my hand against the wind as I light the end. I take short little puffs, stoking the cherry to life.

"Skunky," Linc says, wrinkling his nose, and I burst out laughing.

"That means it's the good stuff, Preppy."

Once the blunt is burning to my satisfaction, I lean back and inhale deeply, holding it in. I close my eyes and listen to the sounds of the forest, letting the weed do its job and relax me further, melting my worries away.

Before I pass it to Linc, I make sure he knows what to do. "Just take one small hit and blow it out. Don't hold it in like I did. I don't want you to cough. You might still, but just go easy. You can have a bigger hit the second time if you want."

He nods a few times and takes the blunt from my fingers. He stares at it blankly for a second before putting it to his lips and inhaling softly, blowing the small puff of smoke out right away. A few little coughs escape him, but nothing too bad. He takes another hit, this time longer, and holds it for a few seconds before blowing out a larger cloud of smoke.

Linc turns his head, coughing roughly into his elbow as he sticks his arm out, handing the blunt back to me.

I chuckle and take it from his grasp. He's gonna be so fucked after that. We should probably head to bed soon.

Without taking my eyes off Linc, I take another slow pull. When he's finally done coughing, he slouches back in his seat with his eyes closed, chest heaving.

"You okay over there, dude?" I can't help but smile at the dazed look in his bloodshot eyes when he finally turns and stares back at me.

"M'fucked," he mumbles in an uncharacteristically husky tone.

I choke on the hit I'm holding until I'm coughing as hard as he was. When I finally compose myself, I put the blunt out in the glass ashtray that was out here.

"You just said fuck," I tell him in a scratchy voice.

"Huh?" he asks, lids going half-mast, looking pretty fucked out of his head. And everything's hitting me all at once, too.

"Nevermind," I rasp.

I stagger to my feet and grab Linc's forearm, pulling him up. He wobbles slightly, and I sling an arm around his shoulder.

We both need to chug some water, but other than that, I'm ready to pass the fuck out.

CHAPTER SEVENTEEN

REMI

Not having drunk enough for a hangover, I wake toasty and comfortable, cuddled under a thick, homemade quilt and a firm body.

My brain stalls, doing a double-take at that thought. There's a warm, hard body on top of me, with an even harder appendage digging into my morning wood.

Linc.

I crack one eye open and peek under the covers. At least we both have our underwear on. And socks. We have those, too. But that's it. We must have gotten hot in the middle of the night.

I squint at the old, weathered-wood clock on the wall. It's eight thirty, and the rest of the class isn't due until ten. We have plenty of time to get up and ready.

Linc's out cold, snoring slightly, face tucked into the crook of my neck. Each exhale tickles my skin, causing my already hard dick to twitch against his. He's only an inch or two shorter than my six feet, but his trim body is so much leaner than mine. I wrap my arms around him while he continues to sleep. My nose burrows into his soft hair, inhaling his fresh, citrus scent that still lingers despite the blunt we smoked last night.

He doesn't move, so I trail a feather-soft touch down his spine and up again.

He finally stirs, wiggling against me, rubbing our cocks together. Only the thin cotton of our underwear separates us.

I bite my lip and grasp onto his hip, stalling his movements before I accidentally come. I want him to be awake and conscious the first time we get off like this. And preferably with no fabric between us.

Keeping hold of his hip, I use my other hand to give his plump little ass a nice squeeze.

He moans and ruts against me.

Okay, bad idea, Remi.

My hips automatically thrust back. It's out of my control, like a reflex. I couldn't stop it if I wanted to. He moans and whimpers, my grip on him tightening.

"Wake up, Preppy," I grit out.

Fuuuck. He needs to wake up. Right now. My balls are tingling.

And then he does, pushing up slightly, his sleepy, confused eyes peering down at me. "Remi?" he breathes, flushed and sweaty.

"Morning," I croak, and I can feel the heat rising in my cheeks—a rare occurrence for me.

A hoarse laugh erupts from deep down. "I would say, 'this isn't what it looks like,' but. . . It's exactly what it looks like."

He tucks his face into the crook of my neck and groans, his warm breath tickling my skin.

I squeeze his hip to get his attention, caressing the smooth skin and running my hand up his back and down again. "Hey. Don't be embarrassed. I'm not. Well, not really. Besides the fact that I almost just came from grinding on a sleeping boy. That's kinda fucking creepy."

His tinkling laughter is a beautiful melody I want to capture and preserve forever. Trap it in a little glass jar like the lightning bugs dancing outside. I love his voice, his laugh, his eyes, his smile. . . Fuck, he's captivating. And it's hard not to be completely and totally obsessed.

I distract myself from the overwhelming thoughts that I'm not prepared to deal with and ask the question I really need to. The important one. "So, now that you're awake. Wanna come?"

He giggles some more, nodding his head into my neck.

"You cussed last night, by the way." A random memory pops into my head at that moment, and for some reason, I feel the need to voice it.

"I did?" he sounds aghast or some shit, making me chuckle.

"Yup, said the F-word, too. The worst one. The big baddie."

He covers his eyes and groans. "I don't even remember that."

"I'll agree to pretend it never happened because I had goals, Preppy. Plans to make you say 'fuck' in even more debauched ways." His embarrassed groans turn into horny whimpers before I even finish my sentence.

I'm pretty sure you can't have sex without saying the word "fuck" at least once. We'll see. I'm here to test that theory. And hopefully soon.

I squeeze his ass again, excited by thoughts of fucking him. "Kiss me," I demand.

He peers at me with a hand in front of his mouth and shakes his head. "Mornin' breath," he mumbles from behind his fingers.

I roll my eyes and smirk. "Quit overthinking everything, Linc. You wanna come or what?"

He keeps his hand in front of his mouth but nods enthusiastically.

"Then kiss me. I don't give a fuck about morning breath." I pull him by his ass, grinding our erections together and causing us both to gasp. "Let's come like this. But without the clothes," I declare boldly. We haven't gone that far yet, skin-to-skin.

"I got tested before I left Detroit, and I'm good. I haven't been with anyone since. And I know you are, too, obviously. But I just wanted to let you know that you're safe with me. I mean that in every way possible. Okay?"

"Okay," he whispers back with a shy smile that's completely at odds with the lust darkening his gaze.

And then my hands slide into the waistband of his briefs, giving his bare ass a squeeze before I push them down low enough for him to kick off.

"I wanna play with this ass so bad," I tell him, rubbing his cheeks tenderly before squeezing them harder, causing him to whimper and buck against me. "But we'll save that for another day."

I thread my fingers through his silky tresses and pull his head down for a searing kiss, rolling us so I'm on top now. His legs automatically part for my hips, cradling them between his thighs. My gaze tracks his body, from his pale pink nipples begging for attention to the long, lean cock jutting straight out at me.

Fuck, this is so hot.

Reaching for the bedside table, I grab Linc's glasses and

the small bottle of lube I stashed there yesterday afternoon. "Here, Preppy. I want you to see what I'm about to do to you. To us."

He slips his glasses on with a crooked smile, and I shove my underwear down. The lube is cool and wet when I squeeze a generous amount into my hand, settling myself between his legs once again. I lean down on one forearm and slot our dicks together, gripping tightly.

The sensation has us both groaning out loud. I silence him with a kiss while I continue to run my hand over both of our cocks in a somewhat exploratory way.

Linc pants and moans beneath me, wrapping his legs around my hips and thrusting with the movement of my hand. We both pick up our pace, rubbing against each other.

"Oh, holy fuck. I'm not gonna last, Preppy. Keep doing that."

"Remi," he whimpers, digging his heels into my ass as I jerk us harder, the wet slurps pushing me higher. I let more of my weight fall onto him as I lower myself enough to nip and bite at his earlobe. I start to twist my hand as we both fuck into it, and the feeling has my balls instantly drawing up. And it must for Linc, too, because not even two seconds later, he's coming all over my hand and dick. I can feel his cock pulsing against mine, and I squeeze tighter, prolonging his orgasm and triggering my own. My grunts are muffled against his neck as I bite down, causing him to whimper. My release mixes with his, and our bodies become a sticky, cum-covered mess.

I roll off of him, breathing heavily, and hold my hand up between us. My entire palm glistens from the lube, and stringy cum drips from between my fingers. I glance to my left and smirk. Linc's nose wrinkles in disgust, just like I thought it would.

"Who's showering first?" I ask with a teasing lilt.

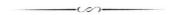

The trails are muddy after last night's thunderstorm as we trudge our way to the campsite where we're meeting the rest of the class. The crisp mountain air smells like damp earth and decomposing vegetation, and the thick mud makes a squelching sound under my hiking boots.

Lincoln says this is the central meeting point between the cabin rentals. There's also a main lodge with a cafeteria where we'll have meals, but I guess Dr. Benson wanted to meet outside first.

Linc and I are ten minutes early, per his insistence, and he strolls over to our teacher in his olive green L.L. Bean fleece and straight-fit gray cargo pants tucked into hiking boots.

My lip quirks because he looks cute. A little nerdy but cute, nonetheless. His hair is askew, the auburn strands hanging haphazardly over his forehead, adding to his innocent appeal.

I sit on one of the slightly damp, sawed-off logs acting as a bench. Six of them circle a fire pit that's outlined with medium-sized stones. Looks like it could be fun. Add a little booze and some weed, and anywhere can be a good time.

Linc stiffly shakes hands with our teacher, and I snort. So fucking proper and polite. But the fact that he's actually a freak in bed, and it's just for me. . . Shit. My dick starts to harden. I adjust my jeans and stretch my legs out, watching him talk animatedly about. . . I don't really know what, actually. Probably leaves or some shit.

A few minutes later, Lincoln wanders over and plops down next to me, dropping his backpack filled with supplies we might need for our project. Mine, of course, has drinks and snacks.

"You didn't come say hi." He frowns at me, not understanding my *I don't give a fuck* attitude when it comes to anyone in a position of authority. He's never been in trouble; he wouldn't get it. When you've had adults telling you you're bad your entire life, you start to believe it, and you get just about fucking sick of it.

"I'm sure he'll call attendance. What else do you want me to do?" I ask with a little more bite than I mean, but if he expects me to be buddy-buddy with any of our teachers, we'll have to agree to disagree. That is a hard pass for me.

"Okay, class!" Dr. Benson's booming voice has Linc whipping his confused eyes forward to listen intently to whatever *rules* he needs to give us.

"It's good to see you all made it out. I'm going to do a quick roll call for formality's sake."

Dr. Benson gets through all twenty-something names relatively fast, and then he's going over which trails we're allowed to take and which ones to avoid. I see Lincoln taking frantic notes next to me, so I don't bother. No point in both of us doing it.

"And lastly, I want all of you to team up with another pair to make a group of four. At least until we reconvene at lunch. More brains equal fewer chances of getting lost, mauled by a bear, or falling off an unseen cliff. And please, for the love of God, do not do any of those things, people. I really do like my job." Linc titters next to me, along with all the girls, and I can't help but snort a laugh, too.

"I'll meet you all at the main lodge in five minutes," Dr.

Benson says. "If you can't decide on groups, I'll pick for you. But keep in mind, this is only for an afternoon. I really hope that you can peacefully coexist with any two of your peers for such a short amount of time. But alas, you are indeed teenagers, and I understand the turmoil that can come with it." He gathers his things but then snaps his fingers several times. "Oh! And don't forget to grab a can of bear spray from the basket on your way to breakfast!"

Bear spray?

What the fuck is that?

In less than thirty seconds, everyone has paired up, scurrying away to eat. Which now leaves us with exactly one option.

Connor and his meathead friend wander over, hovering above us while we sit perched on the log.

Fuck that.

I jump to my feet, forcing him to step back so we aren't face-to-face.

"Guess y'all are with us," he declares, sounding like he's been punched in the nose one too many times. He eyes Linc up and down in a somewhat threatening way, and it grates on my fucking nerves. Especially when I see Lincoln squirm uncomfortably in his seat, lowering his gaze to the ground.

"Guess so," I agree, but fuck, man. I do not want to spend my morning with this tool, and it's clear that Lincoln doesn't want to either.

"Well, whenever we've done groups like this in the past, we just rotate. And only one person is out on the trails at a time. Dr. Benson will never know."

"That's dangerous and defeats the purpose of extra safety precautions." Lincoln surprises me by speaking up.

"No one asked you, Safety Patrol," Connor sneers.

"What?" Linc asks, scrunching his brows adorably.

"You probably jerk off to a list of rules—"

"Hey!" I bark, cutting him off. "Get to your point."

I let the ribbing slide because although he is a complete asshole, he hasn't said anything outright hostile yet. And I'm ready to let these fuckers go do their own thing so Linc and I can do ours. He's been looking forward to this trip and seeing the leaves all week. I'm not going to let Connor ruin that for him.

"We can take turns and do less work this way."

I don't even have to consult with Linc. This isn't work for him; this is fun. He's excited, and I'm excited for him.

"No thanks, dude. You guys can do that. I'm no snitch. But we're gonna do our own project."

Connor's blond brows crease in the center, like he can't understand how I could possibly want to do all that work. And yeah, maybe a week ago, I would have had that same mentality, but not now. Not with Lincoln.

He practically glowers at Linc as if it's entirely his fault that they now have twice the work to do. And I raise one eyebrow in a silent question, tugging on my eyebrow stud.

Are we going to have a problem here, Connor?

"It's settled, then. Let's go eat." The big guy with him grunts, turning to march up the hill toward the main lodge, unbothered by the exchange. Well over six feet tall, he definitely looks like a linebacker. I eye him speculatively, wondering if I could take him in a fight. I have the weirdest urge to jump on his back just to see how many seconds it takes me to choke him out. I think I could have him snoring on the ground like a three-hundred-pound baby in less than ten seconds.

Connor's lips flatten into a thin, straight line, and his

irritated gaze darts between Linc and me. His lip curls
before he storms away. As if we give a shit that he's
annoyed or inconvenienced by his own fucking laziness.

"Catch ya later, Con!" I call after him, smirking.

Only when he's out of sight do I peer down at Linc,
who's still sitting on the bench next to me. With a soft
smile, I ask sweetly, "Hungry?" As if none of that just
happened.

The beaming smile I get in return is answer enough.

Linc and I finished documenting today's group of leaves
sooner than anticipated because he's a fucking genius, so
we went to the campsite earlier than planned.

The object of my friendly obsession is sitting on the log
beside me, reorganizing his backpack with a protein bar
sticking out of his mouth. A slender finger nudges his
glasses up before flipping through our collection for a
second time.

Each leaf sample is meticulously stored in a clear baggie
and labeled with neat, precise handwriting. Lincoln
included the scientific and common name, color descrip-
tion, and date collected. He is diligent, detailed, and thor-
ough. Just as he is in other, more sexual aspects of his life. I
smirk to myself.

"Crap. I think I left the red oak leaf at the final bench.
That's the last one we need for today's grouping, and it was
perfect," he pouts. Fuck, I'll do anything for him when he
pouts. Including searching a forest for one particular leaf,
just to make him happy.

I hop off the log and head for the trail marker. "I'll get

it!" I holler, convinced I actually know what an oak leaf looks like now, thanks to Lincoln.

The uneven ground makes it more difficult, but I jog back to the bench where we last worked on our notes. I instantly spot the large, bright red leaf sitting undisturbed on the seat and sigh in relief. That was easier than expected.

Leaves rustle, and twigs snap behind me, alerting me to someone's presence.

I whirl around, instantly on guard and ready for anyone or anything—even a fucking bear, thanks to the trusty repellent in my hoodie pocket.

I breathe a sigh of relief when it's just the annoying douchebag and not a fucking grizzly or Unknown. Connor smiles wide like we're old pals or some shit, which is different from the hostile vibes he was giving off this morning when Linc was there.

"Hey, Rem!" I want to roll my eyes but abstain. Why do these tools automatically think we're friends? As if I'm actually one of them. It's laughable, really. I guess Brandon didn't relay the fuck-all-the-way-off memo to him. Shitty friend. But no surprise there. He was probably embarrassed at how he nearly pissed his pants. Didn't want his friend to know.

"Sup, Connor? Where's your partner?" I already can't remember the big dude's name, or maybe I never knew it.

"Oh, Gus is on his way here to meet me now. So we can return to the campsite as a pair. We took turns, and he's been at the cabin getting high for the past hour and a half. As soon as we eat, it's my turn," he tells me, grinning with excitement.

I can't deny the logic in that or the fact that I plan to do the same after dinner. But his next words crush any hope I may have had that he's not actually a vile cuntbag.

"I'm glad I caught you alone, bro. I just wanted to say sorry you got stuck shacking up with the goody-two-shoes gay boy. That's gotta be hella awkward morning wood." He chuckles casually like it's not a horribly offensive thing to say.

This would normally be the moment that I loudly and *violently* declare my bisexuality, but no one knows Linc is gay. He hasn't come out, and I know he's not ready. I'd only be confirming this asshole's hate speech, and I refuse to do that.

So instead, I settle for the violence-only option as rage burns through my veins, igniting my fury. The gruesome imagery flashing through my mind is urging me to risk everything and jump-kick Connor straight in the face.

I have zero tolerance for homophobic bullshit, and I react on instinct. My right hook lashes out lightning fast, cracking into his jaw hard enough that pain splinters through my knuckles and up my hand. His head snaps to the side, but he recovers quickly, spitting a mouthful of blood onto the mud below.

It was a warning shot. A punishment of sorts. I know he's heard the rumors, and although not all of them are true, they aren't all lies, either. I will lay his fucking ass out if he comes at me.

Connor stands there frozen for a moment, dull brown eyes staring back at me in shock. A skinny trail of blood drips down his chin, speckling his white hoodie with crimson droplets.

The reprieve lasts all of three seconds, and then he launches himself at me. I side-step, shoving him forward and causing him to trip over his feet. He faceplants to the ground comically. I can't believe this tool is the school football star.

"Fucking rookie move, Con," I taunt because I don't give a single fuck about his feelings.

He scrambles to his feet, but the slick mud has him slipping, and he falls to his knees instead.

"Stay down, you little bitch," I grit out. "That punch was me letting you know to watch your fucking mouth. I won't tolerate hate of any kind. Especially involving my friends."

His normally pale skin is mottled red, and his nostrils flare like a bull ready to charge.

I'm reckless. Impulsive. And I wave the red flag.

"I expected you to hold your own in a fight," I goad. "But, let me tell you. I am less than fucking impressed, *bro*."

That does it, and Connor lunges for me in one smooth motion. It catches me off guard for a split second, and he manages a solid punch. Right in the gut.

Oof.

I double over, wheezing as the air is forced out of me. Cradling my stomach, Connor sees his opening and takes it, delivering a swift uppercut straight to my face. I stumble back a step, hands instantly in guard position.

Motherfucker!

I reach up, lightly touching my tender cheekbone. I have enough experience to know that'll most likely turn into a black eye. And Mom is gonna be on my ass about what happened.

Blood whooshes in my ears, and my vision tunnels. An inhuman roar bursts from my lips, untamed and animalistic. I tackle him to the muddy ground with a splat.

Straddling him, I rear back, intending to slam my fist

into his nose. He throws his forearms up, blocking me before I make contact.

While he's guarding his face, I land three punches in quick succession to his ribcage. Not hard enough to break anything, but he'll definitely be uncomfortable in his football pads for a week or two.

As expected, Connor attempts to block his torso, exposing his face.

I plan to make the little bitch even more nasally.

Before I can take my shot, two massive arms rip me away, stealing the air from my lungs.

I slam my head back, attempting to head-butt whoever-the-fuck just snatched me up, but I miss.

"Stop it," a deep voice growls, giving me a little shake.

Fucking Gus.

His thick-ass arms are banded tightly around me, hauling me backward as I struggle wildly. He's just too fucking big.

Connor scrambles to his feet, clutching his stomach, blood dripping from his mouth.

"Put me. The fuck. Down. Now," I say with clenched teeth, squeezing my hands into tight fists as violence hums under my skin. Anger and fury vibrate beneath the surface, waiting for his grip to go slack. All I need is for Gus to relax for one second so I can slip out of his clutches. Maybe throat-punch him. Or maybe a rear-naked choke hold. If I can get that just right. . . It would be lights out in a matter of—

"I can see you plotting. Stop it," he rumbles.

"How can you see my face when you're behind me?"

His meaty arms tighten around me in warning. "Shut up, you little shit. I don't know what Connor did to piss you off, but we have rules around here. Now, I'm going to let you go. And both of you are gonna control yourselves. We have a game next weekend, and we need Connor. So if you go after him again, you and I will have a problem." He lets go, shoving me away roughly.

"Then put your boy on a fucking leash and muzzle him!" I shout.

Gus stabs a thick finger at Connor when he advances on me. "Hey! You! Go stand by the fucking bench! Goddamnit!" He runs his hand over his close-cropped hair, and his deep brown skin glistens with sweat like this situation is causing undue stress.

"New kid!" he barks.

"It's Remi." I grit my teeth in annoyance but listen anyway.

"The rules here are we don't fight at school. We don't risk our futures at the academy. If you got beef and wanna fight, you come to me."

"Come to you?"

"Yes. Me. I run things around here. Fights." He huffs out an annoyed breath, crossing his arms in front of his barrel chest.

Okay. So I definitely misjudged him. Not a meathead at all. Because this is fucking genius. This is fucking *perfect*.

Gus turns to the bloody-mouth douchebag seething on the other side of the trail from us. "Connor. If you wanna fight, you know the drill, man."

Connor's jaw is clenched so tightly I can practically hear his teeth grinding. "Fine. A thousand bucks."

A thousand bucks? Say what?

"Tomorrow night, then. A one thousand dollar wager. Winner takes all, plus a percentage of bets. We'll hold an impromptu fight night in the woods. There's an old barn twenty minutes down the road. It's abandoned but not too run-down. All the local kids use it to hang out and get wasted, so you'll have a bigger audience. More bets. More money." His eyes shine with greed and a manic sort of excitement that I can relate to.

Knock Connor out fair and square *and* earn twenty percent of the money I owe Mom?

"I'm in."

CHAPTER EIGHTEEN
LINC

By the time Remi comes back from the trail with the missing red oak leaf in hand, Dr. Benson and half the class have already arrived at camp. The sun is starting to set, and the thick forest surrounding us further blocks the last bit of golden light. But it's not too dark to see the disheveled state he's in. My eyes immediately track his mud-caked clothes and the red mark blooming across his cheekbone, right under his left eye.

Movement at the treeline has my attention switching to Connor and Gus, who emerge looking just as rough.

Everyone goes quiet.

"Don't tell me it was the bears," Dr. Benson tries to joke, and a few kids snicker.

"Nope. It was the cliff. Connor almost fell off, and I had to save him," Remi deadpans.

My curious gaze flicks to Connor, and his jaw ticks, the pinched expression on his face showcasing his true feelings. His knuckles are a little red, just like Remi's, and he has dried blood smeared across his chin.

It's obvious Remi is lying. My eyes dart to Dr. Benson next. I blink rapidly, awaiting his response.

A heavy sigh escapes him, and he shakes his head in that disappointed-parent way that I hate so much.

"Connor?" Dr. Benson asks, expecting to hear his side of the story.

"It's true," he says between tightly clenched teeth. "I. . . *fell.*"

"Gus? Do you have anything more enlightening to share with the group?"

"Nope."

Dr. Benson pinches the bridge of his nose, closing his eyes and inhaling a long breath before releasing it as an exasperated sigh. And I don't blame him. I would be frustrated, too. Hopefully, Remi will open up to me later. I really don't want him to be in trouble.

"Well, if no one needs medical attention, there's nothing else to do here. Go eat." He waves his hand in defeat and stalks away, muttering under his breath.

Remi plops down next to me, leaning forward with his elbows on his knees. He stares into the campfire, seemingly lost in thought.

Connor is on the other side of the fire pit from us, flames dancing across his skin and mirrored in his normally dull eyes. They're alight with vengeance, searing me with promises of future pain. Whatever happened between the three of them, I'm pretty sure it had something to do with me. I swallow roughly and try to get Remi's attention.

"What happened?" I whisper, nudging his leg with my own.

He gazes at me intently, the pale moonlight reflecting in his dark eyes ominously.

"Don't worry about it. I'm handling it tomorrow." A slow smile curls his lips until he grins with all his teeth.

I frown but don't push for answers since we're surrounded by so many curious eyes. I'll just ask again later. When we're alone. Because I'm not so sure I like the sound of that. And I *definitely* don't like the look in Connor's eyes as he shoots lasers at us from across the fire.

It's a mild October this year, and the summer's warmth has lingered longer than normal. The fireflies continue their dance, the flickering lights putting me in a trance as the crickets join in on the evening concerto.

The fire hisses and pops while hot dogs sizzle and marshmallows burn.

Classic American camping food at its finest.

Not that I would know.

"You ever had a s'more?" Remi asks as he side-eyes my attempt to spear a hot dog with my skewer. I stab three holes through it before I finally get it secured.

We've been having a good time since Connor quickly made his food and stormed away with Gus hot on his heels. I don't think anyone here wanted his negative energy around anyway. I don't know how Gus puts up with him, acting as his keeper like that. Connor is a loose cannon, and he's always aimed at me.

Remi leans down to whisper in my ear. "You're scaring me with the way you're handling that weiner, Preppy."

I giggle, holding the massacred hot dog over the open flame anyway.

"I've never cooked hot dogs like this. And no, I've never

had a s'more, either," I admit, answering his earlier question.

He makes a whistling noise through his teeth. "All kinds of firsts for you this week, huh?"

I can't stop the laugh that pours out of me, even as a hot flush burns my cheeks, scalding my skin with embarrassment.

Movement out of the corner of my eye catches my attention. Dr. Benson watches me from two logs over with an unreadable expression.

My smile falters. I'm not ready for my favorite teacher to know I'm gay. I only came out to Remi a few days ago; I can't just jump into the deep end. I need to wade in slowly. And the only two people who I can think of to come out to next are Grady and Sierra. I know they'll accept me for me, and I probably should have told them by now anyway.

"So, you're okay with losing an hour of life just to have dinner tonight?"

"Huh?" Remi's strange question pulls me from my inner dilemma.

He chuckles, firelight dancing in his eyes. Even in the darkness, I can see that the delicate skin under his eye is starting to bruise.

And then it dawns on me. The morbid statistic I gave him about hot dogs on our very first date. Wait, no. I mean day. Our very first *day* hanging out.

Not a date.

Our not-date.

Oh God, I have no idea what's going on.

I duck my head slightly and chuckle. "Oh, right."

I pull my hot dog out of the flames, stick it in a bun, and slide the skewer out. I shrug. "I'm too hungry to care at the moment."

I add a single stripe of ketchup, shoving half of it into my mouth and biting down. Mom's not here to see me eating like a heathen, so it doesn't matter.

"Preppy," Remi practically purrs.

His deep voice is a warm caress shielding me from the cool nighttime breeze.

I swallow the massive bite in my mouth before turning to look at him, our faces less than a foot apart. He gazes back at me with a salacious stare that has my stomach tightening. His wickedly sensual mouth curves into a sly, knowing grin.

And that grin is telling me we need to go to the cabin. *Now.*

A throat clears, pulling us both from our lust-fueled trance.

"May I speak to you for a moment, Lincoln?"

"Y-Yes, sir," I stutter uncomfortably, running a hand through my messy hair and trying to get thoughts of Remi out of my mind before I get a hard-on in front of our Environmental Science teacher.

Dr. Benson's eyebrows crease in the center when I don't move. "Alone?"

I don't know why I do it, but I glance at Remi again. This time for reassurance. The processed meat I just ate turns into a lead weight in my stomach at the thought of what Dr. Benson might ask me.

I swallow roughly. I'm stuck to the log and glued to Remi's side.

"Lincoln. Now, please." He sounds annoyed at me. He never sounds annoyed.

Remi subtly nudges me, his arm pressed against mine, silently telling me to move. I take a deep breath and stand, turning to set my plate down on the log.

My eyes flick to Remi's as I do. He winks at me and mouths, "You got this."

A small smile tugs at my lips, and I feel a little better as I follow after our teacher to a private corner of the campgrounds, away from the fire and listening ears.

Most kids have retired to their cabins, ready to enjoy what is essentially a house with no parents. But some people are definitely still hanging out while they eat.

"I see you've become quite close with Remi."

Does he know?

How could he know?

I rack my brain for any memory of when one of us might have slipped, and I come up empty.

"We're friends," I say, folding my arms across my chest. I hate how defensive I sound. It's not like me, and he knows it.

Dr. Benson sighs, rubbing his forehead like he's ready for this day to end. "Lincoln. I want you to be careful. Remi isn't like the other kids here—"

I cut him off right there. "Yeah. He's not a bully or a jerk."

"Maybe not, but he's still trouble. Do you know why he left Detroit?"

I purse my lips and look to the side, peering into the dark abyss of trees. I don't answer him because no, I don't know. Remi and I haven't gotten that deep yet.

"Well, I'm not at liberty to discuss what happened, but I'd advise you to find a new friend. After what I saw tonight, he's walking a fine line with expulsion, and it's concerning. You've been on the straight and narrow your entire high school career, and I'd hate to see things change now, so close to the end. I know your parents. And I know the strict path they have you on for Columbia. You don't want to get mixed up with someone so volatile. So dangerous."

I wouldn't normally talk back to a teacher like this, especially one I thought I respected so much. I'm more of a quiet listener. Non-confrontational. But Dr. Benson needs to know he has Remi pegged all wrong.

"He doesn't judge me. Doesn't think I'm a *freak*. And he's nicer than ninety-nine percent of the students here. And you're wrong about my parents, too. They actually love him."

I grin, realizing he doesn't know who Remi is, and I get to be the one to tell him.

"He's Mr. Keller's grandson."

"Richard Keller?" he asks, eyebrows shooting up his forehead.

"Yep," I say with a pop.

"Wow. Interesting. And unexpected." His eyes dart back to Remi and mine follow.

He's sitting by the fire, legs stretched out in front of him while he assembles another hot dog. His hoodie is off, warm enough from the mild evening and heat from the fire.

My hungry eyes trace over him. His long sleeves are pushed to his elbows, showing off the tattoos decorating his smooth skin. I watch in fascination as he adds every condiment known to mankind and takes a big bite—relish and mustard overflowing onto his fingers.

He sticks his middle and index fingers into his mouth and pulls them out slowly, glancing up to look at us in the process.

My tongue darts out to lick at my dry lips. Thinking about Remi shoving those thick fingers somewhere else has my dick instantly plumping up.

Good grief.

I clear my throat awkwardly, hoping no one can see the inappropriate semi in my cargo pants.

Dr. Benson and I look away quickly, although I know we were staring for different reasons.

"I still think you need to be careful, Lincoln. I'm not trying to upset you; again, I can't tell you much. But he does seem to leave destruction in his wake."

"Can I go back now?" I nearly cut him off.

That's not fair. What he said is not fair at all, and I don't like it.

He sighs wearily again, and I swear he's going to leave this trip with his first gray hair. "Yes, Lincoln. Just. . . watch your back around him."

"You've got it all wrong. Remi's the one who's been watchin' my back, Dr. Benson. *The only one.*" I take a step backward, away from him. "I'll see you at breakfast. Have a good night." I spin on my heel and march back to the campfire, intent on leaving.

"Try it." Remi holds his arm straight out at me as I step closer. Toasted marshmallow goo and melted chocolate ooze from between two golden graham crackers. It looks pretty good but. . . messy.

"I'm full."

"A bite. . ."

I shake my head, plopping back down next to him for a moment.

He lowers his voice. "For me?"

His eyes dart back and forth between mine before flicking down to my lips for a brief second. And I know he's thinking the same thing as me.

Kiss me. Please, just kiss me.

Would it matter?

Do I care?

I lean forward and take a bite of the gooey concoction instead. If only to please him. The burst of sweet flavors on my tongue has me closing my eyes and humming while I chew.

"Good boy."

His voice is low, sounding smooth like honey, and I whimper, forgetting where we are for a moment. No one can hear us over the crackling flames and hushed murmurs of multiple conversations.

"Let's go home," I say, feeling brave.

Remi stuffs the entire s'more into his mouth and jumps to his feet in one smooth motion.

I burst out laughing at his antics, drawing attention from the surrounding students. And Dr. Benson. The more time I spend around my new friend, the less I care what others think, including my parents. Well. . . I'm still working on that one. It's only been a week.

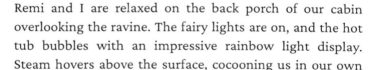

Remi and I are relaxed on the back porch of our cabin overlooking the ravine. The fairy lights are on, and the hot tub bubbles with an impressive rainbow light display. Steam hovers above the surface, cocooning us in our own little world.

I'm enjoying the rum and Coke Remi made. It's not too strong this time, and we're getting high again because. . . well, because Remi insists that he needs it after today. And judging by the black eye that's starting to darken, I think he's probably right. And me? I'm just going with the flow for once in my life. If my new friend wants to get high, then so do I.

He licks the joint paper before sealing it, his wet tongue

gliding along the edge, teasing me as I visualize what else he can do with it.

Remi finishes rolling the joint and offers it to me, warm water bubbling around us. I hold it with the dry part of my lips as Remi cups his hand and flicks the lighter.

"Take two small puffs until you see the cherry glow red."

Following his directions, I get the joint going, and I don't even cough this time.

I pass it to Remi and slink down into the bubbling water, letting the jets soothe my sore muscles from hiking all day. I close my eyes, leaning against the headrest. Pot and alcohol swirl in my system, the steam fogging up my head until I nearly slip under the water as I start to doze off.

"Whoa. Whoa." Remi slips a strong hand under my armpit and hoists me up, holding the joint up and out of the water with his other.

"Don't pass out in a hot tub, Preppy," he scolds before placing the joint between his lips and, using both hands to lift me up, lets the water guide me until I'm straddling his lap face-to-face. I make an embarrassing squeak at being manhandled like this, but my dick starts to fill and presses against his. We didn't bring swim trunks, so we're both in underwear, only the thin, wet fabric separating us.

Feeling brave, I take the joint from his lips and stub it out in the ashtray he set on the deck railing. I grab his face and kiss him hard, rocking my hips into him. My cock automatically seeks friction.

The playlist switches to a new song. The slow, sensual sounds of "Push Up" by Ne-Yo and Trippie Redd pour out of the hot tub's built-in Bluetooth speakers.

Remi takes control, his tongue spearing into my mouth, leaving me breathless. His hand rubs my back up and down, caressing me before going lower, his fingers slipping beneath the waistband of my boxer briefs.

I pull my mouth from his, trailing kisses along his sharp jawline to his ear. I nibble and bite and grind my dick against him shamelessly.

"Touch me," I moan.

His nimble fingers descend until they slip between my crease, ghosting over my hole. I spread my legs wider, arching my back and begging for more.

He rubs and circles, and we kiss messily, but he never applies more pressure like I want him to. I want to know what it feels like. I *need* to know what it feels like.

"Remi," I whine.

"We need lube, Preppy."

I push back against his fingers. "No. It's fine. The water's fine."

Groaning like it pains him to do so, he slips his hand out of my underwear, resting his forehead against mine.

"You're killing me, Linc. We need lube. I won't hurt you." His voice is deep and velvety, full of emotion stronger than simple lust. It's a heady feeling.

"Bedroom. Now," he demands.

We leave the music blaring, water bubbling, and our drinks melting as we jump out of the hot tub in a rush to take this to the bedroom.

CHAPTER NINETEEN

REMI

Water drips everywhere as we kiss and stumble inside, slipping on the hardwood floor. I nearly faceplant, both of us laughing as we attempt to climb the steep stairs to the loft. We strip our wet underwear off and fall on the bed in a tangle of limbs and sloppy kisses. I'm so fucking hard and so fucking ready to take this further.

Here, in the privacy of our own cabin, we can *really* get to know each other.

"I'm going to finger your ass now, Preppy."

"Oh God," he whimpers, his mismatched gaze soft and hazy. The innocent look has my balls fucking aching.

"Lie on your back. Bend your knees and spread your legs." Shame and desire war in his eyes, but he scrambles to obey. I settle on my stomach between his legs, unable to deny myself the clear bead of precum oozing out of his slit. I lap it up with one long lick, and Lincoln groans, fisting the rumpled bed sheets we left unmade this morning.

He stares down at me, and I meet his gaze. His beautiful dick twitches between us, vying for my attention. I keep my eyes locked on Linc as I continue to lick and suck at his cock while he whimpers and moans. Pulling at the sheets. Tugging at his hair. This boy is losing his goddamn mind, and I'm the one doing it to him. Pride swells inside me.

I suck hard, pulling off with a pop and causing an adorable squeak to escape his lips. He's panting and desperate at this point, so I don't take long when I wrench the side drawer open and grab the small bottle of lube.

Squirting a generous amount onto my fingers, I settle on my heels between his legs. I've never done this to someone else before, only myself. But I like to think I know what I'm doing. My dick is so hard, and I reach down, giving it a tug.

"I want you to relax, Linc. Okay?"

He nods enthusiastically, biting his lip as he peers at me from behind his cute-as-fuck glasses.

"Like, really relax," I say, rubbing the soft, barely-there hair on his leg. "Because this is gonna feel kinda weird at first. But then it'll feel really, *really* good. Just trust me."

He inhales a deep breath, and I take that as my cue to push one finger into his tight asshole, causing him to close his eyes and whimper.

Fuuuck. He's so tight and hot. The way his ass squeezes just one single digit, I can't even imagine how it would feel gripping my dick. I start to fuck him slowly with my finger, making sure not to touch his sweet spot yet.

"That's it, you're doing so good," I croon, encouraging him before I slip a second finger in. He spreads his legs wider, throwing his head back and moaning wantonly while he rocks his hips, humping the air. His arms are plastered to the bed, fingers spread, palms flat like he's trying to prevent his mind, body, and soul from floating away. His dick stands straight up, leaking more precum. I can't help myself and lean down, swiping it up with my tongue just to toy with him.

A few pumps later, I curve my fingers, grazing his prostate and lighting him up. He immediately cries out, his hole clenching tightly around my fingers.

"Fuck!" he shouts, and a sly grin warps my lips.

Mission accomplished.

But I'm too hard, too worked up, to point out that he indeed just said "fuck" while in the throes of passion. Just like I said he would.

"Wh-what is that?" he chokes out while I continue to nail him with every thrust of my fingers. It's torture not to have my cock in his tight hole right now, but I know he's not ready. Especially for *my* dick.

I push one of his bent knees even further up with my free hand while I better acquaint him with his prostate.

"*Ungh!* Oh, fuck! Don't stop!" He's whimpering and whining and thrashing around on the sheets.

Holy shit, this is sexy.

I *definitely* don't stop.

Sweat beads on my forehead and trickles down my temple until it soaks into the already damp hair curling there.

"Fuck me, Remi. Oh, God. Fuck me. *Pleeease.* I need your cock." He's nearly in tears, pulling at his hair while his eyes plead with mine.

I never slow the pace of my fingers.

"Preppy," I say, gritting my teeth. "I want to so bad, but you're not ready. You can't go from fingers to dick in the same day," I try to explain to him.

And then I make a hasty, split-second decision that has never felt so fucking right for once in my life.

Impulsive. That's me.

And I've learned to embrace it.

"But you could always fuck me."

And then he's coming on a strangled gasp. Hot ropes of cum shoot from his cock, landing on his abs.

My fingers slow, and my jaw drops.

I didn't even touch his cock.

He didn't even touch his cock.

No one touched his cock.

And he came.

Fuuuck.

Aftershocks cause his asshole to pulse around my fingers, and it's so goddamn hot.

So. Fucking. Hot.

I slip them out while he lies there panting, his chest rising and falling rapidly.

"N-now?" he asks, eyes wide and maybe a little terrified.

I hover on my knees while I leisurely stroke my own dick. "You're not ready for this cock, Linc. But I've been using my fingers for a while now, and I'm definitely ready for yours," I say boldly. "If you wanna give it to me," I add, making him whimper. His deflating erection starts to fill again.

"I do. Fuck, I do." He slaps a hand over his mouth at the curse that slips out.

A deep, sultry chuckle pours out of me, and I crawl up his body between his spread legs. His sticky cum smears between us as I settle my weight on top of him. I lean down and pepper little kisses over his face before pulling back.

"I love that you feel comfortable enough to let it slip. As you should. And knowing that you only curse around me and not other people gets me hot, Preppy. Knowing that it's only for me when those pouty pink lips murmur *fuck me. . .*"

I grind my erection into his, causing a small gasp to escape his swollen lips.

"And I will, soon. But right now, I can't wait to feel your cock stretching *my* ass open," I tell him, nipping at his bottom lip. I've never shied away from dirty talk, and for some reason, it makes me even hotter to see the embarrassment and lust battling in his eyes.

I sit up and tug on his hand, pulling him from the bed with me. "Let's clean up first."

We hurry downstairs to the only bathroom in the cabin, inconveniently located on the first floor. We promptly clean up, and then I push Linc against the wall before we even make it two feet down the hallway. I slam my lips to his, our semi-hard cocks grazing. I plunder his mouth, spearing my tongue in and out in a filthy imitation of the real act.

The act of fucking.

The real act that's about to go down.

In like five minutes.

Fuck. I can't make it upstairs.

I can't do it.

I need his dick in my ass right now. Fucking *yesterday*.

It doesn't have to be all pretty hearts and flowers and rainbows for me. I want it down and dirty. Rough and passionate. I want it to *hurt* so fucking good.

"I want you to bend me over the back of the couch and fuck me hard, Preppy," I say breathlessly, pulling away from his kiss-swollen lips.

His owlish eyes stare back at me, unblinking, and I know I'm going to have to guide him through this. He's never fucked anyone before, guy or girl.

But I get impatient with my balls so close to a nuclear meltdown. Grabbing his hand, I tug him down the hallway and past the kitchen until we find ourselves standing on the fluffy beige rug in the living room. My toes curl into the soft fibers in anticipation of what's to come.

My chain wallet is sitting on the coffee table. I swipe it up and toss him the little packet of lube from inside, tucked next to a condom.

What?

I always like to be prepared.

And the lube is *finally* coming in handy.

"Here," I say, and he catches it, gazing down intently, probably reading the fucking instructions or some shit.

"Don't overthink it, Preppy. Remember how it felt a few minutes ago, and just do that for me."

I bend over the back of the couch and present myself to him, peering over my shoulder to make eye contact. His beguiling mix of vulnerability and strength is shining through.

"Okay," he whispers, but I think it's more to himself.

He runs a tentative hand up and down my back, giving my ass a little squeeze and causing a shiver to run down my spine.

I hang my head. The absence of his dick in my ass is pure torture.

"Lube, Linc."

Then I hear the packet tear, and a cool drizzle runs down my crack and over my balls.

Lincoln rubs it in. *Everywhere.*

My balls. My dick. Then up to my asshole.

He swirls his finger around, teasing me like I did him, and I groan out shamelessly.

I've never had anyone touch me like this. I can hardly fathom it.

He easily slips one finger in, pumping it a few times. My breathing picks up, and I push back against him, needing

more. He adds another, stretching me wider, but not wide
enough.

"Like this?" Linc asks, panting and unsure. Almost as
worked up as me. He curls his fingers, hitting that special
spot deep inside me, and I cry out.

"*Ungh!* Oh, fuck. Yesss. Just like that, baby. One more."

I grit my teeth while he maneuvers a third finger into
me, stretching me to the limit and getting my ass open and
ready for his cock.

"That's enough," I rasp, nearly gasping for breath as he
pulls his fingers out, and I feel the cool air against my sensitive flesh.

"Your cock, Preppy. Now." I glance over my shoulder,
and he's just standing there with half-lidded eyes, his
gorgeous cock pink and swollen. He's staring at my asshole,
and that has my dick throbbing.

I tip my ass up even more, arching my back. He bites his
lip, his hooded gaze meeting mine. A soft, smooth hand
grasps my hip and holds me steady while he grips the base
of his cock with the other. He steps forward, aligning
himself with my hole.

Our gazes lock as he pushes into me ever so slowly.
Gently. Tenderly.

The moment stretches on infinitely. Silently.

Not even the harsh breaths sawing in and out of our
chests can be heard.

Then finally, *finally*, he's fully sheathed inside of me. To
the hilt.

I close my eyes and groan, dropping my head between
my shoulders. I almost can't believe this is happening.

"Move, Preppy. Please," I moan out. And he does,
moving slowly, barely pulling out.

It's not enough.

"Harder. Fuck me harder, Linc. You won't hurt me."

He whimpers. "I won't last."

"Me neither. Doesn't matter."

He grasps my hips with both hands now, digging his blunt nails into the skin. Linc pulls out until just his head is left and then slams forward, shoving me into the couch.

"Fuck, yes," I grunt. Needing this more than I realized. The tension wound up inside me is a tight coil ready to snap.

I brace my arms against the couch, meeting him thrust for thrust as he plows into my ass just the way I wanted him to.

His hips move faster, harder. His thrusts become more erratic as he nears the edge of oblivion. It makes my ass throb and my balls tingle, so I reach under and squeeze the base of my dick so I don't nut too soon. I want us to come together.

He's ruining me for anyone else. And I can't find it in me to care at all.

CHAPTER TWENTY

LINC

I'm having sex.

      Losing my virginity.

      Fucking.

Good grief.

I release his hip to run one hand all over his muscled back, never slowing my pace. He's so much bigger than me —not taller, but broader—and I'm having trouble wrapping my mind around the fact that this is actually happening right now.

Even though I can see it.

Hear it.

Feel it.

My rhythm stutters as my eyes zero in on the point where we're connected. The point where my dick is sliding in and out of his tight hole.

Because I'm inside of him.

Oh God. I'm inside Remi Michaels.

The emotions soaring through me go beyond desire, lust, or arousal. And it's those deeper feelings that finally push me over the edge. Not the vise-like grip choking my cock or the warm heat of his body.

Nope.

It's the full-circle realization that I don't want to be friends. Or best friends. I want to be more, so much more. I'm talking life-altering, soul-consuming, the I-can't-breath-without-you type of more.

Because that's exactly how it's been since I met him. A *week* ago.

My hands grasp his shoulders, and my hold on him tightens. I pull back, slamming home one last time as my breath leaves me in little airy moans timed with the pulsing of my cock deep inside him.

And then Remi is coming with a grunt, the slick sound of him stroking himself echoing with our heavy breathing as his hole clenches me tightly.

We stay connected, and I collapse on top of him—both of us draped over the back of the couch. And I have the fleeting thought of, "How do you get jizz out of upholstery?"

"Holy. Fucking. Shit. Preppy." He's panting, his chest heaving from the post-orgasm endorphins.

I nuzzle my nose into his neck. He smells like sweat and sex and cedar and *Remi*.

Reluctant to remove myself from his body, I stay on top, wrapping my arms around him and squeezing tightly. "You're just an illusion. No way you're real. You can't possibly be real," I whisper.

Remi's low, seductive laugh surrounds me, seeping into my senses and filling my mind with a heady mix of arousal and. . . *safety*.

Because that's how he makes me feel. Safe. And turned on. So freakin' turned on.

Even though I just came twice, my dick already starts to plump up again.

I might have a problem.

Pulling out before I get too hard, we both groan at the foreign sensation.

My legs are shaking, steps like Jell-O, as we round the couch and collapse onto the soft living room rug.

Remi tugs me to him, and I lie on my side, draping a knee over his thick thigh. He hugs me closely, whispering into my hair.

"That was real, baby. No doubt about it. Your dick was in me. *Fucking me.* My ass will feel the proof of that for the next couple of days," he says. "And I fucking love it."

I swallow thickly at his use of the endearment *baby*. It's not the first time he's said that.

But that's not what friends say. . .

Feeling like someone's tickling the inside of my stomach, I sit up too quickly, swaying a little.

"Whoa. You're a little cum-drunk and maybe a little drunk-drunk, too," Remi chuckles, guiding me back to his embrace.

Maybe I am.

I take a deep breath and melt into him, enjoying the security of his big muscly arms and the hard pec under my cheek.

But then I remember the cum drying on the rug. . . and the couch. . . and *us.*

"We need showers," I blurt.

Remi leans over the wide oak table, reaching for the ketchup. I don't miss the slight grimace on his face as he readjusts his position on the unforgiving metal chair.

I feel a little bad, but he asked for it that hard. And I feel less bad when he smothers his poor over-easy eggs with ketchup.

That's just wrong. And gross.

I take a sip of my orange juice just as Connor walks by, kicking the leg of my chair and causing me to jerk forward. Luckily only a few drops dribble down my chin onto my black fleece.

"Oh. Whoops. My bad," he deadpans.

Remi jumps out of his chair in one smooth, silent movement like a viper ready to strike. But before anything can happen, and I have to try and stop it, Gus steps in between, separating them.

"Remember the rules, new kid," he rumbles in Remi's face.

"It's fine. I'm cool. Just. . . keep your boy on a leash. Like I said yesterday."

Connor growls, adding to the argument that he indeed needs to be leashed. He tries to step around Gus, but Gus swings one of his tree-trunk arms out, stopping him.

"Both of you, cut it the fuck out. It's only a matter of hours until you can hash this out officially. I don't want to have to step in between you again. Man up and handle yourselves, for fuck's sake."

Gus turns around and gives Connor a shove toward the exit, pointing. "Go, dude. Take your break first, and chill the fuck out. We'll switch off in two hours."

Connor doesn't even acknowledge his friend. He only sneers at us before storming away.

"Fight starts at ten-thirty tonight. But get there thirty

minutes early. I'll text you the address. There's a neighbor-hood behind the woods where you can park and cut through."

Gus and Remi exchange numbers while I just sit at the table, the pancakes I ate turning into a cement block in my stomach.

They clearly just fought yesterday. And now again tonight. . .

I hate it.

His left eye is already turning black and blue, and his knuckles are slightly swollen.

"Why?" I blurt out, and Gus flicks his gaze to me. He's never been cruel. In fact, there have been a handful of times when he found out about something Connor or Brandon did and tried to reverse the damage. Little does he realize the scars they've left are mostly internal. I know he's just trying to get through school with a football schol-arship to a good college and get drafted into the NFL. Everyone knows this about Gus. And I really can't fault him for trying to keep those two jerks in line. They're part of that equation for him. Even if they're my tormentors and half the reason for the spiraling mess of loneliness I've been drowning in.

Before Remi came along, I had to fight all of my fights alone. But now, I have someone in my corner, tapping in at a moment's notice.

"That's Connor and Remi's beef. Not mine," Gus replies evenly, never one to give secrets away. Respectable, I guess.

Before I can ask, Remi murmurs softly, "We'll talk about it later, Preppy." I know the delicate tone and nickname don't go unnoticed by Gus. But once again, he doesn't gossip, so I tamp down the anxiety starting to bubble up.

Gus gives Remi one of those weird straight guy hugs,

slapping each other on the back hard enough to knock someone like me over.

"My money's on you. Don't disappoint me."

He says it quietly, but I still hear it.

And then he's strolling off toward the lodge exit. Gus Stevenson—cataloging leaves by day and, apparently, maintaining an elaborate underground fight league by night.

I'm feeling brave, so I ask again, now that Gus isn't here. "Why are you fightin' Connor? I know you did yesterday. *Everyone* knows you did."

He opens his mouth to answer, and I just know it won't be the truth.

"Friends don't lie to friends," I declare boldly.

"I. . ." His eyes dart away from mine, showcasing an uncomfortability that instantly puts me on edge. The metal chair squeaks as he sits back down and tucks himself into the table.

His gaze is hesitant and unsure. "He just said some things that weren't acceptable, is all. And I had to let him know that."

"Remi. . ."

Why is he being so vague?

This isn't like him. He's blunt and to the point.

"He didn't accept it. And now we're gonna attempt to work it out again. Tonight."

I still have the sick feeling in my gut that this is all my fault. That this is all happening because of me, and I hate it. I don't want Remi to fight. I don't want him in any more trouble when I know he ran away from something bad. He may be tough, with a devil-may-care attitude, but someone has to look out for him, too. And I don't think anyone ever has.

"I'm coming with you."

"No, you're not. Too dangerous." His response is swift and direct.

"It's not your decision, Remi."

"Preppy—"

"I know it's about me," I say, cutting him off. "So, I'm coming. I'm not letting you go alone."

He sighs, sounding resigned.

"I won't be able to focus on the fight if you're there, and I have to worry about you."

"And I won't be able to sleep knowing you're out there alone, with no one who truly cares about you." I roll my lips inward, worried I just revealed too much too soon.

"Lincoln." This time his tone is soft, careful.

He threads his fingers with mine under the table so no one can see.

I know the look in his eyes. It's the same one shining from mine.

If only he could kiss me.

Right here. Right now.

But there are so many reasons why we can't. Why it's just not the right time to come out. The main one that we aren't even boyfriends, no matter what my heart craves. And I'm still not ready for my parents to find out, either. They have expectations of me that I'm pretty sure don't involve me being gay. And if Connor or Brandon found out. . .

"I care about you too, Lincoln. A lot. And that's why you can't come." Remi's words cut my spiraling thoughts off.

All brainwaves cease.

He cares about me. *A lot.*

If he keeps looking at me with that smoldering stare, I

might spontaneously combust. And I know the heat in his eyes is reflected in my own.

I tear my gaze away before I get a boner at the breakfast table.

I clear my throat awkwardly. "Then at least tell me why you're doin' this." If he won't budge on letting me go with him, maybe I can get some answers.

He squeezes my hand where it rests on his lap under the table, gaining my attention once more.

The fire burns out, but he never takes his eyes off of mine.

"He called you 'the gay boy' and made some lame ass joke about us staying together and morning wood."

I feel the blush settle into my cheeks, ashamed.

"He's said worse," I mumble, accidentally letting it slip out.

"I'm going to kick his fucking teeth in tonight," Remi rumbles in a low, deep voice.

"Don't!" I shout a little too loudly, gathering the attention of a few students nearby.

I lower my voice and duck my head. But I can't cut the frantic tone. "I know you left some bad stuff behind, and I know you're not ready to share. That's okay. But please, *please*, do not get into any trouble or, God forbid, get hurt because of me."

"Chill, Linc. I'd be fighting him even if he wasn't talking shit. I like it. *I crave it.* And I need the money, too."

He needs the money?

I scrunch my nose. Mr. Keller has millions. How could Remi possibly need money now?

At my confused expression, I get another vague answer. What I expect is a half-truth.

"I owe someone important to me, and I handle my debts."

I open my mouth to respond, but he cuts me off.

"If you're done with breakfast, I'm ready to go."

I take the hint and drop the conversation. We have a full day of hiking and collecting the remaining leaves ahead of us. Tomorrow we turn in all of our samples before heading home. This is our last chance to find everything, and I am once again chomping at the bit to get started.

———— ∽ ————

The rest of the afternoon and evening went by quickly and without any Connor sightings. We crossed paths with Gus and some other classmates a couple times, but other than that, we were mostly alone. Even snuck in a few stolen kisses.

The lodge cooked a massive farewell dinner for us, grilling out steaks, chicken, and baked potatoes. Other than a few glares that Remi wasn't fazed by, Connor stayed in his corner of the large cafeteria-like room.

After dinner, we spent a couple hours making out and messing around. Remi needs to recover before we have sex again. I'm a little concerned that his discomfort might affect his fighting ability, but he insists it's nothing. And all I can do is take his word for it and help him in other ways, like the two blow jobs since dinner.

It's nine-fifteen now, and Remi is getting ready to leave our cabin. I'm a little upset that he still insists I can't go.

"I'm going to take a shower. I don't know why, but it's a pre-fight ritual I have to do." He leans in, kissing me slow and deep and spearing his tongue into my mouth, tasting me everywhere. Like he's claiming his prize, and maybe I really am his prize. He is fighting because of me, after all. The thought makes me somber for a moment, wishing I could be there for him. Wishing he'd let me.

The kiss continues for seconds. Minutes. I'm not sure which, but I'm panting. He leaves me breathless and dizzy, stealing every exhale from my lungs with his greedy mouth.

I grasp onto his hard biceps as he pulls away. "I'm going to lie down now," I murmur, and his sensual chuckle washes over me, warming my blood.

"Go to sleep, baby. By the time you wake up, I'll be climbing safely into bed next to you. You have nothing to worry about. I won't bother you before I leave, so just go pass out."

I nod, but he's wrong. I have everything to worry about when he's out there all alone. *Fighting.*

He gives me one more sweet little peck, and I amble toward the stairs like a zombie.

In bed alone, I listen to the sounds of water running through the pipes from the shower, and worry seeps into my skin deeper and deeper with each passing moment.

My earlier sleepiness vanishes as a reckless and completely-unlike-me plan pops into my head. I whip the covers back before I lose the courage to follow through and change my mind. Grabbing my dark jeans and one of Remi's black hoodies, I dig through my bag until I find my black beanie and pull it low, going full incognito. I stuff a few pillows under the covers and fluff them up, just in case.

What? I've never snuck out before.

I tip-toe down the stairs, my socks silent on each step. Even though I know he's still in the shower, I want to be extra careful. My black boots sit neatly by the front door next to Remi's, and I slip them on, completing my all-black super spy look.

I grab my key for the cabin and Remi's big keychain, careful not to rattle it. Silently unlocking his SUV, I set them back down on the little wooden table by the front door and slip out undetected. Key in hand, I quickly lock the cabin, tucking it deep into my boot so I won't lose it, and climb into the trunk of the SUV.

My eyes search for cover, but there's nothing in here. Our stuff is inside, and since this isn't even technically Remi's car, it's clean and free of clutter. I doubt Mr. Keller has even driven it. Probably just Clifford.

With no other option, I curl into the tiniest ball I can manage, pressing myself against the back seat. All I can do is hope Remi won't notice since the windows are tinted black. By the time we get to the barn, it will be too late to turn back. I can ask for forgiveness later. If he's fighting because of me, I need to be there to make sure he's okay.

Because friends should always be there for friends. *Just in case.*

CHAPTER TWENTY-ONE
REMI

My nerves are ablaze, and adrenaline pumps through my veins, leaving me a little jittery. Not to mention the energy drink I chugged before leaving the cabin. I pop another piece of gum into my mouth and tap my fingers anxiously on the wheel as I navigate to the neighborhood behind the old barn Gus told me about.

Under normal circumstances, I would never blindly follow directions from someone I don't know to a fight location that I also know nothing about.

God. If Hydro knew, he'd roast me for being a dumbass.

But this kid goes to the same rich-ass private school as me, and he doesn't seem like a bad guy. Not like his little puppy dog bitch, Connor. Brandon, too.

Money and the need for revenge drive me harder than any common sense. Gus had the chance to jump me back on the trail when he caught me off guard and snatched me up like a punk-ass kid. I believe him when he says they have rules. If they fight at school, they risk their futures. So even though my future after school isn't planned out, and I have no clue what I want to do, I can respect that he has a dream.

Besides, this fight is exactly what I was looking for, and it practically fell into my lap. Just like Lincoln. With each passing day, it feels more and more right to be here in Hunter Springs. Like it's where I should have been all along. My entire fucking life.

Siri tells me I have arrived at my destination. I continue down the silent street until I find a darkened strip of houses where either no one's home or everyone's gone to sleep. I park on the street between two box-like houses where all exterior lights have been turned off. Only the silver glow of moonlight illuminates their small size and the looming forest beyond.

Before getting out of the car, I spit the giant wad of gum into an empty can in my cup holder. There's always a low level of anxiety humming under the surface on fight nights. No matter how confident I feel.

I close my eyes and take a deep breath, holding it in before releasing slowly, trying to calm some of these pre-fight jitters.

I check my face in the rearview mirror before I trek through the darkened woods, following a stranger's text message like a complete fool.

Black eye. Messy dark hair. Pale skin. Angled jaw and an angry stare.

Luckily, my eye isn't too swollen. He got me right under it, so it's just my cheekbone that hurts like a bitch. And now I have to be extra vigilant about protecting that side of my face. If he's had any training or common sense, he'll go after that weakness. Just like I'll do to him.

A quick movement in the very back of the SUV catches

my attention, and I go deadly still, unsure if my eyes are playing tricks on me in the dark.

Because if Unknown is here now, then they know Lincoln is at home.

Alone and vulnerable.

Fuck! I should've let him come with me like he wanted to. I could have at least had his back.

I hop out of the car and stealthily creep around to the back. Ready in. . .

Three

Two

I fling the hatchback up in one fluid move and jump in, diving for the dark lump in the corner, hiding behind the last row of seats with his back to me.

Oof!

We collide, and I land on top, straddling the beanie-wearing assailant. I grab his wrists, pinning his hands behind his back roughly.

He grunts, and it sounds. . . familiar.

"Remi, it's me!" a muffled voice shouts.

Lincoln?

Relief floods my veins, cooling the fire raging through my body.

"Preppy?"

I let go of his wrists and flip him over, peering down into my favorite pair of eyes. Confusion clouds my brain when I should be focusing on the fight.

"What are you doing here, Linc, hiding in the back like a stalker?"

He gives a little indignant huff and tries to cross his arms, but I grab his wrists again and pin them above his head this time. I lean down into his face until I see the adorable freckles dusting his cheekbones. His auburn hair peeks out from the beanie and sweeps across his forehead. He's wearing the glasses with the thick black frames tonight, completing his all-black attire.

I repeat myself when he doesn't answer.

"What the fuck are you doing here?" I growl, putting a little bite into my tone and squeezing his wrists a bit harder to test his reaction.

I'm actually thrilled he decided to stow away. I regretted my decision to leave him unprotected when I damn well know someone is after me. What the fuck was I thinking?

He whimpers slightly and bites his lip. Unable to deny myself the pleasure, I slam my mouth on his, slipping my tongue in. I tilt my head to go deeper, letting him know who's in control tonight.

I pull back and roll off of him so I don't have to fight with blue balls. It's getting close to curtain call, and I need to find Gus and figure out if there are any more rules I need to know or if I can just go in there, guns-blazing, and whoop ass.

We lie side by side, cramped in the trunk of the SUV and stare at the dark ceiling. Both of us attempt to catch our breaths from our rough kiss.

"You follow me and do as I say when we're out there, you hear me?" I tell him with all seriousness.

"I will," he replies instantly. "I know it's dangerous."

His hand slides over and grips mine tightly. "I couldn't let you go alone. That's not what a good friend would do," he tells me earnestly, squeezing my fingers. "And friendships go both ways. You've been there for me so much. Now it's my turn to be there for you." He sounds vulnerable, and I process the truth in his words. I've never really had a truly good friend like Lincoln Anderson.

"You're right, and I'm glad you're here, Preppy. Shouldn't have told you not to come." I don't tell him *why* I shouldn't have left him alone. I still haven't told him about the threatening texts. And he doesn't know about my less-than-stellar past, which is more than likely creeping back to bite me in the ass.

Instead, I distract him with a few more stolen kisses. I bite his lip and suck on it gently, easing the sting before reluctantly peeling my mouth away.

"Let's head out. Gus says it's a ten-minute walk."

I stuff my car and cabin keys into my boot, leaving the rest of the bulky keychain behind with my ID. I need to be completely hands-free.

At least I don't have to risk my hoodie now—Lincoln can hold it. I've lost so many good ones over the past year.

And that's another fight night routine of mine—no shirt. No matter the temperature. Even tonight when it's in the fifties. I can't have any fabric restricting me or give the other guy something to grab when I'm fighting.

The walk to the barn is uneventful. We found the trail marker and followed the breadcrumbs of drunken teenagers along the way. Easiest directions ever.

Just under ten minutes later, we hear music thumping before we fully break through the trees. As we enter the clearing, the old barn comes into view. The unobstructed moon illuminates the washed-out gray wood and missing panels. The roof looks intact, so it should at least be dry inside.

We hastily cross the field of dead grass and get a better glimpse inside. The large barn doors are wide open, and it looks like a fucking rave in there. Shadow people adorned with glow sticks jump around to the music as free-standing strobe lights flash chaotically.

What the fuck kind of rich kid shit is this?

Either way, I'm bouncing on my toes, ready to get in there and get warmed up.

We run around to the back entrance to check in with Gus. He's leaning against the side of the barn, thick arms folded across his chest. He, like most of us here, is dressed in head-to-toe black. I walk over and dap him up, excited to get in there.

He side-eyes Linc for a beat but doesn't say anything. I know he's probably wondering what he's doing here and who he's going to stand with while I fight, but I have it covered. Linc's gonna be my cornerman. I just haven't asked him yet.

"Your opponent's already here—"

I snort at him calling Connor my *opponent*, accidentally cutting him off.

He narrows his eyes at me. "He's already here, in the far left corner of the barn. You stay to the right. I'll cut the music five minutes before, and then it's showtime. Yours is the only fight tonight. These Pisgah kids just like to party."

"Got it. See ya in there, dude. Need to get in the zone."

I grab Linc's wrist, not even thinking that we're standing in front of Gus. I just don't want to lose him once we step inside.

Gus's dark eyes bore into me as if he wants to say something. Ask something. But I don't give him a chance. I swing the small wooden door open and tug Linc in after me. It's dark and cramped enough that no one notices when I slip my grasp to his hand and hold tight.

The entire place buzzes with enthusiasm. It's crammed

with kids from the academy field trip and the local public school in town. Bodies grind against each other and jump to the beat. We weave through the pulsing crowd until it dwindles down the closer we get to our corner.

I release Linc's hand before we get there and glance across to the other side to see if I can spot Connor in the darkness. There's enough light in here to see the nasty sneer on his face. And the thing is, it's not even directed at me. I follow his evil stare to the incredible boy next to me.

I pull my hoodie over my head in one smooth move, the heat from all the writhing bodies warming the place considerably. I step directly in front of Lincoln and glare right back, letting Connor see every muscle that's about to fuck him up.

We're pretty evenly matched. He may be an inch or two taller, but I know I have the fighter's edge. He's just a foot-baller who *thinks* he can fight.

I turn my back to him and face Lincoln. He hasn't really said a word. He's taking it all in silently, eyes darting around, cataloging everything. From what I know, he's lived a pretty sheltered life, so this is all new. Hopefully, he doesn't see me differently after. Guess it's better he knows the truth now rather than later.

"Hey, Linc. You mind holding my hoodie and phone?" He shakes his head no, and I hand the items over. The strobes flash around us, lighting up the little flecks of amber in his single green eye. The other is so dark that I can't see anything but my own reflection. I still can't get over the otherworldly quality of his stare. I could get lost in it all night.

I tear my gaze from him before I become distracted and run through some basic stretches. I keep an eye on Connor,

Linc, and the rest of the room. I don't like not knowing anyone here.

I lean in to speak into Linc's ear. "I need a cornerman, and since you're here, Preppy, it's gotta be you."

"A cornerman?"

"Yeah, between rounds. Give me some water, and maybe tell me if you notice anything that could help me win." I cover my mouth with my hand for my next request, funneling my teasing words directly into his ear. "A kiss and a shoulder rub would be nice, too." I pull back, laughing at his wide-eyed look. "Just fucking with you, Preppy."

I back up a few steps to finish my warm-up. Without Hydro, I do the best I can, bobbing and weaving to loosen my muscles while I throw jabs and uppercuts into thin air. I focus on my breathing; keeping it even is the key to not gassing out too quickly.

Linc watches me with a hooded stare as I practice my stance and defense styles.

My black jeans are soft and skin-tight. Easy to maneuver in. And while the rips that run up the front of both legs let my pale skin show through, more importantly, they allow for airflow and movement. We'll also go bare feet—MMA-style. We're free to kick, punch, and wrestle. And I plan to utilize all of it when I beat his ass.

Gus comes slinking through the crowd of swaying bodies lost to the music. He goes to the DJ area, which is just a guy with his laptop and some big ass speakers on stands. The music cuts out, and the mic screeches loudly when Gus tries to speak. We all cover our ears while the DJ makes an adjustment.

Gus taps the mic with a muffled thump. "Alright, alright. Ladies and gentlemen. Tonight we have two Blue Ridge Prep boys here to settle a personal beef. Wager is one thousand dollars for the fighters. All bets are closed, and payouts will be sent via our secure app after calculations are made."

They have an app? For bets?

Fucking rich kids.

Really fucking smart, though. And safe. No cash to worry about if we gotta run.

Good thing I didn't bring any. Not that I have a thousand dollars lying around anyway. But I know I'll win; there's no question about it. Thankfully, only the loser has to cough up the funds.

Gus does his ring announcer routine, introducing me to the crowd of rowdy, drunk teenagers as Ruthless Remi. I glance at Lincoln to catch his reaction, but he's chewing on his lip, arms folded tightly across his abdomen.

I know him well enough by now to know that he's worried. About me.

All I can do is show him how ruthless I really am and end this fight quickly so we can go home and crawl into bed together.

As soon as Gus shouts, "Fight!" Connor and I circle each other in the middle of the barn. Dry hay crunches under my bare feet, and the strobe lights flash, bringing Connor in and out of focus as he approaches me slowly. It's trippy as fuck, and I'm not even high. His bright blond hair flashes, and the evil glint in his eyes has me narrowing my own.

My number one rule is always strike first, so I surge forward with a quick jab. He dodges enough that my fist grazes his face. But it's right where I hit him earlier, and he grunts at the impact.

Knowing I've found my target, I don't even give him a moment to regroup before I hit him with a fierce uppercut to the jaw. He staggers back a few steps, his bare feet kicking up hay and dust.

He regains his footing and spits out a mouthful of blood, twisting his lips into a wicked facsimile of a smile. Then he says something completely unexpected, and I'm too stunned to use the moment to my advantage.

Without taking his eyes off me, he shouts, "Hey, Lincoln! How was that strawberry milk? I hope you didn't give my delivery service a thumbs down on Uber Eats, bro!" He laughs maniacally, completely unhinged and out of control, blood dripping off his chin and onto his bare chest.

He. . . He just admitted to. . . I can't think. Can't process the words that just came out of his vile mouth.

He nearly killed Lincoln, and now I'm going to make him *suffer*.

Rage burns through my veins like acid, and a savage bellow pours from my lips as I dive for him. He's caught off guard, and I take him to the ground, landing with my full weight on top of him. His head bounces off the hard ground, dazing him for a second.

I repeatedly slam my fist into his face while he attempts to block me. He's pathetic, really, but I'm fucked in the head, so I'll drown in his screams and bathe in his blood.

I will fuck him up for what he did to Lincoln.

I want this to hurt. Not just physically. His pride needs to take a beating, too. He thinks he can humiliate Lincoln, so I plan to do the exact same in return. And he just served himself on a silver platter.

I stand above his moaning body. One leg on each side as I peer down at his bloody face. "I already told your little friend Brandon, but I guess he failed to pass the message along. But stay the fuck away from Lincoln. Or I won't stop next time. This is your final fucking warning."

I step over him, and he crawls to his knees, attempting to stand for round two.

I don't fucking think so.

This next one's for his ego.

I kick out, catching him in the gut. He falls back to his ass with a grunt. "Stay down. Before you don't have a choice," I say behind clenched teeth.

I raise my voice for this next part, so everyone can hear. "That's two days now that I've whooped his sorry ass!" I holler. "Gus! Come get your boy before I do something to ruin your football season!"

CHAPTER TWENTY-TWO
LINC

My mind is reeling.

Too many things happened all at once.

As soon as Remi stepped into the "ring," his phone vibrated in my hand. Without thinking, I flipped it over, reading texts from an unknown number on the lock screen.

I told you I don't appreciate being ignored.

Enjoy your little field trip while it lasts.

I'll collect what's mine soon enough. You owe me.

I know I shouldn't have read it, and now I wish I hadn't. But what is going on with him? Is he in trouble? Need money? What can't he tell his grandfather?

Mr. Keller would literally give him anything. *I* would give him anything. But Remi's too proud to ask for help. I know that. He gives it so freely, so generously, yet he won't accept any of his own. But I won't let that stop me from trying.

Between the eerie text messages, Connor's confession, and the subsequent bloodbath. . . I'm speechless. My thoughts are a jumbled mess, and I'm frozen in place. Rooted to the spot. Eyes wide and unblinking.

So when the first police sirens blare in the distance, I don't move. Not even when a stampede of kids rushes toward the big, open barn doors.

I'm knocked into the wall as panicking drunk people push and shove their way past. Every man for himself.

Gus scoops Connor up from the ground, wrapping his near-limp arm around his thick neck and hustling for the back exit, which is where I should be going.

Definitely where I should be going.

Connor's feet struggle to keep up as Gus drags him toward the door. He has to have a concussion. What Remi did was...

Swollen, bloody knuckles wrap around the unblemished skin of my wrist. Caught off guard and on edge, I can't help but flinch dramatically. I peer into eyes as dark as night and hate the hurt that flares there.

Remi immediately releases me, palms up.

"We have to go. *Now.* I won't leave you here. But I cannot get caught, Lincoln. I will go to jail for a very long time if I'm arrested for this shit. Do you understand what I'm saying?"

He's so calm. How is he so calm?

And jail? Oh God, I can't go to jail!

The sirens get louder, wailing in displeasure. My heartbeat whooshes in my ears. Sweat beads at my temples. My limbs shake uncontrollably.

I'm losing it. Full on freakin' out.

"Lincoln! Now!" He tugs my wrist again, and this time I let him. We're the only two in the barn, and the police sound like they're right down the street. The hard bite in

Remi's voice snaps me out of my fear-induced paralysis. I *can't* let him get in trouble.

We take off toward the small door in the back.

"Let's go! Run! Run!" Remi bolts out first and races toward the edge of the clearing. I follow shortly behind, but he's aiming for the dark expanse of forest.

"Remi! Stop!" I reach out and grab his hand, nearly tripping as I try to stop him.

He whips his head back, panting, and blurts out, "I can't get caught!"

"B-but there are bears! This is North Carolina, not Detroit!" I shout between heaving breaths.

"I'll take my chances. *Hurry.*"

Everyone knows you stay on the trails. These aren't residential neighborhood trees. This is a wild and untamed mountain forest.

He laces his fingers with mine, our hands sweaty, but neither of us cares. I'm already on edge; I don't need to add freakin' bears to the mix!

"There are no other options, Linc. I promise I won't ever let anything happen to you." He's using his calm voice again, soothing me. Making me believe him. Believe that he wouldn't let anyone or anything hurt me.

Remi steps into the dense thicket before us, pulling my hand and tugging me with him. Squeezing hard, I don't let go of his hand.

With only the light of our phones to guide the way, this is really eerie. Too eerie. I don't like horror movies for a reason.

"Hold onto me, and don't let go. Do what I say, and we'll be fine," he whispers urgently. I grasp onto the hoodie he apparently had time to throw on during my freakout. And thankfully, his shoes, too.

The forest thickens around us, our boots crunching on leaves and twigs. Running on uneven ground and leaping over fallen branches isn't the easiest path, but I don't think they'll follow us here. Remi is right; it's the smartest and only option.

The rustle of small creatures and our own labored breathing is the only thing I can hear. No more sirens. No other people. It's like we've stepped into another world.

Remi and I weave through the trees, ducking and dodging the tangled branches as they swipe at us. It feels like we've been running for two miles, and I'm not sure how much longer I can go. I don't have the endurance that Remi does.

An owl hoots overhead, startling me. When my legs threaten to give out, I grab onto his hoodie harder and stumble into him, nearly taking us down.

"Whoa. Whoa. Preppy."

He spins around and grabs onto my biceps. He's breathing heavily, eyes gleaming in the harsh light of our phones. It's pitch black out here otherwise. The trees are too dense to allow any moonlight in.

"You okay? I think we lost them," he whispers between heaving breaths.

I lean forward and rest my forehead on his shoulder, letting him hold some of my weight. "I think we lost ourselves. Where even are we?" I whisper back urgently.

"Gus said it's a straight shot through the woods behind the barn, then we'll be back to the neighborhood we parked in. I got this. Don't worry. I won't let anything happen to you, Preppy."

I bite my lip at his possessive words. There's this constant arousal vibrating under my skin every time I'm near him, giving me a half-chub.

And it's not a fear boner.

A low, gruff sound rumbles in the back of his throat, and I step toward him automatically.

"Why didn't you tell me?" he growls, and my lust-hazed brain can't understand what he's asking.

"Tell you what?"

"You know what, Preppy. That it was Connor who knocked you off your moped. Coulda saved me the inconvenience of kicking his ass twice."

"I didn't want you to get into a fight over me, Remi. I know you're not ready to talk about exactly what happened in Detroit, but you can't risk your future over some *bully*. Although, it was kind of amazin' to see Connor finally get his butt handed to him."

I press my mouth to his and walk him until his back hits the tree behind us. I weave my fingers through his messy, soft hair, tugging slightly.

"And hot. It was really freakin' hot to see you defend my honor like that, Remi," I confess breathily.

He groans into my mouth, slipping his tongue in and turning a simple press of the lips into a heated, soul-devouring kiss.

Remi's kiss.

The only way he knows how to kiss.

Good grief.

He completely owns my mouth and then flips us so that I'm the one with my back pressed against the rough tree bark, his thigh between my legs. My already hard dick grinds against that muscled thigh. I grasp onto him like a drowning man clinging to a life raft.

Remi finally pulls his lips away, resting his forehead against mine as the wind howls, rustling the leaves around us. "We need to keep going. We can't do this here."

I nod, adjusting myself against my zipper. "O-one sec," I stutter, still out of breath.

I will my inconvenient erection away, and then we're off again, stealthily slipping through the woods until we burst from the treeline and duck behind a small white fence that circles someone's backyard.

We crawl along the perimeter of the fence until we get to the street. Remi looks both ways, then down at his phone.

My eyes scan the darkness as we stand on the curb in front of someone's house, the faint wail of sirens in the far-off distance.

"There!" I whisper-shout, pointing to our dark SUV parked in an equally dark area between two small, box-like houses only a few down from the one we're standing in front of.

We take off down the street, and I can't help the giggle that bubbles out of me.

Once again, I've never felt so free. So alive.

And it's all thanks to the irresistibly charming boy running and smiling next to me.

Connor and Gus aren't at camp Sunday morning, and I kinda feel bad for Gus. But I'm sure he'll come up with a good excuse and turn in their work on Monday. He won't accept a zero; he has too much riding on school and football.

Remi and I take our time packing up at the cabin, dragging our feet a little because neither of us wants to leave. We enjoy the drive home together with more snacks and more reading. I can see it becoming a thing for us—road trips. Maybe we can go to the beach next. He drops me off at my house before going to his since neither of us has been home since Thursday afternoon.

By the time I'm showered and settled in bed with my Kindle, it's already four-thirty. Mom and Dad weren't home earlier, but I know they expect me to be at dinner at six, which leaves me an hour and a half to get lost in another world. Only I can't seem to focus. My mind just replays everything that happened this weekend. And it's in over-drive doing so. I get whiplash even thinking about what went down.

The sex. The fights. The adrenaline.

It's a heady mix, and I press the heel of my palm into my rising cock, too exhausted to even think about jerking off right now.

I never gained enough courage to confront Remi about the texts I accidentally saw last night. Afraid he'd think I was snooping. I hope he tells me when he's ready because I know he's not the type of guy you can push to open up. But I'm concerned for him and wish I could do more.

I focus on the words in my story, distracting myself from the worry attempting to take over my brain. I let time fly by with alien worlds, faraway solar systems, and time travel.

A loud knock startles me out of a particularly intense scene, and Mom's muffled voice calls through the thick wooden door.

"Dinner's ready early, Lincoln. Come down now, please."

I check my phone. Five-thirty. My stomach grumbles on cue, but her high heels tap down the hall before I can respond.

"Nice to be home, too, Mom. Thanks for askin'. Had a

great time," I mumble pathetically, whipping the covers back. I pad to the closet in my boxer briefs, rifling through all my button-ups, polos, and sweaters that hang at the front.

Suddenly hating all of my clothes, I dig further back until I find a plain black T-shirt, probably a size too small. I pair it with my gray joggers and call it a night. I know they expect me to dress up for Sunday dinner like we always do, but. . . why?

No one else is here except the three of us, and I'm freakin' tired.

Mom's jaw clenches when she sees what I'm wearing. I take my seat at the table, waiting for Dad to say grace.

"This looks delicious, Diana."

Mom serves the pot roast to my dad with a proud smile on her thin face, even though she most definitely did not make it. We have a chef that stops by three times a week, making meals that Mom can pop in the oven for in-between days. She's helpless in the kitchen, but I don't mind because at least I know the food will be edible.

Fragrant smells of rosemary and garlic swirl in the air, and steam rises from the mashed potatoes in front of me. The tender beef is smothered in brown gravy, and the carrots are glazed with honey. I dig in immediately, listening as they discuss whatever new business they've gobbled up. And their plans for the next. Greedy as ever and not once asking me how my trip was.

Did they even notice I was gone? Remember I left?

Maybe not, which makes me sad.

Unless it directly impacts Anderson Holdings or any associated charities, start-ups, or investments, they don't care. Even when it comes to me. Their son.

I'm just a pawn to them. A tool to grow their business and secure its future.

Continuing to eat my dinner, I drown them out, tired after a long trip and a lot of hiking. And orgasms.

I squirm in my seat, desperately trying not to think about the sex part. How unbelievable it was to be inside his warm, tight body. Impaling him with my cock.

Goodness, gracious.

What is wrong with me?

Not at the dinner table. In front of my *mother*.

I shovel more pot roast into my mouth to distract myself.

"Lincoln!" Dad barks, and my wide eyes snap up to his scowling ones.

"Hmm?" I answer, chewing through the mass of food in my mouth, realizing I'm eating too comfortably like I did this weekend. I sit up straighter, fixing my posture.

"Don't ignore your mother."

I swallow harshly, nearly choking, my eyes watering.

"I-I wasn't."

Mom huffs out an annoyed breath. "I said, we're hosting a welcome-to-the-neighborhood party for the Michaels. Wednesday at six p.m. If you would please convince Remi to join you here, Richard and Raina have already accepted the invitation."

Remi will want no part of this, but I do my best to appease them. "I'll talk to him—"

"No excuses. Make it happen." Dad cuts me off with his terse words.

It's what he always says. Just to add another layer of pressure to the situation. And when he's like that, there's nothing else to say but, "Yes, sir."

"You'll text Remi after dinner and let him know. This is important to our family and to our future, Lincoln."

"Yes, sir," I repeat. I'm not sure how a welcome-to-town dinner is so important to our family's future, but I don't argue.

I was planning to text Remi after dinner anyway.

I already miss him.

CHAPTER TWENTY-THREE

REMI

After dropping Linc off at his place, I speed home, ready to crash. I'm exhausted after fighting and fucking around all weekend. I let my duffle bag slip through my fingers and fall to the floor inside the front door, if only to piss Lurch off a little more.

All illegal substances are currently stuffed into my backpack, and I trudge upstairs on autopilot. Ready for a shower and bed. I don't plan to wake up until dinner.

I'm pulled from my nap when my pillow vibrates, startling me. The sun is no longer out, so I'm slightly disoriented as my heart thumps harder, hoping it's not another bullshit threat from Unknown.

I squint at my phone. It's six-thirty, and I'm relieved to see it's a text from Lincoln. A grin automatically tugs at my lips.

Preppy: My parents say they're having a welcome-to-town dinner for you and your mom on Wednesday.

The three dots appear and disappear several times like he can't decide what to say.

Preppy: I'm sorry.

This isn't my ideal Wednesday night. I'll have to skip training again, and after beating Connor's ass, I'm dying to get back into the gym. But I'll do anything for Lincoln.

Me: Don't worry about it, Linc.

Me: I'll be there.

Preppy: Thanks. Did you ice your hands?

I glance down at my swollen knuckles, already knowing the answer to that question.

Me: Aw worried as always.

Me: I haven't but I will.

Preppy: Okay see you tomorrow.

Me: See ya.

There's so much more I wish I could say in these texts. The urge to be more than just friends rides me hard. I didn't think I'd be so emotionally affected by letting him fuck me. But if I'm being completely honest, it was more than just fucking.

I scrub my hands roughly down my face, not used to this many emotions. I tend to brush shit off with humor or lash out with anger. But I've never been more serious in my entire fucking life than when I think about Lincoln.

I grab some bubble gum from my nightstand and shove a couple of pieces into my mouth, chewing harshly.

Backing out of our text thread, I spy a few more I missed while at the cabin. And I realize I completely forgot about Otto texting me that first night.

Shit.

I go to open his messages, but my eyes snag on another thread. From Unknown. My blood turns to ice. Frozen slush slows my pulse until I can hear each and every heartbeat slowly thumping in my chest.

My thumb hovers, unsure if I even want to know.

Tap.

A slew of angry texts.

Threats. Demands.

But there's still no real clue as to who the fuck this is and why they think they deserve *my* money. My *family* money.

Goddamnit. I need a cigarette.

I grab my pack and head downstairs. Mom hates it when I smoke. Lincoln hates it when I smoke. And fuck, I hate it too. But the stress of everything is becoming too much.

"Baby! You're home! How was your trip?" Mom's excitement fades when she sees me storming down the hall. Her eyes track over the black eye, swollen knuckles, and pack of cigarettes in my hand. She doesn't miss a beat.

"Remington Jace! What on earth happened?!"

"Nothing Ma, really." I use the excuse I told Dr. Benson. "You can call my teacher if you want. But one of my classmates nearly fell off a cliff, and I literally saved his life. Okay?"

Dramatic lies. I know.

"Can I please just go have a smoke before dinner? Just one. It's been days since my last. Promise."

She huffs but agrees, running to grab me a bag of frozen peas from the kitchen. She's used to dealing with these types of injuries.

"Ice one of them. Then I'll get you a new bag for the other hand while you eat dinner." She purses her lips, eyeing me with disdain. "I'm no fool, Remington. I know what a fight looks like. God knows you've been in plenty. I just hope you don't end up where you did last time. Because honey, you *are* eighteen now. And there's nothing I could do to help you this time."

I grit my teeth and take the peas from her. "Like I said. I

really did save someone from falling off the mountain. It just looks bad. I'm fine. Really, Mom. Thanks for the peas." I hold them up in silent cheers.

With a dispirited sigh and a half-hearted smile, Mom says, "Everyone's in the dining room. Come in when you're done."

Everyone?

Now it's my turn to sigh. I'm too tired for this shit. Too tired for guests.

----------⌒----------

Laughter and talking filter in from the dining room as soon as I step back inside. There's a deep male voice that's not Gramps, instantly putting me on edge.

I follow the noise, rounding the corner to find Otto De Luca sitting at our dining room table next to my mom. A little too close.

"The fuck is he doing here?" I blurt out before I can stop myself.

"Remington," Mom scolds me, but it didn't work when I was eight, and it damn sure won't work now.

Otto's not the enemy. I know this. He's one of the good guys, for sure. But it irks me that he's here in my house—laughing and *flirting* with my mom—when I haven't even been home more than a few hours.

His dark gaze scans me from head to toe, eyes narrowing on my black eye, bruised cheekbone, and the bag of peas hanging limply in my hand.

"You were a no-show for training, and you didn't reply to any of my texts. So I stopped by Friday night to check in on you. I couldn't, in good conscience, ignore the fact that you were somewhat *missing*." His gray eyes bore into me, delivering some kind of unspoken message.

And then I remember his words from the gym before I ran out of there like my ass was on fire.

You running from someone, kid?

He knows more than he should, and it makes me uncomfortable. But at least he's keeping his mouth shut and not snitching based on a hunch.

And I'm not running—just on edge and ready to fight. That's all I can do. This unknown *fuck* isn't getting a dime of *my* family's money.

I brush it off, along with his concern.

"And I'm sure it was a convenient excuse to see my mom. You got hearts in your eyes when you found out she was back in town." I smirk like the smartass I can't help but be.

My rudeness doesn't phase him, and he continues on undeterred.

"Your mother assured me that no news means good news when it comes to you."

"Yeah. I don't need a babysitter."

Otto sits with a flat mouth, arms folded tightly across his chest. He doesn't look mad, but he's definitely not happy with me.

"I thought all teenagers were glued to their phones."

"Not this one. And I was on a nature trip. Becoming one and all that shit."

"You could have acknowledged my concern with a simple reply."

"Get off my case, Otto. I don't even know you." Okay, maybe that wasn't the right thing to say to the guy who's gonna start training me, and his next words echo my exact thought.

"You're awfully aggressive for someone who practically begged me to coach you."

I can't back down and submit to another man. Not after my father. It's ingrained in me to resist.

"And you're hella forward, being in my house and all."

He chuckles to himself. "So much fire." He eyes my knuckles again. "Channel it into the ring next time, and then we'll talk. You're too reckless. You need to learn control."

Before I can go off, Gramps comes bustling out of the kitchen with two flowered potholders on his hands, wearing a matching apron, and clutching a giant pot of what smells like chili. Lurch is behind him with a serving platter full of cornbread and a giant salad bowl.

Gramps sets the huge pot on the table and proceeds to ladle generous helpings into the orange ceramic bowls already set out. The spicy aroma of braised beef, peppers, onions, and tomatoes filters into my senses, clearing some of the annoyance stewing there.

"Where's my boy?" Gramps asks, and I swear the wall surrounding my heart—built by a scared and alone and *hurt* sixteen-year-old boy—takes a direct hit. A huge chunk crumbles away, and I again feel a pang of sadness for not having grown up here with Gramps.

With Lincoln.

Mom's eyes dart to me, and Richard follows her gaze. He sucks in a sharp breath and hurries over to me, gently clasping my chin to get a better look. I turn my head, pulling my face out of his grasp, uncomfortable with the attention.

"It's nothing," I mumble, not really feeling like lying for a third fucking time. I'm really just peopled out at this point. I need my bed, the dark, and my headphones to decompress before school tomorrow. But I need food first.

I quickly step around him and sit across from Mom and Otto. Richard follows suit and takes his place at the head of the table next to me.

Lurch sees my face and the thawed peas I just plopped down on the table, dripping everywhere. His lip curls, and he practically raises his nose at me. All I can do is roll my eyes and greedily reach for the platter of cornbread he just set down. Grabbing two with one hand, I drop them on my plate with a thud, little crumbs flying off and landing on the table and maybe even the floor.

His nostrils flare, but he stays silent like always.

Hah. Fucker.

He turns and storms off toward the kitchen, and I smirk, feeling satisfied that I got under his skin once again.

I glance across the table at Mom and Otto. They're both watching me, wearing matching frowns, which is kinda freaky, like they're my disapproving parents or some shit.

"What?" I ask defensively.

Mom shakes her head while scooping salad into her bowl and adding a drizzle of balsamic vinaigrette.

"Remi, dear boy, what happened?" Gramps sounds so concerned. It makes me feel irrationally guilty. I stare into my steaming bowl of chili. I can't look at his face and lie.

"My classmate almost fell off a cliff, and I saved him," I repeat in a droll monotone. So completely over explaining myself.

I can't imagine what everyone at school will say. Especially when they see Connor's face. I have no idea where Gus rushed him off to, and I really don't give a fuck. He got what was coming to him, and it's not going to be pretty.

Gramps doesn't know what to make of me. I know it. He

stares at the bag of peas melting on the table, my busted knuckles, then my black eye.

I wouldn't believe me either.

I scoop up a steaming heap of chili, blowing on it before I take a bite, letting the spicy flavors explode on my tongue.

"Well. That's very heroic of you, Remi."

I snort. I can't help it.

"Thanks, Gramps. This is delicious, by the way," I exclaim, changing the subject. I shovel another bite into my mouth and talk through the burn. "Like really fucking delicious."

Mom and Otto agree, and we all eat in silence, enjoying the food.

Halfway through dinner, my phone buzzes under the table, and my eyes dart to Otto's on reflex. He's already looking at me, dark brows drawing together.

I set my spoon down and slip my phone out of my front pocket. My hand trembles while I press the side button, lighting it up.

My nerves turn to excitement when I see it's not a text but an email. A notification that twenty-five hundred dollars was deposited into my bank account through the betting app that Gus made.

Holy fucking shit.

How did one fight for a thousand dollars turn into this? The bets must have been crazy.

Fucking rich kids.

A new text message pops up, and I swallow thickly. The chili turns to molten lava in my stomach, and my mouth waters with the need to be sick.

I know you're home. Don't get too comfortable.

CHAPTER TWENTY-FOUR

LINC

Monday was a much-needed reprieve from any drama, fighting, or violence. Connor was a no-show at school, and Gus was pretty tight-lipped about everything. Remi tried to get some information out of him, but Gus is not a sharer. He won't budge.

The hallways pulsed with whispers of what happened, creating a living, breathing thing that morphed into wild rumors like a horrible game of telephone. Remi doesn't mind. He seems proud of his reputation.

Now it's Tuesday morning, and I'm standing at the bottom of the steps, waiting for Remi to pull through the roundabout and pick me up for school.

The neon green Camaro comes speeding up the drive-way, coming to an abrupt stop in front of me. Without needing an invitation at this point, I open the passenger door and slide into the buttery soft seats, smiling at Remi.

"Good mornin'."

"Missed you," he replies, leaning over to peck me on the lips. It's so casual, like something a boyfriend would do, and I know the lines are starting to blur.

Every cell in my body thrums in excitement at the thought of being Remi's boyfriend.

Could that really happen?

"Missed you, too," I whisper back shyly, a warm, fluttery feeling inside.

"Tryin' out the Camaro again?" I ask, smoothing my hand along the supple leather. I need to change the subject before I read more into his words than I should.

"Nope. She's mine now. Gramps cornered me after dinner last night and made me choose. First thing that popped into my head. And I think she's a winner." He pats the steering wheel lovingly.

"She is," I agree. The vibrant car is a show-stopper, just like Remi himself. It's a perfect fit.

"How's Betsy Anne?" I ask about my own beloved ride.

"Should be back from the shop any day now. I'll drive her over." He grins at the wide smile stretching across my face. I miss my moped, and there's not too much time left before winter sets in. Although, I like carpooling with Remi more.

"Thank you for handlin' that so my parents didn't find out. They didn't want me drivin' a moped in the first place, and I can't deal with another *I told you so*." I don't tell him that the only reason they would even care is because they don't have another heir. There's no one else to take over Anderson Holdings. Just me. Whether I want it or not.

"No problem, Preppy. And it was Gramps, really. You know how he is."

I nod in understanding because, yes, I do know how he is. Unmatched generosity.

As we arrive at the academy and park, I notice a crowd of people forming in front of Caldwell Hall. We immediately jump out, and I sling my messenger bag over my shoulder, smoothing down my slacks and straightening my blazer. After a few days of casual hiking clothes, it feels weird to be back in uniform.

Remi and I walk side-by-side toward the commotion. He runs his finger down the center of my palm, causing a little thrill to shoot through me.

"Twenty bucks says it's Connor and his busted-ass face."

I giggle at that, not taking the bet because I'm pretty sure he's spot on with that guess.

Sure enough, Connor leans against the flagpole with Gus and Brandon on either side. Half the football team surrounds them, along with what appears to be half the senior class.

He has a split lip, two black eyes, and a huge nose brace taped to his face. His arms are folded across his chest, and he looks pissed as he sees us approaching. Maybe a little scared, too.

I glance at Remi, and the giant grin on his face is just asking for all kinds of trouble.

"Ladies and gentlemen!" he roars, cupping his hands around his mouth like a megaphone.

Oh no. This can't be good.

"To clear up any rumors for those who weren't there Saturday night. This. . ." And then he motions toward Connor's face. "This is what happens when you talk shit to me and think you can bully my friends. And if you wanna try me, take it to Gus. I'll pencil you in."

Connor's already mottled face turns bright red, and he lunges toward Remi. Gus holds him back with a thick arm, and Brandon just sneers at me.

Coach De Luca takes this moment to storm out of the

front doors, his booming voice cutting through all of the shouts and jeers. "Enough!"

He points to his football players. "Get to class. Now!"

Then he turns his frustrated glare to Remi and me, and I swallow thickly, not used to being in trouble. "You two, follow me."

Remi looks at me and shrugs, following Coach until we get to the spare room outside the guidance counselor's office.

"Sit. Both of you."

We don't.

Coach sighs like he's exhausted, even though the day hasn't even begun. "Remi. Your grandfather asked me to watch out for you before you even got here, and I see I've been doing a piss-poor job of that."

"Whoa. Whoa. I'll stop you right there, Coach. I don't need another man looking out for me. Never had one my whole life, and don't need to start now. I have everything under control."

Coach's jaw clenches tightly, and his nostrils flare. "Doesn't seem so by the looks of it." He nods toward Remi's black eye and bruised knuckles.

Remi opens his mouth to speak the same lies that we've been telling everyone about Connor nearly falling off the mountain, but Coach cuts him off. "I spoke to Dr. Benson and my brother. Don't bother with your excuses, son. We all know you were fighting. If you wanna fight, you need to do it the right way. And that does not include pummeling my football players and ruining my season. You need to start training with Otto after school. Funnel that anger into a proper channel. The ring."

I just stand here silently, fiddling with the hem of my blazer. An awkward fly on the wall, as per usual.

The warning bell rings, the shrill sound deafening as it blares from the speaker right above the door.

Thank goodness.

"Appreciate the advice, Coach. But I already have plans to train with Otto. You're wasting your breath 'cause there's nothing to worry about. And you can tell that to Gramps, too. If he's checking up on me or some shit."

Remi strolls out of the room, and I follow after him. Coach isn't happy, judging by the harsh slash of his mouth.

After a rough start to the morning, the rest of the day passes smoothly, and now I'm sitting on a small set of bleachers in front of the sparring ring Remi is currently practicing in. We're at Otto's Boxing Club in Asheville, and I'm making flashcards for our Chemistry exam this week. It's the best way for Remi to memorize the material. It's always worked for me, and I'm determined to help him graduate with more than just passing grades. I want to show him how much potential he has. How smart he actually is.

Although it's been a little hard to concentrate, if I'm being honest.

I push my glasses up and stare some more. He's only wearing a pair of tiny athletic shorts and black training shoes. He's gotta be doing this on purpose.

Remi's sweaty, well-defined muscles are on full display. My eyes trail greedily over his shoulders, pecs, abs, and those delicious obliques. And the V.

Holy hotness.

The V.

I bite the tip of my pen, remembering the tight heat of his body. The feel of his mouth on me. My mouth on him.

This big, tough boxer is soft for me.

Only me.

I adjust my Chemistry textbook, covering the erection uncomfortably straining against my zipper and focus on my work. Determined to help Remi in any way that I can.

Eyes down, I spend the next thirty minutes cranking out these flashcards, practically ensuring Remi's success. I can't wait to see the smile on his face when he realizes he can do it.

I glance up, and Remi is closer now, bouncing on his toes, unable to stay still as Otto messes with the tape on his wrists. Otto slips the gloves on, tightening them as he leans down to murmur something to Remi and then adjusts the headgear. I like that Remi has proper gear now.

"I love the mean fuckers. The really big, really angry ones that think no one can beat them. Those are my favorite. To them, I'm the little guy, and maybe I am. But I've always loved a good David and Goliath story."

Otto chuckles, handing Remi his mouthpiece. "Alright, kid. But this is same weight class sparring. So let's focus on what we learned today and try to put it into practice."

The next fifteen minutes are spent with Remi circling and jabbing at a guy similar in size. I can tell he's getting bored and frustrated that this guy won't fight back. The jittery energy of his stance is a dead giveaway of something to come.

His eyes are like twin pools of calm, undisturbed water before you throw a stone in and watch the ripples spread outward. And as soon as that happens, it's chaos.

"Come on, man!" he shouts. The sound muffled around his mouthpiece. "What are you waiting for?" Remi motions toward himself with his gloves, and the other guy lunges.

It happens in less than three seconds. Remi delivers two

quick jabs to his ribs, ending with a hard blow to the face. Probably harder than he should since they're just sparring.

The guy stumbles back, clearly dazed, and trips into the rope. He gets tangled and bobs there awkwardly.

I can't help it. That embarrassing, inappropriate laugh makes an appearance, and a huge giggle bubbles out of my throat.

I slap a hand over my mouth, my cheeks burning hot.

Remi's laugh is a little unhinged as he calls for the next challenger. Ready for more.

"Alright, that's enough," Otto reprimands him, but I see the little smile on his face. He's as impressed as everyone else.

CHAPTER TWENTY-FIVE

REMI

I t's Wednesday evening, and I'm standing on Lincoln's doorstep with Mom and Gramps. I adjust the stupid skinny black tie around my neck, annoyed to be wearing one outside school. Apparently, Richard had a collection of new suits made for me while I was out of town last weekend. I can at least appreciate the fact that most of them are black, and they fit impeccably.

Lincoln's mother, Diana, answers the door in a navy wrap dress and forced smile. Her hazel eyes track over all three of us, and I guess we pass her inspection.

"Hello. Welcome. Come in, please." Short and clipped. Just like the tapping noise her stilettos make on the hard-wood floor as we follow her into the formal living room.

Robert is pouring what appears to be three fingers of scotch at the bar cart and joins us from across the room.

He immediately shakes my grandfather's hand with calculated enthusiasm. "Richard. So good to see you. It's been too long. Can I get you something to drink?"

"No. No. I'm fine until dinner. Thank you."

He looks to Mom next, who politely shakes her head no.

"I'll take a scotch," I chime in, figuring I'd give it a shot. This night would be a lot easier to handle if I could have a drink.

Lincoln's dad laughs it off like I'm joking, but judging by the slight blush on Grandpa's cheeks and Mom's narrowed eyes, they know I'm not.

Gramps steps in, steering the conversation back to pleasantries. "It's good to see you both, as well. Diana, you look lovely as always." He hands the bouquet of wild-flowers to Lincoln's mom, who accepts them with another artificial smile.

"I know you've already met my grandson, Remington," he says with a proud grin that makes me a little uncomfort-able. Guess no one told him about the mix-up I had with the Andersons when we first met. If they want to move on and pretend it didn't happen, fine with me.

"I'd also like to introduce my daughter, Raina."

Apparently, Lincoln and Grady's families moved into this strange little *neighborhood* five years after Mom left, so they don't know her. And I'm hoping that means they don't know our fucked up family history, either.

Linc's parents are a lot older than my mom. Let's be real. *Everyone's* parents are older than my Mom. So they politely accept the bottle of wine she gives them and attempt to engage in more small talk. Even though I'm pretty sure she's feeling just about as out of place here as I am.

While they converse, my eyes scan the room, searching for the object of my obsession. They land on Grady and Sierra instead, perched on the edge of the living room couch. Both are equally dressed up as me—Grady in a char-coal gray fitted suit and Sierra in a simple, knee-length black cocktail dress.

Lincoln told me exactly who would be attending this intimate little dinner. So the tall, handsome man in a bespoke suit with blond hair and hazel eyes is none other than Sean Walker, the twins' father. Their mother, Kendra, is dressed in a beautiful and respectful red pantsuit, complementing her golden brown skin and diamond jewelry. Her dark hair is pulled tightly into some fancy twist to match her daughter's. They definitely look like a power couple, standing there casually sipping their drinks.

Lincoln strolls into the room then, looking dapper as ever. He joins me, standing close by my side. His classic navy suit fits him flawlessly. His auburn hair is parted and styled to the side like it was the first morning I met him. And he has the sexy black-framed glasses on again.

He looks *good*. Really good.

"Hey," he whispers, brushing his hand against mine.

"Hey," I reply, lightly trailing a finger down the center of his palm in response. It's getting harder and harder to remember why we haven't moved this friendship into a relationship. But now isn't exactly the time to figure it out.

"Remember, Remi. In our families' world, it's all about rubbin' elbows with the right people. My parents don't believe in doin' big business over the phone or email. Or even video calls. They're old school. So any dinner, any social interaction, is an opportunity to weave their way into someone's good graces. They're sharks in the water, circlin' their prey, and they won't hesitate to bite."

His enchanting gaze bores into me, so fucking alluring, and he smiles crookedly.

"Ready to meet your other neighbors?"

"Let's do it, Preppy."

We leave our families chatting and walk side-by-side over to Grady, Sierra, and their parents.

"Mr. and Mrs. Walker, this is Remi Michaels," he says with a proud smile that makes my abs tighten.

I step forward and shake Mr. Walker's hand first.

"Well, if it isn't the man of the hour. It's great to meet you, Remi. And please. Call me Sean." He shakes my hand with a strong grip, but I squeeze harder. I *always* squeeze harder.

Sean seems genuine, as does his wife when she introduces herself, insisting I call her Kendra.

Linc and I pile onto the couch with Grady and Sierra while Sean and Kendra take armchairs across from it. They ask me the usual questions—how am I settling in, and how's school? I give them pretty generic answers.

"So, Remi. Has Richard shown you the ropes at all? Keller Industries is a massive enterprise. Unfortunately, with many leaking tributaries. There's a lot for you to learn."

My hackles rise at that, even though Lincoln warned me how this dinner will most likely go. His parents are strategic as fuck. That's all there is to it. And I'm sure their best friends and business partners, the Walkers, are no different.

"Honey, leave the poor boy alone. He's hardly settled in and has clearly been through an ordeal." She turns her caring eyes toward me. "Sweet pea. I'm sorry, but I have to ask. Are you alright? What happened?"

It's been days since the fight with Connor, but I still have a black eye. My knuckles are barely noticeable. So, I don't hesitate to feed her the bullshit story about how I saved a fellow classmate from nearly falling to his death last weekend.

She eats it up, too, as does Sean. I feel a little bad when I glance over and catch the frown on Grady's face before he schools his features, giving me a nervous smile instead.

Shortly after that, Sean and Kendra excuse themselves to say hello to my mom and Gramps. As soon as her parents walk away, Sierra calls me out on my bullshit in that soft-spoken way of hers. "Everyone knows that story isn't true. Even the teachers."

I chuckle because it started as a joke and spiraled into a lie I've had to repeatedly tell, knowing it's not at all believable. I feel like fucking Pinocio or some shit. "Hey. It may be a shitty lie, but it worked, and that's all that matters."

"I heard some crazy stuff went down in Pisgah," Grady says, leaning forward eagerly. "Is it true you did that to Connor's face?"

My grin is cruel, but one of the rules of Gus's fight league is *deny, deny, deny*.

"Nope. Wasn't me."

Grady's golden eyes flash to Linc, but he doesn't question me. I can tell he's definitely still intimidated. He'll warm up to me over time. I'm sure of it.

Still looking at Linc, Grady says, "I want to go next time."

"Me, too," Sierra echoes her brother. "I'd like to see the neanderthals in their natural habitat. Just once. For curiosity's sake."

"Oh. I see how it is, Sierra. Neanderthals, huh?"

She covers her mouth with a hand, giggling as the rest of us chuckle. She's not really wrong.

"The gang's all here," Gramps says, smiling wide as he takes a seat in one of the oversized armchairs across from the big couch. "Looks like the four of you are fast friends already. Just how it should be. Our future leaders."

"Um. Yeah. Sure." I sit up straighter as Mom and the rest of the parents wander over. The Andersons and Walkers have strange, hopeful expressions as they take in the four of us lounging comfortably and laughing together.

And then it hits me.

"Is this neighborhood some kind of cult or something? Is that what actually happened, Mom? Did you escape a cult with your unborn child?" I gasp and clutch my chest, acting like a complete smartass in front of everyone.

Oops.

"Cut it out, you little shit," Mom retorts, accidentally letting the curse slip. I burst out laughing at the stunned faces around me.

So fucking uptight.

Diana clears her throat awkwardly and announces that dinner is ready before we follow her into the dining room.

The bright chandelier illuminates the otherwise dim room, creating a calm and relaxing ambiance that showcases the beautifully decorated table. Fall leaves and tiny pumpkins dot the orange fabric draped along the center, and cream candles are interspersed throughout.

Damn.

Diana is good. I'll give her that. I can see how they lure people in, win them over, and buy them out. Lincoln's right. Sharks. In a really good disguise.

The table is already set with what appears to be a full Thanksgiving-style meal—complete with turkey, stuffing, mashed potatoes, and of course, macaroni and cheese.

We take our seats, and I grab the one next to Lincoln. It's torture seeing him all dressed up, looking handsome as fuck, and not being able to touch him.

Grady sits on my other side, with Sierra across from us and all of the parents at the end.

"This table is absolutely stunning, Diana," Mom gushes. "And the food smells amazing. Thank you again for having us." She's trying to be extra polite after slipping up and cursing at me earlier. I have to bite my cheek so I don't snort at her syrupy sweet tone.

"Thank you, Raina. I can't take credit for the food. We have a five-star personal chef for that. But I do love a themed party. And I couldn't help but go autumnal with the décor. Then I figured we could have a month-early Friendsgiving of sorts."

"Oh. It's a gorgeous idea, Diana. I love it," Kendra coos.

Everyone else agrees about the beautiful table and theme. Because, well, it is. Luckily, the turkey is already carved, and we start circulating platters of food. Soon, my plate is overflowing with Thanksgiving goodness.

When the clanking of utensils and the soft murmur of individual conversations take over the room, I lean into Lincoln, whispering in his ear.

"This dinner got me thinking, Preppy. I wanted to let you know that I'm thankful for you. And I guess the academy, too. For assigning you as my student advisor. Because honestly, Linc, you're the best thing that's happened to me in a really long time." I punctuate my declaration with a firm squeeze to his upper thigh.

He stares back at me, and we're lost in our own world for a moment. A million light-years away. His eyes flick to my mouth and mine to his. Tempting me.

I know he can't exactly respond appropriately right now. Neither of us can. But I'm starting to realize I can't handle *just friends* anymore. I mean, who even wants that? Is it him? Is it me? Because I don't think either of us *ever* wanted this relationship to be platonic.

"We'll talk later," I whisper, then sit up straight again.

Across the table, I find Sierra watching Linc and me with her perfectly arched brows pulled down in the center.

I ignore whatever she may be thinking and take another bite of the stuffing.

"What are these little chewy things in the stuffing?" I ask no one in particular after swallowing a mouthful of said chewy things. "They're fucking good."

"Giblets," Diana replies drolly.

I hum my response, not really knowing what that means. I devour another bite dripping with savory home-made gravy. So fucking good.

Lincoln giggles in that awkward way I love so much.

"What? What is it?" I mumble around my mouthful.

He continues to chuckle adorably, and I love making him laugh, so I keep going, unconcerned by the uptight adults around us.

"Tell me, dude. Is it intestines or something? Fuck, are we eating the turkey's asshole?!"

Lincoln bursts out laughing, as do Sierra, Grady, and, unsurprisingly, my mom.

I never claimed to be well-mannered, mature, or even civilized. Maybe they'll leave me off the guest list next time. Somehow I don't think I'll be that lucky.

"It's gizzards, hearts, and liver, Remi," Sierra informs me in between giggles.

"Hmm. Well, after thinking it was the asshole, I'm cool with that." I stab a few of the tiny pieces of meat and chew dramatically. "Still good." I grin wide, finally pulling a chuckle from Gramps.

I won't apologize for my language or my jokes. I realize I can be a "love me or hate me" type of person. And it's really up to them which they choose. Not me.

After my outburst, I keep quiet and finish my meal. Robert and Sean have been schmoozing Gramps the entire time, and it's getting kind of annoying. I can see why it's been a while since he's come over to see his *neighbors*. They're a lot to handle. And from what I can tell, Gramps is just a homebody now.

Mom has been uncharacteristically quiet the entire night, which is somewhat strange. I can tell this whole situation makes her uncomfortable. This is exactly the type of environment she ran away from. It doesn't help that she's at least a decade younger than Diana and Kendra.

When everyone finishes dinner, the chef brings out an entire cart full of dessert. And it's all pie—from pumpkin to cherry and even pecan.

I settle on a piece of classic apple with a heaping scoop of ice cream.

As everyone settles in with pie and after-dinner espressos, Robert stands from his spot at the head of the table and dings his wine glass with a butter knife. We quiet, giving him our full attention.

"I want to thank you all for coming. It's been a great evening spent with great company. And before we all part ways for the night, I'd like to announce something very exciting, for all of our families. As we know, reconnecting and growing relationships is an integral part of life and business. So, with that being said—in addition to welcoming Raina and Remi to Hunter Springs—Diana, Sean, Kendra, and I would like to announce the official courtship of Lincoln James and Sierra Marie. With the intention of an engagement upon Sierra's high school completion and enrollment into Columbia alongside Lincoln. We'll have a grand wedding after college. But I'm getting ahead of myself," he chuckles like he's not completely controlling and destroying his son's life in one shitty fucking speech.

Jesus Christ.

They've planned their childrens' entire futures. And judging by the wide-eyed girl in front of me, neither of them had a clue. I know Linc wouldn't have kept this from me. The thought doesn't even cross my mind.

"With Anderson Holdings and Walker Industries inevitably merging into one, and the budding friendship between our boys, Richard, I hope you will strongly consider coming into business with us. Allow us to purchase majority ownership of a few of your key businesses. Let us show you what we can do. How we can potentially double profits in the first year alone. And Sean can look into any possible corruption. You need help, Richard. And we can provide that. If you'll let us."

So selfish. They don't care about Lincoln or Sierra's happiness. They don't care about Gramps. They just care about his businesses. His money.

And securing their own future.

Gramps looks uncomfortable. Mom looks a little upset —probably feeling empathy for Sierra. Grady looks bewildered, and Sierra is shell-shocked. But Linc. . . I turn my head to the boy next to me. His jaw is clenched tightly as he stares vacantly at the untouched pumpkin pie on his plate.

He's already checked out, and that worries me.

But I do know my place. Sometimes. When it's important. And right now isn't the time for me to speak up. No matter how badly I want to. This goes way beyond what I can handle, so for now, all I can do is reach under the table and give his leg a reassuring squeeze. Let him know I'm here for him.

We'll figure this out.

Together.

CHAPTER TWENTY-SIX

LINC

After everyone went home, including Remi, I retreated to my room. To the relative comfort of familiar darkness. But nothing can take my mind off what my parents announced at dinner.

A courtship. With a girl. And not just any girl. My best friend who's more like my sister.

I've finally started to live my life and embrace who I truly am, and they throw *this* at me? Without any warning? Or even the courtesy of a simple discussion. Then they just leave and go to Asheville for the night.

Why am I even surprised?

I didn't miss the deep concern swimming in Remi's eyes when I said I was tired and wanted to go to bed. Alone.

I know he wanted to stay, and I wish I had let him. I can't stop tossing and turning as negative thoughts consume me—telling me I can't be who I want, love who I want, or even have the future I want.

It's all controlled by *them*.

Hatred for my own parents churns in my gut. It's a seething, swarming mess of emotions. I can't pretend anymore. Pretend to be this perfect son with every aspect of his future mapped out. An engagement with Sierra. Columbia. Marriage. Take over the family business. Produce the next generation of Andersons.

The thought of actually living this lie makes me sick. I clamber out of bed and rush for the bathroom, turning the faucet to cool. I cup my hands underneath, drinking handful after handful until the need to throw up recedes.

I can't live my life for them.

What's the point?

My thoughts are spiraling, and I've been in my head all night. Circling around and around, unable to pull myself from the hopelessness plaguing me. It's too much. It's *been* too much. For a while now.

My fingers slip into my hair, rubbing my scalp back and forth, messing everything up.

Something inside me cracks.

A guttural scream tears from my throat before I lose all composure and lash out, smashing my fist into the perfectly imperfect reflection in front of me. A spiderweb of cracks fills my blurred vision before the sharp pain registers. I whimper and cradle my hand to my chest.

I slip my phone from my hoodie pocket and tap my favorites. I only have one.

He answers on the first ring, voice hoarse and groggy from sleep. "Linc?"

The tiny numbers in the corner of my screen tell me it's two in the morning.

"Remi." It's a strangled whisper, ending with a loud sob. But I'm in too much pain, physical and emotional, to care how I sound.

"Lincoln, what's wrong?"

"Can you come over? It's unlocked." I rasp in a choked voice.

"Already on my way." Keys jingle, and a door slams in the background. My phone clatters to the floor. I have no energy, so I slump against the wall and slide down until I'm sitting in a heap on the cold bathroom floor.

Who knows how much later, the door pushes in, and the light flips on. A sharp gasp echoes around the otherwise silent room, pulling my attention to Remi. His eyes are focused on the cracked mirror speckled with dots of red. His gaze tracks those droplets, following them down to the counter, over the sink, and across the otherwise pristine white tile floor.

I'm tucked into the corner of the room, knees bent, arms folded on top. My bloody hand hangs limp, dripping into the crimson puddle below.

"Lincoln. Fuck, Preppy. *What did you do?*" The urgency and pain in his tone are like a punch to the gut, and I struggle for air.

"I'm fallin' apart on the inside," I whisper, admitting that I can't handle all this pressure anymore.

"It hurts. *Everything hurts.*" The last bit escapes on a tumultuous breath filled with pain of the non-physical variety.

He drops to his knees beside me. "Let me see your hand." Remi gently grasps my wrist, setting my palm in his so he can inspect the damage.

His usual grin is nowhere to be found. Instead, his sharp jaw is clenched tightly, and his eyes are focused on my torn flesh.

"We'll figure this out. I promise you, Lincoln."

He says that now, but what if this ends when he sees how broken I am? When he decides he's had enough friends with benefits? And just wants to be friends. Or maybe not even that.

The intense pain at that thought spears through me, stealing the breath from my lungs.

A life without Remi.

Going back to what it was before him. The loneliness.

I can't do it. I won't do it.

I need him.

Remi's soothing voice pulls me back to the present. "Focus on me, Linc. Focus on my words. I need you, too. I've needed you every moment of every day since the second I spotted you pulling into school on your moped. I could *never* forget you. Not in a million years. Do you understand what I'm saying?"

Oh, God. I said that out loud.

My breathing picks up, turning ragged, and my heart hammers violently against my ribcage.

A cool palm touches my cheek, guiding my gaze back to his.

Everything feels disjointed, out of touch.

"I need you," he repeats.

I hear his words. But they don't sink in.

He reaches out and places his other hand over my heart.

"I fucking *need* you, Lincoln Anderson," he whispers passionately, never taking his eyes from mine.

Remi's heartfelt words cut through the panic in my mind like a knife. Slicing away my worry and replacing it with calm.

"Y-you need me?" I ask through wet, snotty sniffles, certain that I couldn't possibly hear him right.

"Yes, Lincoln. Probably more than you need me. Like I said at dinner, you're the best fucking thing that's happened to me in a long time. Probably ever." His dark eyes shine with undeniable, irrefutable truth.

"Now, please, let me take care of you. I fucking *hate* seeing you hurt like this, Preppy. Once was too much. Twice is hell. A third time might kill me, so please be careful with yourself. You're important to me."

Remi helps me up from the floor, and I move on autopilot. Dizzy from his words, I add them to the jumble of thoughts spinning around in my mind. To say I'm overwhelmed is an understatement.

We move to the sink, and he places my hand under the slow stream. I watch as the water rinses the blood away, revealing two small gashes along my red knuckles and already bruising flesh.

I barely react.

His brows draw together, probably remembering how much of a baby I was over a few scratches last week. I close my eyes tightly, compartmentalizing the stinging pain and everything else until I'm left numb again.

Unfeeling.

"Things could have gone a lot worse here, Preppy. You could have broken your hand or gotten glass stuck under your skin."

Opening my eyes, I glance down at the white bandage wrapped around my hand and the bag of ice perched on top. I blink rapidly, clearing some of the fog from my mind.

Huh? When did that happen?

I'm sitting on the bathroom counter in my tiny purple briefs and tall white socks. Remi stands in front of me, thick arms folded tightly across his chest as he stares at me with a deep frown and concerned eyes.

"Are you back with me now? I was worried there for a minute. You completely checked out."

"Y-yes. Sorry I'm such a mess," I apologize, lowering my eyes to my lap, embarrassed at everything that happened tonight as the shock of it all starts to wear off.

"Hey. You are not a mess. Don't ever apologize for your emotions. And don't ever feel like you need to hide them from me." He steps between my spread thighs. Rough palms cup my cheeks, lifting my gaze. "You are one of the strongest, most resilient people I've ever known. All the shit you've been through since I met you is more than anyone should have to handle."

He leans in and presses a tender, barely-there kiss to my lips. "You're incredible, Lincoln."

Another kiss. This time to my cheek. "Strong."

My other cheek. "Honorable."

My forehead. "Intelligent."

Both eyes. "Unique."

And back to my lips. "Undeniable."

I whimper at his soft words. My cock fills until it's tenting my briefs, attempting to free itself.

It feels like we've come full circle, back to the first time in my bathroom when he cleaned my wounds and healed some of my heart and soul on the first day of school. And here he is doing it again, not even two weeks later.

"Y-you really mean all that?"

"I never say shit I don't mean. You know that."

"You're the one good thing in my life, Remi. The only thing. And that's scary. Because I don't want to lose you."

"How would you lose me, Linc? I only just got here. I'm not fucking going anywhere. Whether you like it or not, I'm in your corner."

I reward his sweetness with a half-smile, but I'm still worried.

"How am I supposed to get out of this mess? And without hurtin' Sierra, too."

"We tell them the truth."

"What truth?"

"We're dating."

"D-datin'?" I sputter.

"Yep. Boyfriends."

My mind stalls out, convinced the trauma of the past week is causing me to hallucinate my own desires. It's the only logical explanation here. The *only* one.

"Think about it. Our first date was at the arcade, along with our first kiss. We've been on vacation together. Fucked. Met each other's parents. We've pretty much been boyfriends since day one. Just on an accelerated timeline or some shit."

He. . . he's not wrong. I've felt it all along.

"Boyfriends," I echo. It sounds good. It sounds *right*.

A weight lifts, and there's a new lightness in my chest. Hope and excitement swirl inside, giving me a newfound energy.

This fast, passionate flame burning between us has utterly consumed me, leaving me empty and aching for him.

I lean forward on the counter and slam my lips to his. Abandoning the ice bag, I wrap my arms tightly around his neck, careful not to bump my hand. He kisses me back fiercely, tongue licking at the seam and invading my mouth.

He stops for a moment, resting his forehead on mine. "When will your parents be home?"

"They're in Asheville for the night," I pant.

And then he's kissing me again, lifting me up. I wrap my legs around his waist, grinding my hard cock against his abs as he carries me to the bedroom.

"My boyfriend," I whisper, needing to say it out loud again.

"Yes. Your boyfriend. All yours. Only yours," he mumbles back.

His rough, hard exterior is tempered with tenderness when it comes to me. And there's just something so attractive about that. Knowing he's soft for only me.

"I want my boyfriend to fuck me," I murmur into his open mouth, still rubbing myself against him.

Right now, I just really need him to show me how much he needs me.

"Fuck, I love it when you curse, Preppy. Gets me so fucking hot," he growls, sending shivers down my spine.

He lays me gently on the bed, cradling my head like I'm breakable. Or something precious.

I scoot backward until my head is resting in a cocoon of pillows as Remi crawls toward me, eyes smoldering. My thighs automatically part for him as he continues moving until he's settled against me in just his boxers.

"Are you sure you're ready for this? And today? After everything?"

"Now more than ever, Remi." I nip his bottom lip. "Show me you need me, too. Prove it to me."

Before I can even utter the word "please," Remi seals his lips to mine, kissing me again.

Soft kisses trail down my body, licking and biting at my nipples, making me squirm.

"You like that?" he asks.

"Mm-hmm," I hum.

He sucks one into his mouth, and my hips flex, cock pulsing.

"Ooooh," I moan wantonly. I never knew having my nipples sucked could feel so good.

"Fuck. You're sexy," Remi whispers, hot breath ghosting across my sensitive flesh, his words empowering me.

Remi continues with his trail of kisses until he reaches my underwear. I lift my hips, and he slips them off, wasting no time dragging his tongue up my cock. He swirls it around my crown, teasing me before swallowing me to the hilt and holding his mouth there for a few seconds.

I'm on edge. Ready to explode.

Remi pulls off with a loud pop, and I whimper, breaths heaving. "I was... about... to... come."

"I know," he says mischievously. "Now get on your hands and knees, and tip your ass up for me. I need to work you open really good. It's gonna be a tight fit." His grin is wicked, but his eyes are full of something much deeper. Something I think I feel, too.

I swallow thickly at his dirty words and roll over, peering over my shoulder with half-lidded eyes. I'm ready for more butt stuff.

I trust him.

CHAPTER TWENTY-SEVEN

REMI

"Arch your back and stick your ass out. I wanna see that untouched hole."

He hangs his head and groans out my name. I'm sure his face is as red as his hair, but he obeys, spreading his legs more. I get the sexiest view of his tiny pink hole, begging me to open it up.

I climb between his thighs, squeezing his cheeks and spreading them apart. Leaning in, I swipe my tongue across him, and he jolts.

"*Oh, hell.* W-what was that?" he mumbles into the pillow, pushing his ass toward me, asking for more.

"My tongue, Preppy. Now just relax and let me get you ready for my cock."

He nods his head, his body visibly slouching. I lick him again, running my tongue along his taint, then back to his hole, where I circle his tight pucker, softening him up. I apply pressure, spreading him with my thumbs until the tip of my tongue slips in.

"Yesss," he cries in pleasure. Legs shaking, he holds still

as I continue to fuck him with my tongue until he can't take it anymore and starts to rock his hips.

I decide to let him come before I fuck him, so I slip my tongue out, reach around and grasp his cock. It doesn't take more than two pumps before he's spilling all over my hand and the sheets below.

I sit back on my haunches, inspecting his slightly open hole. "You've loosened up. I'm gonna keep going, okay?"

He hums his consent, wiggling his ass for me. I chuckle, giving it a playful smack. I gently press down on the middle of his back. "Stay on your forearms, but keep your ass in the air for me, baby. I'm gonna stretch you open more."

Using his own cum, I circle his hole. He's soft and relaxed from my tongue, so I easily push into him. His moans are unrestrained, lustful sighs that light my fucking insides on fire.

Goddamn, he is fucking sexy. He doesn't have a clue.

His asshole clenches around my finger, so I add another, wanting to feel the pressure of him squeezing me. He easily accommodates another digit and moves against me, rocking himself back on my fingers.

"That's it. Ride my fingers. Keep fucking yourself, Linc."

I keep my fingers in his ass while I lean over and rummage around his bedside drawer for the small bottle of lube I put there.

I squirt an unnecessarily large amount over his hole and slip another digit in, stretching him wider. He cries out, legs trembling.

I stroke his back while I press feather-light kisses down his spine. I curve my fingers, lightly grazing the spot I've been avoiding.

"*Ungh!* Oh, God! There!" he yells. And I'm so glad we don't have to worry about his parents hearing us.

"Do you want to come again? Before I fuck you?" I grit out, ready to get my dick inside him. It'll be a tight fit, but I think he's ready now, judging by the sight before me.

"No. I want your cock in me. Now." He's practically slamming himself against all three of my fingers, so I slip them out.

He whimpers my name.

"I know. I know," I murmur, squirting even more lube into my hand to stroke myself first.

I press my tip to him and rub in slow, teasing circles. I taunt him with the soft, silky glide of my cockhead down his crease and over his hole, driving him wild with need.

I push forward slightly, finally giving him what he wants, but there's resistance. I pull away, unwilling to hurt him even a little. I switch back to my fingers, scissoring them this time, pushing the limits of his body.

"Relax for me, baby." I rub up and down his spine, worshiping his soft skin and every single freckle adorning it.

He's groaning and whining and making all kinds of sexy little unintelligible noises while I try to get him ready to take my cock.

"Shh. That's it." I pull my fingers free and continue to whisper reassurances, squirting even more lube directly onto his gaping hole. I line my cock back up, pressing forward ever so slowly. My crown starts to ease in. He's squeezing me so fucking tight it almost hurts.

"Just a little more." My breath is a ragged, desperate thing.

"I can't do it. It's too big," he whines.

"You can. It's almost in. Just bear down." I stroke his hip, and he pushes against me until I slip past the tight ring of muscle. He cries out, swallowing me into his body.

I pause, continuing to rub his side tenderly. "You okay?" I breathe out.

"Y-yes. *Oh, God.* Give me more," he begs.

I close my eyes and let my dick fill him, fully sinking into him. His breath hitches, his body gripping me. All of me.

Holy fucking hell.

He's the tightest thing I've ever felt. Squeezing my cock like a vise. Nothing can compare. *Fucking nothing.*

"Still okay?" I murmur before I start moving.

I know I'm big, and my dick is *all* the way inside him right now. My brain almost can't compute that I'm actually in there. *In his ass.*

My boyfriend's ass.

He turns his head to peer at me over his shoulder, eyes half-mast. "Fuck me," he rasps, in a needy demand that has my balls drawing up and my cock pulsing deep.

I can't express the feelings raging through my body and mind as my hips pull back until just the tip is in. His mismatched gaze bores into me as I surge forward, giving him my entire length in one solid thrust. His mouth drops open, and his eyes roll into the back of his head. His forehead falls to the bed, and the rest of what he moans and shouts is an inarticulate mess.

But it's the sexiest thing to see him so untamed, so carefree.

"Oh fuck, Preppy. You're a sight to behold right now." I grit my teeth and close my eyes for a second, trying not to come from the erotic sight in front of me and the enthusiastic groans pouring nonstop from Lincoln's lips.

I reach my arm around his hip to grasp his cock with one hand, stroking him in time with my thrusts. My other hand roams across his stomach, and his lean abs ripple under my touch.

"Ohhh. Remi. Fuuck! Fuck me harder!"

I curl around his back, relentlessly pounding into his ass, and bite his ear. "Told you I'd make you say fuck while I fuck you," I growl, eliciting more whimpers from him.

I band my arm across his torso and pull him up so we're both on our knees, his back to my chest. I thrust harder, finding that perfect angle, making his whole body jerk.

"*Ungh!* Fuuuck! There!"

My fingers dig into his hip, my palm splayed and pressing into his belly as I fuck him fast and hard.

"Good boy," I rasp into his ear, nipping at it. I nearly jizz from my own fucking words.

"Oh God, Remi. Don't say that. I-I won't last," he whines.

"You're so good. Taking this cock." I continue to grunt filthy words as I plunge in and out of him. Praising and rewarding him with every thrust into his hot, clenching body.

And then his hole is pulsing around me, and my nuts draw up. We both come together with strangled cries.

"Now that you've had a little taste of both, what do you prefer, *boyfriend*?

At his quizzical look, I clarify.

"Top or bottom?"

Even after *everything* we just did, everything we've *been* doing, his cheeks still pinken adorably.

I think I know what *I'm* feeling. And I hope it aligns with his desires.

"Oh. Um." He ducks his head and peeks at me from under his auburn lashes, glasses off.

"I like both. But I really, really like what we just did. I guess I'm more of a bottom?"

"Yeah?"

Oh, hell yes.

He nods, a small yet confident smile gracing his lips. "Yeah."

We're lying on our sides in his bed—faces inches apart —with a clean change of sheets and fresh showers. It's almost four in the morning, but we're both a little wired from the sheer amount of drama in our lives. Not to mention the buzzing of the texts I've been avoiding from my jeans that are in a heap on the floor. I have to focus on Linc right now. My boyfriend.

Not Unknown or my family issues.

"I think I'm more of a top, myself," I volunteer, leaning forward to lick at his mouth. He kisses me back, and I casually suck on his tongue before pulling back and carrying on with the pillow talk.

"Seeing your asshole stretched open with my cock? Feeling you grip me like that? Fuck. I could come just picturing it in my head, Preppy."

He giggles softly. "Stop before I need you inside me again. My dick's already half-hard."

I reach down and cup him. "You're more than half-hard," I growl. "But we need to talk about a couple of things before we sleep. You need rest and to recover." I roll to my back, staring at the ceiling fan circling slowly above us.

"Since the plan to get you out of this bullshit courtship is to just tell the truth, I say we start with Grady and Sierra. Since you planned to come out to them anyway, this is just forcing your hand earlier than expected. But it'll be okay; I'll be there with you. And I'll be there when we tell your parents. I got your back. Always."

"Okay. I can text Grady to meet up after school."

"After the gym. Because you're coming with me again. And as soon as your hand heals, you're training with Otto and me. No more studying and making flashcards on the sidelines. You need a healthy outlet. And punching mirrors isn't it, Preppy."

He scoots into me, and I slip my arm around him, pulling him tightly to my body. He hides his face in the crook of my neck. "Just hold me. Please. I can't talk about that part right now."

"Don't be embarrassed, Linc. It's a step above punching a brick wall, and I've been there myself. There's no judgment here. Ever. I just want to make sure you're okay. You have a boyfriend to lean on now." I kiss the top of his silky auburn hair, inhaling his fresh citrus scent.

"Let me hold some of that weight for you."

CHAPTER TWENTY-EIGHT
REMI

Lincoln agreed to skip first period after everything that happened in the middle of the night. We needed to sleep in and get more rest, so Dr. Benson better not give us shit the next time we see him. Lincoln already told me he warned him away. Told him to find a new friend, someone other than me.

What-the-fuck-ever.

The rest of the short school day flew by, and now we're stepping into Otto's gym. The little bell above the door chimes, and Sasha looks over, her smile dropping to a frown as her eyes dart to Lincoln's bandaged hand, then immediately over to me. Accusing almost.

She's only four years older, in her final year of pre-med at a local college, but she's definitely taken on a mama-bear role when it comes to us, especially Lincoln. I don't really blame her. I've also felt the need to protect him since day one.

"Hey," I whisper into his ear. I don't want him to hear any of this. "Go ahead and take a seat by the treadmills. I'll be over there in a sec."

He nods, adjusting his glasses and messenger bag, scurrying over to the bench by the warm-up equipment. He says a quick hello to Sasha, ducking his head along the way.

"Remi. What the hell happened?" Sasha hisses under her breath. She's tried to get information out of me ever since I came back from the trip with a black eye. She knows I've been fighting. It's obvious.

"Linc isn't fighting, is he?"

"No," I grit out. "Hell fucking no. Look, where's Otto? He needs to hear this, too."

"I'm right here. What's going on?" He strolls over in his usual tank top and joggers, like the rest of his employees. His thick brows are pulled down in the center, and his gray eyes dart between Sasha and me.

I sigh heavily. "Lincoln's hand is bandaged up because some shit went down with his parents last night—"

"They hurt him?!" Otto shouts a little too loudly.

"What? No!" I peer around him to check on Linc. He's got his earbuds in. *Good.*

"Listen. Don't ask me to tell you what happened. It's not my story. All I can say is, he needs a healthier outlet for the shit he's dealing with."

That's as much detail as I'm willing to give them, only because I know they truly care. "So when he's feeling better, we're gonna start training together. Here, with you."

That pulls big, genuine smiles from both of them, just like I knew it would.

"But I'm not pushing him to start soon. It's on his terms. When he's ready."

They both nod enthusiastically. "Of course, hun. We would never pressure him. I'll just keep buttering him up with my homemade protein cookies and winning personality. He can't say no." Sasha laughs warm-heartedly, heading over to Linc, where she plops down next to him on the bench. She bumps her shoulder into his and says something before he pulls one of his headphones from his ear and hands it over. She bobs her head to the music, smiling and saying something else to him. He laughs, a slight blush settling on his cheeks. I love that he has another person enamored with him.

He's remarkable. Something uniquely special. And everyone should know that.

Otto and I stand here for a moment, watching them.

"So, you into my mom or something?" It's a random transition, I know. But if we're talking about shit, I'd like to know.

He turns his head, peering down at me from his six-and-a-half-foot height.

"Would it bother you if I was?"

I shrug. "Nah. Not really. I know I've given you some shit, but you're a good guy, Otto. She's still married to my dad, though. And he's a shithead. You know that, right?"

He grits his teeth, clearly unhappy with the idea. "Yes. I know. But your mother and I have a history, as I've briefly told you. We went to school together. Grew up together. I was devastated when she left, and I won't let her go again. Not without a fight. And I *don't* lose."

Shit. That just got deep.

"She knows this?" I ask curiously. Mom can be tough. A little standoffish. And Otto seems a little more in touch with his emotions, although he's clearly still a badass.

He nods. "She does."

I hum my response. Guess I've been so preoccupied with my new boyfriend and my own issues that I didn't realize how serious things were getting with them.

"Okay. Well, then, is this you asking me for my blessing?"

He barks out a loud laugh. "Yeah, kid. I guess you could say that. So what'll it be?"

"Like I said, you're a good guy. And she's never had that. So, if you treat her right and take care of her, you more than have my blessing. Even if it might be a little weird when I start seeing you at the breakfast table Sunday mornings."

He belts out another deep chuckle and slings his massive arm around my shoulder, putting me in a half-hug, half-headlock embrace. "You're something else, kid."

"Something else spectacular," I grin, slipping out of his hold and grabbing his wrist. I twist his arm, pinning it behind his back, forcing him to bend forward and submit. I know he could take me if he really wanted to, but probably not now that he's trying to bang my mom.

Some of the guys around the gym cheer and yell, attempting to egg us on.

"Alright. Alright. You got me. I'm tapping out, kid."

I shove him away, laughing. "Lame."

He straightens and chuckles at that, shaking his head.

I narrow my eyes on him. "What? You don't think I could take you?"

Before he can answer, my phone buzzes twice in my back pocket. I freeze, slipping it out on autopilot. It's gotten to the point where I *have* to look now. I can't *not* look. I went from actively avoiding the messages, and even my phone, to needing to know what they say immediately. In case he's outside my house or some shit.

See you this weekend.

Don't make any plans.

My throat dries out, making a weird clicking noise as I try to swallow. I can feel the blood drain from my face.

"Remi. Tell me what's going on. Let me help you." Otto's low, urgent tone tears me away from my screen.

"What are you talking about? It's fine. Just spam."

My phone vibrates again.

I can't understand how Unknown is getting past all of my blocks. Does this psycho get a new phone each time he texts? Or is he stealing them?

What the fuck is even happening?

This fucker is *terrorizing* me.

My palms are sweaty, and I nearly drop my phone, fumbling it so badly that Otto grabs it out of the air before it smashes onto the unforgiving ground.

I snatch it out of his hand, not wanting him to get a glimpse of the threatening texts. "Thanks, man."

My eyes glance down, unable to stop myself.

How are you enjoying that big house on the hill?

Fuck! These psychological games are bullshit. I got enough of that from my old man growing up; I don't need it from this unknown asshole.

Otto side-eyes me and purses his lips. I know he wants to say more, but I'm not willing to involve him or my mom just yet. I can handle this. I hope.

"I'm ready to punch something now," I say instead, heading over to Lincoln sitting alone, quiet and reserved. He's reading through our English homework, munching on Sasha's oatmeal chocolate chip cookies, looking adorably sexy.

"Ready to watch me kick some ass, Preppy?" I grin down at him as he peers up at me with chipmunk cheeks that turn pink.

———— ∽ ————

Before we finished at the gym, Linc wanted Otto and me to show him some basic self-defense moves. Nothing intense —no punches, just a few easy blocks and basic escape maneuvers. He seemed to enjoy it and is open to the possibility of training. So I'm hoping he'll try a little more each day. But it's still his choice.

Afterward, I dropped Linc off at his place and went to mine for dinner with Mom and Gramps. I'm dying to question her about Otto, but I'm pretty sure she'll question me about Linc if I do that. And this relationship is all on his schedule—when he wants to come out and to whom—not mine. Because I'm cool with whatever.

I am bisexual and proud, and I am definitely Lincoln's boyfriend and proud. I will climb Mount fucking Mitchell and scream from the top of my lungs to the entire state that I am Lincoln Anderson's boyfriend.

But until he's ready, I won't.

Speaking of coming out, Linc's parents are unfortunately back in Hunter Springs tonight, so he has to sneak out to link up with Grady and Sierra. He texted me to meet him in the woods behind my house, and he'll show me the way to some secret spot where the three of them hung out as kids. Away from their lonely homes and nosey parents. And I'm definitely curious to get a glimpse into his past.

Preppy: Walk straight back from your deck. I'll find you.

Following Linc's directions, I start walking down the trail, using the light from my phone to help guide me. The trees rustle in the wind, carrying scents of damp earth and pine. I pull my hood up and stuff my free hand into the leather jacket I threw on. The late October air is finally cold enough for another layer.

Not even one minute into my hike, Lincoln steps out of the trees like some ginger-haired woodland nymph.

"Hey."

I stop abruptly, stumbling back a step. *"Jesus Christ!* Are you trying to give me a heart attack?"

"Sorry," he giggles, reaching forward to thread his fingers with mine. "It's this way." Linc nods his head to the side, shining his flashlight into the dense, untamed part of the forest, leading us off the beaten path.

Now I'm *really* curious about where we're going.

"Where are you taking me, Preppy? I'm getting excited. And kinda turned on." He tugs my hand harder, pulling me after him while he laughs freely. The sound is like a balm to my soul and a firm squeeze to my dick.

"My secret lair. To have my wicked way with you. *Again,*" he teases, and I love it when he can just be himself. Free to laugh, free to flirt and joke.

"Oh, fuck yeah. Use me, baby," I tease back. His giggle turns into a snort, and he trips over a log on the ground in front of us. Before he can fall, my arm whips out lightning fast, and I pull him to me, spinning us until his back is pressed against the tree trunk.

"Told you I'd always have your back," I whisper over his lips, staring into his mesmerizing eyes lit by the soft glow of the moon barely peeking through the thick trees.

I dart forward, licking at the seam of his mouth. He kisses me back, our tongues tangling. Before we get carried away and someone gets fucked against the rough bark of this old oak tree, I peel my lips away, resting my forehead against his instead.

"You feeling okay about tonight? About telling your friends?"

"Yeah. Think so." He smiles softly and pecks me on the lips. "It's not as scary knowin' I have you there with me. As my boyfriend."

"Good," I growl, nipping his lip one more time before stepping away and letting him lead us through the forest. To his *lair*.

We step over fallen logs and duck under hanging branches until we reach a small clearing in the woods. The most magical treehouse I've ever seen comes into view.

Built around a massive oak tree, a small wooden house sits untouched by time other than the vines crawling over the roof, weaving their way through the wooden slats. The quaint structure is illuminated with draping fairy lights and flickering lanterns. A spiral staircase made from natural wood leads up to a small porch full of colorful pillows. I feel like I'm in another world. A book or some shit.

It's the most extravagant and fantastical child's playhouse I have ever fucking seen. But I guess I *would* think that when my comparison is a cardboard box and a blanket.

"They're already here," he whispers unsteadily.

"It'll be fine. You know it will." I squeeze his hand in mine before dropping it.

"Okay. Let's do this," he says, more to himself.

"I'll go first." I climb the surprisingly sturdy stairs, popping my head through a small hole in the deck. Grady and Sierra sit on a pile of pillows and blankets, with several lanterns surrounding them.

"Hey guys," I say casually, hoisting myself up. I reach down to grasp Lincoln by his forearm, helping him into the treehouse, carefully avoiding the bandage around his hand.

We crawl over to the twins, sitting down across from them.

Sierra's dark hair is down in loose, glossy curls tonight, and her face is void of makeup. She's wearing plain black leggings, Chucks, and a Blue Ridge Prep hoodie. She looks so young like this but beautiful as always. Grady is in comfortable dark sweats like Linc and I, and they're sitting there waiting for us to take the lead.

"Oh my gosh, Linc! What happened to your hand?!"

We didn't see the twins at school today, and I'm sure Linc didn't tell them over text that he punched his bathroom mirror.

"It's nothin'," he mumbles, tucking his hand into the giant pocket of his hoodie.

"It's clearly somethin', Lincoln James!" she scolds him, using the middle name and everything. Pink settles into his cheeks, and he blushes adorably, ducking his head.

"I just. . . I kind of had a freak out last night," he admits, not making eye contact with anyone, and I'm a little surprised he's going to tell them.

"Why? Because of us? I mean, because of what our parents said?" She places her cute little hand on his arm, and I automatically stiffen, even though I know it's completely unreasonable. She doesn't know he's gay. She doesn't know we're together. And she's been nothing but sweet to him his entire life. I know this. But the caveman in me wants to beat on my chest and yell that he's mine.

"Y-yes. Because I can't do it, Sierra. I can't live a lie that big."

There's an extended pause, and no one says anything or moves a muscle.

"I-I'm gay," he blurts, and it's a little smoother than when he came out to me, but not by much.

"Oh, Linc." Her hand slips to his uninjured one, and she squeezes, her brilliant smile stretching wide. "I'm so happy you felt comfortable enough to tell me. To tell us." She nudges her brother. "Right, Grady?"

He clears his throat, swiping his floppy curls away from

his forehead, only to have them fall forward again. "Y-yeah, man. Really, that's great."

Lincoln subconsciously leans into me, and her inquisitive amber eyes don't miss a beat, landing straight on mine.

"And you. . .?"

"Bisexual." I grin mischievously.

Her lip quirks. "And you two. . .?"

"Are boyfriends," Linc blurts out again.

"*Ohmygod!* Oh my God! OH MY GOD! I knew it! Well, I didn't know it, know it. But y'all just hit it off so fast. Your friendship has been a relationship the whole time?"

We look at each other and shrug. "Pretty much," I answer truthfully.

She squeals, doing some kind of weird happy dance on her pillows.

"Well, I'm happy if Linc is happy. And it really seems like you have been the past couple of weeks."

"Thanks, Grady," Linc mumbles, and I wrap my arm around his shoulder, pulling him into me now that we don't have to hide.

Sierra squeals again and claps her hands together. "You two are so freakin' cute together! I'm goin' to die!" I roll my eyes at her dramatics.

"In all seriousness, y'all don't have to come out to our parents if you're not ready. We can pretend, Linc," Sierra offers in her usual sweet, mild-mannered way. "I'm okay with that, for now."

She's absolutely gorgeous, inside and out. And I feel the need to protect her, just like I do Linc. They share an innocence and vulnerability that vultures like Brandon like to prey on. Not under my fucking watch.

"Thanks, Sierra. But, I'm done livin' my life for them. We're not hidin' this, and we plan to start tellin' people,

soon. But if you could just keep it under wraps for now. . ."
His mismatched gaze bounces between his friends, the soft
orange glow from the lanterns highlighting the golden
flecks in his emerald eye. I can't stop staring at him. I clear
my throat before I tongue him in front of his friends and
give Grady a stroke and Sierra a lady boner.

"Of course," Sierra agrees, and Grady nods his head.

"Should we do a group hug or some shit?" I ask, only
slightly joking. I'm down if they are.

CHAPTER TWENTY-NINE

LINC

After coming out to Grady and Sierra last night and having them be so accepting, I feel lighter and more myself as the four of us eat our lunch, discussing the next *Call of Duty* release. It's Friday, and I'm looking forward to a peaceful weekend hanging out with Remi. Grady and Sierra, too.

"Maybe we could all meet at my house and go swimmin' tonight? Order pizza and game?"

"That sounds awesome, Preppy. I could use some chill time."

"Me, too. We haven't swam together in years, Linc," Sierra says, and Grady hums his agreement.

Our weekend plans get interrupted by a cold, callous voice that causes a knot of worry to form in the pit of my stomach.

"How can you even be friends with him?"

My cheeks burn as humiliation washes over me.

Remi sits up straighter, muscles tense and ready to strike. Brandon is oblivious to the apex predator in front of him, scoping out the best way to take down his prey.

He continues on, unaware, spewing his hateful vitriol at my *boyfriend*.

"He thinks he's too good for everyone else here. Living up on his hill like he's above us. Never hanging out with anyone. Never inviting anyone over. Never going to any parties. Makes me fucking sick. Stuck-up little prick." He turns his angry sneer to me, hatred seeping from every pore.

"Did you know your dad bought my dad out of his own business this week? Our entire family legacy. *Gone.* Taken by force. Bought out from right under his nose. Swallowed up by *Anderson Holdings.* Now there's nothing left for him to pass down. Your parents are fucking soulless bastards. Just like you. Except they're manipulative and calculated. *You.* You're just a fucking robot." He practically bares his teeth at me, and I can't help but shrink back into Remi as Brandon looms above me.

I never react to him. Never give him the satisfaction. I choose to suffer in silence and remain quiet in the face of my bullies, but I know it pushes his buttons even more.

Carry on. Keep strong.

"Whoa. Whoa. Back the fuck up. Right now, Brandon," Remi barks, grabbing hold of my chair and sliding it away from Brandon's spiteful presence. The metal legs screech across the cafeteria floor, garnering more attention.

Remi jumps up, placing his body between Brandon and me and hollering for Gus, who rushes over from across the room where the other jocks are sitting with mocking grins on their faces. I don't know why when the jerk at the center of them all is sitting there with his face all busted up. By Remi. *My boyfriend.* My overprotective-hothead-with-a-heart-bigger-than-most boyfriend.

I'm tempted to just tell everyone we're together right

now. Get it over with. But I can't risk it getting back to my parents before I tell them myself. My best hope for something amicable coming out of this is to be honest and tell them as soon as possible. Sierra and I will not be putting on a charade. Not even for one night.

Gus's dark eyes track over the drama-fueled scene in front of him. Sighing heavily, he asks, "What now, new kid?"

"Dude. It's not me. I swear. It's your bullying, bitch-ass teammates that keep harassing me and my friends. We were just sitting here eating lunch. Minding our own fucking business. As usual. But this fuckface just *loves* to come over and talk shit."

Remi turns his cold stare to Brandon. "Fuck your family's company, you prick. We don't give a shit. That has nothing to do with Linc. Or me. Or Grady and Sierra. And since you can't listen and back the fuck off. . ."

Folding his thick arms across his chest, school blazer nearly bursting at the seams, Remi glares at Brandon but speaks to the whole room.

"I formally challenge Brandon Fuckface Halliday to a duel. A fight to the death!" he bellows, throwing his fist up in mock triumph. Remi cackles wildly, the sound echoing around the nearly silent cafeteria.

Brandon pales, eyes darting over to Connor's ruined face, then back to Remi. His mouth opens and closes a few times like he wants to protest but knows that will only make him look weak.

"Twenty-five hundred plus bets," he adds, a confident smirk tugging at his lips.

"What'll it be, Brand?" Gus asks impatiently. "I have a spot open tonight. Otherwise, you'll have to wait two weeks. I got family stuff going on next weekend."

Swallowing thickly, Brandon hesitantly agrees, looking way less sure of himself than when he came sauntering over five minutes ago, threatening me. I hate that Remi is fighting because of me *again*. I hate it so, so much. But there's nothing I can do. He won't let Brandon or Connor or anyone else get away with bullying.

Remi is a crusader, a fierce champion. *My champion.*

And maybe I just need to get used to that.

———————⁄∽⁄———————

My parents are in New York for the weekend at some kind of Columbia Business School alumni function. I'm just thankful they didn't drag me along. Probably because of the unsightly bandage around my knuckles that I told them happened when I accidentally closed Remi's car door on my hand. It wasn't a far stretch from something that's happened before, so they didn't even bat an eye. They just turned their noses up at me, like the fact that I hurt my own freakin' hand *disappoints* them.

It makes tonight easy. Remi didn't have to sneak in, and I didn't have to sneak out. We had to take a rain check on swimming, though. But we did talk Grady and Sierra out of coming to the fight. I feel bad for telling them maybe next time because, in all honesty, I'm hoping there won't be a next time. But they're only seventeen, and Remi can't watch out for all three of us *and* fight. It's not fair to him.

This time his friend Ivan will be there. I only know him as the stoner kid with blue hair, but I'm supposed to stand with him so Remi can focus on the fight. And I'll do it. Because as much as he hates seeing me hurt, it feels even worse to watch someone hit him. To see the deep bruises mottling Remi's pale skin and know there's nothing I can do. It's a helpless and vulnerable feeling. One I don't wish to experience regularly.

We're lounging in my room, wasting time before we head out. I swivel around in my desk chair. "Remi, you really don't have to fight because of me." I have to reiterate it. I just have to.

He's sitting on the end of my bed, leaning over to lace his boots up tightly, even though he takes them off before every fight. His dark hair is raven black after his shower, and the wet strands hang limply over his forehead. Tiny droplets land on his bare chest, trickling down his sculpted body, and I can't tear my eyes away. He looks so freakin' good in his fight gear. My dick starts to harden while my body does the complete opposite and practically melts to the ground in a puddle of boneless flesh.

"It's not just because of you. I know I haven't been completely open about what happened before I left Detroit. Didn't want you to think less of me, I guess."

"I would never think less of you, Remi. *Never.*"

"I know that now, Preppy." His deep voice rolls through me, caressing me with its sincerity.

"But the gist of it is, I got arrested for fighting. Mom and I needed money. Dad was a deadbeat before he left, and we couldn't count on him for shit. I had no choice but to help pay the bills. After the arrest, she spent most of her money on my lawyer, which is why I need five thousand dollars. To pay her back. I already have half."

"But she doesn't need that money now. *You* don't need that money now."

"Look, I don't expect you to understand. It's just something I have to do. For my own peace of mind. I pay my debts. Always have. And I owe her a lot more than that if I'm being honest with myself."

"Remi. You're her child. You don't owe your mom anything. And I'm sure she knows that."

"Well, regardless, this is happening. I'm fighting tonight. For the money." His lips tug into a teasing smile. "And for your honor."

There's no stopping him when his mind is set. I can only be there to support him, and I will. "But after this one. . ." I trail off, hoping he'll agree to stop.

The fact that Remi's already been arrested makes me really, really uneasy. His urgent words from that night in the woods, lost in a haze of panic at the time, trickle into the forefront of my mind.

I cannot get caught, Lincoln. I will go to jail for a very long time if I'm arrested for this shit. Do you understand what I'm saying?

And not juvie. He's eighteen now, so he'll go to prison. I can't lose him when I've only just found him.

Once he pays his mom back, he won't need the money. And once he fights Brandon, there's no one else he needs to protect me from. Connor and Brandon are my main tormentors. *Were* my main tormentors. Because after tonight, they'll both be put in their places. And when they find out Remi's my boyfriend. I'm hoping they'll stay there.

"I'll think about it, Preppy."

I guess it's better than a *no*.

He finishes lacing his shoes and grabs my bare foot off the ground, tugging me over to him. The desk chair offers no resistance, and I squeak embarrassingly loud, gripping the armrests as I'm wheeled over.

He places my foot in his lap and begins to massage it sensually.

"You don't have to do that, Remi," I say over a moan as he rubs his thumbs up the arch of my foot.

"I like to. I like making my boyfriend feel good. And I like mapping every little freckle on your body. Even these cute little ones on the top of your feet." He lifts my foot and presses a soft kiss right on top. "And I like touching you." He smirks, continuing his massage up my calf, kneading the muscle before working his way up to my thigh. "Everywhere."

I tip my head back, staring at the ceiling for a second. His expert touch is getting me all worked up. I spread my legs, tenting the thin cotton shorts I've been wearing around the house without my parents home.

"We don't have time," I gasp as he slips his hand under the hem of my shorts, immediately grabbing hold of my cock. His eyes dart to mine, excited.

"No underwear?" he asks, sounding slightly impressed.

I shrug. "We're home alone. Why not?"

He slips to his knees, peering up at me. "You'll be quick, right? I'm feeling like a pre-fight blowie might give me some good luck."

I giggle, hoping that sucking my cock can be his good luck charm. I nod enthusiastically and lift my hips, allowing him to slip the small blue shorts down to my ankles. Remi starts to lift my T-shirt, so I help him, pulling it over my head with one hand. I lean back in the desk chair and peer down at him.

He sits there for a moment, and my gut heats at his slow, visual sweep of my naked body. The savage heat flaring in his hooded eyes scorches my insides, stealing the air from my lungs.

"Suck me," I whisper bravely, needing his mouth on me right now.

"I'm gonna suck you so hard, baby. And I plan to be

balls-deep inside your ass tonight, Preppy. Celebrating our win."

His dirty words have me aching for him, and I thrust my hips forward.

"Please," I moan, wanting it all. The thought of Remi sucking me off, then taking my hole again tonight makes my cock pulse.

My eyes roll into the back of my head when he swallows me down, bobbing his head quickly.

"*Oh God,*" I cry. He didn't even give me a chance to work up to it. Just started sucking me hard.

He tightens the suction, pulling a long, drawn-out groan from me. My balls draw up and unload instantly. I don't think he's prepared for my cum to spurt into the back of his mouth, so he gags. His throat undulates against my cockhead as he swallows, and I come harder, load after load filling his mouth until it's dribbling out.

He pulls off and swipes a finger across the corner of his mouth, scooping up my cum and holding it out for me. I lean in and suck his finger down to the knuckle, releasing it with a loud pop and swallowing my own spunk for him.

"Good boy," he rumbles, making me whimper.

Why do I like that so much? What is wrong with me?

Remi stands, digging the heel of his palm into his erection, trying to adjust himself against his zipper.

"Let me take care of that for you." My voice sounds low and husky and so unlike my normal tone that I giggle and clear my throat.

"Sorry. Um. Did you want me to help you with that?" I nod to the giant boner trying to escape his pants.

"Nah. It'll keep me worked up. Angrier. Aggressive. Ready to kick Brandon's ass so I can come home and fuck yours," he teases and *gah*, his dirty words get me every time.

"Go get dressed," he rumbles, and I jump out of the seat, semi-hard cock hanging between my legs as I scurry to grab a change of clothes for another fight night in the woods.

CHAPTER THIRTY
REMI

"What? Don't look at me like that, Preppy." I lower my voice as I slip into the same side of the booth as Lincoln. "I can't even touch you from all the way over there. It's too far."

I just finished the easiest fight of my fucking life, and now we're grabbing a quick bite in Asheville before heading back to Lincoln's place.

I had a sound strategy tonight. No hits to the face. Take Brandon down and make him submit MMA-style. I was *not* going to allow him to add another bruise to this handsome mug.

Clearly, he wasn't expecting that. He was expecting a fistfight like they all do. I asked around. In Gus's fight league, no one takes it to the ground. Most of these assholes are football players from Blue Ridge and one of the private schools here in Asheville Gus has a connection with. They may know how to punch and block, but their ground game is weak. Tonight proves that.

I had Brandon down in the dirt in the first five minutes and passed out in the next two. He refused to submit, so it's his own fault he had to take a nap like a little bitch.

We didn't stick around for the fallout, the other fights, or the afterparty. It's over. My winnings will be deposited into my bank account by Monday morning, and the only person I want to hang out with is sitting next to me.

"You know I have trouble keeping my hands to myself. And I'd rather enjoy my food than be miserable sitting all the way over there," I tell Linc in a hushed whisper. "See? No one will even know if I do this."

I slip my hand underneath the table and cup his junk lightly. He jerks and sputters, his eyes darting around the nearly empty diner.

"Remi," he hisses under his breath. "W-what are you doin'?"

I remove my hand, and Linc visibly relaxes. "I'm just fucking with you." I squeeze his thigh as our server comes over with a bright smile and big hair.

"Hey there, sugarplums. How y'all doin' tonight?"

I glance from her nametag to her hot pink lips, bright blue eyeshadow, and bleach-blonde hair with bangs teased to heaven.

Jesus. Tammy Lynn is *Southern.* And Tammy Lynn is stuck in the fucking eighties.

"We're doing great, Miss Tammy. How's your night been going?"

Even though she's older than my mom, she blushes, straightening the little white apron tied around her waist.

"Oh. Well, it's been alright, I suppose. Thanks for askin'. Now, what can I get for ya?" She smiles warmly, crinkling the skin around her eyes.

Linc tries to order grilled chicken breast and veggies, but I inform him that only greasy, fatty food is allowed after eleven at night. Sugar, too. So I order two double cheese-burgers, chili cheese fries, and chocolate and strawberry malts.

Wildflower's Cafe is quirky and rustic, with an artsy vibe. It's located on the end of a strip of businesses that are closed for the night. If they didn't have one of those classic neon lights reading *Open* stuck in the window, we would have missed it on this dark and deserted side of town.

The place is filled with fresh, colorful wildflowers. Local art covers every inch of the wall—from graffiti work to framed paintings and canvas watercolors. The lighting is dim and relaxing, with only small orange lanterns on each table and larger pendulum lighting above the long bar.

It's definitely a hole-in-the-wall, which usually has the best food.

Tammy brings the malted milkshakes before the meal, setting them down before us.

Chocolate for Linc and strawberry for me.

We both thank Tammy and take long sips of our shakes, humming at the flavor.

"We can share," I offer, nudging my glass toward him. "The strawberry is really good. Bet we're getting all our daily calcium, too," I tease because it's just so easy, and it also kinda gets me hard.

He glances around quickly, then leans in and wraps his soft pink lips around my straw, pulling hard and moaning at the taste.

Fuuuck.

"Shit, Preppy. How was that so hot? My blue balls were already aching." I grin at him and wink, making him duck his head and laugh lightly.

We're nearly done with our food when a group of girls

comes in giggling, taking a corner booth on the other side of the room. A couple smile and wave, and I give them a nod in return. They may have been at the fight if they're out here this late.

After a few more glances and giggles, the redhead leaves her friends and approaches our booth.

"Hey," she says with a brilliant smile, self-consciously adjusting the strap of her purse. "I'm Heather."

"Hey, Heather," I reply in a friendly tone, somewhat amused by this until I notice Linc shredding his napkin into tiny ribbons.

"Um. So my friends and I do this thing where every Friday night, each of us has to do something we're scared to do or something we want to do that we may not normally do that puts us out of our comfort zone so I was just wondering... Are you seeing anyone?"

Fuck. That was exhausting to even listen to. And I really only caught the last part.

Linc stiffens at her question, the tattered napkin frozen in his grip. I give his thigh a reassuring squeeze under the table.

"I am, actually."

"Dang. Of course you are," she chuckles. "You're way too hot to be single. Well, she's a lucky girl."

"Boy. He's a boy," I clarify, and it feels pretty fucking good.

Then Lincoln does something that completely surprises me. He slips his arm from under the table and drapes it over me, squeezing my shoulder possessively.

"*My* boyfriend."

Holy fucking shit. I'm instantly hard. Full-mast, salute your shorts, raging-boner-digging-into-my-zipper type of hard.

"Oh. My. God. You two are so hot together!" she gushes while clapping and bouncing in her Uggs.

"Thanks," we say in unison, like a couple in tune with each other, and I am into it.

Heather gives us another beaming smile. "Well, enjoy your meal." As she wanders away, I catch a "So hot" under her breath, and I can't hold back my snort.

When she's back at her table, safely across the diner, I turn my heated gaze to Linc. "Did you just publicly claim me?"

He gulps and nods, chewing on his bottom lip. My gaze zeroes in on the pink flesh, and my dick pulses in my jeans. I adjust myself against my zipper and throw two twenties on the table, knowing I'll be swimming in cash after tonight. Even after I pay Mom back.

"Bathroom. Now," I growl.

I need my boyfriend. I can't wait until we get back to his place. The fire blazing through my veins is too hot to put out.

We silently slip out of the booth and sneak back to the bathrooms near a side exit.

"Scratch that. My car."

I change course and tug on his good hand, steering him toward the exit. We slip into the cool night, soothing our overheated skin. I shove him against the rough brick wall in the dark alleyway between the diner and the neighboring strip of businesses and grab fistfuls of silky auburn hair. I kiss him stupid, pressing him against the wall with my body.

"Well. Well. Well. What do we have here?" a deep male voice jeers from somewhere behind me.

I immediately spin around, sheltering Linc between my

body and the wall. Keeping him out of view of this sneering, voyeuristic asshole.

"Who the fuck are you?" I demand.

A man with yellow teeth and a stained white tee steps forward, staring me down while speaking to his equally disgusting friend. "Think Logan knows his boy's a faggot?"

I growl, muscles taut and ready to defend. I don't like this at all.

He's getting too close.

The other guy speaks up, his greasy brown hair slicked back and his tracksuit oversized and sloppy. "Your pops sent us. Wanted to deliver a message. Let ya know he ain't playin' around about the money." His thin lips turn into a victorious snarl when he sees the color drain from my face. "And it's not just the two of us. We have backup. So don't try anything."

The cogs in my mind spin, clicking into place as I piece it all together.

Of course.

Of. Fucking. Course.

Dad found out we left Detroit. About Mom's family. Our money. *Everything.*

He's the one who's been harassing me. Threatening me. Threatening Lincoln.

I'm going to fucking murder him.

A humorless laugh churns in my stomach, escaping my lips on a bark and sending chills down my spine.

"You can tell him—"

I don't even get the chance to finish my sentence. The guy with yellow teeth strikes out faster than I can process, punching me twice in quick succession. My head whips to the side, the harsh blows stunning me. I stumble back a step, bumping into Lincoln.

He's crowded us into the wall.

Cornered us.

I need to think fast.

"Run!" I yell as I lean down and ram my shoulder into his flabby gut like a pro football player, shoving until the prick falls flat on his ass, with me on top. I punch him square in the nose, blood instantly gushing out as he wails and clutches his face. Before I can get another shot in, I dodge the boot from above, quickly rolling to my feet.

I glance behind me. Linc is stuck to the wall, eyes wide and unblinking.

Fuck! He didn't run!

I reach back and grab his hand as I take a hard hit to the ribs, but I keep moving because I've had way worse. I tug Linc behind me and kick out, nailing the bastard in the kneecap with my heavy boot. He cries out, crumpling to the ground.

"You little faggot shit!" he hollers, grasping his leg. His screeching voice echoes down the alleyway like nails across a chalkboard. "Carl! Get up, ya fuckin' pussy! Grab them!"

Carl can't get up. He's moaning on the ground, clutching his gusher, bright red blood seeping between his fingers as it pours from his most likely broken nose. I didn't hold back. *At all.*

"Run, Preppy!" I shout, tugging him along, trying to snap him out of it. He can't freeze up. We absolutely cannot let these homophobic pricks deliver their "message." I *refuse* to see him hurt again.

We race past the incapacitated assholes. There's a clear path to make our escape. My breath saws in and out, my thoughts a jumbled mess. The only thing I can focus on is getting Linc *out.*

Just before we reach the exit, two more goons step into

view. I skid to a halt, Linc bumping into me from behind and clutching onto my hoodie.

"Back to back," I shout, and he listens, remembering some of the basics from his defense lessons with Otto. We slowly turn in a circle. Bloody-nose Carl, Tracksuit, and the two new slimy douchebags surround us.

I can't figure a way out.

My heart pounds wildly in my chest, banging against my ribcage.

"We can't take them all, Preppy," I whisper so only he can hear. "I'm going to lunge for the skinny prick in blue. Create a distraction. And you're going to run."

"Like hell I am, Rem!" He lowers his voice, whispering urgently. "I'm not leavin' you. Don't ask me to." His voice cracks, full of anguish, and I swear it crumbles another piece of the wall surrounding my heart. And I feel so fucking vulnerable right now. So fucking *raw.*

Our choice is made for us when one of the new guys lunges for Lincoln. I intercept him, smashing my fist into his temple and knocking him out cold.

"Do it! *Go, Linc, go!*"

He takes off down the street, and I breathe a sigh of relief just as someone grabs ahold of me from behind.

I don't even care what happens to me as long as Linc gets away.

We wrestle for what feels like hours until I finally get him into a headlock. This asshole's had training, unlike his friends, who look like the walking dead ambling toward us —bloody and broken. He slips out of the hold easily and shoves me away.

I stumble for a moment, faking him out and crouching like I fell. He reaches for me, but I spin around and punch him twice in the face with a one-two combo. He falls to the ground in a crumpled heap, and I take the opportunity to race down the dark alleyway to my freedom. And *fuck*, this is bringing up way too many unpleasant memories.

The other three assholes are long gone. They must have slipped away during our scuffle. I saw Lincoln get away, but my mind spirals into the *what-ifs*.

I need to find him. *Now*.

The street lights are conveniently burnt out, and the world around me is eerie as I sprint down the sidewalk looking for Linc. I slip my phone out of my pocket, my heart beating a nervous staccato inside my chest. I nearly fumble it when I see the message on my screen. From my fucking scumbag prick of a *dad*.

Gotcha!

That sonofabitch mother fucker!

I'm going to commit patricide when I find him.

That's it.

I'm going to fucking jail.

For real, this time.

Before I can even click on Preppy's name, I hear grunts and shouts. I bolt toward the commotion, running down another fucking alleyway before slamming into a chain link fence. The jolt is startling, snapping me back to that moment in Detroit before I got arrested. I blink rapidly and shake my head.

"Lincoln!" I shout. The word is a desperate plea as I watch Carl and the other new guy pin him to the wall, a small trail of blood trickling from his nose.

His scared eyes dart to mine, silently pleading for help. Rage and fear battle inside me, slicing me deep with their harsh truths.

He's hurt again. Because of me.

Because of my fucking scumbag father.

"Watch me fuck up your little boyfriend," Carl sneers.

He pulls his fist back, slamming it into Linc's stomach, causing him to lurch forward with a pained grunt. They let him go, and he falls to the cold cement, curling in on himself.

I go bat-shit. Ape-shit. Horse-shit. *All the shits.*

I fucking lose my mind and escape my body.

There's no other way to explain what happens next as a warrior cry pours from my lips. I take a running leap at the trash cans and dumpster, climbing them like fucking stairs to heaven before I jump to the fence.

Carl moves to grab Lincoln again, and in a split second that feels like twenty, I leap from the top and onto Carl's back, taking him down with the force of my weight. He crashes to the ground with a sickening thud, cushioning my fall. I hop up, but Carl doesn't move. He's out cold on the dirty fucking cement where he belongs.

"Remi! Watch out!" Lincoln shouts in a raspy, strained voice. I spin around but don't quite dodge the blade slashing out at me. It cuts through my hoodie, grazing my side.

Fuck!

Searing hot pain shoots through me, and I stumble back, clutching the wound. Before this asshole can come at me again, he crumbles to the ground. Lincoln stands behind him, eyes wide, hair and glasses askew, a random two-by-four in his trembling hands.

Holy fuck that's hot.

He tosses it to the ground with a clatter. I rush to him, cradling his face with one palm.

"Preppy—"

"Did he get you? Are you okay?" he interrupts.

"I'm fine," I lie. "Are you?"

He coughs out a wheezy breath and wipes at the blood trickling out of his nose.

Why does bad shit always follow me? This is all my fucking fault.

"Y-yeah. I've never been punched in the face before." He sniffles, causing more rattling coughs.

"First and last time," I growl. "That is never fucking happening again."

He leans into me, resting his head on my shoulder. Short breaths puff against my neck. "Can we go back to the car now?" he whimpers. "I want to go home."

"We can't go back to the car. We can't go anywhere near Wildflower's again. We don't know where the other two are or if there are more," I whisper urgently, grabbing his hand and getting the fuck out of here.

We limp along the darkened edges of the sidewalk, out of the probing view of the scattered streetlights. We're leaning on each other at this point, both of us dragging ass.

I pull my hand away from my side, and even in the dark, I can see the shine of blood on my palm. I swallow thickly and press it back. It's not deep, but it won't stop bleeding.

"Can you find Otto's from here? Are we close? I think we were close if we didn't run too far." But he knows Asheville better than I do.

Linc squints up at the next street sign.

Marigold Avenue.

"Yes! It's only a few blocks from here!" he wheezes out.

A sigh of relief pours from my lips as a wave of exhaustion hits me. I know Otto stays open late on Fridays. I just pray he's still there and that we can make it that far.

CHAPTER THIRTY-ONE
REMI

After what feels like five miles, we finally get to Otto's. The giant sign is off, but the dim overhead lights are still on, illuminating the empty gym. *Please be here. Fuck, please be here.*

I bang on the door with the hand not clutched to my bleeding side. If they're in the lounge room, there's no way they'll hear. But I can't stay upright any longer. Tonight's events and the blood loss are catching up to me. I lean against the rough exterior wall, sliding down until my ass hits the pavement.

Linc does the same, leaning his head against my shoulder. It's eerie out here, completely silent other than the annoying buzz of a flickering street light.

I nudge him. "Hey, don't go to sleep."

"We've been in fight-or-flight for too long, Remi. Our adrenaline is crashin' hard. I'm tired."

"I know, baby," I murmur softly, letting go of my side so I can pull him into my arms, not giving a shit if I'm smearing blood on him.

I slip my phone out of my hoodie pocket. Ignoring all texts, I open the phone app and scroll to Otto's name.

"Remi?" he answers on the first ring, voice dripping with concern.

"Out front," I grunt before ending the call. I can't do phone conversations at the moment.

Not even thirty seconds later, I hear the lock click, the bell chiming as the door opens, and Otto steps out.

"*Jesus Christ, kid!* What the fuck happened?" Otto shouts at us, his voice echoing into the night.

"Just help me get him up," I grit out between clenched teeth as I try to contain the fresh hell burning me from the inside out where that fucker got me with his knife. It's not too deep, just a flesh wound. But I might need a few stitches because I'm *still* fucking bleeding.

"Linc. Wake up." I shake him gently to rouse him, careful not to agitate any injury he might have sustained before I showed up. When I think about how many hits he may have taken or what horrible things they probably said to him, I want to scream and shout and burn the fucking world down.

I wince at the movement, my hand automatically darting back to the wound on my side.

"Help Linc. *Please,*" I beg, and I don't even care if I sound pathetic. He's hurt again, and it's all my fault. I'm bad news for him. I shouldn't have forced myself into his life like this. I brought this on him, and I don't know if I can forgive myself.

"Please," I implore him with my eyes, letting him see the desperation there. "I never ask for help, but look at us, Otto. We fucking need some."

He squats down in front of us, pushing the hair back from Linc's forehead and examining his sleeping face.

My eyes flutter, and I shut them for just a minute. Barely even a second.

"Remi. . ." Otto says urgently, like it's not the first time he's tried to get my attention. His hand is on my shoulder, shaking me slightly.

"Huh?" I ask numbly. Exhaustion is taking over.

"You need a hospital. I'm taking you both. *Now*."

My eyes pop open. "No! No hospital. They ask too many questions." The disappointed look in his eyes is something I'm not used to.

"Don't look at me like that, Otto. I didn't start this. My *dad* sent them."

"Your dad?" The confusion on his face morphs into anger, his gray eyes turning to molten steel.

"Yeah. And they fucking jumped us. *For being us.* If you catch my drift."

Do I really need to spell it out to him?

"They called us fucking faggots, Otto."

"Fuck, kid." He rubs his hand down his face, scratching at the dark stubble peppering his chin.

"Where are they now?" he asks, peering over his shoulder at the dark street.

"Scattered around the alleyways near Wildflower's. Probably off licking their wounds."

"How many?" His tight jaw barely allows the words to escape.

"Four. Now get us inside. Please. No hospitals," I repeat, feeling impatient that we're still on the cold cement outside.

"Remi. You're looking too pale, kid. I don't know." He's hesitant. Understandably so. I would be too. But I *can't* go to the hospital.

"They'd call the police for a 'stab' wound. I'd go to jail," I say wearily.

Too much fucking talking.

"Stab wound?! What the fuck, Remi! Why didn't you say something?"

He looks horrified as he leaps up and shoves the front door open, hollering for Sasha. I vaguely remember that she's on her way to medical school.

She sprints outside in her normal leggings and employee tank top with a purple fleece that matches the purple in her hair. She gasps as she takes in the pitiful sight the two of us make right now.

I smile up at her nonetheless. "Stitch me up, Doc." I remove the pressure from my side and show her my palm glistening with blood. I think it's almost stopped now.

"Remington! *Oh my God!*" she cries out dramatically.

An awkwardly timed giggle rings out next to me, and I peer at Linc from under half-closed lids.

"She full-named you," he whispers before promptly lowering his head back to my shoulder.

"Otto, help Remi. I can get Linc."

They manage to get us up and shuffle into the gym. Otto locks the door and turns the lights off, ushering us back to the break room with a flashlight he keeps at the front desk.

"I have blankets in the closet. Let's get them on the couches." Otto's talking to Sasha as I lean heavily on him. He pulls me in, taking the extra weight, and an uncomfortable lump of emotion forms in my throat. The stress of the last couple of weeks—hell, the last couple of months—is catching up to me. I try to be inconspicuous, but I'm pretty sure the quiet sniffle gives me away.

"Come on. I got you," he whispers, guiding me to where

Sasha has already laid out soft-looking plaid blankets for us. Lincoln is settled onto a couch, eyes closed.

"Is he okay?" I grit out. Sasha slips his shoes off and pulls another plaid blanket on top of him.

"He said he got punched in the stomach and the face, but he's fine. Just exhausted. I'll get him an ice pack for his nose."

"Well, can't you check him for internal bleeding or some shit?" I grumble.

He sits up, pulling the blanket to his chest and tucking it under his chin. He peers at me with sleepy yet lucid eyes.

"I don't have internal bleedin'. *Okay?* So, please just sit down. I'm worried about *you*. You're *bleedin'*. A lot, Remi." His eyes dart to my hand that looks like I dipped it in dark red paint.

I continue to stand here, leaning heavily against Otto. I stare back at Lincoln, cataloging his features. He's drained, and I can see he's crashing as hard as I am.

"Alright," I concede, somewhat satisfied that he's really okay.

Otto and Sasha gingerly slip my hoodie and T-shirt over my head, helping me lie on the couch. I examine my side, hissing at the slice in my skin. It's shallow but also pretty long. I'm lucky it missed the Detroit skyline tattoo that wraps around my torso. This is gonna leave a gnarly scar, and I woulda been pissed if they fucked up one of my tats.

Linc gasps from across the small living area, lying on his own couch, which is perpendicular to mine.

"It looks worse than it is, Linc. I promise," I whisper softly, and Sasha glances between us. She rifles through the first aid kit, looking for supplies to fix me up.

"Shit, Otto. You don't have it."

"What do you need?" he asks intensely. "If it's not there, I'll call Sterling."

"What? No. No. No. Why would you call Coach? Don't do that." I cannot deal with his know-it-all ass right now.

"He was a field medic in the army in Afghanistan, Remi. That's why. He still does medical work with the VA, so he might have what Sasha needs."

"I need Dermabond. This is a clean, straight line; it's not jagged. So glue is ideal." Then she turns to me. "You don't need stitches, hun. They're painful and unnecessary. You'll be able to do everyday activities while you heal, as long as you're careful not to pull the glue."

I nod. "Call him," I grit out, knowing I need help. Being able to move around without stitches would be best. Especially with my asshole prick of a father still out there. I clench my jaw thinking about all the texts and bullshit he's been tormenting me with.

"I'll make the call. Sash, disinfect that. Stat." Otto nods toward the gash, grimacing.

"On it," she replies, pulling on disposable gloves and filling some kind of giant syringe-looking thing with hydrogen peroxide. She ambles over to me with an apologetic look on her face.

"I'm really sorry, hun. There's no way around it, and this is gonna hurt like a bitch."

I laugh at her bluntness, but it quickly turns to a shout and a curse as she squirts hydrogen peroxide directly into my wound.

Hot stabbing knives. Red hot blades slicing me open. It feels like my skin is melting off as liquid fire is poured inside.

"Fuuuuck," I groan. Black spots dance across my vision.

Linc is still awake, watching me with tears pooling in

his eyes. I close my own tightly and face the ceiling. I can't see him like that while this agony burns through me. It's more than I can handle.

"I'm sorry, hun. It had to be done. I figured it's best to just rip off the Band-Aid." She soaks up the bloody mess with a white hand towel and presses a large gauze pad to the wound.

"Is that what they teach you in pre-med? *Just rip off the Band-Aid?*"

Jesus fucking Christ, that hurt.

Before Sasha can answer, Otto comes bursting back into the room. "Sterling's five minutes out. He was in town doing some work at the VA hospital after football practice, and he's got what we need. And Remi, I know you're tired, so I told him what you've told me. But he's going to need answers, too. The full story. Especially if we aren't taking this to the police."

"Remi? Lincoln?"

Coach Buzzkill is here. The quiet reprieve and short nap have ended. I peek one eye open and see Linc snoring softly, mouth wide open, glasses askew. My mouth quirks at his adorableness, even though my side is throbbing. I need a joint or a cigarette, but first, I need my fucking skin glued back together.

"Shh," Sasha hushes him. "They're resting, and Lincoln is out cold. Bless his heart. Let him sleep."

They rustle around in the kitchen area, speaking quietly until Coach and Sasha come back, gently rousing me. Coach informs me of every step of the process as he holds the wound tightly with one hand and applies the glue with the other.

"All done," he says, snapping the rubber gloves off. "No need to wear a dressing over it, either. I'll check on it next week. Let me know if you see redness or swelling. But you'll be okay."

"I'll get ya some cookies and juice since you did lose a bit of blood," Sasha says, ruffling my hair like I'm five years old and just fell off my bike. I let her, appreciating everything she's done for me tonight. Everything they've all done.

"Ok. I need answers. What's going on, Remi? Talk to us so we can help you," Coach says.

So I do. I tell them about the threatening texts that started shortly after we moved here. How they've been escalating. Even though I'm sure the De Lucas already know, I tell them about getting arrested for a violent offense in Detroit, which is why I can't involve the police. They would assume the worst of me like everyone always does. All the hard work Mom did to keep that bullshit off my adult record would be for nothing. I'll go to fucking jail.

And finally, I recap everything that went down tonight, minus fight night in the woods. That has nothing to do with Dad's goons chasing us, and I'm not going to snitch on myself more than I already have.

Instead, I lie and say we were at a party, and that's why we were in Asheville eating at Wildflower's so late.

I don't leave the homophobic slurs out of my story, either. Even though I hate the pity lurking in their eyes, I'll take that over hate. All I see is acceptance and worry when I scan the three people in front of me. Another part of the wall crumbles, and I let a few more people in.

"We need to create a plan of attack," Coach states,

sounding matter-of-fact and pragmatic. Very militaristic, now that I can make the connection.

"Agreed. We need to find Logan before he finds us," Otto says.

"Take out the leader, and the rest will fall away. They'll have no motivation." Coach is pacing, one hand on his chin like he's deep in thought. "I'm just not sure how we find him."

"For starters, I'm staying with Raina until this all blows over." Otto turns his gaze on me. "I'm not leaving you, your mom, and Richard alone and vulnerable."

"Understandable and admirable," I murmur.

"Look. It's really late. Lincoln is passed out, and Remi is nearly there. Let's reconvene in the morning to figure out how to search for Logan. Our first line of defense is Otto staying at the Keller estate. Tonight, the boys are safe sleeping here. And that's all we can do for right now," Coach says, stepping in and ending this long night from hell.

Everyone agrees, slipping out of the break room to allow Linc and me to sleep undisturbed. They probably went into Otto's office to discuss this fucked up situation even more. I know I have to tell Mom and Gramps that Dad is coming for me. Coming for the money. But not tonight.

I'm too tired to care as I let the peace of oblivion steal me away.

CHAPTER THIRTY-TWO
REMI

It's Saturday morning, and we're snuggled up in my bed in our boxers. Sasha drove my car home, and Lincoln and I rode with Otto. No one wanted to let us drive, and I don't blame them. We snuck in early before Mom or Gramps were even awake.

I made Otto promise to let me talk to my mom first. No matter his intentions, this isn't his family or business. It's not his place to tell her what happened—that her lying, cheating, soon-to-be ex-husband has been threatening her son. My father had me jumped last night and nearly stabbed, too. Fucking scum of the earth. I hope he shows up here. I fucking *hope*.

Lincoln's parents are still out of town and completely out of the loop as usual. How can they continue to neglect him yet try to control him at the same time? My heart hurts when I think of how he must have felt as a child in that environment. What kind of sick, twisted psychological bullshit is that? It's not happening under my watch.

My side aches as I lie here stewing over everything that's happened. Everything with Linc's shitty parents, the asshole bullies, and my psychopath of a father. It's fucking ridiculous, and I just need a moment's peace for once in my life.

I pull Linc closer, nuzzling his neck as I curl my body around his leaner frame, spooning him. He's my peace. The best thing in my life. Our connection is so deep it fucking resonates in my bones.

My thoughts waver as much as my fingers as I run my hand over the curve of his hip and down his thigh, feeling his soft skin and making sure he's okay. That we're here. Together. We made it out. Because fuck, my mind keeps going to some pretty dark places of what *could* have happened. What *almost* happened.

"You okay?" he whispers, voice still a little raspy from lack of sleep and, well, general fucking trauma.

I hate that I brought this on him after everything he's been through with Connor and Brandon. And I know I don't even know half of what they've done to him over the years. Whether he believes it or not, he's strong, and he holds his pain deep like I do.

"Talk to me. Please." He rolls over and faces me, both of us on our sides. Tucking one hand under his cheek, he reaches out and places his other palm tenderly on my face, cupping my bruised jaw.

"You can be vulnerable in front of me. You don't have to be so tough all the time. Let me fight for you sometimes, too. Show me what's underneath all this beautiful art." He slides his hand down my neck and across my shoulder until he's caressing my bicep and tracing the details of my tattoos. His fingertips circle the life-like compass on my forearm.

"What's this one mean?" His voice is soft and earnest, like he really wants to know.

"To guide me. Show me where to go when I'm lost," I murmur. Our eyes lock, and an intense energy pulses between us. So strong it's tangible

"And are you lost now?" There's hope in his tone.

"Not when I'm with you," I confess, blinking away the moisture pooling there.

Lincoln grabs my hand, squeezing gently. "Show me everything inside your soul, Remi. Let me carry the burden with you, handle the lows and celebrate the highs. We're a team. Can't you see that? We've been a team since day one."

He's completely taken over my brain. His honest, caring words and kind, innocent eyes break every last barrier away, causing unwanted memories to surge to the surface. Things I've kept buried so deep, telling no one.

Fear and anger and a million other emotions swirl around inside me, tangling together until they form a knot in the pit of my stomach. My dad is still out there, and knowing this has me on edge. I just need to talk to my boyfriend.

"I don't even want to tell you all this. But I need to get it out. *Fuck, Linc.*" I peer at him with pleading eyes that I know are swimming with tears. "I need to get it out," I say again, this time in a defeated whisper.

I close my eyes and focus on my breathing instead of the whirling torrent of emotions inside me. It all pours out. *Everything.* I start with my dad's gradual decline into alcoholism until he became a drunk deadbeat with no job, living off of his own wife and son.

Lincoln's beautiful eyes shine with unshed tears when I start to tell him about the abuse.

"He started hitting me when I was sixteen. First time it ever happened was because I didn't put his beer in the fridge, and he had to drink it warm all night. Things like that. Mom was never around; she worked all the time. And that's not her fault. It was his. *Everything* is his fucking fault."

And then I tell him the worst of it all. Something I've never told a soul. The horrible memories I usually push away rise to the surface and won't let me continue to ignore them. I squeeze my eyes shut as they take over.

———— ⟳ ————

A rough hand clasps onto my upper arm, yanking me from my pull-out sofa bed and out of a deep slumber. "Did I say you could take the car, you little shit?" a raspy voice sneers.

I'm disoriented from sleep and make the mistake of answering the question truthfully. "Huh? You did say I could, Dad."

He shakes me roughly, and spit lands on my cheek as he drunkenly yells at me to shut the fuck up. The smell of stale beer wars with the stronger, more pungent odor of sweat.

"Don't talk back to me, smartass. If you wanna take the car without asking. . ." He drags me behind him through the living room, grabbing the car keys from the hook by the door. Dad's so much bigger than me. I'm helpless to do anything but flail behind him the entire way. "Then go sleep in it," he finishes and opens the front door. The keys go flying down the dirty outside stairwell that drunks and junkies like to piss in, landing with a clunk at the bottom.

Then he starts to pull me toward the stairs, too.

"Dad. Please. I'm sorry. I won't do it again," I plead, trying to placate him, even though I didn't do anything wrong. I've had to walk on eggshells around him lately, and I should've known better than to disagree with him just now.

We're getting closer to the steep concrete stairs, and I'm starting to freak out about what he's doing. He usually just smacks me upside the head or punches me in the stomach. I dig my heels into the ground, bare feet scraping against the rough cement. "Please, Dad. Stop!"

He grunts at the force required to drag his sixteen-year-old son against his will. "I. Said. Go. Sleep. In. The. . ." and then I'm airborne as he drunkenly shouts the word "Car!" at my flailing body.

There's a millisecond when my brain computes what is about to happen, and I twist just enough for my arm to take the brunt of the fall instead of the back of my head.

Crack!

Pain radiates up my left arm in hot, stinging waves. The burning agony pulses from the tips of my fingers to the top of my shoulder, and I cry out sharply, gasping for air.

I make the mistake of looking down at my unnaturally angled arm. My eyes bulge at the gruesome sight, and my mouth waters with the need to empty my stomach.

I stare at the brown water stains peppering the crumbling ceiling as spiders and moths continue on with their nightly business, completely oblivious to the boy lying in shock at the bottom of the stairs.

The pain is starting to wear off, or maybe I'm just going numb. I sit up and scoot back, cradling my fractured arm to my chest until I lean against the wall. I don't even have a phone to call for help.

Or shoes.

Maybe if I just rest my eyes. . .

―――――― ∽ ――――――

A soft hand cups my cheek. "Open your eyes, Rem. Let me see you."

My eyelids slowly flutter open, blinking at the moisture on my lashes. A few droplets fall, and *fuck*, I'm not sure if I've ever cried in front of another person before. But the shame and anxiety I expect aren't there as I peer through waterlogged eyes at the amazing soul in front of me. I turn my head and nuzzle into his hand, kissing his palm.

"Linc," I rasp, voice horse from a long overdue release of emotions.

"I'm so sorry, baby," he whispers, and the endearment makes my stomach bottom out.

"I'm so fuckin' sorry that happened to you," he curses, running his hand down my neck and over my shoulders. "That you had to suffer that much. In silence, too."

There's a heavy pause—the air thick between us. He's also suffered in silence, in his own way. His controlling parents. The bullies. The isolation. The loneliness. It's probably why we connected so instantly. We're kindred spirits, and I'm never fucking letting him go.

"Thank you for openin' up to me. I want you to know that you can tell me anything. *Anything*, Remi. And I'll be there for you because no one has ever cared for me the way you have. No one has ever *seen* me the way you have. Truly and completely."

Fuck. I fall hard and complete—somewhere far away. I swear all I'll ever need is the light emanating from Lincoln, from his heart and soul. With every passionate moment and traded truth, we become more entwined. There's no going back. He's mine. I fucking *love* him.

I lean forward and slam my lips to his, needing to forget every grizzly detail that just flew through my mind.

"I need you," I say urgently, and he moans into my mouth, thrusting his hips forward, trying to grind his dick against mine.

I roll him to his back, peeling our underwear off before I crawl between his spread thighs, and we're skin to skin. I'm careful not to pull at the wound in my side too much as I lower my body on top of his. "I need to be inside you, baby," I rasp, and I can hear the torment in my voice.

"Yes. Please," he moans into my mouth. We're breathing each other's air as we kiss desperately. My dick is so hard I'm about to bust, so I peel my lips away, panting heavily.

"Wait. You're hurt, though," he says in a strained whisper. I know he wants this as bad as I do.

"Don't care," I grunt, and it's not just my dick taking control; it's my heart, too. I *really* need him right now.

"I do." The barely-audible words sweep through me, warming my soul and stealing my breath.

"I know, baby." I rest my forehead against his. "I know. I'll be careful."

Linc reaches over and grabs the lube from the bedside drawer, handing it to me. I squirt more than I need onto my fingers, and he grabs behind his knees, holding his legs back and open. Pleasure floods my veins at the sight of his tight hole on display for me, his cock thick and engorged, jutting straight up from his hips.

I lean down, giving his flushed cock a soft swipe of my tongue, swirling around his sensitive head. He twitches, and I smirk, focusing on what I want to play with. His ass.

I rub the lube all along his crease, teasing him. He pulls his knees back even farther, trying to get me to touch him right where he wants.

"Remi," he whines, eyes pleading.

I peer up at him, tapping my finger against his tight little hole. "You want me here?" I ask, making him squirm.

Before he can answer, I sink one finger deep inside of him.

"More," he demands, throwing his head back wantonly. So greedy for my fingers. For my cock.

I add another, pumping in and out of him a few times. His moans turn low and guttural when I add a third.

He's rocking against my hand, three fingers shoved deep inside, stretching him wide. He's so fucking hot like this. Full of confidence, nothing holding him back. Nothing between us. No clothes. No secrets. Just my best friend. And he's all fucking mine.

I gently slip my fingers out and squirt more lube on my cock. I line up with his hole and lean forward on one forearm, sealing my mouth to his.

"Bear down," I breathe out as I slowly push my way inside. My cockhead finally slips past the tight ring of muscle, and his body pulls me in. Both of us groan low and long at the sensation. His hot body squeezes me in a death grip, and I have to pause for a moment so I don't nut.

I need this moment to last. To feel close to him. *Love* him.

This deep connection thrumming between us is more than just a physical bond. It's a thread between two souls that recognize each other. Found each other. Our scars stitched together, entwining us. *Forever.*

I'm thrusting into him in long, slow strokes, showing him how much he means to me.

"Faster," he pants, locking his legs high around my hips.

I angle my hips and pick up the pace. "*Ungh!* Remi! Don't stop," he chants.

He wraps his arms around my neck, clinging onto me with a heady desperation that has my dick swelling even more. Linc burrows his face into my shoulder, grunting with each thrust. We're in this moment together. Just him and me. Nothing but harsh breaths and sweaty bodies and heartfelt words whispered between us.

"*Fuck.* Lincoln. I love you. *I love you so fucking much.*"

A high-pitched, keening cry erupts from Linc at my confession, his asshole clenching tightly around me, cock spurting against our stomachs in searing hot pulses.

I'm right behind him, coming on a ragged shout. My dick pulses deep in his ass, coating his insides with my cum.

We stay frozen for a moment, breaths heaving as I lie on top of him.

"My dick's not going down. I just love you too fucking much," I say, pulling back an inch and pushing forward again. His eyes roll into the back of his head, and he moans, squeezing his legs tightly around my waist.

He focuses on me again, his mismatched gaze boring into the very fiber of my being.

"Good. Because I love you too, Remi. *So much.* And I want you to show me again."

He rocks his hips into me, pushing me deeper, and now *my* eyes are rolling into the back of my head.

I pull out, ignoring the pressure tugging at my wound, and very carefully roll, flipping us so he's on top now. I sit him right on my cock, impaling him in one smooth motion. I don't even add more lube. My cum oozes out of him, making filthy, squelching noises that get me even hotter.

"I love doing this. Love fucking you. *Love you,*" I grunt as I put my feet flat on the bed and tilt my hips, making sure to nail his prostate on every thrust and not giving a single fuck about the delicate skin that's glued together on my side.

I wrap my arms around his back and curl my hands over his shoulders, gripping him more tightly as I press all the way in, grinding my pelvis against him, getting as deep as I can.

"Love you, too," he moans, breath sawing in and out. I yank him down and seal my lips to his, our kisses raw and carnal. Invading. My tongue plunges into his mouth in time with my cock thrusting into his ass.

He reaches between us, tugging on his cock. The sticky mess from his previous release smears between us.

We continue to fuck slowly and deeply as we whisper "I love you" in-between filthy pleas and dirty words.

I'm never letting him go. Never letting anyone else hurt him. This is forever for me.

The orgasm that rolls through me this time is slow and languid. It's not the intense explosion like the first time, but a long-lasting, feel-good release.

"Take this cum. Filling you up again. Such. A. Good. Boy," I grit out between a tightly clenched jaw.

The praise pushes him over the edge, and he comes with a whimper. His hole squeezes my sensitive cock almost painfully.

I slip out, wrapping my arms tightly around him as we both breathe heavily. Neither of us cares about the mess this time, not even Linc. Our emotions are high, and our love is deep. *Real.* I will do anything for him. Tell him anything. My deepest darkest secrets. I would jump off a cliff if it meant he didn't have to.

"I love you, Lincoln Anderson," I say one more time, squeezing him tightly, but he's already starting to snore lightly.

"So. Fucking. Much." My voice cracks, unable to hide the utter truth of my words.

CHAPTER THIRTY-THREE
REMI

The gash in my side throbs as I gingerly sit down in the overstuffed leather chair. The double dicking-down I just gave Lincoln probably didn't help the situation, but I wouldn't take back everything we just did. Everything we just said.

I love you.

I said it. He said it. We said it.

It's like we couldn't stop once we started—both of us unfamiliar with hearing or saying the words.

Linc went home before his parents could return from their trip and wonder why he isn't sitting at the table in a suit and fucking tie, waiting for dinner like a good boy. I hate that he's over there dealing with them alone, but at least I know he's safe. Away from me and the threats that follow.

I asked Linc not to say anything about what happened to us in Asheville, which he easily agreed to, not wanting to talk to them about much of anything really. Luckily, his face doesn't look like mine. The slight purple bruising under-neath his eyes could be dark circles from stress and no sleep. It's not a far stretch, and I'm sure his parents won't notice anyway.

I still haven't spoken to Mom and Gramps about what happened. I'm not hiding per se, but with all this drama, I just need some time to escape. A quiet place to sort through these overwhelming thoughts. And up until ten minutes ago, I had no idea this place even existed.

We have a library. A full, two-story library, complete with a rolling ladder that I know Lincoln will love. Mahogany bookcases with elegantly detailed woodwork fill every inch of wall space, and file boxes and precarious old newspaper towers are stacked in the corners. The smell of dusty old books is quite soothing, and I lean back, pulling my leather jacket more tightly around me. The house is drafty, and these big, unused rooms get chilly. The fireplace is cold and empty, but there's no way I can start one in my current condition.

I have a lot on my mind since I found out my father tried to have me jumped and held for ransom last night. Or jumped and robbed. *Murdered?* I don't even really know. All I know is he's the one who's been threatening me with these unknown text messages.

He obviously found out about the money, correctly realizing that Mom and I are now the heirs to the Keller fortune. I have no clue how she kept it from him. Or me. The fact that she comes from money, not just regular money, but the "my butler lives on my estate in a separate house" type of money. It's a huge secret to keep.

As I sit here stewing, I get more and more angry at her.

Why did she do this?

The entire reason those scumbags came after Linc and me was because of the decisions she's made.

As if my thoughts alone conjure her, the large wooden library door pushes in, squeaking on its old hinges.

"Remi, baby. You in here?" Mom's soft voice rings out, echoing around the spacious room.

I'm tempted not to answer, but I call out anyway.

"Here, Ma!"

She follows my voice until she walks around my chair, and the warm light of the small table lamp I turned on illuminates my bruised and battered face.

Mom gasps, her hand flying to her open mouth.

"Remington. What happened?" she asks, taking the seat next to me and hesitantly reaching out toward my cheek.

I dodge her touch.

"What do you think?" I reply tersely.

"I think you've been fighting again."

My lips flatten into a thin line. Of course she does. And I was, but it still pisses me off.

"Your husband says hello." I know I'm being an asshole, but I'm rattled. And he's still out there.

Mom gasps again. "You saw your dad?"

I turn my icy glare on her, my fingers curling into fists until the bite of my nails into my palms calms the storm raging inside.

"No," I say through clenched teeth. "I met his *friends*." I emphasize the word "friends" sarcastically before motioning to my face. "And they had a message to deliver."

"There must be a misunderstanding, Remi. Logan would never do something like that. Sure, he wasn't always reliable or faithful, but he's never put his hands on us."

"There's no misunderstanding, Mom. He did this, and he's still out there, coming for me. You hid this whole other world from him and me. Now he knows we have money, and he wants it."

"Remi—"

I cut her off, needing to get more off my chest. "They jumped me. *And* my boyfriend. *Lincoln.* They fucking jumped *Lincoln*, Mom."

"Oh, baby—"

"No," I interrupt her once again. "I could have been here with Lincoln my whole life, Ma! With Grady. Sierra. With Gramps!" I glare at her. "How could you take that away from me?" I don't let her answer; I just keep going. It's a long time coming. "And for what? To run away with your shitty boyfriend who knocked you up?!" I shout at her, past my breaking point. It's harsh. Cruel, really. But she has no clue the hell he put me through these last couple of years.

"Because you would have been *here*! With *her*! As *her* son! Not mine! She wanted to raise you as her own. Or have you not exist at all. . ." She whispers the last sentence, and I suck in a sharp breath.

"What?" I ask, completely confused. We're switching from one fucked up parent to the next, and it's throwing my head for a loop.

"Yes. Please explain. Both of you." Gramps strolls into the library, an unusual fire blazing in his dark eyes. He's switched from doting old Gramps to his problem-solving CEO alter ego.

"Mom," she whispers. "And her ultimatum."

"Dad. And his violent goons," I add ruefully, pointing to my fucked up face.

Grandpa rounds the chair and gets a better look at me. The open curtain allows silver moonlight to pour in, showcasing their handiwork. There's no overhead lighting in this space—only the giant arched windows and colorful Tiffany lamps dispersed around the room.

"Good God," he says in a gasp, eyes scanning my injuries.

"Nope. Just Logan Michaels," I reply with a bite, unable to tamp down the smartass. It's my go-to defense mechanism.

"Your father sent men. . . to do *this*?"

"Yeah. He wants your money. Because *someone* never told him about it." I glare at Mom, and she ducks her head, probably questioning every decision she's ever made and rightfully so. "Or me. And I can at least agree that it was shocking as fuck to find out."

I tuck my arms more tightly around myself, feeling a little vulnerable about this next part. Because I couldn't protect him fully. Because he got *hurt*. On my watch. "And they got Linc pretty good, too. Fucking chased us around downtown Asheville slinging homophobic slurs and everything. Luckily, we were able to get to Otto's. That's the only reason things didn't go worse."

"You went to Otto?" Mom questions, eyebrows pulling together in the center.

I roll my eyes. Annoyed that she asks about him out of all that shit I just said. I may have just put him in the dog house, but too fucking bad.

"Yes. Embarrassingly enough. He was our knight in shining armor. And Coach. And Sasha."

Fuck.

That's humiliating now that I think about it.

Gramps leans against the mantle and rubs his chin speculatively.

"Well, to address one thing at a time. Remi, dear boy, I want to ensure that you know I support you and your life choices."

He gets a fond smile on his face. "I quite like the idea of

having another grandson, and I couldn't have hand-picked a better man for you."

I really wish there was a fire blazing in here because there's nothing else to explain the heat building in my cheeks right now. "Thanks, Gramps."

"You could have told me at the beginning when I insinuated all the girls were chasing after you."

My lip curls into a mischievous grin. "Well, you weren't wrong about that either, Gramps. They do chase me. And I'm bisexual. That means I like guys and girls," I add on. Just in case he doesn't know.

He chuckles heartily, the laugh lines around his eyes crinkling deep. "My boy. I love you all the same. But thank you for sharing that with me. I'm always glad to know more about you."

Fuck, he's the nicest old man in the world. He needs a fucking trophy or some shit.

"Linc hasn't fully come out yet. We told Grady and Sierra, and Otto knows after last night. But his parents don't, and no one at school does. So please don't out him."

Mom clutches her chest. "Remi, give me a little more credit than that, please. You know I would never do that."

"I know, Ma. But it still had to be said."

"I second that. I may be old, but I know that is a terrible, terrible thing to do to a person. I will always have your back. Both of you."

"Just needed to make sure." I'll always have his back.

Gramps speaks up again, leading the discussion and getting us back on course. "Now, for the next topic—Logan. I'm uneasy that he's still out there, so we need to increase security. And I'm not sure I like the idea of Lincoln being alone until this blows over. We can't guarantee he's not a target now. And his parents can be. . . overzealous, to say the least. I don't want to make things worse for him because of this."

I couldn't agree more. He'd be grounded and cocooned in bubble wrap until he's thirty.

"I'll text him. It'll be like a sleepover since Otto's staying, too. They all want to help," I inform them as I message Linc.

Come back over.

On lockdown together.

You gonna S the D?

I follow up with a string of eggplant and devil emojis because even though we just got jumped twenty-four hours ago, if we're on lockdown in this house together, you better believe I'm gonna be in that mouth *and* that ass.

I'm pulled from my phone and my horny thoughts when Richard speaks up again.

"That's a good idea for Otto to stay. I'll speak with Sterling and have Cliff get in touch with a private investigator right away. I know we don't want to involve the police unless we absolutely have to. We like to handle family affairs internally whenever possible."

If "no po-po" is the Keller family motto, I can definitely get down with that.

"Remi, is there anything else you'd like to share about exactly what happened last night? Or any other details that could explain what's happening?"

I contemplate telling them about the abuse—the broken arm—but I can't bring myself to do it yet. Not after everything that's happened, and not after spilling my guts to Lincoln just last night. I can't do it again. No way in fucking hell. I think I'll just let the present serve justice for the past.

"He's a greedy, lazy fuck. And he wants money in any

way he can get it," I mumble, counting down the minutes until I hear the doorbell ring and my boyfriend gets here.

"Okay. Well, now that we have a plan to handle Logan, Rainy, it's your turn. Please explain this ultimatum you mentioned."

"Don't act like you don't know, Richard." Mom lashes out, folding her arms across her chest.

I guess we're just putting it all out on the table tonight. No-holds-barred.

"You ran away to be with Logan. You didn't want to live by our rules."

"Your rules?" Mom sneers.

Okay, this is going downhill fast. And I have the inkling that Gramps feels like he has *two* teenagers to deal with.

"Yes," he replies calmly.

"Your *wife* expected to raise my child as her own. Like some kind of sick and twisted patriarchal-male-heir bullshit."

"*What?*" Gramps and I exclaim at the same time. She said this earlier, and my brain can't compute.

What the fuck is going on with this town?

I'm starting to wonder if it really *was* better in Detroit.

"She gave me an ultimatum to either let her raise my baby as her own, or. . ." Mom trails off, unable to voice what we all know she means.

Get rid of me.

"Needless to say, I left."

She turns an angry glare to Richard. "My own father couldn't even stand up for me."

I see him wince out of the corner of my eye, and I feel bad for the old man, but she does have a point.

"I did try, baby girl. You're both so stubborn—"

"Do *not* compare me to her. I would *never* abandon my

own child. I could believe all of that from her; she always hated me. But with you, it hurt even worse."

"Rainy—"

"Who knows what would have happened to me if Logan didn't step up. Yes, we've had our ups and downs over the years, but we survived and were doing okay there for a while."

She's in denial. That's all I can say. There's no other excuse for it. We were never doing okay. And saying Dad "stepped up" gives the prick far too much credit.

"Don't look at me like that, Remi. I am not talking about the present day. Your father has clearly gone off the rails."

I grit my teeth. He went off the rails two fucking years ago when he started hitting me, but I don't tell her that.

"Rainy. Let me speak for a moment, please. I know things are getting tense between the three of us, but we're all each other has. And we need to work this out."

Mom leans back in her seat, arms crossed and looking more like my sister than my mother. Her sleek dark hair is pulled into a high ponytail, and her oversized sweater and leggings could put her in line at any Forever 21 store across the country.

"I know I was more focused on my companies than my family back then, and I took your mother's word for the truth. She said you didn't want to live with us or follow our rules. That you were moving away to be with Logan."

It's kind of a weak excuse, but if he trusted his wife to handle their daughter while he handled the businesses, maybe we can't blame him.

And it's like he read my mind.

"I know it's not an excuse, but I tried to stop you from leaving, baby girl. Don't you remember me hugging you and begging you not to go? You broke my heart, Rainy."

"No. Your wife broke your heart. I was a *child*. I was scared and alone. I only had Logan, but he was six hours away at the beach. And the way your wife spoke to me was disgusting. She told me to *take care of it*."

She looks over at me sadly, apologetically almost.

"I think she expected me to fall in line and do exactly as she said, like always. But it wasn't her decision. At all. I couldn't stay, not after everything she said. She told me what I did was embarrassing. That I tarnished our family name and became a stain on the Keller legacy."

"Rainy. I didn't know." Richard sounds like he's in physical pain, his voice cracking as he lowers his head, stooping his shoulders.

"I'm so, so sorry."

This whole exchange has me feeling extremely uncomfortable, like I need a joint or a cigarette. Immediately.

This poor old guy has been stuck between his wife and his daughter for eighteen years.

It hurts my fucking heart.

"Your mother passed away two years ago, Rainy. Suddenly. Did you get my letter? Any of them?"

"When the letters stopped for nearly ten years, and I got one out of the blue, I knew it was something important. So, I finally opened one. I just couldn't bring myself to come back here. It was too painful. She died with us both hating each other, and that's something I'll carry with me for the rest of my life. I tried, Dad. I really, really tried." Mom breaks down, and it's hard for me to watch, but this is their moment, so I let Richard be the one to console his daughter.

He crouches in front of her, pulling her into his arms as she hugs a moose-print pillow tightly to her chest.

"Did you know I tried to reach out when I was eighteen?" She sniffles. "I called Mom and invited you to the small wedding Logan and I were finally having. I was so excited and ready to bury the hatchet. Start over. Let you back into our lives. Remi was the cutest little ring bearer with his suspenders and shiny shoes." She smiles fondly at me even though I know this hurts to talk about.

"She told me I was dead to her. That I had died two years earlier when I let some trash defile me and then run off with him."

Richard makes a choking sound in the back of his throat, and I sit forward quickly, worried he's about to have a fucking heart attack or some shit.

Mom doesn't miss a beat, though. She just keeps landing blows.

"I mean, honestly, Dad. What did y'all even tell people when your sixteen-year-old daughter just disappeared?"

He clears his throat and shifts back, releasing Mom from his arms. "You won't like it."

"Tell me."

"She told her friends that you were out of control, got pregnant, and we sent you off to get help while you finished your schooling."

Mom scoffs. "And after that?"

"Then, she told everyone you moved to Michigan and that we visited you occasionally. No one really thinks anything of it anymore. There are only a few people who know the truth."

"Who?" Mom demands, her spunky attitude coming back in full swing.

"We can talk about that later, Rainy."

"No. Let's just finish this conversation now and be done. I'd like to move on from this and not wallow in the past," Mom insists.

Grandpa sighs deeply before saying, "The De Luca

brothers. Their father, too, God rest his soul. I see Sterling regularly, and until recently, it'd been close to ten years since I'd seen Otto."

"Otto. . ." Mom says somewhat wistfully, and I dart my eyes to her right before she drops *another* fucking bomb. Another secret. "I should have chosen him over your father. He was ready to raise you as his son."

"Ma, what the *fuck*?"

Is she really for real right now?

"Otto was one of my best friends. When I found out I was pregnant with you, he begged me to stay. Said he'd raise you as his own. How could I do that to him? To a sixteen-year-old boy? No way. Your father was a sweet talker, said we would build a family together. Just the three of us. And I believed him. Not to mention I just needed to get out of Hunter Springs. It was toxic for me, physically and mentally, and I loved you so much, baby," she says, smiling sadly at me. "I made a decision, and there's nothing else to say."

"And you just cut him out of your life after an offer like *that*? Ma, that's fucking cold-hearted." I feel bad for the guy now. *Jesus Christ*, she tore this town up when she left. And I can't help but feel some residual guilt for it.

"Remi. Do you really think your father would have allowed me to keep in touch with a *boy* from home?" She smiles regretfully, and yeah, she's got a good point. He didn't let her keep *any* friends.

"No wonder you and Otto jumped into things so fast." I had no idea they had so much history. A horrible thought strikes me, and I just need to be sure. "He's. . . he's not my. . . I mean, there's no chance *Otto* could be my father, right?"

She chuckles, and it lightens the tense atmosphere in the room. Even Gramps relaxes his uneasy posture.

"We would only be so lucky, baby. But no, we were never together like that in high school."

"Okay. Just needed to make sure." I mean, we do kinda look alike.

"We can move on from this and heal. I know we can," Richard says earnestly. "We're all each other has, and we're in this together."

Gramps is right, and I'm not going to let my scumbag father take this away from us. This is *my* family now. And Lincoln and Otto are included in that.

"Well, my side is aching like a bitch, and Linc should be here any minute, so can we hug and call it a night or some shit?"

They both laugh freely, and it feels good to clear the air between us. I truly hope we can move on from this.

CHAPTER THIRTY-FOUR
REMI

Two weeks have passed since the attack in Asheville, and the P.I. Gramps hired isn't any closer to finding Logan. I've decided I won't call him Dad anymore. He lost that title a long time ago and sealed the deal when he had Lincoln and me jumped. So now it's either Logan or scumbag prick.

The only detail the investigator has managed to find is a one-way bus ticket from Detroit to Asheville. Purchased in my father's name, with cash. So we know for certain that he's here with his *friends*. And the fact that he's just *waiting* to make a move sets my nerves on edge. More psychological games, but at least the texts have stopped.

Otto has stayed over the entire time, practically moving in. He and Mom are getting closer, and I'm not mad about it. He's been an important support system for her during this craziness, and for me and Gramps, too, if I'm being honest.

I just wish Lincoln could be here every night. He stays over whenever his parents are out of town. And on the nights they are home, Gramps has extra security discreetly stationed outside their gates. It's not ideal, but it's all we can do for the time being. No one wants Lincoln's parents or the community to find out about this. It would be a scandal, a hit to the Keller family name, and Gramps doesn't deserve that. We came here for help and, I think, reconnection. Maybe even a fresh start. Neither of us intended to bring this drama to his doorstep.

So far, it's worked to keep things quiet. No one knows that the entire Keller estate has been in a state of unease for the last two weeks—on edge and waiting for Logan to make his move. Otto and I hate it. We're both firm believers in the strike first motto, so being a sitting duck doesn't sit well with us. Even Lurch has been tense, checking the security alarm and cameras constantly.

I know the cops will inevitably get involved once Logan shows up, but Gramps promises nothing will happen to me. I've done nothing wrong. His connections on the force already know what's happening, and he's paid them generously to keep it quiet.

We filled Grady and Sierra in on everything. We couldn't let them think we were ghosting them. But it's not worth the risk to their safety to hang out while there's still a threat. Logan could be watching us, and I won't put the twins in danger.

Something's going to happen, soon. I can feel it in my bones. A storm is coming. Logan isn't done. He didn't just accept defeat and run home to Detroit. No fucking way. He came for money, and the greedy fuck won't leave until he tries his own hand at taking it.

It's Friday night, and Linc's parents are in New York for the entire weekend, so he doesn't have to leave the estate. I can keep him tucked safely into my bed, with my dick nestled in his ass for the next two days.

We're cuddled up, watching the new *Game of Thrones* show. Lincoln is snuggled into my side with his head on my chest and his thigh thrown over mine. His delicate hand rests on my abdomen, just above the waistband of my boxer briefs. He scratches lightly at the hair there as I draw lazy circles on his soft skin with my fingertips.

"Even though a lot of bad things have happened in the last month, I wouldn't take any of it back. I'd go through it all again, just to know you. To love you," I murmur into his hair.

"Me too, Remi. I love you more than anything." He punctuates his words with a gentle rock of his hips, grinding his semi into my thigh.

"Yeah?" I ask, already knowing the answer.

"Yes. So fuckin' much."

He's started cursing more when it's just the two of us in bed. And it gets me so fucking hot to know those filthy words only leave his mouth for me.

I roll him to his back, trailing wet, open-mouthed kisses down his lean body until I get to his little briefs I gave him with the periodic table printed all over them. I smirk, feeling supremely satisfied that he loves them so much and knowing I have five other pairs of scientific underwear in my closet for him.

I nuzzle him over the fabric, breathing in his heady scent of male musk and fresh citrus soap. I hum in approval before peeling them down, freeing him.

His cock twitches, stretching longer before my eyes. I lean down and swirl my tongue along the crown, feeding his length into my mouth. I bob my head, taking him deep before pulling off with tight suction. He moans wantonly, reaching out for me.

"When I'm done, I'm gonna paint your fucking guts with my cum."

And then I dive back down, sucking him into the back of my throat and swallowing against his tip. He cries out, grabbing onto my hair and tugging hard. Lincoln fucks into my mouth until he comes, spurting down my throat and nearly choking me with his jizz. I swallow every last drop, loving his taste. His flavor.

His breaths are uneven, but he's ready for more. Linc rolls over, crawling to his hands and knees and arching his back, presenting his ass to me. His cock hangs half-hard and glistening between his legs. I skim my fingers down his spine, ready to show him just how much I truly fucking love him.

A rattling noise rouses me from sleep, and I roll over, pulling Lincoln's back to my front. I drift off again until I hear the same scratching sound before the bedroom door clicks open.

Like a specter from the past, my father steps forward, seemingly out of nowhere. His dark, messy hair is pulled into a top knot, and it looks like he hasn't shaved since he got here two weeks ago. His smile is all teeth—evil and conniving, making me feel like the spawn of Satan himself.

"Hello, Son," he says in a chilly tone that sends ice down my spine.

My heart jumps into my throat, and my mouth goes dry. As much as I talk a big game, to see him standing here in my room, with a *gun* pointed at me and my boyfriend. . .

Fuck, I'm rattled.

"Stand up," Logan demands, motioning with the gun.

He shuts the door quietly behind him, not taking his eyes or his aim off of me.

I hate that I'm frozen, but he's the one person on this planet that can really fuck with me. Really get inside my head. And what the hell can I do against a gun?

"Be a good son for once, and do as you're fucking told! Stand. Up!"

Linc startles at his angry shout, sucking in a breath when he opens his eyes to a strange man with a gun at the foot of our bed, lit only by the moonlight streaming in from my open curtains.

"Shhh," I whisper into his ear. "Just do what he says. Don't try anything. Let me handle it. I love you, baby."

"Enough! You don't want to test me, Remi. Your little boyfriend stays here." He waves his gun toward Linc, threatening him, finger on the trigger like the dumbass he is. "If you don't want him hurt, don't call the cops, and don't tell your whore-of-a-mother or her new *boyfriend*."

I clench my jaw, growling under my breath as I wrap my arms around Linc and pull him close.

"I'm scared," he whispers, his body trembling in my arms.

Logan won't touch him. I won't allow it. No one else will ever harm a hair on his beautiful auburn head. I will riot for him. Fucking kill and die for him, all in the same breath.

And my father is completely oblivious to that fact as he continues to go off on a rant, speaking about Mom like *she* was the one cheating and being a deadbeat this entire time, not him.

"Stop," I growl, unable to listen to it anymore.

He barks out a cruel laugh. "Always were a sensitive little mama's boy." His vicious smile turns into a snarl. "But when you look weak, I look weak. Now get the fuck up." He starts around the bed, toward Lincoln's side.

I jump up immediately, unconcerned by my near nudity in the tiny black boxer briefs I'm wearing.

"Okay! Okay!" I hold my hands up in front of me in mock surrender. I won't ever surrender to him.

"I'm up. Just leave him alone. This is between us."

My father laughs maniacally, completely off his fucking rocker. He shakes his head and mumbles something that sounds like "so fucking gay" under his breath.

"I'll stay here and keep lover boy company, so make sure you don't do anything stupid," he sneers. "I'm guessing you know all of your grandfather's security codes." His teeth peel back even further, adding to his menacing glare. "Now go empty his safe and grab all of his watches. And pocket watches. I really like this silver one with my son's name on it. Seems like it was made *just* for me." The twinkle in his eye is like a steel blade, ready to strike where it hurts, cutting to the quick.

My hands curl into fists, which he doesn't miss, laughing cruelly as he slips *my* pocket watch into his jacket. The pocket watch that Gramps just gave me. The pocket watch that means *so* much to him. A family heirloom he had specially engraved for me. He even added a chain long enough to hang out of my pants, just like "kids do these days," as Gramp says.

If Logan didn't have a gun on me, he'd already be unconscious. But he does, so I have to stand here while he continues to talk shit. I know he's trying to get a rise out of me.

"I couldn't help but notice he likes quality timepieces, so I think I'm gonna cash in on the family antiques. Claim my own inheritance. Maybe even grab one of those weird fucking bird clocks on the wall downstairs. Don't think he'd even miss it."

"We're not your family," I snap, unable to stop myself. Feeling protective over Gramps and his clocks and his *money*.

Logan rears his hand back and slaps me across the face. My head jerks to the side from the impact, cheek stinging. The familiar metallic taste of blood fills my mouth, but at least he didn't cold-cock me with his pistol.

"Don't talk back, you little shit. You'd do well to remember that."

I clench my jaw tightly, molars grinding in restraint. If he puts that gun down, I will fucking *murder him*. With my bare hands. Lincoln's quiet sobs have rage burning through me. My eyes narrow in on my target.

"Now listen up. Keep quiet, and we can go our separate ways after this. I won't bother you again. You can live your *homosexual* life," he sneers, eyeing my nearly naked body, then Lincoln tucked in bed with the covers pulled to his chin. "And you can tell your mother to send me the divorce papers."

He's fucking delusional if he thinks he's going to take *anything* from my family and walk away a free and *unharmed* man.

"I only want you to share a little bit of the wealth. For putting up with your disobedient ass for eighteen years. I don't think that's too much to ask for, Remington. Do you?"

I know better. I fucking *know* better. But it still doesn't stop the aggressive words from tumbling from my lips.

"You're. Not. Getting. Shit."

He huffs out a disbelieving breath, flinging his hands up in the air in a fed-up way. I take the opportunity to dive for him while the gun isn't pointed at either of us.

Pop!

It fires as I make contact with my father's stomach, taking him down with a grunt. The steaming hot piece of metal skitters away, stopping under my desk in the corner.

I vaguely hear shouting and yelling from outside the bedroom and down the hall. But my ears are fucking *ringing* because of the pistol that just went off a foot from my face.

I'm disoriented as Logan rolls us, striking me in the face twice, this time with a closed fist. Before he can take another shot, the door bursts open. Suddenly, he's ripped away from me as Otto tackles him to the ground.

I stare at the ceiling, breaths ragged. My heart ricochets around inside my chest. Linc crawls over to me, still in his periodic table underwear, and pulls me into his lap, cradling my head.

"Remi," he whimpers, hand hovering over my bruised cheek. "Say somethin'," he pleads, eyes darting over to the commotion and then back down to me.

I can feel blood dripping down from a split in my eyebrow, but at least he didn't get my piercing. I'd have been extra pissed if he ripped that shit out.

"Have to help Otto," I mumble, shaking off the shock. I sit up a little too quickly, and my vision wavers.

"You're not okay," he implores, trying to get me to stay back with him. But Logan's on top now, and I *need* to get up.

"I'm fine, baby. Trust me. Stay here." I crawl over to Otto on my hands and knees before grabbing my father's arms and wrenching them behind his back.

Otto clambers to his knees and rears his fist back. "For Raina. And for the son that should have been mine all along."

Fuck. Did he really just say that?

My father cackles like a lunatic as he continues to struggle against me, but he's gassing out. It doesn't matter that he's bigger than me. "Ahhh. The new boyfriend. Enjoy the whore. She's the reason I'm here right now. It was really convenient, actually. The alarm was off. The dumb bitch never remembers to—"

Otto slams his fist straight into Logan's face with a sickening crunch. I let go, and he drops to the ground in a pathetic heap. I stagger to my feet just as Lurch barges in.

And holy fucking shit, Clifford.

He's got his own piece, equipped with an extra-long silencer aimed straight at the pile of trash by my feet.

That is. . . unexpected. And completely fucking badass.

Lincoln tip-toes over, curling into my side and handing me a pair of athletic shorts that I quickly slip on.

"Threat contained, sir," Clifford speaks into a tiny earpiece I've never noticed before and wonder if he's had it this whole time.

Lincoln must notice my confused expression because he whispers into my ear, "Clifford is part of Mr. Keller's secret security."

"Huh," is all I can say. I wasn't expecting the uptight man to go all James Bond, but damn, my respect for him just skyrocketed.

"I've reached out to Richard's contacts on the force. This will not be called in like a regular domestic disturbance. But you will need to stay and give your account, young sir. And I've called the family doctor over." He eyes me like he expects me to object, but I'm too fucking tired. It's the middle of the goddamn night, and my adrenaline is starting to tank.

Linc and I leave the bedroom and my unconscious father behind. I don't want to be in the same space as

Logan when he comes to. I've had enough of his hate my entire life; I won't spend any more time around it.

I grab Lincoln's hand, squeezing tight, both of us lost for words. The weight of what happened is heavy and unyielding. That was close. *Too close.*

We go downstairs, heading toward the kitchen to grab a bag of ice and find Mom and Gramps.

And if I have to speak to the police, I'm gonna need a fucking sandwich and a cigarette.

In that order.

CHAPTER THIRTY-FIVE

REMI

It's been a week since my father's arrest, and things are finally starting to settle down around here. Logan was detained on a slew of charges, including assault with a deadly weapon, attempted robbery, breaking and entering, and a whole heap of domestic abuse charges considering it was his own son he smashed in the face. He's looking at spending the next ten years in jail, if not more. Let's hope he's old enough to learn his fucking lesson by then and not come for me or mine ever again.

Mom has already filed divorce papers with help from Gramps and his courtroom connections, and Otto still stays over on the nights he's not at the gym. It sort of feels like a real family, and I think Mom and Otto feel it too. It's another thing set right in the universe. Another thing that should have always been.

Mom and Otto.

Me and Lincoln.

All of us, *home*, in Hunter Springs, with Gramps. Who successfully kept everything under wraps might I add. The

Andersons, the Walkers, and the entire town are none the wiser to yet another Keller family scandal.

But what we *can't* keep under wraps any longer is Lincoln and my relationship.

We *have* to tell his parents.

Lincoln and I are ready for it to be done. Sierra has been smoothing things over on her end, placating her parents with small fibs to keep them happy. And as soon as we come out to his parents tonight, we'll start holding hands at school. Maybe even kiss. No big announcement for our peers. It just is what it is.

If anyone has a problem, they can take it up with me, and I'll take it up with Gus. I'm not fighting anymore. After everything that happened, I made a promise to Lincoln. No more fight nights. Instead, I'm focusing my energy on looking into who's running Keller Industries. But I still train with Otto, so I won't hesitate to defend my boyfriend's honor and our right to be together, unbothered. And I never back down from a challenge.

No one will fuck with Linc ever again. Not under my watch. Connor and Brandon have backed down since getting their asses whooped, unwilling to start on either of us and suffer more embarrassment. Don't blame them. They're pathetic and should just stick with football.

"Is my tie straight?" Linc asks for the millionth time.

"Yes, Preppy. Come here." I hold my hand out, and he places his palm in mine, fingers trembling.

I'm perched on the end of the bed, waiting for him to finish getting ready for dinner at his house. I pull him between my spread thighs, settling my hands on his waist. I peer into the eyes that I love so much. "You look amazing. Really, Lincoln. And you don't need to worry about what your parents think anyway. You're not living your life for them anymore, remember? You live for you."

I place my hand over his heart and his over mine. "For us."

His heart beats steadily as he stares at me, chewing on his bottom lip.

"This is *your* life, *your* happiness, not theirs," I say, reinforcing what he needs to hear every now and then.

He leans down, pressing his lips to mine, breathing into my mouth. "I love you, Remi. You're my happiness."

"Love you, too," I respond, grabbing him by the hips until he's straddling me in his suit and tie. I band my arms around him tightly, squeezing him to me.

"So fucking much."

"Sean, darlin', would you pass the risotto, please?" Kendra asks, her dark hair slicked back into a neat bun on the back of her head.

She scoops a small portion onto her plate, then motions to Linc sitting next to her with me on his other side. "Want some more, sweet pea?"

"No, thank you, Mrs. Walker," he responds politely with a stiff smile on his handsome face. His knee bounces under the table, and I settle my palm onto it, letting the weight calm him.

I lean in, subtly whispering into his ear, "Relax, Preppy. Everything's going to be fine."

I glance across the table and lock eyes with Sierra. The parentals are chattering away next to us. She knows the questions are coming soon. Either her parents or Linc's will ask about the courtship unless we spill the beans first.

Before Linc can gather the courage and grab the metaphorical bull by the horns, Diana speaks up.

"So, how has the courtship been going for you two? Lincoln, have you taken Sierra out on a date yet? I'd like to hear about it." Diana doesn't miss a beat, and I can see the sweat beading along Lincoln's temple. I stroke his leg, letting him know I'm here for him. Whatever he wants to do. However he wants to handle this.

"No, Mother. I haven't," he replies calmly, in complete contrast with the raging emotions I know he's keeping a tight hold on inside.

Diana releases a heavy sigh, slowly shaking her head like she's just so disappointed. It's hard for me to sit back and wait for him to get his words out. But I will. I'd wait forever for him.

"And why not, Lincoln James?"

Everyone's eyes turn to Linc, waiting. Sweat forms on his upper lip, and he adjusts his tie, tugging at his collar. His knee starts bouncing like a jackhammer again, vibrating my arm.

Diana doesn't give up. "Don't be disrespectful—"

"I'm gay!" he shouts.

Shit.

He did it *again*. Just blurting out his sexuality like that.

The table pauses, and all utensils cease their movements as the reality of the situation settles around us.

Robert laughs, actually fucking laughs. If he wasn't Lincoln's father, he'd be face first in his risotto. "No, no. That's not possible. You must just be confused. Going through a phase."

"These types of things will work themselves out," his mom adds with an awkward little chuckle, glancing at her best friend, like she's embarrassed by her son.

Fuck that.

Fuck *all* of that.

I push away from the table, my heavy chair scraping against the hardwood. "Don't tell him he's confused, and definitely do not tell him it's a phase. *He's my boyfriend.*" I pin my disgusted glare on Robert.

Kendra gasps, and Lincoln's parents cease their awkwardly rude laughter. Sean has a blank face, and Grady and Sierra's matching amber eyes dart around the table nervously.

Robert's shock morphs into a Grinch-like smile. All conniving teeth and greedy eyes.

He changes his tune quickly, just like he did when he learned I was Richard's grandson and not an intruder.

"Of course, it's not a phase. Excuse me for that."

It's close to an apology but still fake as fuck.

"You're only saying that because you've been on Gramps's dick for years. Trying to get your grubby hands on *my* family's profits."

He sputters, his mouth gaping like a fish. "That's. . . I'm not. . ."

Kendra speaks up then, her dark eyes warm and kind. "I can see the spark, and I'm happy for you boys."

Sean clears his throat. I can tell he's a little uncomfortable by the news, but there's nothing but respect in his hazel eyes. "Yes. Robert, you need to back off and let the boys breathe. Be themselves. There's no need to pressure them about the future right now. And Sierra, honey, I need you to know something. Your mother and I only agreed to this courtship because we truly believed you and Lincoln had feelings beyond friendship for each other. We didn't. . . We didn't know your orientation, Lincoln. And I apologize.

And I'll apologize for my friend because we all know he won't."

Look at Sean. Taking one for the team.

"Thank you," I reply, giving him a tight nod. He's never done anything to wrong me. Or Kendra. I won't disrespect them.

Lincoln pulls from my strength and stands next to me, linking his fingers with mine. "We're in love," he declares boldly, making me feel proud of how far he's come from the shy, stumbling boy I first met who was so far in the closet he couldn't see the light of day. "And I won't let any of you tell me who I can be with."

"For how long? How long have you been together?" Diana asks quietly.

"Since the beginning," we say in unison, and I squeeze his hand. It's true. We've been boyfriends since I gave Linc his first kiss in the arcade photo booth. We just didn't see it yet.

"Well. I'm not against homosexuals or anything," Diana says, smoothing down the sleeves of her crisp white blouse, starched to hell.

I snort. "Great. Glad we cleared that up. Maybe we can work on more progress at a later date. This therapy session is over." I turn to our younger friends.

"Twins. Wanna come to my house? Play the new *Call of Duty*?"

"S-sure," they both stutter, rising from their chairs and joining us on our side of the table.

"Listen up. This is the future of your companies. The future of Keller Industries. Right here. Right now. Standing before you. Robert, I can see the wheels turning, and I know what a conniving snake like you is thinking—you now have an alliance with Keller Industries. And maybe you're right.

Maybe Linc and I will get married one day and merge the companies. But the point is—this is *our* life, not yours. You can't control your sons *or* your daughter." I look at each of them in turn. "This is twenty-twenty-two people. Let's get with it, for fuck's sake."

I've had enough; my tolerance for assholes is really low lately. The four of us head for the door, leaving the parents gaping after us, and I must have a problem or some shit because I fucking love shocking people.

After Grady and Sierra leave, Lincoln and I head down to the kitchen for a quick snack before bed. It's a Friday night, and he doesn't have to report home anymore. His parents know we're together. My family knows we're together. And it feels fucking good.

"How'd the dinner go?" Mom asks, sitting at the kitchen table with a glass of wine and her iPad.

Otto stays late at the gym on Fridays, so it's her "girl's night," as she likes to call it, which just means her latest romance novel and a drink. Usually wine.

"My boys!" Gramps shouts before I can answer Mom, strolling into the kitchen in his go-to beige cardigan, tan slacks, and old-man slippers.

"Sit. Sit." He ushers us over to the table with Mom. "Tell us how tonight went, and I'll whip up some grilled cheese for everyone. How does that sound?

"I'll take two!" Mom says in an unnecessarily loud voice.

I snicker, "Tipsy, Ma?"

"Remington Jace! You are not one to talk after you got

shitfaced in front of your grandfather within a few days of meeting him."

"Touché, Ma. Touché."

She got me there.

Gramps laughs at the kitchen counter, and Lincoln giggles next to me.

"You never told me about that," he says through laughing breaths.

"Yeah. I guess it wasn't my proudest moment. Not to be a downer, but that was right after Logan sent me some of the first threatening texts, and I was kinda fucked up in the head about it."

Lincoln lays his head on my shoulder, grabbing my hand under the table and squeezing gently.

"Oh, Rem. I'm sorry. I shouldn't have teased you," Mom fusses.

"Nope. It's all good. Really. Let's not bring up the scumbag prick again," I say, changing the topic back to food. "I'll take two grilled cheeses as well, Gramps."

"Um. Can I just have one, please, Mr. Keller?"

I chuckle at his adorableness and trace my finger down the center of his palm, making him shiver and sit up straighter.

"Well, tell us how the dinner went," Gramps says as he starts to slice chunks of cheddar and gouda, the thick brioche bread already slathered with butter and ready for the skillet.

"It was alright. Not too bad, really. The Walkers were pretty cool about it," I tell him.

"My parents were jerks until they found out Remi is my boyfriend. They seemed to accept that I'm gay after that. But it just felt fake because I know they aren't really happy for me. They don't *really* want me to be with another man. Even if that man *is* the heir to Keller Industries."

"Oh, sweetie. I'm sorry," Mom says warmly, and I appreciate her soft tone with him. "I'm sure they'll come around. It sounds like they're taking steps toward acceptance."

"Yeah, hopefully." He smiles, but it's a little strained.

"They will. It'll be fine, Linc. We're living life for us now, remember?" I run my hand up and down the soft fleece of his plaid pajama pant-clad thigh.

I'll remind him as many times as he needs.

Every day for the rest of our lives if it's necessary.

My mom's attention is back on her iPad and wine, and Gramps is busy with the food while the skillet sizzles away, the rich smells of decadent cheese and melted butter filling the air. I continue my caress under the table until I cup his junk, settling my hand there. I prop my right hand under my chin, waiting casually for my food as if nothing debauched is going on under their noses.

His cock swells under my touch, and I keep my hand there, squeezing ever so gently. He whimpers, and I cough to cover it.

"Hmm?" Mom looks up, eyes slightly glassy.

"Nothing," I smile sweetly at her. "Stomach just grumbled. Hungry."

"Should be soon," she says absently before taking another sip and focusing back on her book.

I keep my hand still and lean into his ear. "You're being so fucking good for me," I say in a barely-there whisper.

I sit back just before Gramps places a platter of delicious-looking grilled cheese sandwiches in front of us. As soon as we eat, I'm taking my boyfriend back to my bed.

Because although we may have just met a month ago, there's an entire lifetime we missed out on.

We may have started this whole thing as friends with benefits, but that was just a ruse—a farce. He was in my air space from the beginning, flying undetected, and we were going to collide sooner or later. It was inevitable. Our collision of souls. Two people meant to be in each other's lives from the beginning.

And there's nothing left to do but make up for lost time and love him with every fucking fiber of my being.

EPILOGUE
LINC - ONE YEAR LATER

"I got an A on my Molecular Biology exam!" I exclaim, bursting into our dorm room and slamming the door shut behind me. I set my helmet on the small corner table next to Remi's. Mr. Keller surprised him with a matching black moped for his graduation present, and they've been the perfect fit for campus life. It's different here—not like high school. No one cares. No one judges us. We can be gay *and* ride mopeds.

"Of course you did. You get As in everything you do, Preppy. Including sucking cock," Remi teases, and I blush at his dirty words, loving when he talks so filthy.

We decided we wanted the full college experience. We're not missing out on anything. So even though neither of us *needs* to be cramped in this tiny dorm room together, sharing a bathroom, we *want* to be.

He said he'd follow me anywhere, so it was up to me to choose our college. Well, that and his grade point average. But thanks to his awesome student advisor and the additional AP science classes, it was pretty high. Remi had no problem getting accepted, and I couldn't be more proud of him.

We ended up staying in North Carolina, but on the opposite end of the state from our parents. I enrolled in the Marine Biology program at a private coastal college, forgoing Columbia and my parent's desire for me to get a business degree. Remi chose to pursue his degree in Exercise Science *and* Business, following me to the beach.

We love it out here; it's impossible not to. Grady and Sierra fell under the spell of this place's charms when they helped us move into our dorm room. And now they can't see themselves anywhere else. Much to their parent's dismay, I'm sure.

For now, Remi and I are just taking things day by day. We don't need to have the rest of our lives planned out at nineteen. We have our whole futures ahead of us. And it's not up to anyone else what we decide to do with those futures. But we aren't turning our backs on the family businesses. That wouldn't be smart. What we *will* be doing is running them the way we want, when we want, and investing in projects that we're passionate about.

Remi and I encouraged Mr. Keller to hire new people and start vetting the Keller teams before high school even ended. Turns out there *was* corruption. The northeast team was siphoning profits and funneling two percent into offshore accounts, which may sound small, but from the massive collection of businesses they were managing, it was in the millions. There's no recovering those losses, but the head of the snake has been severed, and Keller Industries is continuing to flourish. And until Remi is ready to jump in, Otto and Sterling have stepped up, helping Mr. Keller get a better handle on everything—supporting him and assisting in the decision-making. He needs people who care about him, who he can trust, and that's the four of us.

As far as my family business, my parents continue to do well, still chasing after Mr. Keller and his companies. They're more than ever determined to get a piece of the pie, but until Remi and I get married, they'll probably continue to chase their own tails.

Mr. Keller doesn't trust them. And neither do I.

But he *does* trust Remi and me. So when we take the reins, we won't let him down.

"How was your Anatomy exam?" I ask, plopping down on his twin-sized bed while he mashes buttons and kills hordes of zombies.

"Think I aced it. Want me to show you what I learned about the human body, Mr. Advisor?" He tosses his controller to the side as his character goes down in a swarm of bloody faces and gnashing teeth.

He rolls on top of me, pressing my body into the bed with his full weight as he cages me in with his forearms. Remi's gotten more ink since high school, adding the silver pocket watch his grandfather gave him, the chain wrapping around his forearm. I kiss his neck, trailing my tongue up the new designs on his neck and loving how sexy he looks.

His grin is crooked and captivating. "I can show you where your prostate is." He leans down and licks at my mouth. "In case you forgot."

My head bobbles so fast that I get dizzy. "I forgot. I definitely forgot."

Remi chuckles, leaning in to kiss me deeply. "I fucking love how eager you are for ass play," he growls into my mouth.

I am. I'm completely obsessed with butt stuff. Anytime

he touches me there, it inevitably leads to me shamelessly begging for his cock.

I open my legs, cradling him between my thighs, but there's too much between us. Too many clothes.

"Off." I tug at his T-shirt impatiently, and he pulls it over his head with one hand behind his neck.

My hands trail up the ripples of his abs, over his pecs, and around his shoulders. I'll never get tired of feeling his muscles and touching his body because I never in my wildest dreams thought a boy like Remi would be interested in a boy like me.

We slip out of the rest of our clothes, and Remi grabs the bottle of lube from his bedside table. I bend my legs and spread them further apart in anticipation.

"I need you to be quiet this time. If the RA comes banging on the door again while I'm nutting, I might punch him in the face. With my dick out."

I giggle at the memory of the most awkwardly timed orgasm in history. Remembering Remi's strained "O" face while Tommy, the annoying RA, banged on our door has me laughing even harder.

"Don't laugh at me when I'm about to have my dick up your ass, Preppy," he teases with a half-grin.

His cool, slick fingers caress my hole, and my laugh immediately dies out with a moan. He presses one, then two inside of me, and I'm humping against them, trying to get him deeper.

"Need you," I moan.

"I know, baby. Almost there." His intense gaze locks onto my face as he savors my every reaction.

He adds a third finger, and then he's twisting them, stretching me open, and it feels so freakin' good.

My needy, desperate-sounding pants should be embarrassing, but they only spur Remi on, pushing me higher. He thrusts harder, pumping his fingers in and out of me, but it's not enough.

"Need you inside me. Please, Remi," I moan unabashedly. "Want your cock."

He slips his fingers out and scoops me up under my butt, lifting me before I even have a chance to cry out at the emptiness.

"Hook your legs over my shoulders," he rasps out, and I obey.

He squirts more lube into his hand, stroking his length before lining up with my hole. Remi presses forward, practically folding me in half, his cock slowly sliding in and stretching my body to its limits. We groan in unison, my cock dripping and my balls drawing up tight.

He pauses for a second, letting me adjust before he's drilling into me, hips working like a piston.

"So. Perfectly. Tight," Remi grunts out between hard thrusts.

"More," I whisper. Wanting it all. Wanting his cock as deep as it can go. Wanting to *feel* our connection. Our love.

He lifts my hips higher and adjusts his position, angling his thrusts just right until he completely bottoms out. He pauses there, keeping me filled up.

I cry out, unable to contain my sounds of pleasure. My legs are a quivering, shaking mess. My chest heaves, lungs working overtime at the exquisite pressure against my prostate.

"Shh. Baby. You gotta be quiet," Remi gasps. "Fuck. *Goddamn,* you're tight."

He's so far inside my guts I can taste him. His length pulses as he grinds his pelvis against my butt, rubbing the coarse hair nestled around the base of his cock against my sensitive rim.

"It's so deep. You're so deep. So big—"

He pulls out and slams forward.

Again. And again. And again.

"Ungh! Ohmyfuckingfuck!"

I curl my hands into the bed sheets as Remi leans forward even further, grabbing hold of the headboard and grunting with his effort to fuck me as hard and deep as he possibly can. Giving me everything I asked for. *Begged for.*

I whimper as my eyes roll into the back of my head, and I just lie here, folded in half, *taking it.* Taking *everything* he gives me because he lights me up, steals my breath, and completes my soul. He's it for me. My forever.

I don't even need him to touch me. The moment I feel his hot cum spurt into me, his cock pulsing, I'm flying. Soaring past the sun and the moon and the stars. Maybe even to another dimension.

My cock is still twitching with aftershocks when Remi pulls out, lowering my trembling legs to the bed. He collapses next to me, chest heaving, just like mine. Both of us are covered in a light sheen of sweat.

Good grief, that was intense.

I roll over, tucking my hands under my cheek, staring at his strong profile. "I love you, Remi. So fuckin' much," I curse, just because I know he likes it.

He turns his head, his lip pulling up on one side. The eyebrow stud that I love so much glints under the harsh fluorescent bulbs of our dorm room. "Yeah? Well, I fucking love you with all of my motherfucking heart, Preppy." His smile turns into a full-on Cheshire grin, and he leans forward to kiss me softly.

"Be right back."

Remi hops up, half-hard cock hanging thickly between his legs, and slips into the bathroom to clean up.

He comes back and gently wipes me down. My cheeks burn as he inspects my body to make sure I'm okay, which I assure him I am.

Remi settles back into bed and opens his arm for me. I scoot into his side, settling a hand on his chest and my leg over his thigh. We fit perfectly like this.

"So, I made plans for fall break. And I think you're gonna be excited," Remi says as he draws lazy circles over my hip.

"You did?" I ask, still a little breathless.

"Yeah, baby," he croons, caressing my body reverently. "The Buffalo Bungalow is all ours. For a whole weekend. You. Me. One cabin. One bed. Alone."

I lift my head, peering up at him, knowing my eyes are alight with excitement. "Yes, please!" I shout unnecessarily. It wasn't even a question.

He chuckles, leaning down to nip at my lips. "Might even let you fuck me over the back of the couch again," he teases, giving me his signature wink that makes me melt every dang time.

I get those fluttery feelings thinking about Remi letting me inside him again. It's only happened a few times since we lost our virginity together in the cabin last year. He tends to top, and I tend to beg for it in my bottom. So it just works.

"What about your family?" I ask. "We promised we'd come home for Thanksgivin' and spend it with them."

"We will. We're leaving after dinner. And after we stop by your place to say hello to the Walkers and your parents. And you better believe I'll be bringing the booze and weed, Preppy."

I hum, not disagreeing in the slightest. I'm not afraid to have fun anymore. Let loose a little. We've both changed a lot in the past year, overcoming so many of our own personal obstacles and starting the journey toward healing our traumas.

Our love may be new, but it's forged deep, battle-hardened and practically indestructible. We've been through so much together. Each trial, each tribulation, has been a testament to the strength and resilience we recognized in each other from the beginning.

I roll on top of him, grabbing his wrists and boldly pinning them above his head, something I don't normally do. "Are you really goin' to let me bend you over the couch again?" I ask breathlessly. Ever since he said that, my mind has replayed the mental images I saved from last year at the cabin. I can't wait to go back to the place where it all started.

"Fuck yeah, Preppy. And you can bet your ass I'll be bending you over, too," he practically growls. "Not sure I plan to step one foot outside the cabin unless it's to fuck you in the hot tub or smoke a blunt." His wolfish grin is disarming, and I already know I'll go anywhere with him or do anything he asks of me.

Our trust runs deep, and our loyalty never wavers.

This isn't about doing what's right or wrong. Good or bad. It's about doing what makes us happy. What fulfills us and brings us joy. This is our life, and we'll live it how we damn well please.

Do you want a super spicy 2k-word bonus scene from Remi and Linc's return to the cabin? Subscribe to my newsletter!

ACKNOWLEDGMENTS

First, I need to say thank you to my shy, lonely boy and my recklessly playful bad boy. This second book was difficult for me on many different levels, but in the end, Remi and Linc told their story and earned their HEA! And I just love them so much!

My beta readers. Elizabeth, Morgan, and Kat. You ladies are amazing and validated me so hard! Thank you for your support and encouragement and for all the ridiculous and immature things we laughed about for way too long. Like twenty-four hours too long.

Elizabeth, my wifey. Once again, thanks for being the first person to read this story. I don't see this changing anytime soon, so I appreciate you for the supportive bestie that you are!

Silver Grace. You are a star! Thank you for taking my long-winded emails about the cover and bringing our bad boy to life. Because Remi is just perfection. And can we please talk about the pocket watch tattoo on his forearm! I don't know how you do it, but thank you for being so amazingly talented!

Molly, there's no one else I would trust to help deliver the best story that these boys deserve. Remi and Linc mean so much to me, so thank you for caring and for all your hard work!

To all of my Bookstagram friends, author friends, and

reader friends, your friendships and messages bring a smile to my face every day!

Joelle, thank you for being one of the first authors to reach out to me about Cali Boy! I'm so grateful that we've become friends. You are always there to listen, offer advice, and answer questions. For real, thank you for answering all of my questions!

And an extra special thanks to Rikki for always being there to cheerlead, pump me up, and match my energy! It's been awesome getting to know you, and you've been a big support for me in finishing this book!

Loren, thanks for being you and for your support and encouraging words. I'm so glad we've become friends, and I'm really excited for everything to come!

Finally, to you, the reader, if you've gotten this far, please know that you are so very appreciated! I love seeing every review, edit, and comment on social media, and I am so grateful for each recommendation! I hope you stay on this wild ride with me, even when I come out with vampires and werewolves. Peace!

ALSO BY CHARLI MEADOWS

The Loyal Boys

Cali Boy

Bad Boy

Lost Boy

ABOUT THE AUTHOR

Charli Meadows is an obsessive reader, avid Bookstagrammer-turned PA, and now an author herself. Lover of all things romance, she plans to write a little bit of everything but make it sweet and spicy.

Living in North Carolina with her husband and young daughter, you can usually find Charli working her boring corporate job or at home playing video games. When she's not reading, writing, or daydreaming about books.

Subscribe to my newsletter! Join my Facebook Group!

37925696R00220

Contents

1

Introduction to Weather

Text: Introduction (pp. 4–5)
Vocabulary Words:

atmosphere

climate

blizzard

Discussion Questions

1. Locate the vocabulary words in the glossary. Write the definition for each.

2. Name three ways that weather can affect our daily lives.

3. Paul says, "All things were created by God, things in heaven and on earth, visible and invisible" (Colossians 1:16). Would you consider wind to be invisible? Why?

4. How is the Holy Spirit like the wind?

5. How long have seasons existed on the earth?

6. As a result of Adam and Eve's sin against God, the weather was affected. What do you think the weather would have been like if man had never sinned?

Text: Chapter 1—God Created (pp. 6-7)

Vocabulary Words

ultraviolet light

carbon dioxide

ice age

tide

---

nitrogen

ozone

oxygen

pollution water

vapor

latitudes

Discussion Questions

1. Locate the vocabulary words in the glossary. Write the definition for each.

2. What effect does the moon have on the earth?

3. What would happen to the earth if the moon were farther than 240,000 miles away?

4. Why do the sun and moon look the same size in the sky even though they are not?

5. Earth spins on its axis once every day. Why is that perfect for weather on Earth?

6. Why is the tilt of the earth's axis important to our weather?

7. What percentages of various gasses comprise our atmosphere?

8. Why is it important for fair-skinned people to apply sunscreen when out in the sun for extended periods of time?

9. How many meteors hit the earth's atmosphere each day?

10. What happens to most of these meteors?

2

Chapter 2
Part 1

Text: What Causes Weather? (pp. 8–9)

Vocabulary Words

Coriolis force

precipitation

axis

equator

Discussion Questions

1. Locate the vocabulary words in the glossary. Write the definition for each.

2. Name the seven main components of weather.

3. What are the five main forms of precipitation?

4. What happens to sunlight that reaches the ground?

5. What is infrared radiation?

6. How does infrared radiation affect the temperatures in summer and in winter?

7. As the air is forced upwards from the Coriolis force, what is formed?

Text: World Climate Zones (pp. 10–11)

Vocabulary Words

ice cap

arid

tropical

humid

subarctic

tundra

Discussion Questions

1. Locate the vocabulary words in the glossary. Write a definition for each.

2. The weather may change from day to day, or season to season, but climate is the average weather condition for a particular place at a particular time. Look at the world climate map on page 11. Locate where you live. By using the key at the bottom of the map, classify your climate. Describe it briefly using five words.

3. Are there any tropical rain forests found in the high or mid latitudes? Why?

4. At what degree latitude are most of the earth's deserts found?

5. How does the distance from the ocean affect the weather?

6. How do mountains affect the climate?

3

Chapter 2
Part 2

Text: Weather Facts (pp. 12–13)
Vocabulary Words

monsoon

typhoon

Discussion Questions

1. Locate the vocabulary words in the glossary. Write the definition for each.

2. What was the highest recorded surface wind speed?

3. Why does the air above snow stay so cold?

4. Which two American states tied for the largest amount of rainfall in one hour?

5. Where is the lowest air pressure found (naturally) on Earth?

6. Why is the Antarctic ice sheet called a polar desert?

7. Write a poem about your favorite weather fact. Remember, poems don't have to rhyme, but they should express a strong feeling or emotion.

Text: How to Read a Weather Map (pp. 14–15)

Vocabulary Words

cold front

dew point

meteorologist

warm front

Discussion Questions

1. Locate the vocabulary words in the glossary. Write the definition of each word.

2. What are two types of weather observations?

3. How often are the measurements taken for each observation?

4. What role do computers perform in predicting the weather?

5. Even with a computer, why is it sometimes difficult for a meteorologist to predict the weather?

6. Suppose you are planning an outdoor activity, such as hiking or camping, for the next day. When you watch the weather report, do you hope to see an approaching high pressure or low pressure area? Explain your choice.

7. Look at the graphic symbols on page 14 that are used by weather forecasters. Design some new ones that could be used for the following weather conditions: sunshine, partly cloudy, rain and thunderstorm.

Text: Jet Stream (pp. 16–17)
Discussion Questions

1. What is the jet stream?

2. What causes the jet stream?

3. What is the average speed of the jet stream during the summer and winter months?

4. What effect does the jet stream have on the weather?

5. Which direction do storms generally move?

6. Does the wind speed stay the same in the jet stream? Explain your answer.

7. Why are jet stream charts important to meteorologists?

8. How fast would a balloon circle the world if placed in the jet stream?

Text: El Niño (pp. 18–19)
Vocabulary Words

El Niño

plankton

Discussion Questions

1. Locate the vocabulary words in the glossary and write the definition for each.

2. Name at least three unpleasant effects of El Niño on the lives of people in Peru and Ecuador.

3. What are some of the things that scientists are trying to learn about El Niño?

4. Why is the warm weather condition of El Niño not good for fishermen?

Unit One Quiz

Questions

1. What effect does the moon have on the earth?

2. Why is the tilt of the earth's axis important to the weather?

3. Name the seven main components of weather.

4. What are the five forms of precipitation?

5. How does the distance from the ocean affect the weather?

6. Why is the Antarctic ice sheet called a polar desert?

7. Which is associated with good weather, high or low areas of pressure?

8. What is the jet stream?

9. What is one of the major problems that El Niño brings to people in Peru and Ecuador?

4

Chapter 3

Text: Water in the Atmosphere (pp. 20–21)
Vocabulary Words

condensation

evaporation

Discussion Questions

1. Locate the vocabulary words in the glossary. Write the definition for each.

2. Half of the water for rain or snow comes from plants, wet ground, rivers and lakes. Where does the other half come from?

3. When ocean water evaporates into the air as water vapor, what replaces it?

4. Where the water table is deep in the ground, the land is dry. Where in the world is this the case? (Use the map on page 11.)

5. Runoff from rainstorms carries chemicals from the soil to the ocean. If the chemical composition is off-balance and becomes harmful to plankton, how could the rest of the ocean suffer?

Text: Clouds (pp. 22–25)
Vocabulary Words

cirrus clouds

convection clouds

cumulus clouds

fog

relative humidity

stratus clouds

Discussion Questions

1. Locate the vocabulary words in the glossary. Write the definition for each.

2. How do clouds form?

3. Which holds more water: warm air or cool air?

4. What do fog, mountain clouds, convection clouds, and frontal clouds all have in common?

5. What are the three basic cloud types?

6. When are cumulus clouds usually seen?

7. Which of the three basic cloud types contain ice crystals?

8. Which cloud type is found at low altitudes?

9. Clouds are classified according to their _____ in the sky.

10. Which two cloud types may contain rain?

Text: Warm Fronts and Cold Fronts (pp. 26–29)
Discussion Questions

1. What is a warm front?

2. What causes most cloud and precipitation formation?

3. What force pulls water droplets to the ground?

4. What are the indications of an approaching warm front?

5. What weather conditions occur along with a warm front?

6. From which direction do cold fronts usually come in the northern hemisphere?

7. Which is more dense: cold air or warm air?

8. During summer, what weather conditions indicate that a cold front is passing through?

Text: Fog (pp. 30–31)
Discussion Questions

1. List and describe the four types of fog.

2. The air can hold no more water when it reaches its
    _____.

3. When could fog prove to be hazardous to people?

4. What is the difference between fog and clouds?

5. Which types of fog occur over water?

6. Which types of fogs occur over land?

5

Chapter 4

Text: Thunderstorms (pp. 32–35)
Vocabulary Words

electricity

thunderstorm

Discussion Questions

1. Locate the vocabulary words in the glossary. Write the definition for each.

2. Where do most of the world's thunderstorms occur?

3. From which cloud type do thunderstorms develop?

4. Why is there a better chance of a thunderstorm occurring in the afternoon than in the morning or late at night?

5. What causes a cumulus cloud to change into a huge towering cumulus?

6. Why does a cumulus cloud stop growing when it hits the stratosphere?

7. In what ways are thunderstorms blessings from God?

8. How can thunderstorms remind us that God has promised to never flood the earth again?

Text: Lightning (pp. 36–37)
Vocabulary Words

electrons

static electricity

Discussion Questions

1. Locate the vocabulary words in the glossary. Write the definition for each.

2. How is lightning like static electricity?

3. What is thunder?

4. What does lightning sound like when it is near?

5. How fast does thunder travel?

6. Which travels faster: thunder or lightning? Why?

7. Are electrons negatively charged or positively charged?

8. Is the ground positively charged or negatively charged?

9. What are some problems with the following theory? Lightning is formed when electricity builds up in the cloud as a result of ice particles collecting.

10. A large amount of energy is released with each lightning bolt. If scientists could somehow harness this energy, in what ways could it be used to help mankind?

6

Chapter 5

Text: Dangerous Thunderstorms (pp. 38–39)

Vocabulary Words

flash flood

updraft

downdraft

Discussion Questions

1. Locate the vocabulary words in the glossary. Write the definition for each.

2. What percentage of yearly thunderstorms in the United States are considered dangerous?

3. How has God provided for our safety in dangerous weather?

4. What conditions are needed for a thunderstorm to develop? What is needed for a severe thunderstorm?

5. What geographical features contribute to severe thunderstorms in the United States?

6. Which regions of the United States receive the highest number of severe thunderstorms?

7. Look at the map of the United States on page 38. Florida has the most thunderstorms per year. Why?

8. Which three states have fewer than ten thunderstorms each year?

9. Name three reasons that flash floods occur.

10. Nearly half of the people that die in flash floods do so in their cars. In your opinion, how could such future deaths possibly be prevented?

Text: Hail and Wind Damage (pp. 40–41)
Vocabulary Word

hailstones

Discussion Questions

1. Locate the vocabulary words in the glossary. Write the definition for each.

2. Which cloud type is associated with hail?

3. Describe the formation of a hailstone.

4. What factors determine how fast hail falls to Earth?

5. If you find a hailstone consisting of a large amount of cloudy ice, what can you deduce about how it was formed?

6. True or false: all hailstones are smooth and round. Explain your answer.

7. What damage can be caused by hailstorms?

8. Describe three safety tips helpful for those experiencing a hailstorm.

9. What damage can be caused by a windstorm?

Text: Tornadoes (pp. 42–47)

Vocabulary Words

Doppler radar

supercell

tornado

Discussion Questions

1. Locate the vocabulary words in the glossary. Write the definition for each.

2. What is the difference between tornadoes and hurricanes?

3. What is the difference between how tornadoes and thunderstorms form?

4. Who are storm-chasers?

5. A tornado forms in a certain spot under a thunderstorm. Where is that spot?

6. Describe the most-dangerous tornadoes. Tell what they look like, how fast they move and how far they can travel.

7. Why are tornadoes considered unpredictable?

8. What does a "tornado watch" indicate?

9. What does a "tornado warning" indicate?

10. What makes a tornado visible?

11. Where do the largest number of waterspouts occur?

Unit Two Quiz

Text: pages 20–47

Questions

1. Describe the path that a drop of water takes as it cycles through the atmosphere.

2. What are the three basic cloud types?

3. Under what conditions are most clouds and precipitation formed?

4. What is the difference between fog and clouds?

5. From which cloud type does a thunderstorm develop?

6. How is thunder created?

7. What three conditions are needed to develop a thunderstorm?

8. During the formation of hail inside a cloud, what processes are happening to the water drop as it travels to the top of the cloud?

9. How is lightning similar to static electricity?

10. Name one reason that a flash flood occurs.

11. What is the difference between tornadoes and hurricanes?

12. What does a "tornado watch" indicate?

13. What does a "tornado warning" indicate?

7

Chapter 6

Text: Hurricanes (pp. 48–53)
Vocabulary Words

Intertropical

Convergence Zone

tropical depression

tropical storm

hurricane

Discussion Questions

1. Locate the vocabulary words in the glossary. Write the definition for each.

2. What is a monsoon?

3. List and describe the three storm types that occur in the tropics.

4. How are hurricane hunters similar to tornado chasers?

5. How are scientists able to predict the months during which hurricanes will most likely form?

6. Where is the eyewall located in a hurricane?

7. How does barometric pressure affect wind speeds in a hurricane?

8. What do the Japanese call a hurricane? The Australians?

9. What causes nine out of ten deaths in a hurricane?

10. What causes the sea level to rise as a hurricane passes overhead?

11. What were the geographical and economic factors in Bangladesh that caused so many deaths during the hurricane of 1970?

12. What killed most of the people who died after Hurricane Andrew passed through?

13. What is the National Weather Service's National Hurricane Center?

14. How has this agency been able to save lives?

15. How is Doppler radar useful in tracking hurricanes?

8

Chapter 7

Text: Winter Storms (pages 54–59)

Vocabulary Words

ice storms

Northeaster

sleet

wind chill factor

Discussion Questions

1. Locate the vocabulary words in the glossary. Write the definition for each.

2. What causes the earth's seasons?

3. What causes temperatures to be cooler in the winter?

4. What causes temperatures to be warmer in the summer?

5. What are the seasons in the tropics like?

6. Why do the west coasts of the United States, Canada and Europe very seldom have snow?

7. What would happen if snow melted as soon as it hit the ground?

8. Describe some benefits of winter rainstorms to the southern United States.

9. In California, what problems result from heavy rainstorms?

10. What weather conditions determine if a snowstorm is called a "blizzard"?

11. What is a "Northeaster"?

12. What causes ice storms?

13. What problems do ice storms and winter storms cause?

9

Chapter 8

Text: Wild Weather (pp. 60–63)

Vocabulary Words

chinook

winds

Santa Ana

winds

St. Elmo's Fire

ball lightning

Discussion Questions

1. Locate the vocabulary words in the glossary and write the definition for each.

2. When does "St. Elmo's Fire" normally occur?

3. What causes the continuous rainfall at Mt. Waialeale?

4. Which American state has both a rain forest and a desert?

5. What is a foehn wind?

6. What cloud type makes up the foehn wall?

7. What are foehn winds called in the United States?

8. What damages can chinooks cause?

9. Describe the effect an arctic cold front has on the Great Lakes area.

10. Describe a "lake effect snowstorm."

11. Describe "ball lightning."

Unit Three Quiz

Text: pages 42–63
Questions

1. What causes the earth to have seasons?

2. What causes temperatures to be cooler in the winter?

3. What causes temperatures to be warmer in the summer?

4. What weather conditions determine if a snowstorm is called a "blizzard"?

5. What is a monsoon?

6. How are scientists able to predict the months during which hurricanes will most likely form?

7. How is Doppler radar useful in tracking hurricanes?

8. What is a foehn wind?

9. Describe the effect an arctic cold front has on the Great Lakes area.

10. What is a "Northeaster"?

10

Chapter 9

Text: Climate in the Past (pp. 64–65)

Discussion Question

1. Why do scientists believe the earth's climate may have been different in the past?

For more information, read about Buddy Davis's Alaskan dinosaur adventure in *The Great Alaskan Dinosaur Adventure!*

Text: Noah's Flood–Key to the Past (pp. 66–67)

Discussion Questions

1. Why is it important that one understands the assumptions one has about the past?

2. What does the uniformitarian model assume about the past?

3. What does the biblical view assume about the past?

4. Why is Noah's Flood considered key when understanding past geological events?

5. What are some problems with trying to fit uniformitarian assumptions into the biblical view?

6. Why is there, technically, no such thing as "prehistoric past"?

See also www.AnswersInGenesis.org/Flood, www.AnswersInGenesis.org/geology, www.AnswersInGenesis.org/fossils

Text: The Ice Age (pp. 68–69)

Vocabulary words

permafrost

bogs

Discussion Questions

1. Locate the vocabulary words in the glossary. Write the definition for each.

2. Describe how Noah's Flood caused the Ice Age.

3. How long did the Ice Age last?

4. Why has the Ice Age ended?

For more information, see www.AnswersInGenesis.org/IceAge and www.AnswersInGenesis.org/mammoth

11

Chapter 10

Text: Future Climate (pp. 70–73)

Vocabulary Words

---

greenhouse warming

environment

fossil fuels

ozone

Discussion Questions

1. Locate the vocabulary words in the glossary. Write the definition for each.

2. Why should the Ice Age be considered a "one-time" event?

---

3. How does carbon dioxide affect the earth's atmosphere?

4. What causes the amount of carbon dioxide in the atmosphere to increase?

5. What are potential effects of increased "greenhouse" gases in the atmosphere?

6. What variables can cause fluctuations in the thickness of the ozone layer?

7. Explain how the existence of the ozone layer presents serious problems for those who believe in evolution.

12

Chapters 11–12

Text: Observing the Weather (pp. 74–77)

Vocabulary words

weather vane

thermometers

barometer

weather balloons

rain gauge

Discussion Questions

1. Locate the vocabulary words in the glossary. Write the definition for each.

---

2. You are able to observe the current weather situation in just about any part of the world by logging on to weather.com. For one week, chart the weather pattern of a place on the opposite side of the world from where you live. How does it compare to the weather in your area?

Text: God, Creation, and You (pp. 78–79)
Discussion Questions

1. God gave Adam dominion over His creation (Genesis 1:28). How should we apply the "dominion mandate" to our lives today?

2. Define "pantheism." How is this different from the biblical view of God?

3. Even more important than caring for the earth itself is caring for the eternal lives of those who live on the earth. How are you involved in sharing the good news of the Creator who became our Savior with those around you?

Unit Four Quiz

Text: pages 64–79

Questions

1. Contrast the uniformitarian view of the past with the biblical view of history.

2. Describe how the Flood of Noah's day would have initiated an Ice Age.

3. Why should the Ice Age be considered a one-time event?

4. How does the ozone layer impact life on Earth?

5. How does the "dominion mandate" God gave to Adam apply to our lives today?

6. Describe some of the observations you've made with your own weather station.

Answer Key

Lesson 1

Introduction

1. See glossary.

2. Accept reasonable answers. Examples: daily activities, how we dress, our moods, work to be done, travel, play.

3. Wind is invisible because we cannot see it. We can feel it and see the effects of it around us.

4. Accept reasonable answers. See John 3:8.

5. Seasons have come and gone since at least Genesis 1:14.

6. Accept reasonable answers. Examples: Perhaps beautiful with year-round growing seasons.

God Created

1. See glossary.

2. The moon causes tides in the ocean.

3. The oceans would become very polluted.

4. The sun is 400 times the size of the moon and 400 times further from the earth.

5. If the earth were to spin slower, the light side of the earth would be too hot and the dark side would be too cold. If it were to spin faster there would be fierce winds on the face of the earth.

6. A smaller tilt would result in the higher latitudes being

too cold which would bring about an ice age. A greater tilt would result in unstable climates.

7. Oxygen 21%; Nitrogen 78%; Argon 0.9%; Water vapor and carbon dioxide 0.15%

8. The sun emits dangerous ultraviolet rays that can cause skin cancer and damage skin, hastening the effects of aging.

9. 20 million.

10. Most burn up before they hit the ground.

Lesson 2

What Causes Weather

1. See glossary.

2. Wind direction, wind speed, visibility, amount of water vapor (humidity), air pressure, cloud condition, air quality.

3. Rain, freezing rain, snow, hail, drizzle.

4. Some is absorbed, some is reflected. Of the absorbed sunshine, some becomes heat energy, while a portion is turned into chemical energy stored in plants.

5. Invisible rays transmitting heat energy, given off by the land as it cools down at night.

6. If days are long and nights short during summer, more heat is gained by sunshine than lost by infrared radiation. It works the opposite in the winter.

7. Clouds and precipitation.

World Climate Zones

1. See glossary.

2. Answers will vary. Accept reasonable replies.

3. Tropical rain forests are found near the equator where it is both very warm and wet.

4. Thirty.

5. The closer to the ocean, the wetter the climate.

6. Mountains are cooler and wetter, while the land downwind from mountains is drier.

Lesson 3

Weather Facts

1. See glossary.

2. 280 mph.

3. Snow reflects 90 percent of light energy back into the atmosphere.

4. Missouri and Hawaii.

5. The center of a tornado.

6. The Antarctic ice sheet normally only receives an inch of precipitation per year.

How to Read a Weather Map

1. See glossary.

2. The two types of weather observations are surface observations and upper air observations.

3. The measurements are taken hourly for the surface and twice a day for the upper.

4. Computers draw weather maps and solve equations that tell the estimated position of the jet stream, the fronts and pressure centers in the future.

5. Meteorologists do not know enough about the

atmosphere nor do they have enough observations. They need bigger and faster computers. Even then, the weather is so complex and chaotic that there will always be substantial limits as to its predictability.

6. High pressure areas are generally areas of good weather.

7. Accept reasonable answers.

Jet Stream

1. The jet stream is a ribbon of high-speed wind in the upper atmosphere.

2. A jet stream is caused by the differences in temperature between the tropical and polar latitudes.

3. The speed of the jet stream is 90 mph during winter and 35 mph during the summer.

4. The jet stream can cause storms (low pressure areas) and cold and warm fronts and steers storms.

5. Storms move generally from west to east.

6. The wind speed varies with areas.

7. Stormy weather can usually be found associated with certain portions of the maximum wind.

8. Fourteen days.

El Niño

1. See glossary.

2. Poor fishing, heavy rains, flooding, thunderstorms and mud slides.

3. Research scientists are trying to find out what causes an El Niño, how far the influences may extend and what effect the two El Niños have on global weather.

4. The warm water is poor in nutrients so there is less

plankton and therefore fewer fish.

Unit One Quiz

1. The pull of the moon on the oceans is the main cause of the tides.

2. A smaller tilt would cause the higher latitudes to be too cold. This would bring about an ice age. A greater tilt would make the climates more unstable.

3. The seven components of weather are: wind direction, wind speed, visibility, water vapor, air pressure, cloud condition and air quality.

4. The five forms of precipitation are: rain, freezing rain, snow, hail and drizzle.

5. The closer the distance to the ocean, the wetter the climate.

6. A large portion of the Antarctic ice sheet normally receives an inch of precipitation per year.

7. High pressure areas are generally areas of good weather.

8. The jet stream is a ribbon of high speed wind in the upper atmosphere.

9. El Niño brings poor fishing, heavy rains, flooding, thunderstorms and mud slides.

Lesson 4

Water in the Atmosphere

1. See glossary.

2. It evaporates from the ocean.

3. Rainwater.

4. See semi-arid and arid climates.

5. Plankton is the bottom of the ocean food chain. Sea life depends on it for survival.

Clouds

1. See glossary.

2. Clouds form when the atmosphere can no longer hold all of the invisible water vapor so it condenses into water droplets or ice crystals.

3. Warm air.

4. They are all formed by moist air cooling enough to form clouds.

5. Cumulus, cirrus and stratus.

6. Usually on a bright, sunny day.

7. Cirrus.

8. Stratus.

9. Height.

10. Cumulonimbus and nimbostratus.

Warm Fronts and Cold Fronts

1. Warm air pushes the cold air back and warmer air rises above it.

2. Most clouds and precipitation are formed as air rises into the atmosphere.

3. Gravity.

4. We can tell when a warm front is approaching by the type of clouds observed – high clouds first, then thicker and lower clouds.

5. When the warm front is close, the clouds are low and precipitation falls.

6. North or west.

7. Cold.

8. Thunderstorms.

Fog

1. Evaporation, advection, radiation, upslope.

2. Point of saturation, dew point.

3. Accept reasonable answers.

4. Fog is a cloud that forms on the ground.

5. Evaporation and advection.

6. Radiation, upslope, and advection.

Lesson 5

Thunderstorms

1. See glossary.

2. Tropics.

3. Cumulus.

4. Because updrafts that cause thunderstorms occur more often when the ground is warm than cool.

5. Three conditions: (1) A large difference in temperature between the ground and upper troposphere, (2) plenty of moisture in the lower atmosphere, and (3) a trigger— a process to start the thunderstorm.

6. Because the stratosphere is warmer than the air immediately below it.

7. Thunderstorms provide summer water, cool the earth, and clean the air. They also balance the earth's electricity and provide fertilizer.

8. Rainbows are sometimes seen with thunderstorms (Genesis 9:11–17).

Lightning

1. See glossary.

2. Both lightning and static electricity involve electrons that travel from a negative to a positive area liberating energy.

3. Thunder is the sound of air expanding as the temperature increases due to the lightning bolt splitting the air.

4. A sharp crack.

5. The speed of sound, 750 mph (1200 kph).

6. Lightning travels at the speed of light which is a million times faster.

7. Negative.

8. Positive.

9. Small clouds can generate electricity. Electricity can form without ice crystals. There are cases of positive charges, and scientists can't explain it.

10. Reasonable answers are meeting the energy needs of cities or an alternative to fossil fuel.

Lesson 6

Dangerous Thunderstorms

1. See glossary.

2. Ten percent.

3. He has given us the knowledge and ability to predict dangerous weather patterns so we can protect ourselves.

4. The combination of warm earth and moist air creates thunderstorms. Severe thunderstorms require this condition along with a strong updraft and a strong downdraft.

5. The two features are (1) moist air from the Gulf of Mexico and (2) the warm earth of the plains.

6. These regions are the southern and central midwest.

7. This is true because warm moisture from the Gulf of Mexico moves east across Florida and Florida stays warm most of the year.

8. California, Oregon and Washington.

9. (1) Slow moving thunderstorms drop an unusual amount of rain on a small area that cannot be absorbed by the ground. (2) Two or more gully-washing thunderstorms hit the same spot, one after another. (3) Heavy rain falls on rapidly melting snow.

10. Accept reasonable answers. Possibly by paying more attention to weather forecasts or by not taking chances unnecessarily while driving in flash flood conditions, such as not driving across a road when water is flowing over it.

Hail and Wind Damage

1. See glossary.

2. Cumulonimbus.

3. As a small water drop is blown upward inside a cloud, it collides with other supercooled drops, growing larger.

4. The speed of the downdraft determines the speed of the hail.

5. The cloudy ice is caused mainly by rapid freezing, trapping many air bubbles.

6. False. Hail comes in strange shapes, sometimes with ragged edges.

7. Answers should include crop losses, property damage, injury and possible death.

8. Accept reasonable answers.

9. Losses include damage to mobile homes, roofs and airplane crashes.

Tornadoes

1. See glossary.

2. Tornadoes are relatively small, while hurricanes cover hundreds of miles.

3. For tornadoes, the updraft must be halted for a while by a layer of warm air just above the ground.

4. Storm chasers are professional people who try to get as close to a tornado as possible so they can film and take pictures of it.

5. Tornadoes form under the thunderstorm where there is little rain or lightning, in the southwest part of the storm cloud.

6. The most dangerous tornadoes are thick, black clouds that are 2,000 feet across. They spin at 250–300 mph. They move about 50 mph across the land. They can travel for 100 miles and have a damage path of over 1 mile wide.

7. Tornadoes can change shape as they move. They can also go back up into the cloud and to the ground again.

8. A tornado watch indicates conditions are right for a tornado to form.

9. A tornado warning indicates a tornado has been spotted

or seen on Doppler radar.

10. We are able to see tornadoes because of condensed water vapor, dust and debris.

11. The largest number of waterspouts occurs in the Florida Keys.

Unit 2 Quiz

1. The water drop cycles from the ocean to the land to the ocean again.

2. The three basic cloud types are cumulus, cirrus and stratus.

3. Most clouds and precipitation are formed in areas of rising air in the atmosphere.

4. Fog is a cloud that forms on the ground.

5. A thunderstorm develops from a cumulus cloud.

6. Thunder is created when a lightning bolt splits the air. The temperature causes the air to expand at a rapid rate causing the sound we hear.

7. The three conditions needed are warm earth, moist air and a trigger.

8. As the drop of water travels upward, it collides with other super-cooled drops, all the while growing bigger.

9. Both lightning and static electricity involve electrons that travel from a negative to a positive area, liberating energy.

10. Flash floods occur when:

    1. Slow moving thunderstorms drop an unusual amount of rain on a small area that cannot be absorbed into the ground.

2. Two or more gully-washing thunderstorms hit the same spot, one after another.

3. Heavy rain falls on rapidly melting snow.

11. The difference between tornadoes and hurricanes is that tornadoes are small, while hurricanes cover hundreds of miles.

12. A tornado watch means conditions are right for a tornado to form.

13. A tornado warning means one has been spotted or detected from Doppler radar.

Lesson 7

1. See glossary.

2. A monsoon is six months of rain in the tropics.

3. Tropical depression (rainstorm with winds of 38 mph (60 kph) or less), tropical storm (heavy rain and winds between 39–74 mph (60–120 kph), hurricane (very heavy rain and winds of 75 mph (120 kph) or greater).

4. They both chase after dangerous storms, hoping to gather information.

5. They have learned that most hurricanes form after the ocean water warms up past 80°F, so hurricanes are more likely to form during months when water temperatures are above this.

6. The eyewall directly surrounds the center, or eye, of the storm.

7. The falling barometric pressure in the middle of the mass of the hurricane causes the winds to increase.

8. Typhoons; willy-willies.

9. The rising ocean water on land (storm surge) causes 90 percent of the deaths.

10. Extremely low air pressure inside the hurricane.

11. The country is very flat, and there was no way to warn the people of Bangladesh because they did not have modern communication systems.

12. Most were killed by touching downed electrical wires.

13. It is a governmental agency that issues watches and warnings to the people of advancing hurricanes. They use the latest technology to do so.

14. It has been able to give 24-hour warnings of approaching storms. The people are able to leave their homes to go to safer areas until after the storm has passed.

15. When a hurricane draws near, Doppler weather radar tracks the storm's details.

Lesson 8

1. See glossary.

2. Earth's seasons are due to the tilt of its axis.

3. Shorter days (with less sunshine) and longer nights cause cooler temperatures.

4. Longer days allow more sunshine to warm the ground and atmosphere.

5. No seasons or very small changes in the temperature.

6. Warm winds from the ocean blow onto the land keeping it too warm for snow.

7. Plants and animals would not be protected from harsh winter weather. We would have no storehouse of water in the mountains.

8. It adds to the water table and replenishes above-ground water sources.

9. Erosion and even mudslides.

10. Winds over 35 mph and poor visibility.

11. A storm that moves northeast along the east coast.

12. A temperature inversion, so rain falling into below-freezing temperatures of the lower atmosphere becomes supercooled. Supercooled droplets freeze when jostled, sometimes before they hit the ground (ice pellets or sleet) and at other times on objects (freezing rain–very hazardous!).

13. Accept reasonable answers. Examples: auto accidents, property damage, personal injury or death due to the freezing temperatures.

Lesson 9

1. See glossary.

2. It occurs during the last phases of a violent thunderstorm.

3. Trade winds pick up great amounts of water vapor as they blow across the Pacific Ocean. The water vapor condenses as the winds move up the mountainside, forming clouds that quickly develop into thunderstorms.

4. Washington.

5. A relatively warm and dry wind that is descending down a mountain front.

6. Cumulus.

7. Chinooks (a native American word meaning "snow eater").

8. They can fan grass fires out of control. They can blow

vehicles off the road or damage homes. They can cause rapid condensation of water vapor, leading to lowered driver visibility as car windows turn white.

9. Arctic cold fronts cause high evaporation rates, triggering heavy snowstorms once they hit land.

10. Winds blowing from the west pick up moisture as they cross the Great Lakes and cause snowstorms in places up to 100 miles (160 km) downwind from the Lakes.

11. It is a glowing ball of electricity that occasionally forms during thunderstorms.

Unit Three Quiz

1. The earth's seasons are due to the tilt of its axis.

2. Shorter days (with less sunshine) and longer nights cause cooler temperatures.

3. Longer days allow more sunshine to warm the ground and atmosphere.

4. The weather conditions during a blizzard are winds over 35 mph and poor visibility.

5. A monsoon is six months of rain in the tropics.

6. Scientists have learned that most hurricanes form after the ocean water warms up past 80°F, so hurricanes are more likely to form during months when water temperatures are above this temperature.

7. Doppler weather radar can track the details of a hurricane and thus provide warning to the population of an area threatened.

8. A foehn wind is a relatively warm and dry wind descending a mountain front.

9. Arctic cold fronts cause high evaporation rates as they pass over the Great Lakes, triggering heavy snowstorms once they hit land.

10. A storm that moves northeast along the east coast.

Lesson 10

Climate in the Past

1. Warm-climate fossils have been found at high latitudes. Fossilized swamp cypress trees have been found in the Arctic Islands. Old river channels have been found in the Sahara Desert. Woolly mammoth bones have been found in Siberia.

Noah's Flood—Key to the Past

1. The beliefs one has about the past will affect how one interprets the evidence. We should be aware of our starting assumptions so that we understand how they are affecting our interpretations.

2. "The present is the key to the past"—i.e., the slow and gradual geological processes we sometimes observe today have been forming rocks, etc. this way for millions of years.

3. The Bible view is that creation took place approximately 6,000 years ago, and that God judged the entire Earth with a world-wide Flood during the time of Noah, approximately 4,500 years ago.

4. The vast amounts of water and sediment produced during the Flood would have had catastrophic effects in re-shaping the geology of the earth. Many of the geological processes that occur slowly and gradually today would have taken place quickly during the Flood.

5. A straight-forward reading of the Bible shows that the earth is around 6,000 years old. It does not allow for the "millions of years" demanded by the uniformitarian view. See www.AnswersInGenesis.org/low_view for additional insights.

6. The Bible provides the history of the universe from the very beginning. Therefore, there is no time that is *before* history, or "pre-history."

The Ice Age

1. See glossary.

2. The ocean waters were warm from volcanic and tectonic activity (Note: much of the Flood waters came from under the ground), thus causing vast amounts of evaporation. As the water vapor blew over the cooler continents, it condensed as snow, continuing to fall in the northern latitudes year round. The piling snow eventually compacted into ice.

3. About 700 years.

4. The volcanic and tectonic activity that began during the Flood soon slowed. The rapid evaporation slowed down as the warm oceans cooled. The associated warming of the air, and the increased sunlight reaching the ground as the atmospheric dust and gas decreased, caused the ice sheets to begin to melt.

Lesson 11

1. See glossary.

2. The Ice Age was caused by the Genesis Flood. Since God promised to never again send a Flood of world-wide proportions, the conditions for starting another Ice Age will never again be present.

3. It helps to keep the atmosphere warm. As the amount of CO_2 in the atmosphere increases, the temperature of the earth's surface will increase.

4. Burning fossils fuels, cutting down trees.

5. Droughts may occur, hurricane activity may increase, ice sheets may begin to melt.

6. The amount of ozone found in the stratosphere is cyclical. Air circulation causes mixing of ozone. Certain chemical reactions can cause fluctuations, as can volcanic dust and gases.

7. Ozone is made from oxygen, yet oxygen supposedly could not have been present in Earth's original atmosphere, as oxygen destroys the compounds from which life allegedly evolved. But without oxygen, there would be no ozone layer, thus allowing harmful ultraviolet light to destroy the chemical compounds from which life allegedly evolved.

Lesson 12

God, Creation, and You

1. We have the responsibility of caring for the earth, as far as it is possible for us to do so, by cleaning up pollution or litter, etc. See also www.AnswersInGenesis.org/environmentalism.

2. Pantheism is the belief that everything is God. The Bible teaches that God and His Creation are *distinct* (Genesis 1, John 1:1-3), and that the essence of idolatry is giving worship to created things instead of the Creator (Ex. 20:4-6, Rom. 1:23,25).

Unit Four Quiz

1. Briefly: The uniformitarian view is such that things originated on their own over millions of years, and that death, disease and suffering have always been a part of history. The biblical view states that God created a perfect world in 6 normal-length days around 6,000 years ago; that death, disease, corruption and suffering entered the world after Adam rebelled; that the Flood of Noah's day formed a majority of the rock layers and fossils we find today and initiated the Ice Age.

2. The ground would have been cooler and summers much colder. The oceans would have been warmer. Snow would have fallen in the northern latitudes year-round.

3. The Flood, which provided the right conditions to initiate the Ice Age was an one-time event.

4. The ozone layer protects the earth from harmful ultra-violet rays.

5. Christians are to take care of the earth and everything on it, including the atmosphere.